ALSO BY JULIA GLASS

Three Junes
The Whole World Over

I See You Everywhere

JULIA GLASS

I See You Everywhere

PANTHEON BOOKS, NEW YORK

Copyright © 2008 by Julia Glass

All rights reserved. Published in the United States by Pantheon Books, a division of Random House, Inc., New York, and in Canada by Random House of Canada Limited, Toronto.

Pantheon Books and colophon are registered trademarks of Random House, Inc.

Grateful acknowledgment is made to Jalma Music for permission to reprint an excerpt from "Green Grass," written by Tom Waits and Kathleen Brennan, copyright © 2004 by Jalma Music (ASCAP). Reprinted by permission of Jalma Music.

The following pieces were previously published in slightly different form: "Husbandry" in *American Short Fiction;* "Coat of Many Colors" in *Bellingham Review;* and "Now Is Not the Time" as "My Sister's Scar" and "The World We Made" as "The World We've Made" in the *Chicago Tribune;* "I See You Everywhere" on *FiveChapters.com;* "The Price of Silver" in *Five Points;* and "A Door to the Sky" in *The Southampton Review.*

ISBN-13 978-1-60751-929-4

Printed in the United States of America

For Carolyn
and Robert

Don't say good bye to me
Describe the sky to me
And if the sky falls, mark my words
We'll catch mocking birds

—From "Green Grass,"
by Tom Waits and Kathleen Brennan

I See You Everywhere

Swim to the Middle

1980

I avoid reunions. I'm not a rebel, a recluse, or a sociopath, and I'm too young to qualify as a crank, even if it's true that I just spent the evening of my twenty-fifth birthday not carousing with friends or drinking champagne at a candlelit table for two but resolutely alone and working, glazing a large ovoid porcelain bowl while listening to Ella Fitzgerald sing songs by the Gershwin brothers. (A crank could never love Gershwin.) My one real boyfriend in college, just before we broke up, told me I'm nostalgic to a fault. He professed contempt for what he called "the delusional sound track to our parents' deluded lives." He informed me that you can't be nostalgic for things that had their heyday before you were so much as born. Just about any member of my family would have laughed him out the door and down the garden path.

Family reunions are the worst—all that competition disguised as fellowship—and they're also the hardest to avoid. But when my father's Great-Aunt Lucy died last summer, there was an inheritance at stake, a collection of antique jewelry. Not the glossy priceless stuff—no diamonds, tiaras, or niagaras of pearls. Not things you'd sell but things so deliciously old-fashioned and stylish that to wear them makes you feel like a character from a Jane Austen novel or a Chekhov play. The one piece I remembered most vividly was a cameo, two inches square, ivory on steel-blue Pacific coral, a woman's face inclined toward her hand, in her slender fingers an iris. Aunt Lucy had worn that cameo day and night, winter and summer, on lace and wool. Maybe she'd left us a charm bracelet, maybe earrings of garnet or Mexican silver, but mostly I wondered about that cameo. And wanted it. I'd wanted it since I was a little girl. One of my earliest memories is of sitting on Lucy's lap, squirming to find a comfortable spot on her bony thighs yet happy to feel her kind honeyed voice in my hair as she talked with the other grown-ups gathered on her porch. She did not object to my poking and fingering the cameo, probing its fragile details: the woman's eyelids and earlobes, the cuticles of her nails, the harmoniously wandering tendrils of her hair. She let me borrow it once, for a family dinner at a country inn.

Because Lucy never had children, not even a husband, my father long ago became the one who kept an eye on her in the last decades of her very long life. Geographically, he was the closest family member by far; out of a large, tenaciously Confederate clan, they were the only two living anywhere you can count on snow. Once Dad decided to stay north, after earning two degrees at Harvard, the family lumped him together with Lucy: "How are the defectas faring up yonda?" a cousin might ask Dad at a wedding in Memphis or Charleston. Happily, their proximity blossomed into genuine affection.

So Dad was the executor of Lucy's will, which emerged from her bureau drawer along with a letter to my father that she'd written a year before she died. It began, *To my splendid grandnephew Beauchance: Before I take my irreversible leave (which I suppose I will now have taken, strange to think), I am seizing this lucid moment to write down a few matters pertaining to the house and my ragbag possessions therein. I have little doubt that I shall have left the house in a rather sorry state, for which I apologize. Be charitable, if you can, to any bats or raccoons which may have colonized the attic or basement (though none to my knowledge have done so), and please take Sonny's word on any tasks for which he claims I still owe him payment; our mutual accounting has grown slack if not capricious. . . .*

Over the phone, Dad read me the letter in its crisp yet meandering entirety, stopping now and then to chuckle. I heard no tears in his voice until the end, where she wrote, *Whatever modest adornments pass for jewelry, I leave to your daughters, Louisa and Clement. I did not become as intimately acquainted with them as I would have liked, but I did know the satisfaction, one summer to the next, of seeing how they grew; as I wish I had seen you evolve in your youth. I wish I had known much sooner, Beau, that you would become the facsimile of a perfect son, a gift whose pleasures I wish I had been blessed to know firsthand.*

His voice cracked on the word *gift*, as if he didn't deserve such gratitude, my father who will do just about anything for anyone, driving my mother crazy with all the favors he does for everyone else (including, as she likes to say, any random citizen of Outer Slobovia and its most godforsaken suburbs).

I decided to fly across the entire country because I couldn't bear the thought that if I didn't show up in person, my sister might inherit everything—including that cameo—by default. On the plane, I tried to decide which of two equally vulgar motives, materialism or spite, had compelled me to buy a ticket I couldn't afford to a place where I'd see no one I wanted to see. My life was not, as people like to say, in a good place—though, ironically, the place where I lived at the time happened to be Santa Barbara. So I made excuses and timed my visit to avoid the masses of cousins, aunts, and uncles who would descend on Lucy's house to grope the heirlooms by day and drink too much bourbon by night. I may share their Huguenot blood, but not their bad taste in booze and their glutinous drawl. I will never forget how, when our grandmother died two years ago, the family marauded her New Orleans house with no more respect than the Union soldiers who stripped us all bare a century back. You'd think, with all our costly educations, the reconstructed Jardines would avoid civil wars. Well, ha. There was an ugly brawl, which featured weeping and a smashed lamp, over the Steinway grand. Someone with Solomonic intentions actually went so far as to crank up a chain saw. I could not deal with that type of gathering all over again. Whether I could deal with Clem remained to be seen.

My sister had been living with Aunt Lucy for what proved to be her final summer. After Lucy's death, Clem stayed on while the relatives passed through, finishing up her summer jobs before heading back to college for her junior year. During the days, Clem worked in a bike shop and volunteered at a sanctuary for recovering raptors: birds, she'd explained when I called, that had been shot, struck by small planes, tortured by teenage boys. In the evenings, she kept an eye on Lucy—until her sudden death at the beginning of August. Not that our aunt was infirm, incontinent, or witless, but for the last several months of her life she was afflicted with an obstinate restlessness that sent her out after dark on urgent eccentric missions. Winooski, Vermont, is a snug, friendly place, so she wasn't likely to be mugged or abducted. Nevertheless, reasoned Dad, who could say she wouldn't do something drastic like sell her last shares of Monsanto and Kodak, head for the airport, and unintentionally vanish?

I'd hardly spoken to Clem since moving out west two years before. After college, in pursuit of a man I'd prefer to jettison from memory, I hauled my pottery wheel, my heart, and my disastrously poor judgment from Providence to California. It was completely unlike me to do anything so rash; maybe, subconsciously, I was trying to get back at Clem by pretending to *be* Clem, to annoy her by stealing her role as devil-may-care adventuress. Whatever the reason for my tempestuous act, it backfired. Three weeks after I signed a lease and bought a secondhand kiln, the boyfriend shed me like a stifling, scratchy-collared coat. To keep up with the rent I'd fooled myself into thinking he would share, I gave up my car. After that, I sold a pitcher here, a platter there, but to stave off eviction I wrote articles for a magazine that told workaholic doctors what to do with their leisure time. In college, I'd been just as good with words as I was with clay, and one of my Brit-lit classmates had started this odd publication. People had laughed, but subscriptions to *Doc's Holiday* sold like deodorant soap.

Thus did I hold starvation at bay, but I also felt like the work kept me stuck in a place where I ought to love living but didn't. Everything out there unnerved me: the punk shadows of palm trees slashing the lawns, the sun setting—not rising—over the ocean, the solitude of the sidewalks as I rushed everywhere on foot, carless and stared at. My inner compass refused to budge. *North!* it kept urging me. *East!* I'd just come to the conclusion that I didn't belong there and never would, and I was feeling uncomfortable in my work, both kinds, but I had no intention of letting Clem in on my angst. My plan was never to trust her again, never to fall for her charms the way everyone else, especially men, seemed to do so fervently. And to snare that cameo. Maybe a string of pearls. Oh, Glenn Miller. I love him, too. What's life without a little delusion?

IF YOU'RE TO HEAR LOUISA'S VERSION of what went on last summer, you will also be hearing mine. Louisa's worst side is the one I call the Judge. À la Salem witchcraft trials. There's this look she gets on her face that tells the world and everyone in it how completely unworthy it and they are to contain or witness her presence. *Beware!* says that look. *The Spanish Inquisition was Entenmann's Danish!*

Her new life in Santa Ladeedabra did not seem to have mellowed her out one iota, because when I pulled up at the airport, that's the look she was wearing, firm as a church hat, beaming her world-weary scorn clear across the state of Vermont. I was late, okay, which didn't help. It didn't help either, I know, that it was me picking her up.

I wonder sometimes what kind of sisters we'll be when we're ancient (if we ever are). Olivia de Havilland and Joan Fontaine: before that visit, you'd have bet the hacienda we'd end up like them. Cold? Suspicious? Resentful? Ever notice how sisters, when they aren't best friends, make particularly vicious enemies? Like, they could be enemies from the time they lay their beady little eyes on each other, maybe because their mother makes them rivals or maybe because there's not enough love to go around and—not out of greed but from the gut, like two hawks zeroing in on a wren—they have no choice but to race for it. (Laws of nature, pure and simple. Be vigilant and survive. Altruism? A myth. Share? Oh please. Whatever it is that feeds the hunger, dive-bomb first, philosophize later.) Or maybe they grow apart in a more conscious way, maybe because their marriages clash: the guys they choose see each other as losers or sellouts; the women are helplessly loyal. But that's not our story. No husbands yet, not even a hint of husband.

I've always been the favorite—our mother's, at least. Partly, it's the animal thing: Mom grew up on a storybook farm where animals ruled life more strictly than clocks. And I happen to be the one who set my sights that way. Saving animals is all I've ever wanted to do. In fourth grade, I asked Mom to give me all her shoe boxes. A hospital: that was the plan. I cut windows in the ends of the boxes and stacked them in the bottom of my closet like high-rise condos. My first baby bird got the penthouse. Next day, he was dead. They almost always die, I'd learn. But that didn't stop me. "You're my daughter, all right," said Mom when she saw what I'd built (though her tone made me wonder if the likeness was such a good thing).

Louisa thinks this makes my life easy—being the favorite. She doesn't realize that once you're the disappointment, or once you've chosen a path seen as odd or unchoosable, your struggle is over, right? On the other side of the fence—mine—every expectation you fulfill (or look like you might, on purpose or not) puts you one step higher and closer to that Grand Canyon rim from which you could one day rule the world—or plummet in very grand style.

IN THE CAR, I let Clem do the talking. She was late to pick me up, and I was glad: it gave me a reason to sulk until I could get my bearings. I was glad to be back in New England, but I was cross-eyed with fatigue. I cannot sleep on planes. So Clem filled me in on the reading of the will and what she called the Great Divide: relatives clutching lists, drawing lots, swarming the house like fire ants. But this time there were no dogfights; everyone, said Clem, remembered the piano brawl.

I hadn't seen the place in five years, and when we arrived, I just stood on the walk and stared. It's a Victorian, more aspiring than grand, and it had always looked a little anemic, but now it was a wreck. The sallow paint, formerly white, hung off the clapboards in broad curling tongues, and the blue porch ceiling bore the crusty look of a cave complete with stalactites. The flagstones were fringed with moss. The front steps sagged. That the lawn had just been mowed made the house look even more derelict. "How could Dad let her live this way?" I asked.

With the edge of a sneaker, Clem swiped cut grass from the steps. "She insisted. She felt safer this way. No one busts in if they figure you can't afford a paint job." She shrugged. "Makes sense to me."

"But I remember this caretaker guy. . . ."

"Sonny?" Clem laughed. "Lou, do you know how old *he* is now?"

I walked ahead of her into the house. I braced myself for cobwebbed sofas, curtains spattered with mildew, but I was shocked again. The antique tables were polished, the upholstery taut and preened, the glass over the samplers and watercolor seascapes shimmering with leafy reflections. The floor, once oak plank covered with dark orientals, was now a bright field of linoleum, great black and white squares, stretching from parlor to kitchen. I dropped my bag. "What the hell happened here?"

"She told me she always wanted to live inside a Vermeer." My sister watched me for a moment. "I mean, you're the artist, you can relate."

"Vermeer? This is Captain Kangaroo."

"It was an experiment," said Clem. "Don't be so uptight."

I walked on through the dining room. The same old salt-pocked captain's table and the five-foot brass candlesticks supported by turbaned Moors now resembled pieces on a chessboard. But the kitchen had become the most eccentric room of all, a time warp. The cabinets were the ones I remembered, their rumpled glass panes framing porcelain platters, ranks of translucent teacups, curvaceous tureens (of which, I now realized, I would have liked to claim a few). In the center of the room, like a relic of Pompeii, the same claw-foot bathtub held court: no faucets, a rusted gas-jet heater below. When I was little and we stayed here, Dad would haul water from an outdoor pump and turn on the gas. After turning it off, he'd press a towel or two against the bottom so Clem and I could bathe without scalding our bottoms. Beyond the pump was an out-house shrouded in lilacs. When Dad insisted on plumbing, Aunt Lucy balked. The compromise was one toilet, a washing machine, and a kitchen sink; after that, to fill the tub, she'd hitch a garden hose to the tap in the big soapstone sink. "Luxe de luxe! Just splendid! My dears, you haven't a clue what modern *feels* like," she'd say. "To you, it's the air you breathe. To me, it's a foreign country, an Oriental language."

But the long wooden counter, with its century of scars, now stopped at a double-door frost-free Amana, imposing as a glacier. Lined up along the back of the counter, cheek to cheek, were several brand-new culinary contraptions. A Cuisinart, a coffee grinder, and a microwave, followed by a small turquoise missile whose function I deduced only from its name: Juice King. At the very end, a circular machine with a plastic dome. When I peered inside it, Clem said "It makes bread" and opened the freezer door. Stacked inside were dozens of foil-wrapped cubes. "She sort of stopped sleeping at night, so sometimes I'd stay up, too, and we'd, like, improvise. She never settled for plain white or wheat, no plain *any-thing*. I'd be a wreck at work the next day, while she'd sleep away the morning. But we had a blast."

Side by side, we examined the contents of the freezer, its chilly white mist scorching our skin. Each loaf was labeled in Lucy's Christina Ros-setti cursive on first-aid tape: ZUCCHINI-BIRDSEED, BANANA-MAPLE RYE, ZUCCHINI-CHOCOLATE, PRUNE-PECAN-CASSIS. "Harvey's Bristol sourdough wheat?" I read aloud.

Clem reached past me and took it out. "Awesome with cream cheese. We'll have it for breakfast." She closed the door, leaned against it, and folded her arms. Standing there, she looked for just a minute like our mother, sure of her place in a world where she'd landed almost by acci-dent. I laughed.

"Oh good," said Clem.

"What?"

"You didn't leave it behind after all."

"What?" I said again.

Clem walked toward me and pretended to pull something out of my breast pocket. She held it up, the invisible thing, and shook it in front of my face. "Your sense of humor." She put it back, giving my pocket a tender pat.

I felt the air shift between us, as if we were finally together somehow. This wasn't what I wanted. I walked across the room and looked out the window at the backyard. I counted four bird feeders, all filled. My sister, Saint Francis of Assisi.

"The cousins missed you," said Clem. "Too bad about your deadline. Couldn't you just have brought your typewriter out on the plane?"

I sat on the edge of the tub. I could tell her that I didn't work well away from home, but it would have been a lie, and it might have started a real conversation, which I was doing my best to avoid. "How come the place isn't looted?"

Clem pointed to the kitchen table and chairs. I noticed then that everything wore a claim: a tag or strip of tape marked RACINE, JACKIE J., GAIA, BEAU, and so on. The shippers would pack it all up the following week, after Clem left for school. My father would return, to hire painters and talk to real estate agents.

Clem hadn't taken her eyes off me. She'd spotted my resistance, and I could tell she was contemplating the challenge. "So, you buying me dinner tonight?"

"If you're buying tomorrow. I don't remember owing you any favors," I said.

Her smile opened wide. I've always envied her those perfect teeth: small and square, lined up straight as rails in a banister. "Deal," she said.

FUN WAS THE LAST THING I expected when Dad roped me into this babysit-the-family-dowager job. But free rent all summer in Vermont: who'd say no to that? So I figured, okay, my hot date's gone to Alaska to make big bucks on a rig, not an adventure I cared to join, even if I could've schemed the airfare from Dad (and I would have), and this way I could work with all these amazing creatures—owls, hawks, and falcons, something I couldn't get paid for without a fancy degree—and maybe get in some serious cycling. Aunt Lucy knew this guy who ran a bike shop; his dad had been her gardener when she'd bothered with a garden. Fine, I figured; so I'd spend the summer fixing things—rusted derailleurs and bent spokes, cracked beaks and fractured wings, my great-great-aunt's delusions. Bikes and birds I could deal with. Dementia? Well, I'd play that one by ear.

Lucy was ninety-eight and a half years old when she died. She was still sharp, if a little slow on her feet, even surprisingly strong. Walking, she reminded me of a cat on a skinny branch: agile but cautious. She ate her meals at normal hours, but she'd be wide awake for most of the night and then sleep, when she did, during the day. That was her only weird habit. I thought back then (back then!) she made an excellent argument for avoiding marriage and babies, and I told my Catholic boyfriend as much. (Luke still goes to church when he goes home. Which I try to ignore.) If she was ever lonely or bored, she didn't say. The day I arrived at the house, a UPS truck was pulling away. Lucy was on the porch pushing a humongous box through the door, one careful inch at a time.

"Hey, let me do that!" I shouted. I dropped my backpack on the sidewalk.

She looked down at me and said, "Hello, dear one. I am in the process of newfangling my life." Without waiting for me, she went back to her task. When I got inside the door, she had just pried the packing notice from its sleeve. She held it at arm's length. Her face lit up like a flare. "Oh splendid!"

I stood beside her as she pulled an X-acto knife out of her apron pocket and removed its cap with her teeth (her *actual* teeth, believe it or not). Slowly, and with a concentration that totally canceled out my presence, she slit the tape. When she pulled the box open, Styrofoam peanuts exploded upward, reverse confetti. "I hate these dingbats, don't you? They end up all hither and yon. Like water bugs in a tornado." The cap in her teeth whistled as she spoke.

"Yeah, and you know," I said, "they'll outlast our species by about a million years. The dingbats *and* the water bugs." I picked a few off her dress.

She really looked at me then, as if I'd passed a silent test. "I liked the old newspaper stuffing," she said. "I liked looking at the stories, especially when they came from towns that one is never likely to visit. 'Mayor's Nephew Charged with Poultry Theft.' 'Tree Surgeon and Dog Catcher to Wed in Fall.' 'Cattle Drive Causes Interstate Mayhem.' Serendipity and fluff. Not always inconsequential, but never of tragic proportions." She capped the knife, straightened up, and looked me over. "You have been sent here, young lady, to curtail my amusement. Your father was frank about that. He has also canceled my American Express. As if I were squandering an imperial nest egg. I tolerate Beau's meddling because he does it from afar. But yours: we'll have to see about yours. You are the slippery slope toward one of those, I believe they're called 'home health attendants'?" She sighed, leaned over, and pulled a tapered plastic tube from the box. She held it up like a flagstaff. "Noses down behind cushions!"

Jesus, I thought, I'm spending my summer with an old lady who goes into raptures at the sight of a new vacuum cleaner.

At least she wasn't in diapers.

So my great-great-aunt, who still wore lace-up pointy-toed boots and long-sleeved, ankle-length dresses in June, had become the consummate consumer. It was like she'd lost her virginity and discovered the tyranny of lust. She loved paging through catalogs, but her new favorite thing was getting out her '66 Ford Fairlane after dinner and driving to Burlington, where stores stayed open late because of the students. These shopping trips—for which she refused to call the guy who was supposed to drive her places—were what Dad called her "nocturnal missions" (innocent pun, I'm sure). They were the main reason he wanted her under surveillance. So Lucy and I made a deal. I drove, and I had veto power over purchases that were outrageously impractical or way overpriced. I'd come back from the bird station about six-thirty and put our frozen dinners in the new microwave. I'd talk about birds; she'd talk about books. She liked poetry and war memoirs, a weird combination, and lately she'd begun to subscribe to magazines like *Architectural Digest* and *House Beautiful*. "A curiosity," she said, "the way my aesthetic urges have veered toward the palpable." After dinner I'd make her peppermint tea and then, most nights, she would look at the grandfather clock before the just-emptied cup touched its saucer and say, "On your mark, Clement dear!" By the time I pulled the car out of the garage, she'd be standing out front with her purse—excuse me, *handbag*.

That was my life for two months. Except for the absence of Luke, I would gladly have lived like that for a year.

CLEM PUT ME in the room that was, a very long time ago, Aunt Vetty's. Vetty was Lucy's sister, who lived here, and died here, way before I was born. On the bed lay the green and yellow wedding-ring quilt Aunt Lucy said Vetty had made to honor her marriage (before it turned sour). Her quilting hoop still hung on a hook behind the door. Her brush and comb lay on the bureau, her Bible on the washstand, her dresses and shoes inside the wardrobe with the streaked milky mirror. Newly taped to the mirror was a hand-lettered decree: CONTENTS TO GAIA: HANDS OFF! Gaia, who's my age, is a second cousin who dreams of becoming a Broadway costume designer. Sometimes I worry that artistic grandiosity runs in our blood. Which isn't to say my cousin has no talent. It's me I worry about. Do I feel I am somehow entitled to live with an immunity to rules? There's a lot of that in our family. Sometimes when I'm at the wheel, mesmerized yet alert to its rapid spin, hands shiny with cocoa-colored mud, I wonder. Am I talented? Am I a fraud? Am I grandiose?

In Vetty's room, the only other sign of change was a faintly darker oval in the wallpaper over the bed: the ghost of Vetty's husband, according to Dad. Aunt Lucy, he says, took the cad down when her sister was dead, face turned up toward that picture, not even an hour. Dad says she actually scolded the picture. When he tells the story, he holds the imaginary portrait before him and whispers, with the utmost contempt, "Begone, poltroon." We don't laugh, because we know what Aunt Lucy sacrificed on account of that man.

In our family lore, she is a saint, a crackpot, or a militant lesbian ahead of her time; take your pick. If she had stayed where she was meant to stay—if she had married as she was expected to marry, raised a family, and ushered her offspring into society—she would have reigned over a sun-filled French Quarter town house, complete with lacy gridwork, gilt chairs, a world veiled by white oleander. Tante Lucidité, we might have called her. Or maybe she wouldn't have lived so long. Maybe we'd never have met her.

It starts like a fairy tale. There were, once upon a time, three sisters in the Jardine family: Vetty, Amy, Lucy. Vérité was the oldest, Amitié followed two years behind, and Lucidité, spark of sentiment, trailed them by twenty more. There was also a son, Vetty's twin brother, Aristide (my father's father's father). Aristide had the anxious honor of being the first Southerner accepted at West Point after the Civil War. As the only member of his class to inherit the pain of cultural as well as military defeat, Aristide was an object, variously, of his fellow cadets' pity, esteem, and scorn. His eventual popularity was hard won and, as a result, never taken for granted. After rising through the ranks faster than any of his classmates, he wore four stars by the time he was fifty and, on November 11, 1918, in Rethondes, France, played a critical role, with his plantation manners and flawless French, in closing the deal on the Armistice.

For Aristide's graduation, the family commandeered a first-class train carriage north, the women flaunting every amber bead and tiny pearl that remained of their semiravished sugar fortune (that blue cameo, I imagine, riding the proud throat of my great-great-grandmother Théa, barely pregnant with Lucy). They'd stuck it out beyond the terrible losses of the war, refusing to turn tail and head back to France, as so many of their compatriots did. They would show these Northerners that they had done far better than merely survive.

During the festivities, the Jardines must have stood out like peonies in goldenrod, strolling the campus and praising the sights, exclaiming at everything in their patrician drawl, fussing with fans and parasols. Aristide's best friend, Josiah Moore, squired the two sisters about with their brother whenever the parents' energies flagged. Bantam-chested and big-chinned, blond but with a Venetian's dark eyes, Josiah looked tremendously virile in his uniform. (Who can know what his smile was like, how devastating, when all that remains to us now is a shady quick-silver image on glass, a portrait taken the day of commencement?) A week after the Jardines returned to New Orleans, Vetty fled north again to elope with Josiah. She wrote to her family from Boston, requesting their love and forgiveness.

What she got was a thorough disowning. It was one thing, in 1881, to share education and martial fellowship with one's vanquishers and quite another to marry them, let alone on the sly. Over the next two decades, Père Jardine rebuilt his fortune, cane by cane; Lieutenant Aristide Jardine helped bring in Geronimo; Amy married a grapefruit czar and had the first three of five children; young Lucy grew up and was groomed by mother and older sister for a glorious debut. She knew of her eldest sister's existence only through whispered remarks outside her home. The way Dad tells it, Lucy was popular and pretty, poised for a momentous engagement, when a letter arrived from Vetty, opened only perhaps because its postmark was a riddle. Vermont? Who knew anyone there?

Vetty's husband had left her. Childless, she could not bring herself to ask his family for help, and she was afraid she might not survive another winter by herself. She was too distraught, she said, to travel home on her own and did not know, besides, whether the family would take her back in.

Meanwhile, her sister Amy was pregnant for the fourth time—as it would turn out, with twins of her own—and her mother's help was indispensable. Père Jardine had a business to run, and Aristide was about to set sail for a tour in the Philippines. So a bold nineteen-year-old Lucy volunteered to make the trip, with a trusted servant as companion, to bring home a sister she'd never even known. (Is this tale Victorian or what?)

How it happened that the servant returned to New Orleans several months later without either sister isn't entirely clear. But in the end, what we do know is that Lucy stayed in Vermont to care for Vetty, a woman who made herself scarce, preferring to stay in her room and quilt, her stitching a method of mourning away the rest of her life.

About the forlorn, mysterious Vetty, rumors still thrive: that Josiah left her far earlier than she claimed, nearly as soon as she was disowned, because money was all he'd been after; that she had a child who died as an infant; that Josiah ran off with their maid after getting the girl pregnant. Whatever Lucy knew, she kept to herself. When I asked Dad why he didn't get her to tell the whole story, he said, "Louisa, we live in an age when keeping secrets is out of fashion, and that's a shame. If she wanted to tell us, well, she would."

More than once, I've listened to my relatives squabble inconsequentially over the meaning of Lucy's choice, as if she made it last week. Some say she was a foolish martyr who inherited the loneliness she deserved; others that she was a wise, willful woman who saw and took her best chance at freedom from a life of luxurious monotony. Others insist that she was simply a good girl who honored—as so few children do these days, they'll say with a sharp mournful glance at members of my generation—the Most Important Thing: loyalty to blood, cost be damned. Some of the younger cousins are certain that Lucy was gay, perhaps dallying with her own sister. I don't believe any of this; I believe she was swept along on a tide, like most of us. There you are, diligently swimming a straight line, minding the form of your strokes, when you look up and see, always a shock, that currents you can't even feel have pulled you off course.

A WEEKEND, a whole *weekend*, with Louisa? What a sourpuss she had become. But I was stuck playing host, so I asked for the afternoon off from the bike shop. That morning, I was slicing the loaf I'd thawed and Louisa was sleeping off jet lag when who should call but Ralph. Ralph and Hector ran the raptor station. They're zoology grad students, muscular outdoorsy guys you'd never guess are lovers unless you've been to their house and seen their water bed (king size, spread with a polar bear hide). Ralph wears a diamond the size of a peppercorn in his left ear, but he also has a tattoo—a blue cormorant—on the opposite biceps. Ralph's run the Iditarod, and Hector, from Portuguese New Bedford, dresses like an off-duty fisherman—clean but hardly stylish. When Ralph asked if I wanted to go out and hear a new band, all I could think was that my prayers had been answered. I wrote Louisa a note and left to put in my grease-monkey time at the shop.

Lucy liked my mechanical know-how. She treated me like a free electrician, plumber, you name it: an all-around Ms. Fix-It. This was her subtle revenge for my treating her like I was her probation officer, no matter how nicely. If I came home for lunch, I'd find a sandwich, a bottle of beer in a bowl of ice, and a note that said, *Clement dear, the drain in the sink seems a mite sluggish; could you give it a thorough snaking?* or *Do you rewire? The tasseled lamp by the pink chesterfield has a new habit of winking.* Lucy would be asleep in her room, so she never asked me in person. I could have stayed in town all day, but the weird thing is, I began to look forward to going back at noon: I liked the green breezy silence on the porch, liked finding that beer, liked peeking through Lucy's bedroom door to make sure she was breathing. Maybe this was the closest I'd ever come to having a child.

But nothing surprised me more than how much I got into the after-dinner shopathons. By early July, I was an ace chauffeur and personal shopper. At first, we just hunted down gadgets: man, was she obsessed. Like the juicer, which I tried to talk her out of. She had to ask me what it was for, and when I explained how it was mostly for health fiends who live on carrot juice and have orange skin on the bottoms of their feet, she said, "My carrots will never be anything other than boiled." But she put her hands around the barrel of that thing and said, "Don't you adore its sheer presence? So exquisitely masculine! A stevedore. A *gigolo!*" In her mouth, that word was a delicacy, a chocolate-covered cherry, and she gave me a new smile—hardly the smile of a maiden aunt—so I overrode my own veto. (Things I did veto: a pasta maker, an electric corkscrew, an automated shoe-shine.)

Her obsession sent us back to the same three stores again and again; after two weeks, she'd seen everything there was to see. So one beautiful evening—dry spruce air off Lake Champlain, sunset scorching the water flamingo pink—she steers me down a street of hippie boutiques, those places where simply stepping inside to browse makes you smell like a swami for days. I figure she must sense this because at first she just peers through open doors, makes disapproving remarks ("Clutter, clutter" or "Whose attic exploded here?" or a tart "Re*mark*able"). But then she says, "Here we are!" like she's a regular, and pulls me into a pack rat's trove of gauzy dresses, earrings like chandeliers, and a million doodads for smoking pot. I'm nervous she'll ask me what all the bongs and pipes and clips are for, but she's staring at the ceiling—a fleet of Chinese kites. She points to a black one, a twisting dragon with scales painted in gold. It's incredibly cheap for something so cool, so handmade, I guess because the paper's fragile and it isn't expected to fly. I warn Lucy, but she says she's too old for flying kites; she wants to hang it over her bed. (We know who'll get to do that.)

While the salesgirl wraps it—in a slo-mo dream haze and I know, or smell, exactly why—Lucy wanders around the store. "Is this *la mode* these days?" She pulls a minidress, all tiny brown paisleys, off a rack. Then she turns toward a mirror and holds it against her chest. Her laugh is soft and husky. The dress does look silly against her navy-blue dowager special, a tailored thing from about the year my sister was born, shoulders straight from the Super Bowl, neck closed with this old-fashioned cameo she wears all the time: some dainty damsel sniffing a flower. But right then, for the first time, I see my great-great-aunt as more than a charming fossil. Her face is so wrinkled, it's a geology unto itself, and her hands are knobby and speckled as driftwood. I'd bet she's lost five inches in height—never too tall to begin with. But she stands upright and slim, wears her hair in a neat silver twist, and smiles sometimes like she's sixteen, so I think, Why the hell not?

I lead her to a back corner, a rack of dresses on sale because they're outdated, last spring's longer style. I pick a dark purple one with red flowers, crinkly rayon with a loose waist and sleeves. Lucy jiggles the tiny bells that hang from ties at the neck. She looks cautiously approving. "So?" I say. "Try it on."

She tells me emphatically that she's past the days of undressing outside her own room. But I can guess her size—like, *teensy*—and nine dollars is worth the adventure. When I point out it's a two-for-one sale, she says, "Very well, then this one, too." The second dress is equally modest, but it's an electric maharani green shot through with turquoise, like the sea off Martinique at noon. It comes with a long gold sash. As she strokes the sash, laughing quietly at herself, it makes me think of all the years she's lived and all the people who've passed through her life—just countless—because I'm pretty sure that none of them ever saw the Lucy I'm seeing tonight.

I SLEPT TILL ELEVEN, infuriating myself. Clem was gone, but she'd left out that eccentric bread, cream cheese, maple butter, and coffee in a brand-new Swedish coffeemaker. I poured a cup and took her note onto the front porch. The house wasn't far from the street, but thanks to Aunt Lucy's hands-off approach to the landscape, it was hidden by holly trees that had knit their branches into a daunting fortress.

Clem had made plans with two guys named Hector and Ralph, and did I mind? My first reaction was, *So what if I do?* The second was, *Which guy is she involved with?* Clem is never without a boyfriend or two. She's not beautiful, exactly, but she's tall and strong and has the kind of hair— dark and dense—that lends itself to tossing. She's physically daring, if rarely graceful, runs and throws like the boys (fast and far, which they so predictably mention, tripping over themselves with adulation). I'm not so tall, not so strong, and my hair, ruly and just barely blond, doesn't toss. I decided that whichever guy was hers, I would do my best to steal him, just for a night. I was determined if not optimistic.

After toast and more coffee, I toured the house. Clem was staying in the bedroom next to mine. It looked like a college lair: whirlpool of sheets, sneakers, and books. Clem's books are detective novels and nature guides: everything you ever wanted to know (or not) about dolphins, comets, birdsong, and the endangered flora of northern New England. The dresser was strewn with earrings—wooden tigers, silver parrots, soapstone Eskimo fish—and the floor with bikini underpants, glossy and black like her hair.

But Aunt Lucy's room was where I wanted to snoop. Partly because I wanted to see what treasures, if any, were left behind, but mostly because she'd always been such an enigma. After her sister's death—sometime back around World War Two—Lucy started sleeping in the den, off the parlor. The furniture was heavy and dark, the linens starched and wedding white. The quilt on the bed was white on white, a grapevine, one of Aunt Vetty's. The wallpaper, a mesh of spidery ferns, gave the room its only color.

In the past, the dresser had held only practical things. Lucy did not like displaying photographs, least of all any including herself. So, no effigies of family on the dresser, but tucked in the frame of the mirror was a picture of Jimmy Carter, a recent cover from *Time* magazine. On the lace runner below, among soft-bristled brushes and silver-capped jars, a cassette player loomed like an urban intruder, one of those new macho machines resembling a suitcase. Some of the tapes stacked beside it were classical—Chopin, Mozart, Puccini—but the ones on top included Bob Marley, Bruce Springsteen, the Grateful Dead. When I pushed PLAY, Van Morrison filled the room, a song that went off in my memory like a flashbulb: back in college, a picnic in Boston Garden, roast beef subs, screw-top chablis. The swan boats gliding in a blur behind willows. "These Dreams of You."

Over the bed hung a kite, a dragon with a twisting tail, suspended from the ceiling with hooks and fishing line. On the side table, a wind-up alarm clock had stopped at 9:21.

The dresser drawers were empty, except for the brittle paper liners patterned with tiny violets.

"The jewelry," said Clem, "is in the bank." She stood in the doorway.

I closed the top drawer. "That's not what I was doing."

"I know." Oddly (mercifully?), she didn't sound sarcastic. "I'm trying to hang on to her, too. All the little details. The quirks. Really, though, she didn't leave much of herself—her *self*—behind." Clem walked back into the parlor and looked around. "She used to make me lunch. I suppose we'll have to go out. We have a lifetime supply of bread, but nothing to go between it."

"I think I saw soup in a cupboard," I said. "When I was looking for sugar."

Clem laughed. "That's right. You take *sugar*."

"What's so funny?"

"Oh, just everything."

"Death is funny?"

"Sometimes, Louisa, yes. As a matter of fact. But that's not what I meant."

∽

"AVIAN AEROBICS," I explained to Louisa. "Physical therapy."

Ralph held a peregrine falcon while I exercised the newly healed wing, flexing it away from the body and back, away and back. Lance (Ralph gave all the birds Round Table nicknames) knew the routine by now, but still you had to be careful. Back in June, a barn owl had nailed me. I thought he was small enough for me to handle alone; next thing I knew, he snatched a leg free and sank his claws a good inch into my arm. I managed not to scream; a struggle would have ripped me to shreds. Hector, precise and silent as a surgeon, pulled the foot free one sickle-shaped talon at a time.

Louisa was finally out from under her portable storm cloud. She seemed thrilled by everything we showed her. But she was weirdly overdressed—in this practically see-through white dress, long gold earrings that Lance would gladly have swiped in a flash; I could see his cold laser glance captivated by the glint as she laughed. She stood back when I brought him out and turned down my offer to help feed our orphaned cygnets.

Ralph explained how Lance had been caught in a ground snare set for wolves, how he'd fought and broken his wing in two places. Lance is one of Ralph's miracles. Unlike most of our birds, which end up in preserves and zoos, he'd get released back into the wild.

"He's magnificent," Louisa said to Ralph.

"They drove this guy down from Canada; they know we don't fool around," said Ralph. He put Lance back in his cage.

"Tell her about the redtails," I said.

This was our favorite success story, but really it was Ralph's. The previous fall, before I arrived, he had rescued a female red-tailed hawk with a torn foot. She'd been a star inmate at the sanctuary when I came. Ralph adored her, but he was careful not to tame her. Two weeks after I got there, she was ready to go home. "So we drive her in on this long bumpy road," said Ralph, "in a big cage in the back of the truck, and she's bouncing like crazy, and she's calling out in protest—or that's what I think till I cut the engine and I hear the calling back, and it's coming from up ahead. And we look up and we see . . ." Tears began to fill Ralph's eyes, the way they did whenever he told it. "It's her mate. He's waited all this time. Eight months! They're calling back and forth—it's earsplitting—and then we can actually see him up there. We let her go, and she flies up to meet him and . . ." He lifted one hand in a soaring motion.

"Off into the sunset," I said. "Romeo and Juliet." I got teary, too.

"Except with a happy ending," said Louisa. "Wow."

Ralph wiped his eyes. "I can't believe what I *do*."

After I met Ralph, it took me a while to figure out why he's so likable, so effortlessly cool: it's because he's brilliant at what he does but without a speck of modesty, false or real. He never stops asking questions. Hector's just as smart, but he's shy. He has this kind of honest stealth and a soft voice that transfixes the birds into stillness whenever he holds them. A matter of soul, not technique.

The band wouldn't go on till ten, so after we locked up the station, we took a six-pack and a bottle of wine to the lake. We found an empty stretch of smooth gray rock, its surface striped with raised white welts as thin as twine. Louisa told Ralph about her pottery, how she'd been in a bunch of shows, though never her own. I'd seen the announcements on the fridge at our parents' house. Louisa never sent them to me. Most of her pots are tall and curvy, like skinny people in a fun-house mirror. When you see them, you can't resist smiling. You'd think they were made by someone who's perpetually sunny.

At the end of telling us about her life, Louisa sighed loudly. "But the truth is," she said, "I can't stop missing the East. I'm hopelessly Yankee."

And how, I could've said. But I said, "So move back. Before you fall for the wrong guy and get stuck there. Isn't Santa Barbara like the capital of golf? That's all you need: some golfer who can't see his white shoes over his beer gut."

Ralph laughed. Louisa gave me her iron-maiden look. "*You* try to change coasts when you're always on the verge of broke."

"I *am* always broke."

"You're a student," she said. "That doesn't count. Dad bails you out."

"So, he'd bail you out, too."

"I wouldn't let him."

I couldn't help laughing. "You wouldn't . . ."

"Wouldn't what?"

"You shouldn't be so proud, is what I meant to say." I'd been about to say that she didn't seem inclined to let anyone do much of anything for her.

"What I am is practical. I have to make a living. Save some money."

"No offense," I said, "but making pottery is practical?"

"Shouldn't you be in New York?" asked Hector before Louisa could answer me. "Isn't that the place to be an artist, to be taken seriously?"

"I like New York, but"—she groaned—"I wanted something different. Well, different's what I got. Different as in irrelevant." She shrugged. "But I'll figure it out. I don't mean to complain. And you"— she turned to include Ralph—"you guys are an inspiration."

She asked Ralph about his thesis. He's studying birds that nest on Lake Michigan, how pesticide residues weaken their eggshells. Tests of local topsoil show evidence of, among other poisons, a compound that was used to kill boll weevils ten years before and no farther north than Georgia. Louisa nodded sincerely, saying things like "Incredible" and "That is such important work" and "People have no idea." Her aggressive flattery put me on edge.

I interrupted. "You know what blows me away about Ralph? He's run the Iditarod."

"Once," said Ralph, his mouth full of pretzel. "It was fantastic, but once is plenty. I like my toes and fingers very much. I find them useful." He wiggled his salty fingers in front of his face. He glanced at Hector, who blushed and smiled.

"The what?" said Louisa.

"It's a thousand-mile race by dogsled," I said. "It makes the Boston Marathon look like a game of Old Maid."

I started to describe how the route retraces the relay that carried a vial of diphtheria serum to snowbound Nome back in 1925, but Louisa cut me off by turning to Ralph and saying, "Did you win?" This is so her, the A student ranking everything in sight.

"Second to last, but you had better believe it, I finished."

Louisa took off her gold sandals and stepped into the water, ankle deep. The low sun shone through her dress. "Do you realize how beautiful this is?" she said, gazing across the lake. She looked good—sexy; tall and curvy like one of her pots—but she also looked absurd, like a Greek goddess who's dropped in to make a little trouble for the mortals below.

Ralph punched me on the arm. "Hey, tomorrow. Let's take her out to the gorge. It's supposed to be a scorcher. I'll bring the boys. And some tunes. You bring lunch."

"Oh. Like, we're women, so we do food?"

"How about, I'm your boss so you do what I say? I'm the one with the four-wheel drive? Clement dear." He'd heard Lucy call me that.

"What gorge?" asked Louisa.

"A place we go when we're tired of the lake," Hector told her.

"When we want a touch of danger," said Ralph in a menacing whisper.

"People dive off this tall rock," I said. "It's incredibly stupid, but too much fun. I did it once, for the rush. A guy was killed last year when he boomeranged back in midair and smashed his skull. He thought he could do a somersault. On top of stupid, he was totally trashed."

"Didn't someone get sued?" Louisa looked queasy.

Ralph said, "This is Vermont, baby. The risks you take are all your own. You break it, you bought it."

Everyone laughed except Louisa.

I GET WEARY just looking at dreadlocks. I keep thinking, How *heavy* is all that hair? How on earth do you wash it? We sat near the stage, so the music was loud enough to boil your blood, and the smell of dope was a fourth dimension. I'm no big fan of Jah, whoever he is, but I did my best to feign a glow. Clem must have caught on when I failed to sing along with the Natty Lads' cover of "No Woman, No Cry." She suggested (she had to yell) that we head over to a bar called the Galaxy, which had, she said (yelled), a "jukebox for white girls."

Well, I said to myself, be what you are.

On the way over, the guys walked together in front of us. Clem whispered to me, "Are you just alone too much these days or what? You are like so . . . I don't know, antsy?"

"Is that a question?" I asked.

"Well, see what I mean?" she said loudly. Ralph turned around to smile at us, then waited to throw an arm around Clem's shoulders. And then we were, thank heaven, at the bar. Because she was right, about my being alone too much. I knew I was being obnoxious, and I didn't care, but what if I couldn't have been otherwise? What if I'd tried to be agreeable but couldn't?

When Marvin Gaye came on, Ralph asked me to dance. He spun me around with such certainty and speed that I was dizzy, but in that happy way when you know you're in the hands of a man who won't bungle the moves. Who dances so well that you do, too, no matter how clumsy you are. He had to be the one, I decided—the way he put his arm around Clem and whispered in her ear—but I liked him, too. I liked the way his thick dark mustache moved when he talked, I liked the passion he had for the minutiae of his work: measurements, in millimeters, of feather-shaft diameter, egg circumference, the width of fledglings' skulls. At first I'd thought of it as a game—a taste of revenge—but now, with the wine singing in my ears, I decided, both overjoyed and mournful, that I was falling for the guy. That morning I'd worked out a scheme: Saturday the view, Sunday the kill, Monday the jewels, Tuesday split town to visit my parents. Now it didn't look so easy.

Between his deft moves, Ralph liked to talk, so he sounded a little breathless. "Nice you two are friends." Spun me out, snapped me in. "I have a brother in Chicago, can't stand the sight of me. Once in a while I try again, but no cigar." Under his arm I soared, as if cast on a reel of silk ribbon.

"We have our moments," I said when I faced him again. "Our differences." I didn't say that lately I'd felt about Clem the way his brother felt about him.

I rolled inside his arm toward his chest in an effortless spiral. I could smell his sweat, just faintly, through his damp plaid shirt. "You know, I met your Aunt Lucy," he said. For a few minutes we were face-to-face. Gently, he rocked the two of us back and forth, his hands clasping my shoulders. *Please stop talking,* I thought. "Man, what a live wire," he said. "Somebody should've studied what her secret was. I'd say I'm sorry she died, but it seems like she lived the life she chose, no other. You know what I mean?"

He clapped loudly at the end of the song, as if Marvin Gaye were right there with us. He took my arm and led me back to the table. I said, "Yes, and talk about a devoted sister."

As I started telling the story of Lucy and Vetty, Clem stood up. She touched my back. "I'm off to lounge in the lounge." She gave us a tiny flirtatious wave. Ralph mimicked her wave in return. My heart sank.

I told the short version of the family saga, because the jukebox was right by our table. I touched Ralph's hand several times. When I finished, my throat was sore from shouting and Clem was still gone. In Ralph's pure, sincere attention to the story (mirrored by Hector), in the way his hand never moved in reaction to mine, I saw that none of his attention had anything to do with me. I was both mortified and relieved. I excused myself.

I found her talking on a pay phone in the ladies' room; she gave me her coy little wave. I heard her say, "Like crazy, you animal you," before hanging up.

"Another one waiting in the wings? You never cease to amaze me."

"Another what? That was my guy Luke. You don't know about him. He's in Alaska for the summer." She turned toward the mirror, arched her eyebrows to put on lipstick. She moved her hips to the music out in the bar and, before closing the lipstick, looped it through the air like a stunt plane, part of her dance.

"Who'd you steal *him* from? Is he a dogsled champion, too?"

Clem giggled. She worked at coaxing her hair behind her ears. "What about me? Think I could do it, Lou, the race to the Pole?"

She offered me her lipstick. Angrily, I took it. It was exponentially brighter than any color I'd ever worn. "You are so stoned," I said. "But, sure, why not? That's you, isn't it? Adventures right and left just begging to let them be yours. Same as all the men."

"Ouch." Clem looked at me in the mirror. "Is this about Mike?"

"No," I said.

"Yes, it is. Christ, it is." She gazed at the ceiling. "I guess I'd be stupid to think you've forgiven me after all this time, right? Did you come out here to, like, reinforce the grudge, is that it?"

"I came out here to pay my respects," I said. "And not to you."

"Oh that is such bullshit," said Clem. "Louisa, are you lonely or angry or both? Or am I deluded when I remember we used to have fun?"

Instead of answering, I looked at myself in the mirror and put on the lipstick. "I don't think so," I said, but I was talking about the color.

"Wow," said Clem. "So. Who gets to be the Soviet Union and who gets to be the U.S.A.?"

A very drunk girl entered the bathroom and stopped to brace herself on the paper towel dispenser. She caught my eye in the mirror and laughed. "Uh-oh," she said. I asked if she was all right, but she was already lurching into a stall. Clem and I listened to her retch. I started for the door back to civilization.

"No," said Clem, blocking my way. "You've got this *idea* of me."

I sighed. "Okay, sure, we did have fun. We used to."

"So, if I say I'm sorry, will you snap out of this funk?"

Another girl came in, calling loudly, "Fran? Fran, are you in here?"

Clem started laughing. The new girl glared at her. As we left the restroom, Clem leaned against me and said in a soft voice, "Listen. I'm trying monogamy on for size. And you know, it's not like I've been . . . promiscuous." She sounded out the word with care. "Which I know is how you see me. Well, you're wrong."

Barry White was singing. Hector and Ralph were dancing. Together.

"Hoo, will you look at those boys," said Clem. "Delicious, aren't they?"

Clem saw my ruefulness, written all over my face. "Guys. Deceptive, even when they're not trying. Always a challenge."

"Well, for some of us."

"Even for *me*," said Clem, barring me with her arm for an instant, to make me look her in the face. "Lou, I am not who you think." I had no answer, and I don't think she wanted one.

I let her lead the way back to our table. We watched the men dance.

Clem said, "If I could steal one of those wonderful guys from the other, I just might."

"So much for your monogamy pledge." But I couldn't help laughing. Mostly at myself.

Mike was the guy she'd stolen from under my nose, two summers before. I was twenty-two; Clem was eighteen. It was the last summer we were both at home, living with our parents. Mike lived down the road. He collected motorcycles, repaired our neighbors' sports cars, and, I'm guessing in retrospect, serviced the neighbors' wives with a parallel expertise. One day I got him to look at my rusty Dodge Dart, which had developed yet another ominous rattle or squeal. In his driveway, I thought those easy smiles were personal, mine alone. We spent one fragrant sticky night on the hammock behind his garage apartment, and oh, what ridiculous notions I had about what that night meant. Two days later, he picked me up on one of his bikes and sped me to a distant beach. We went at each other, clumsy and hot, against a hedge of prickly beach plum.

A week went by; I stayed late a few nights at the museum where I worked, putting up a show of new photographers (which is how I met the one I followed out west—Clem's fault if I factored in Mike and the rebound effect). One night when I got back, the two of them were on the porch. I assumed Mike was waiting for me. After we watched the news together, me sitting tight by his side, he said he still had work to do. When he didn't take me with him, I thought, All right, a little distance is natural. Next night, Clem's bicycle was gone and stayed gone till morning. The phone rang forever at Mike's. The night after that, under a crazy quilt of stars, I crossed five backyards in my bare feet. I heard them long before I saw them, but that didn't send me home. I had to see them with my own eyes, all but naked on the chaise by Dr. Eccleston's pool. Going back, I stepped on a piece of glass.

He had the nerve to come to my parents' Fourth of July barbecue, and Clem had the nerve, even worse, to borrow a dress from my closet. It's quite something, watching your favorite dress make time with the guy you're crazy about—without you in it. I walked right over and threw my Mateus rosé in her face. I drove to the beach and lay on the sand till fireworks erupted from the trees. When I told her she was the scum of the earth, she said I might have a good case.

LUCY'S ROUTINES BECAME MINE, so whenever she broke them, I was thrown off balance. One breezy Saturday evening, once I'd parked the car near the Burlington green and helped her out onto the sidewalk, she said brightly, "No shops, not tonight." She put her arm through mine, the way she asked for support without asking. "Show me the town, Clement dear."

"The town?"

She laughed. "Don't play the innocent. I know a party girl when I see one. Take me to your favorite nightclub, your . . . hangout? Den of iniquity?"

I laughed, too. What was I afraid of?

The Galaxy was filling up fast. We got a few odd looks, but there was Ralph, waving from a table beside a window. Bob Marley was singing "Positive Vibration." Ralph called out, "Cool runnin's, baby!"

"Africa, unite!" I called back, raising a fist. "I know those guys," I said to Lucy, leading her carefully through the crowd.

Ralph and Hector stood up like our fathers would and pulled out a chair between them. They acted like it was the most normal thing in the world, taking your great-great-aunt to your local bar. That's when I really fell for them. Ralph took Lucy's handbag and put it under his coat on the windowsill. Hector insisted on treating us.

Having settled herself and looked around, she turned to him and said, "Africa? Is this Black Panther talk?"

Ralph laughed loudly and leaned close to Lucy. "Mrs. Jardine, it's reggae talk. We're just into the lingo of the music, it's a fantasy. We're too pathetically white to be Rastafarians."

She told him to call her Lucy. "I have never been a Mrs. and will never be a Ms." She frowned. "Rosicrucians, did you say? The Rosicrucians make music?"

"Just listen for a little," he said. "Let me be your deejay." And off he went to the jukebox.

We watched her take in the music and the surroundings. Hector set her cream sherry in the center of a napkin, like a waiter in a white-glove hotel.

Lucy cupped a hand behind her best ear, to hear the music over the voices in the crowded bar. She repeated carefully, uncertainly, " 'In

the abundance of water, the fool is thirsty'? Is that what he just sang?"
She went back to listening, and then she looked at me. "So if I were a
young girl now, this is the music I would like?"

Oh Lucy, I wanted to say, *you* are *a young girl.* I felt so moved by the
look on her face that I couldn't quite answer. I asked, "Well, are you
thinking of, like, revolutionizing your tastes?"

"Revolution is no longer a possibility," she said. "My tastes, like my
bones, fossilized decades ago. Reach a certain age and you are obliged to
become an anthropologist. It's the only way to ignore that the rest of the
world regards *you* as an artifact, that your culture has faded beyond the
horizon, leaving you adrift on your tiny, solitary life raft." She said this
without self-pity or sadness. I'd lived with her for a month and hadn't
stopped to think, till then, that she no longer had any friends her own
age. Not a one.

Ralph returned. "Bob Dylan, the Dead, Marianne Faithfull, Lou
Reed, Al Green, Hendrix. It's a start."

Lucy closed her eyes. She looked as if she was listening in order to
memorize. For Jimi Hendrix, she sat forward and squeezed her eyes
tight. At first, I assumed she found the din of his guitar unbearable. Then
she opened her eyes and said, "He's kissing the sky?"

Her sherry glass was empty; with a slight nod, she passed it to Hector,
who rose at once to get her a refill.

"What a lovely thought. Kissing the sky," she mused, a ghost of southern girlhood in her voice.

Several songs later, she asked me if we could go to a music store the
next day. "You'll remember what we've heard this evening, won't you?"
she said as we helped her up. I assured her that I would.

"Come again, anytime," said the bartender as we passed him.

"I just might," Lucy told him. "I just might become a regular."

But she never did ask to go back. Two weeks later she died, as she
deserved to, in her sleep. I'd made our dinner, poured her sherry, but she
didn't respond to my knocking. The night before, she'd said she was too
tired for a drive, said she'd go to bed early and read. Just after dawn, I was

sure I'd heard her in the kitchen below my room. But the night we went to the Galaxy, she was tireless, as much a party girl in her way as I am in mine. Going home, she made me stop at the all-night Star Market. "Carrots," she said. "I want to try out my little blue gigolo." She waited in the car; when I came back, I noticed that her nose just barely cleared the dashboard.

Lucy insisted on a pitcher, tray, crystal glasses, and mint from the patch that grew wild by the old water pump. I carried this Swanee-style production onto the porch.

"This is like punch! Miraculous! Splendid!" she said. My hands were stained bright orange, along with my Red Stripe T-shirt and most of the kitchen counter.

While I was lighting the mosquito candles, I said, "If this is disrespectful or nosy, just say, but I've been wondering—living here, you know, with you—about Aunt Vetty. She's like this gothic character everyone whispers about. As if she was a ghost even when she was alive. And that spooky room, with all her stuff up there . . ."

"Well, my dear, in every family lucky enough to inherit stories, there will always be specters."

"What inspectors?"

"No, Clement dear." She laughed. "Perhaps I should say, Many a hope chest contains a suit of rattling bones." She sipped her juice, pushing the suspense. I waited. Finally she said, "I used to wonder if your father knew. He's the only one of the current crop who might."

"Everybody agrees you saved her life, that you were incredibly selfless." For the second time that night, but differently, I was nervous.

Lucy looked at me, silent again for what felt like ages. I thought she might be angry until she said, "Do you know, Clement dear, that not one member of this prolific family has ever asked me for my version of events until now? Until you? As if they think I'd keel over from recalling the sheer disgrace of it." She smiled what I thought of now as her little-blue-gigolo smile, practically sexual, a come-on. I thought, sadly, how she never got to use that smile the way it was meant to be used. "Not that I know if I would have told anyone," she said. "There is a secret—only because no one's pried. And which, if you stay up, I see no reason not to tell you. Consider it a dividend of all your hard work. Keeping me in the strait and narrow. I think your father must be pleased."

I waited. I laughed my nervous laugh. "Well, I hope it involves a trunk of money buried in the yard that will support me like royalty the rest of my life."

Right away, I was sorry for the joke, but Lucy kept on smiling, more like a grandmother now. "As you might say, don't I wish." She touched her throat for a moment, the place where she had worn that old cameo before we jazzed up her wardrobe. She kept doing that, always forgetting she'd given it up.

"My sister Vetty was thirty-seven when I met her for the first time," she said. "Imagine that. And all I knew of her till then was that she had done this rash, impetuous, ruinous thing: run off with what sounded to me like a perfectly respectable young man whose only shame was provenance. Isn't that a comic, lamentable slap of fate?" She directed this question out toward the holly trees, the fireflies, the chorus of crickets.

"When I met her, this husband had left her, just as you've heard—no thanks, mind you, to our sanctimonious parents. Vetty and Josiah had no children, but she loved him. Such a passion for such an ordinary man, and oh how she tried to hold him! When he left the army after the Indian Wars, he came home—here—to run his father's sawmill. Vetty was thrilled. He would be safe; they would sleep under the same roof! But after five years he moved across town to look for another bride. I think if she'd had a family to meddle and cajole, events might have turned out otherwise. Never mind, though: he still gave her money, still split her wood, still went to their church—she was the one who had to change pews—but she was alone as could be. The more so for his being near. She had a talent, thank heaven, and by the time I arrived, she had a solid business as a seamstress. She was pitied, but also respected. No one blamed her. Hand of God and such."

I watched Lucy closely. "But you . . . you came up here to rescue her."

"Oh no." She looked at me, this time without a smile of any kind. "I came up here so she could rescue me." Lucy reached down slowly and lifted her glass from the floor. "Another, thank you."

I poured her the rest of the carrot juice. "Clement dear, when I was eighteen years old, I met a man of my own. A man the family couldn't have approved of more! A man with whom I was smitten! Everything splendid! A nascent betrothal in everyone's eyes, as it turned out, but his. There I was, six months later, not a gem on my hand, but pregnant as the sky is blue. So ordinary, as sins go; even *that* seemed sinful, how viciously ordinary it was. The most common of female mishaps. Now, my daddy could bear many less-than-agreeable things, but *common* things, no. My daddy belonged to the same club as my young man's daddy, but they shared no business, so there was no leverage. We were one year into a fine new century. Duels were a thing of the past. And what could possibly make more sense, in my parents' desperation to bury another scandal, than to ferret out and repossess fallen daughter number one to gain a refuge for number two? Logical, don't you agree, Clement dear?" She drained her glass with a flourish and held it tight in her lap.

"Vetty. Imagine how ecstatically she must have awaited my arrival— the sister she'd never laid eyes on, soon to deliver a baby, to give poor Vetty a flesh-and-blood purpose. Misfortune it might seem to some, but to her, it meant reunion with her family and the gift of the child she'd always longed for. As for alibis, I was said to be on a tour of Europe recovering from the attentions of a cad—a colorful affliction at best—and would return to the marriage market evanescent and worldly. I would be fed stories of Paris and Constantinople with which to charm new ranks of suitors. How clever my parents were. How thorough."

"You had a baby?" I said. "You had a *baby?*" I was longing for a beer but didn't dare leave the porch.

"A little boy," she said. Not a hint of tears. She smiled rapturously at the night. "He was with us, Vetty and me, for less than a month when our father arrived. You could have knocked us down with a butterfly wing.

My, but his particular coldness . . . something more climatically suited to these parts than to steamy, gay New Orleans. A gene, I'm thankful to say, that seems to have dwindled into extinction."

She laughed a tight, dry little laugh. "Our father was such a shrewd strategist. I suppose it didn't take him long to see how very *useful* it was that our sister Amy was expecting her fourth child. Aristide, your great-grandfather and my brother, would never have let it happen. He'd always written, secretly, to Vetty and her husband. His twin sister and his best friend from school: the union always seemed right to him. But he was abroad at the time of my calamity, ignorant of the entire affair. I sometimes think my parents sat quietly on their decision till after he had shipped out to the far, far East. So Amy, our favored sister, the only one not to betray and disappoint, well bless her soul if she didn't all of a sudden have *twins*. One quite the bruiser, astonishing! No one ever saw a newborn baby so big, no mother was prouder. She wrote me often, I will say that. She sent me a portrait every year at Christmas: my son in her lap. Sometimes, you know, I think about the pressure on Amy to be the good one, how much more strenuous that must have felt once I fell by the wayside, too."

"Wait," I said. I belong to one of those families in which every single member could produce under torture a flawless family tree, every gnarl and knot in place, reaching back five generations. I was doing some hasty scrambling through the branches. Amy's twins were my great-uncles Charles and Christopher, both recently dead. I asked her, Which one?

"Ah," she said, "here ends my confession, dear one." She handed me her empty glass, stood, and leaned against the back of her chair.

"I won't tell anyone if you don't want me to. I'll keep it a secret." Mentally, I was busy reconfiguring two batches of second cousins; which were in fact descendants of Lucy?

"If you should be so lucky as to live a life this long—that is, if you consider it luck, and I am not saying you shouldn't—I cannot possibly hold you to a promise like that. But promise me this." She put her arm through mine. As she leaned against me, I could smell her gardenia powder, a smell like attic and garden together. "Promise they'll burn me in that splendid green dress you made me buy, the one with the golden sash."

The next day, when I came home for lunch, she looked as if she'd been impatient for me to arrive. She asked if I had time to drive her to the bank. On a table in the living room sat a large box covered with dark green alligator skin. She had no further use for jewelry, she said; it might as well be somewhere safe. Then she reached out and pressed something into my hand. I felt a slight prick and looked down at the old blue cameo. Its sheer familiarity, as something inseparable from her, made me light-headed, yet I felt I had to tell her it shouldn't go to me because I'd never, ever wear it. But she said, "Can you please send this to your cousin Gaia? She likes Victorian. And please insure it, Clement dear."

"For how much?" I asked.

"Oh," she said, waving a hand, "enough to convince the postal service it's too valuable to lose."

After the bank, Lucy said she was too tired to shop for music. I took her home for a nap and went by the sanctuary. When I finished cleaning cages, I drove to the record store on my own. Later, after dinner, I brought the boom box out on the porch. We listened to song after song after song. Bob Marley was in the middle of "Exodus"—I love how he sings it *Exey-duss*, taking that lofty word away from the Bible—when suddenly I got it. My cousin Gaia was Lucy's great-granddaughter. What did this change? Everything and nothing.

I looked over at Lucy, to express to her what I felt more than what I had learned, but she was asleep again. Her body was getting ready to sleep for good. A few weeks later, before the rest of the clan arrived to divvy up the other spoils, Dad and I managed to get ourselves into a canoe without tipping over, to scatter her ashes on Lake Champlain. I had this image of Lucy flitting weightless over the water, that gold hippie sash like a peacock's tail: Lucy, up there, invisible, finding out what it's like to kiss the sky.

~~

WE STRETCHED A WORN CHENILLE BEDSPREAD on a rock beside the gorge, weighed down the corners with six-packs of beer and Coke and a basket of sandwiches (cucumber and chicken between fat slices of Aunt Lucy's sourdough-prune). Except for the surrounding birch trees— which made me achingly homesick for everything northern, everything dependent on frost—the place made me think of somewhere southwest-ern: along a twisting sinew of river, slabs of rock leaned every which way, like a band of precarious drunks. The river flowed down a shadowy corri-dor, some twelve feet wide, with lichen-stained walls. A few people had arrived just before us, so the road leading in was a tunnel of dust, dust that now coated my skin and hair, since I'd ridden in the back of the pickup to be with Ralph's dogs, Tuck and Moe. Along the way, brand-new NO TRESPASSING signs leaned out from the encroaching woods. My backside, thanks to the potholes, felt like it had been shot full of novocaine.

Bodies, half clothed or naked, sprawled on the rocks, soaking up sun. Because of the restless geology here, privacy was easy to come by; as we zigzagged toward Clem's favorite spot, we passed a sudden crevice where a lean brown couple were making love.

Only two or three people were swimming. On my stomach, leaning over the steep drop beside us, I could just touch the surface of the water if I stretched. "Jesus!" I said, electrified by the chill.

Clem had already helped herself to a sandwich. "Oh, you'll go in. It's too hot not to." As if to prove her point, Tuck and Moe plunged, side by side, splashing us all. They panted as they swam, noses tilted toward the sky.

"Oh Christ," said Ralph. He took off his shirt and dove in.

"What's the matter?" I asked.

"There's a waterfall down there, around that corner," said Clem. She sounded nonchalant. "We go through this routine every time, but usually they wait till we go in."

Hector walked the edge of the river, abreast of Ralph and the dogs, who floated down in tandem, cradled on a lazy current. The four of them slipped out of sight where the river made one of its many sharp turns.

Clem saw my anxiety (she always does). "Relax. Farther down, it's not so steep. Hector pulls them out. Ralph gets to push." She laughed. "Hard to believe they once worked for a living, those goofy dogs."

Clem pulled her sunglasses down off her head, over her eyes. She unclasped the top of her bikini, tossed it aside, and lay back on the bedspread. "Cancer, come'n get me."

Her breasts are smaller than mine, but tight and golden, like our father's skin—the Basque in the woodpile, he likes to say. Her nipples are darker, too, a startling purple. I realized that she was significantly older than the sister I'd been determined I would leave behind for good; older than I wanted her to be. She was nicer, which I struggled not to see, but also less relaxed. Above her glasses, I saw the first hint of lines at the peak of her nose.

"Have you thought about the jewelry?" I said.

She raised her head, looked at me, then lay back down. "Not really. It's all in a big leather box we drove to the bank. I didn't ask to open it; that seemed rude."

"Rude never stopped you before," I said, though I found myself speaking lightly.

"Well, yeah, touché, Miss Manners," said Clem. "But you know, family jewels don't exactly fit the life I picture for myself. I mean, rubies on the Outer Banks? Hatpins on Kilimanjaro?"

"When do you plan to be on Kilimanjaro?" I was saying when I heard a loud "Heads up!" Ralph's voice, followed by whooping laughter and a lash of ice water. The dogs arrived ahead of the men and shook themselves all over our small encampment.

"Pigs, you pigs! You boorish Eskimo pigs! Shit!" Clem was on her feet in an instant, clutching a towel.

"Watch your language, missy." Ralph took Clem's towel and wrapped it around her from behind, squeezed her tight in his muscular arms.

"Scrub me down, hot stuff," she said, and twisted inside the towel to face him. Then she pushed him back, threw the towel over his head, and dove past him straight into the river. In the water, her skin turned blue as moonlit snow. The dark bottom of her bathing suit split her body in two. Before she arched back to the surface, I saw the soles of her feet, the dust rising quickly in a cloud, their pallor reflecting the sun.

"She's an athlete, I've always been jealous of that," I said.

"Strong swimmer," said Hector. "But crazy, too. I saw her go off that rock. Her and Ralph. Me? No way." He looked upstream toward the site of the fatal dive.

Clem broke the surface. "Yahoo! It's fuckin' polar down there!"

"Make room," called Ralph, and he dove in again. Hector bent over and untied his sneakers. He set them aside symmetrically paired, then took off his T-shirt, folded it into a square, and laid it on top of the sneakers. If Clem and Ralph made one logical couple, Hector and I would fall together sensibly as well: careful, circumspect. But who was I fooling? I was alone.

"Come on in," said Hector, smiling warmly at me, and then all three of them were in the river, heads bobbing on the surface. Even the dogs had deserted me, still on land but roving their way upstream, hunting for untended food.

Clem was treading water next to Ralph. "C'mon, you overeducated pseudo-bohemian pondscum," she called out.

This was exactly the sort of moment with her that made me feel so small. "Maybe later," I said. "I think I'll read for a little. I don't think I'm hot enough yet."

"Suit yourself," said Clem. She swam after the men, who now sat on a ledge just above the waterline, their legs submerged to the knee.

I lay on my stomach and pretended to read, but I was looking down at the water. Though I'd grown up near the ocean, I had never liked going in over my head. I had seen the rock bottom of the river when I leaned over the ledge, yet I knew that depth is always an illusion; those rocks could have been six or twenty feet down. But come on, I told myself. Here, in front of these two charming, brainy men and my charming, invincible sister, was I really going to lie on this rock by myself, reading *Mrs. Dalloway*?

They talked and laughed. About me, perhaps. I couldn't hear a word because of the hidden waterfall, its steady hiss. Clem gestured wildly, arms waving overhead. Hector smiled at her antics. What story could I have told with such fervor?

I stripped to my bathing suit and sat on the edge. I hate diving because my ears always fill up with water, and this dive was steep. I turned around on all fours and felt for toeholds in the face of the rock. Halfway down, I slipped, scraping my right shin, but I was in the water—which was so cold that my lungs turned to stone. I gasped and clung to the wall beside me. The surface of the river was calm, but my knees were gripped in a taut undertow. I took a deep breath, let go of the rock, and swam as hard as I could. Without lifting my head, I knew I was going nowhere, my stroke too weak to master the current, which seemed to insist that the party was better downstream. When I came up for air, I saw that I was slowly slipping backward, toward the waterfall. I reached out to grab the rock but could find no cracks or ledges. The surface was glassy with slime.

"Hey, you. No big deal, what did I say?" Clem had spotted me. She was grinning. "Come on up here. Fantastic or what?"

I was kicking like crazy, but my upper body was caged in frigid fear. "Where did *you* take swimming lessons?" I heard my sister call out in jest. "Oh, that's right. *Dad* taught you."

My mouth would not form a single word. I saw vaguely that Ralph was frowning, saying something to Clem. She stood up on the ledge and shouted, "You all right?"

All I could do was shake my head. I was still grappling at the rock when I heard her voice again, directly above me. She stood on the edge of the gorge four feet over my head. Then she was kneeling, her dark wet hair hanging down around her face. I could not see her expression. She said, in a low, deliberate voice, the voice of a teacher, "Swim to the middle of the river."

"No," I managed to gasp. "No."

"Swim to the middle, Louisa," she said again, just as calmly, though her voice was louder. "The current is strongest at the edge, where you are."

"Can't be," I forced out. I felt as if I were wearing a medieval corset. My right shin, where I'd scraped it, throbbed with an icy fire. Christ, I thought, all because of a stupid piece of jewelry and an adolescent grudge, I might die. Actually die. I thought, absurdly, of the clear "picture" Clem had mentioned about the life before her. I had no such picture of mine.

"Do what I'm telling you. Now, Louisa." Later, I would remember this moment with exceptional clarity, how her voice betrayed not a hint of panic. Tuck stood beside her, looking down at me with his eerie ice-blue eyes, smiling and panting. I wondered if I was about to suffer the humiliating relief of being rescued by a dog. I wondered how he would do it, what part of me he would grab in his jaws.

I pushed away with my right foot and hurled myself, more than swam, toward the middle. She had been right. The water unshackled me as I left the edge. The middle of the river, a fissure of noon sun, was placid and warmer, and after treading water for a moment to let my muscles find their purpose, I swam slowly upstream. Clem walked with me, the way Hector had walked beside Ralph and the dogs, and then she climbed down where the ledge came closest to the water, where I had watched her telling her antic story, and she reached out to reel me in. As soon as I was sitting beside her, I started to sob.

"I always knew you were a weakling," Clem said, rubbing my back with a towel, "but hey."

I wept into the towel, bent over my lap. Weeping was my only language.

"Seriously," she said, "the current is strong. We've been swimming here for two months. I kind of forgot to warn you, I guess. But you're okay. Aren't you?"

By the time we returned to our picnic, the dogs had staked out the lion's share of the bedspread, and Hector was picking apart his sandwich to give them each a bite of chicken. Ralph put an arm around my shoulders and handed me an open beer. "To immortality," he said.

I sat next to Moe. His hot fur felt glorious against my thigh. When I stroked his neck, he twisted away from Hector and licked my face with abandon.

"Oh my. He's in love," said Hector. "He doesn't do that with everyone."

That's when I lost it again, crying uncontrollably and shaking. I saw Clem not knowing what to do. I wanted to be mad at her all over again, for putting me in this shameful spot, but I couldn't get back there because I had done what she told me to do, and she had been right. Against all instincts, I'd swum to the middle.

"Hey you, you're okay. You really are," she said to me, but she sounded less certain in her chiding. Hector wrapped a second towel around my shoulders. I was thinking how if she wanted the cameo, I'd have to let her claim it now, and then I remembered what she said about hatpins on Kilimanjaro.

Kilimanjaro? And it dawned on me: This was the first time in three years I had an urgent question to ask her, a question to which I really wanted the answer.

Now Is Not the Time

1983

About the only thing we had in common that summer was solitude. Or so I was led to believe. Mine was a solitude of retreat and longing, fraught with wishes and sighs—but Clem's I imagined as sure and intrepid, a flight from everything soft about civilization. I was copyediting ruminations on art. Clem was counting seals. As usual, we exchanged letters. We communicate best by mail. On the phone, we argue. In person, we tend to become sarcastic. Our letters, though, have a touch of romantic collusion.

I had fled my fourth-floor walk-up in Brooklyn to house-sit for Mars and Leah Katz. I hardly knew these people—they were friends of friends, jetting off to romp in the lavender fields of Provence—but I was desperately glad to slip into their easy, aesthetically cushioned life. The Katzes' house, a small Victorian with fuchsias lining the verandah, sits snug on a hill near Long Island Sound in one of those Connecticut enclaves whose elegance is tainted only by the hourly hurtle—distant yet always within earshot—of the trains to Grand Central Station.

From the master bedroom in the turret, I could see a good stretch of sawtooth coast, a boat-specked horizon, and the chocolate haze over New York City. Until recently, Mars was the chef at a famous restaurant in New Canaan. Leah writes gardening books. They were on a two-month sabbatical and had left me a beach pass, a three-speed bike, and ten pages of instructions: she for her lush thirsty flowers, he for his hutches of rabbits, pheasants, and quail. My only regret about leaving the city was that I had fallen in love.

So there I was, sitting plush, while Clem, explorer that she is and always will be, made do in a Quonset hut on the coast of Labrador, someplace so desolate it did not merit so much as a flea dot in my cinder block of an atlas. Her mail went to a post office twenty miles away; a fisherman named Spider brought it up by boat, twice a week or so. He brought groceries as well; in general, he was paid to keep an eye on Clem. But the dangers were nil, she wrote. Her routine was placid, the climate benign. Nothing like the time she'd spent in Barrow: three months of hellish cold, predatory bears, fracturing ice floes, drunks with tempers and knives. There she had packed a shotgun. Here, she packed a logbook, a tuna-fish sandwich, a pair of binoculars, and a tube of Bain de Soleil. Out on the water, the seals made excellent companions. At first because they were curious, and then because it amused them, they followed Clem's boat. Friendly, loud, demanding, they yammered at her all day long. *Before you know it, you're talking back. You say what you have to say. They say what they have to say. Nobody contradicts anybody, nobody gets political. Nobody has any THEORIES. Peace! They have a fine sense of humor, these guys, they even do impersonations. This one bull, I kid you not, does over-the-hill Frank Sinatra. But try to reach out and touch him—vamoose, right down under. Do you know about selkies? Half woman, half seal. I get it now, how the Irish believe in that myth. It's the look in their eyes, like they KNOW you.*

Clem was paid by an international wildlife commission whose name I could never quite remember. Systematically, she was to roam her assigned stretch of coast—on foot; by jeep; in some unobtrusive jalopy of a boat— and tally the various species, both living and dead. An epidemic had struck, killing them off by the hundreds. Clem's mentor, Kurt, is a marine pathologist at Woods Hole, one of those dashing bearded types you're always seeing on *Nova*, valiantly rescuing lost baby whales. Having isolated the virus, he was collaborating on a vaccine. He'd persuaded someone in Washington to foot the bill for inoculation trials. To me, all this fuss seemed bizarre, even improper (money to vaccinate *seals*? what about cancer? what about children starving all over the world?), but I'd met Kurt, so I saw it all clearly. . . . Kurt, on his high scientific steed, writes to Ted Kennedy, explains how all this arctic seal decimation will have a domino effect, threatening the lobster crops of Maine and Massachusetts. Ted is aghast: What, no more thermidor, no more Newburg, no more *sauce diable* at the Edgartown Yacht Club? Out comes the federal checkbook. Strom Thurmond's too busy to notice; he's hard at work trying to vaporize the NEA.

How Clem saw such beauty in all that tundra, how she could live there and keep her wits about her, I couldn't imagine. And how she could abandon Luke—another mystery. Clem's boyfriend was one I'd have kept in my sights. He was smart, tender, strong. A little moody, but how close can you come to perfection? Luke had been devoted to Clem for over three years, since their sophomore year in college. He had begun to talk about marriage. She didn't want to lose him, she told me, so she answered his proposal with a speech that went something like this: "Sure I love you, don't be absurd, but I won't know if this is really *it* for years. Maybe not till I'm forty. If I live that long. It's only fair to warn you." Privately, she worried about Luke's ingrained Catholicism, never mind that he went to Mass only when he stayed with his parents. *Once they inject you with all that superstition, practically straight into your marrow, you are theirs for life. Antibodies to common sense,* Clem wrote to me after they'd been going out together for a year. *Listen to this. Luke told me he grew up thinking that if the communion wafer touched his teeth, he'd get struck down dead by a holy thunderbolt. Is that sick or what? They tell you this stuff when you're five years old!*

But maybe faith, faith of the lowercase variety, gets injected along with all that fear of holy thunderbolts. Because Luke had stuck it out all this time, though Clem was as slippery as one of her seals. Just before I left for Connecticut, he called me up in a funk, all the way from Miami. I was amazed. I was thrilled. "I'm sorry," he said right off, "I'm hammered, okay, or I wouldn't be calling, but everything I'm telling you is true, okay? If there was a decent bridge around here, I'd be standing on the edge looking down. That's how crazy she makes me, that sister of yours." Luke is a graduate student in engineering. Bridges are his main obsession, his passion (aside from my sister).

I said, "Then I'm glad you called."

He said, "I could kill her."

"Well, I've known that feeling myself," I said.

He'd paid a surprise visit to Woods Hole. Clem, he discovered, had taken up with a guy from a construction site who whistled at her legs. They had been hanging out together on Clem's front porch when Luke drove up.

"Maybe they're just friends," I lied. I knew about this guy. Clem said he was funny, uncomplicated, strong. She had a weakness for strong.

"She was sitting in his lap," said Luke. "He looked like a frigging troglodyte."

Clem had apologized to Luke after sending the troglodyte home, but she also told Luke he was a fool. It was nothing, a passing fancy. (That was true.) Anyway, where was *he*? Way the hell down in Florida. If he made a scene, she warned, this was the end. Luke spent the night in the Trailways shelter across from the ferry slips, then left. "Hysterical. She called me hysterical. What goes on in that mind of hers, *what*." He'd called me, I realized, because he needed calming down. In our family, he calls me the Rational One. My dad's the Dreamy One, Mom the Colorful One. Clem's the Wild One—when she's not the Heartbreaker, the Ball-breaker, the Nemesis, the Bitch on Wheels.

"I wish I could answer that, Luke. I think we're friends, but we're not, well, not exactly soul mates. Historically, we're kind of like England and France."

"But you *know* her."

"Better than you?" I said. "Come on. And what goes on inside her head? Who knows? Something way out, I have to say. Something very Robinson Crusoe."

"I wouldn't idealize anybody so moronically reckless."

"If there's one thing she's not, Luke, it's a moron."

"Maybe what I need is a moron. To fall in love with a moron."

"When she's scared, she holds everyone at arm's length. You must know that by now."

"Scared?" Luke laughed sardonically, but he was clearly tired, losing steam. "You know how you get to a point in a relationship where it feels like you're lost in this jungle?"

"Well . . ." Right then, I pined to be that deep into any relationship. I could face lost in the jungle; just show me the jungle.

"No paths. No compass. Can't see six inches ahead of you, branches wapping your face, bugs the size of rodents . . . and . . . tigers watching from the trees . . . This I do not need," he concluded. "Am I crazy, Louisa, like she says?"

I couldn't endure much more of his sodden sorrow. I said, "Look, it *is* you she loves. I shouldn't say it, but I expect to see you married. Not now, not right away, but . . . she hates to admit it, she has these instincts—she fights it, but it *is* you, Luke."

"She told you that?"

"If that's what you want, you just need to be patient." Listening to myself, I was appalled. She had told me no such thing. To Clem, there is no *you* in that singular sense. She's vowed there never will be, though I don't really believe her.

For a few seconds Luke was silent. I could hear him relax, breathing in my consolation. Wasn't I the older one, the wiser one? If only, I thought, if only just once I could feel what it's like to be inside her skin, to live with such intense abandon. Then I would be the wiser without question. Whatever there was to know, I'd know.

Like half the population of New York City, I am a struggling artist, and one of the things I was conveniently doing by holing up in the Katzes' house was taking a break from the struggle. I've begun selling some of my pots—this year I've even had commissions, for a few sets of plates and a huge teapot—but I can't stop wondering what makes me pursue this archaic talent in a city that takes no pity on anything quaint. Yes, there are exceptions like Betty Woodman, who's managed to turn ceramics into high art by covering walls with great saucy arabesques of terracotta glazed in colors straight out of Matisse. Well, she sort of is Matisse;

Matisse on steroids, Matisse up to his elbows in mud. She also has a passion that I wonder if I share.

Lately when I'm working, I feel as if I'm in a play. I love the city, that much I know, but moving there only seemed to exaggerate my doubts about what I do, which sometimes boils down to making the containers from which people feed themselves. That's fine, I suppose, but it feels more utilitarian than anything I ever intended to do when I was a reader, a thinker, a girl who recited poetry to her cat. And it doesn't pay the bills much better than reciting poetry to cats. Fortunately, I have other skills with which to make a living. Because I also happen to like words. So I write a little, and I edit. This is how I came to work for *Artbeat*. It's a monthly magazine, thick with glossy photos of paintings, sculpture, videos, and so-called installations. My job is to pore over the long, contemplative essays on the artists who make them, artists who aim beyond butter plates and mugs. I can carry batches of these essays back and forth on the train, back and forth to the beach.

The editors at *Artbeat* give me what they call the hot-potato essays, the ones that are transparently pretentious (but must be published for various political reasons), bloated with critical ego (often transparently pretentious as well), or just plain poorly written (on a timely subject that can't be reassigned). I deal with meek authors who cannot put a sentence together and with vain authors who cannot put a sentence together. When I have no idea what something means, I am not (unlike the editors I work for) afraid to say so. I am paid to be a verbal backhoe. It's not a job to choose if you need to be loved by the people you work for. That's why the editors give the worst stuff to me.

I had two big essays with me that first week: one about a Scottish artist who makes strange, delightful confabulations from nature—towers of driftwood, gardens of ice, Herculean braids of grasses and leaves—and the other a provocative rant against Jeff Koons, David Salle, and a herd of other artists this critic believed to be the worst case of emperor's clothing in decades. *TONE IT DOWN!!!* the editor in chief had scrawled across the front of the manuscript.

Hugh, the managing editor—who, as far as I can see, is much too nice to work with such sharks—had kindly added, just for me, an illuminating postscript. *Author is protégé of Hilton Kramer.*

One afternoon, as I sat on a velvet chaise in the Katzes' parlor, poking my arms and legs to see if I'd burned myself at the beach, I spent an hour on the phone with Hugh going over specific gripes on the essay about the Scottish artist.

"Hugh," I said, "is the guy allergic to commas? Reading this piece is like reading semiautomatic gunfire. It leaves you mentally out of breath."

"He's very big in L.A.," said Hugh, sounding apologetic.

"And they don't like commas out there?"

Hugh laughed. "I'll have to look into that theory. But he attached this note saying that . . ." I heard him rustling papers on his desk. "Yes, saying that punctuation mustn't be 'impedimentary.' "

Now I laughed. "I'll bear that in mind."

"Oh, listen. Change whatever you like," said Hugh. "I will deal with the fallout. That's my job. Just how about this: how about no semicolons? I know he hates semicolons most of all. 'Roadblocks,' he called them on the last piece we ran."

I agreed to hold back on semicolons. But I love them, I have to confess; I find their particular flavor of hesitation similar to the lip I like to form on the large bowls I make, holding my right thumb up and slightly cocked, a hitchhiker's thumb, as I spin the wheel, as the velvety lavender slip runs over the heel of my hand and down my wrist. The slight return of the lip allows you to hold the bowl securely, carry it heavily laden with apples or oranges across a room. I had brought one of these bowls as a present to the Katzes, and it sat on their kitchen counter. I was using it to hold their mail.

I took a shower and rinsed out my bathing suit. I fed the rabbits and birds their dinner, took out the hose and watered the garden, trying to conjure a rainbow. Half soaked in the end, I coiled up the hose, mixed a margarita, and (there being no Ella Fitzgerald, no Sarah Vaughan) put on Bob Dylan, *Blood on the Tracks.* It's odd to spend your vacation with someone else's music, especially when you're alone. You're free to let loose, unobserved, but someone else has chosen the words you belt out in private, the rhythms you can dance to like a fool.

I opened the front windows so I could hear the music out on the verandah, where I settled myself in the wicker swing. Before me stretched Leah's wide bed of irises, the old-fashioned kind with big parchment petals. Beyond them stretched the lawn, unblemished; a swatch of road; some trees, maples and sycamores; another house; the early evening sky. I squinted until it all closed into glass chips of purple, apricot, cobalt, green. Listening to Bob, I dreamed of Sam.

I met Sam at a May Day party on the roof of his building. Sam is a painter who turns his dreams into comic neon landscapes brimming with colorful people and oddly shaped creatures. They're alien but also alluring, funny and warm. Sam lives in a loft shadowed all day by the Manhattan Bridge. Everything shudders when the subways pass over, including Sam, who laughs all the time. His teeth are white as gulls, a little jagged, and his eyes the color of trout, pewter flecked with green. He is in his late thirties and has a wavy ginger-colored ponytail that nearly reaches his waist. At the party, we had to shout every time a train went by. "Life on the Transit Fault!" he shouted gaily. "Like earthquakes all day long, it's wild!" He said his dreams were full of earthquakes; so then, for the moment, were his paintings: toppling buildings, tidal waves, cars and boats tossed to the sky, yet without any sense of doom. He took me downstairs to see them.

Artists are supposed to be an anguished lot. Not Sam, and that was partly why I fell for him. Also because he was full of surprises. One: that he was from Nebraska. Another: that twice a week he got up at four and drove to a marina at the end of Long Island, a place where you pay to go deep-sea fishing. When he came over to my apartment for dinner, he was all fired up from one of these trips, his nose polished red by the sun. The whole time he seemed to be blushing, hyperactive with rapture. "Thirty-five blues," he exclaimed, "ravenous devils, mouthful of razors!" He showed me a Polaroid of himself on the dock with a fish half as long as he was tall. Over stuffed chicken breasts, I listened to him reel off fishing tales like so many love affairs fondly recalled. Over ice-cream sundaes, I showed him photos of my fruit bowls and teapots and fanciful ewers.

"Your colors are like fog and snow," Sam said softly. "Fantastic and ephereal." He sounded reverent. But did he mean *ephemeral* or *ethereal?* I didn't ask. As happens to me at these moments, I heard my sister scold me: *Loosen up there, Lou.* Another time she caught me acting like a schoolmarm, she startled me out of it with her best James Brown. "Get on the good foot, unh-unh-unh, get on the GOOD foot!" she grunted, dancing like the proverbial funky chicken. She can't sing to save her life.

After putting the dishes in my sink, I went to the bedroom to brush my hair and get my bearings. Now, I thought. *Now.* Breathless, I returned to the living room. There he still was, still glowing, his head tilted back on the sofa: snoring gently to my patterned tin ceiling. That was sometime late in June. Take it slow, I consoled myself. Sam could visit me out in the country, the ideal setting for romance. I pictured us under Leah's pergola, sunset filtered through fragrant red grapes (however inconsistent the season). I thought of Clem, how she would have rolled her eyes and groaned at the image. "Boy," she'd say, "if they're out there to be found, you'll find 'em, the looniest men on earth."

"Oh no," I would tell her, "not this one." And on we would spar.

My sister was named for our grandmother Clement, a Louisiana belle who died of pneumonia when our father was eight. She looks, in the pictures he has, fragile and pale as a new gardenia. You look at her face and suspect this girl will die lamentably young. When my sister was born, she was sick all the time and had violent allergies to everything under the sun. She was practically allergic to *air.* I remember the raised voices, the lurid hospital halls, the frenzy of the too many times she came close to dying. Her face would swell up and she would gasp inaudibly, groping for air. Most vividly of all, I remember our mother's panic (also, my wicked ambivalence). Clem outgrew these afflictions, however, and though she is fast approaching the age at which her namesake died, she is hardly so tragic or fragile; she is about as much a southern belle as I am a Canadian Mountie. Nevertheless, she's had her brushes with fate.

From the time she could crawl, I bullied her, exercising a subtle form of terrorism (games, deceptively pleasant, at which she could never excel). It seemed only fair; everyone else was so deferential. For years, our mother was effusively grateful for every morsel of food Clem could keep down without breaking into hives. Ironically, Clem became extremely plump; when Mom wasn't looking, I'd sing "Clementine" and make her wail. Four years older, I had an easy advantage, and for nearly a decade I could make her do just about anything. I was supreme, in charge. To be fair, I also took care of her. I read to her, watched her on the swings, kept my sadistic urges in check.

Then something shifted. She was stronger than me by the time she was seven, a born wrestler. Suddenly she no longer took my threats seriously. Try as I might, I could not regain her fear, her respect, never mind her trust. Well, I thought, this is what I deserve for being such a tyrant, for having assumed my regime was infallible. Tyrants, no exception, fall.

Clem has called me a loser, a wimp, a hopeless romantic. In return, I have called her a selfish, hard-hearted bitch. She tells me the men I fall for are creeps: pseudo-intellectual, stuck-up, effeminate creeps. Sometimes I look at the latest one and see in a flash that it's true. By that time, however, the man in question has usually vanished, slipped out of sight under the waves.

Nights in the country were long. I would listen to the same records over and over. I was getting used to, even attached to, the music—what I came to think of as Mars and Leah's pothead collection. I even sampled Pink Floyd, though Bob remained my favorite. One sweltering night, I played "You're Gonna Make Me Lonesome" about seventeen times, so loud I was amazed the police didn't show. It was the end of July. I had been there a month and Sam had not called.

Barefoot, I carried my glass of wine onto the lawn. The grass was warm and slick with the day's humidity, the night's first dew. I sang to the rabbits. The light from the house picked out their eyes in the dark like garnets. They watched me, ears erect, transfixed in their little prisons, probably terrified by the crackpot behavior of this weaving, tonedeaf creature. The pheasants and quail slept on through my crooning, heads tucked seamlessly under their wings. "Nighty night," I whispered, suddenly teary. Poor doomed creatures, I thought. I made my way back to the house.

The rear entrance led into a small room that felt dank and medieval. The walls and floors were stone, so the air was always surprisingly cool. In the center stood a long wooden table, rough and gouged, a drain in the floor underneath. Along one wall hung raincoats, ragged elongated sweaters, umbrellas, and scarves. Below these were stacked several cases of wine. I imagined it had once been an icehouse or a larder for onions and turnips.

The rush of cool was a shock. I closed my eyes and felt dizzy. I am going to swoon, I thought, but I didn't. I began to cry, woefully sorry for myself. I went into the kitchen, set down my glass, and rested my head on the telephone.

Don't call him, don't call him, don't call him, I warned myself then. You will have a cup of tea. You will write Clem. You will go to bed. I stood up, stoic, and followed my orders. I'm good at following orders.

Not that I was falling apart. Several evenings, I took advantage of Mars's technospectacular kitchen and made myself elaborate dinners. I used the mortar and pestle, learned to grind my own spices. On sunny days, I biked to the town beach and worked on a new batch of essays. I put a dictionary and half a dozen very sharp red pencils in my knapsack, along with my towel and sun hat. I worked on my lap, Mars and Leah's latest *New Yorker* serving as a blotter beneath the manuscript of the moment. "Articulata" was a piece on the proliferation of text in photography. *Might we see this as a symptom of visual insecurity, or is it the strident, declarative end to our long-running romance with lensmen such as Adams,*

Weston, and even Walker? *Might we venture so far as to interpret this trend—nay, this turning point—as an invigorating divorce of sorts?* I looked up to see a gull eyeing my knapsack, venturing so far as to interpret its bulk—nay, its grease-stained belly—as a food station. "Well," I said loudly to the gull, "might we indeed?" I squawked, and the gull scuttled away. I lay back and put the essay aside, weighting it down with my sneakers. I fell asleep in the sun. I dreamed that the author of the pompous essay turned out to be Sam. "That *we* is not royal," he told me angrily. "It's entirely actual. Look in your *Chicago.*" It turned out that somehow I had the wrong edition of *The Chicago Manual of Style,* that my copy was way out of date. I would lose my job. When I woke, the gull was back, standing at the edge of my towel and staring at me. The obvious question on his mind was *Is she edible?*

I rode back to the house by the longer, scenic route—past the shore-line estates, shingled mastodons waving bright flags—and stopped at the fish market. I love eating fish, but I hate buying it, the raw smell, the iridescent flesh. At Woods Hole, when Clem gave me a tour of the marine biology labs, I said no when she opened the door marked PATHOLOGY. Eviscerated dolphins, I said, were not my cup of tea. "Sometimes I think they are *precisely* mine," said Clem.

But here, at this market, I would linger and pretend to be indecisive. It meant I'd get to flirt, quite harmlessly, with the teenage boys at the counter. Jimmy was my favorite. Arms akimbo, he'd make a John Travolta dance of wrapping the fish, then of taking my money and making change. On his days off, I'd see him at the beach with his girlfriend, an au pair who worked in one of the big shingle houses by the water. He smiled and waved whenever he saw me. At twenty-seven, I must have looked middle-aged to him, so I liked the way he humored me. Often, in a single day, the banter I exchanged with Jimmy and the other boys was my only conversation. Me and those boys; Clem and her seals. I wrote to her, *Celibacy is the pits. Mind if I borrow Luke for a month or two?*

～つ

Sam called in the middle of August. Next Saturday, if the weather was fine, he planned to check out a lake north of where I was staying; could he drop by for dinner? What could he bring? "Just yourself," I said, as my mother had taught me. Bring your earthquakes, I thought as I hung up the phone, hands shaking.

We would have filet mignon, I decided, with parsnip purée and haricots verts à la Marrakesh. I had been browsing through Mars's recipe file in the study off the master bedroom. (Was this a crime? Were a chef's private recipes, I wondered, like a playboy's little black book?) For dessert, nothing too heavy: compote? granita? sorbet? These were fantasies I could fulfill.

Friday night, having put in a good six hours on Hilton Kramer's blowhard protégé and my perfect tan, I was melting chocolate on the stove when the phone rang. *NO*, I practically shrieked aloud. (Three times that day I had called weather, to recheck the forecast: reassuringly, always sunny and clear.)

"Collect to anyone from Carmen. Thank you for using AT&T." Followed by a cascade of mellifluous tones.

"CLEMENT," I heard her yell, impatience loud and clear across the miles of crackling. "I'm in Bar Harbor," she said. "I'm driving down there, can you give me directions?"

"Here?" I said. "To this house?"

"No, to Cape Canaveral. Of course to there."

"I thought you were in Labrador until October."

"Look, Lou, I'm in this handicapped space and I can see the meter maid prowling the lot. I'll explain when I see you."

"Clem, are you okay?"

"I'm fine, Lou. Now's not the time. I'll see you tomorrow."

"I have to tell you, tomorrow's not the greatest—"

"Just get me there from Stamford, okay?" This was Clem's businesslike voice, stubborn, unswayable. I'd heard her use it on Luke.

I gave her directions. I hung up. I scraped out the burned chocolate and started all over again.

~~~

Clem's car is her trademark. It's a green 1968 Alfa Romeo convertible, rebuilt from a virtual junk heap by one of her high school boyfriends. The car had been garaged in Bar Harbor before she took the ferry up north. She pampered that car like a lapdog. When our parents asked her to sell it, to raise money for graduate school, she told them she'd sooner work as a go-go dancer in the Combat Zone.

About three the next afternoon, I heard it roar into the driveway. I walked onto the verandah and waited. I was deeply annoyed by then. I'd assumed she would drive overnight and arrive by morning, giving me plenty of time to get rid of her, at least temporarily, by dinner.

She heaved a duffel bag out of the trunk and started up the hill. She waved when she saw me. At the top of the steps, she threw her bag down and said, "I left without telling Kurt. I'm in deep shit. Got any aspirin?"

"I'm just terrific," I said. "Thanks for asking."

Her laugh sounded oddly compliant.

When I came back from the medicine chest, I found her in the kitchen pouring herself a shot of vodka.

"To you. Port in a storm," she said, and downed it. She took the Tylenol bottle, shook out two, and swallowed them.

"Are you going to explain why you're suddenly here?" I said. "Because in about two hours Sam is arriving for dinner."

"The fishin' magician? Him?"

"Stop being so clever and sit down," I said. She was pacing.

She paced into the living room and sat on the sofa. "I'm in deep shit."

I was not going to play this game. I sat down across from her and waited. Clem closed her eyes and ran her hands again and again through her hair, combing it. In the humidity of summer, her hair goes feral. She ties it back in a knot and leaves it like that for days.

"What I need most is a shower."

"That's fair," I said, and I showed her upstairs.

The water was still running twenty minutes later, and I was in the kitchen peeling parsnips, when I heard the front door open.

"Wow, some place! Hey you!" Here he was, just like that. I was stunned. In the two months since he'd fallen asleep in my living room, Sam's hair had turned almost blond, his skin dark as tea. He set down a compound bucket and kissed me on the cheek. I looked down; the water was silver with fish. He grinned. "More in my cooler. Oh man what a day! What an incredibly, fantastically illimitable day."

"Trout!" was all I could manage to say.

"Cool car. That come with the house?" The front door stood open behind him. His pickup truck was parked behind Clem's Alfa Romeo— right up against its backside, like one animal sniffing another.

Don't get paranoid, I told myself.

"That's my sister's. She's here sort of out of the blue. I wasn't expecting—"

"Well hey, there's plenty to go around!" He tossed his Mets cap onto the hat rack, where it landed on a silk-flowered pillbox. Then he carried his bucket to the kitchen. I heard him set it in the sink. "Somewhere I can clean up? I smell like a trawler!"

I led Sam upstairs and gave him Mars's study to change in. Clem's belongings were strewn in a wanton meander all the way down the hall from the bathroom to the guest room: red sneakers, black lacy briefs, a beat-up copy of *Arctic Dreams.* "Hey," she said, passing us on her way downstairs. She gave Sam a quick smile. I wish I could describe precisely the way Clem greets men; she sort of inhales her hello, in a terse, shy voice as if she's run out of breath. Offhand but riveting. (Oh go ahead: *be* paranoid, I told myself.)

"And hey to *you.* A pleasure." Sam gave her his wide glinty smile in return.

Clem had changed into shorts and a T-shirt. She wore three necklaces, thin gold chains with dangling gilt-edged seashells. "Something else I better tell you now," she said when I came down. "You promise not to blow up." A statement, not a plea.

I gave her a look that promised nothing. I dropped the naked parsnips into a bowl of cold water.

"Sometime probably in like the next half hour, Luke's coming."

"Gosh," I said, "a party."

"I need you to be serious."

"I'm trying hard. But what I need is for you to tell me what's going on."

"I've got to meet him on neutral ground, we've got to talk." Luke was in New Jersey that month, visiting his parents.

"Neutral ground." I thought about that. "Well, I hope we all like trout."

"I'll clean them," she said. "I'm fast."

"Clem," I said, "what aren't you fast at?"

At five o'clock, we rode to the beach in the Alfa Romeo, Sam and I squashed in the back with a hamper of wine and hors d'oeuvres, Clem driving, Luke beside her. Luke strained at cheerfulness. He had arrived looking queasy and, toward me, embarrassed. He could barely look me in the eye as he presented me with a purple begonia plant.

"Me—bait all the way," Sam was saying, "and no apologies. I'm too high-wire to stand around in some tempid river up to my neck in mosquitoes."

"Oh," said Luke, "I don't mean to say that the other kinds don't take skill." He'd been describing how he once tried fly-fishing, how it seemed more like an art than a sport.

"Now deep sea—that's the big challenge for me," said Sam, and then he began to tell what I realized must be his signature story, the time he'd been marlin fishing down in the Keys. This was the second time I'd heard it.

Clem's jaw was set. She drives fast, on the hormones of a teenage boy, right down the middle of the road. She handles the wheel like a baker handles dough: easy, flip, loose.

"Clem," I said, leaning forward, "we're not trying to make a plane or anything." Sometimes this sort of remark will make her drive faster.

"Sorry," she said, and slowed down a hair. "I tend to forget about the battery. It's held in for now with a coat hanger, very makeshift."

Luke frowned, and Clem saw his look. "Lazy, what can I say?"

"Jesus," he said. "One *day.*"

"What's all this?" I asked.

"If you knew the first thing about cars," she said, "you'd know that, at the speed I'm driving over these funky roads, we're in danger of being blown off the face of the earth."

"Oh come on."

"Hey," she said, raising both hands from the wheel, a habit I hate. "It's like this: Car rams through pothole, battery crashes loose. Battery hits road and makes sparks. Sparks fly up and enter gas tank. *Kapow!*"

"Then GO SLOW," I yelled.

"I am." She let up on the gas again. "Some people make such a big deal about dying."

"Ah. James Dean," said Luke, "as we live and breathe."

Sam laughed loudly, then dove back into his marlin safari.

"Are those the World Trade towers? You can see them from *here?*" said Luke. He screened his eyes and pointed toward the far right horizon.

"Don't be silly," said Clem.

"Could be," Sam said. "You can see for eons on a day like this."

"Nah. You couldn't see New York City from here," said Clem.

"The coastline does strange things," I said. "You'd be surprised."

"Strange how?" teased Clem, making an eerie Halloween noise.

Luke insisted, "I'm sure it's New York."

"Probably oil tanks in New Jersey."

"Clem, honey, your geography's warped."

Luke and Clem stood side by side, glumly staring at the ocean, which glittered with the clarity of a gem. Except for two couples walking their dogs, we had the beach to ourselves. I shook out a large bedspread.

"This is heaven, man!" cried Sam, who seemed unaffected by the quarreling lovers' general gloom. He romped around like one of the dogs, then stopped and crooked his hands into a frame. He looked up through it, as if to shoot a portrait of the sky. "Know what I'd like to be able to capture?" he asked me. "Those incredible amazing blue distances—Titian, van Eyck . . ."

"Yeah, great sky," said Clem. "Mare's tails."

"Like writing," said Sam. "Like a coded message from beyond."

"Those aren't clouds," Luke said abruptly. "They're jet trails."

"Guess we just missed an air show," said Clem.

"Look at the way they widen out. Any fool knows jet trails."

"The Brie is melting," I warned.

Luke sat on a towel. Clem remained standing. Slowly, she removed her clothes. Underneath, she wore a black tank suit, oddly modest. She is usually in the smallest of bikinis. Clem loves the sun, and the feeling is mutual.

Luke watched her intently; watched her hands pull down the suit, smooth back her hair, pull it tight to one side and knot it. She smiled at me, an apology. I looked at her scar, always uglier than I have remembered it, parched as old dry bone. Whenever I see her bare legs, I try not to look at it, the way you try not to look at a pregnant woman's belly. To do so is unseemly—yet this, in a way, is what defines her.

"I'm going in," she announced. The rest of us watched her swim far out, swiftly, then settle into steady laps until all we could see was the dip and arc of her arms against blue.

"Would someone like to open the wine?" I asked.

Sam said eagerly, "I'm for that." For a moment Luke remained aloof, staring at Clem. Then he smiled and pulled a Swiss army knife out of his pocket.

"Your sister's been in an accident," my mother said calmly. I had just moved to Brooklyn. I was holding the receiver and looking out the window at a statue of Saint Lucy in front of the church across the street, holding her eyes on a spotlit platter. For a split second, I pictured myself as an only child all over again. That night, I had a dream in which my mother gave birth to a third baby: another sister, without eyes. In the dream, I was enraged, indignant. How dare she.

The accident that caused Clem's injury was surprisingly ordinary. It did not happen the summer she crewed on a barkentine that was caught three days in a freak typhoon. Nor the summer she spent studying raptors, when in fact an owl whose broken wing she was securing with a splint sank its talons clear through the muscle in a forearm (a wound from which she has also kept scars, a faint constellation). Nor, miraculously, during her brief flirtation with hang gliding.

It happened in Michigan, just after Clem graduated from college. She had stayed on an extra week to be with Luke. Afterward, she was to head east, for her first job with Kurt.

Clem and Luke were biking to a lake. Clem, leading, came to an intersection with a street that she thought was one-way and so looked, economically, only one way. But it was not a one-way street, and at that moment a car was approaching from the other direction. If Clem did not have such quick reflexes, she would probably not have survived; but she saw the car from the corner of an eye and, just before it would have smashed her broadside, turned her bicycle sharply away. Still, the car sideswiped her. She might have escaped with bruises if the right front-door handle of the car hadn't been broken. Jagged, it punctured the front of her upper thigh like the teeth of a saw. Running an inch deep, it tore straight down to just above the knee, where, by some fluke of how she fell, it made a U-turn and tore another six inches up the inner thigh, finishing off like a fishhook or a cockeyed smile.

Luke called my parents from the hospital, crying. His fault, his fault, all his fault, he kept saying. Clem downplayed the whole thing. At the site of the accident, according to Luke, she had instructed him—clearheaded; even bossy, I'll bet—how to press his shirt on her wound while they waited for the ambulance. When it came, Luke was the one who fainted. "Hardly any blood," Clem says if you ask her about it.

"Mostly lots of yellow jellowy ooze. All fat. Disgusting more than anything else."

The doctor told our mother that Clem was the sort of patient who gave him migraines. She'd asked him to give her directions on how to change the bandage herself so that she could dash off on some sailboat way up in the maritime boondocks. "Sixty-two stitches!" he kept on scolding, as if our mother were to blame. "Sixty-*two*, if you please!" And frankly, he wasn't confident that the flesh inside the hook of her gash had the blood supply to heal correctly. He wanted her in bed for six weeks. "Two," said Clem. "This isn't a flea market, young woman," retorted the doctor. Three weeks later, she was aboard the *Gannet;* sometimes in pain, but, she wrote, madly in love with the Newfoundland coast. Her leg looked different every day, she said: *like my own flesh-and-blood mood ring. But Dr. Indignant was right about the necrotic tissue. Nasty, but no infection. YES, I am keeping an eye on it, Lou. I do not plan on losing my leg. So no lectures when you write back. Send Almond Joy bars and a really good juicy novel.* I sent her *The Magus.* She wrote back and told me it was perfect.

At the end of the summer, she tore up the card of the plastic surgeon her doctor had told her to call. "I've grown fond of it," she said. "Of what?" I asked, bewildered. "The scar," she said.

"What's *with* you guys?" I whispered. We were in the kitchen. I was putting herbs in the baby Cuisinart. Clem was cleaning the fish. She had washed her hair and it shone like black plumage, matching her short cotton dress. Her necklaces swayed away from her skin as she worked, bent over the sink.

"Nothing. Plenty," she said, not looking up. "Everything's the same . . . nothing's the same. You know. *Plus ça change*, however it goes."

We could hear Sam and Luke, on the verandah. Mostly we heard Sam, off on another of his fishing benders. The man was obsessed. Once in a while, I heard Luke murmur his approval. He was grateful, I think, just to be listening.

"You barge in here," I said, "invite Luke, act like you're running from the law, crash my date. You think you can stand there and tell me nothing?"

"Sorry." The repentance in her expression was so unusual that I had no choice but to buy it. "I *am* sorry. I'll tell you later. Trust me."

We focused on food for a while, working quietly, listening to the men. Now they were talking about New York. Luke was talking about the Verrazano-Narrows Bridge. "I saw it light up once, totally by accident. I was lost in New Jersey, and suddenly I'm driving up on this palisade—Jersey City? I still don't know where I was—and I saw the bridge in the distance, and exactly then the lights went on: from one end to the other, these pale green bulbs, swooping up and down along the spans like a pair of birds flying in tandem. It was . . . I could feel it in my chest—right here—do you know what I mean?"

"Oh I do!" said Sam. "Right there!"

"It was something *else,*" Luke said. I glanced at Clem, to see if she was moved by the rhapsody in his voice, but she was intent on slicing a radish.

"It's sweet, the way he's so openly passionate," I said.

"Yeah. It is." She scraped the sliced radishes into the salad. "What next?"

I gave her a cucumber. "I'm on it," she said.

The kitchen is the only place where Clem still follows my orders. She's a good cook, but I'm better and she knows it. I like it when she phones me long distance for recipes. In her life, for the most part, I feel superfluous.

"Okay," I said. "I may as well ask what you think of Sam."

Clem laughed. "Yeah, you'll hear it if you ask or not."

"So."

"Great eyes. Cute, in a retro-hippie sort of way. Talks like this is nineteen sixty-eight, everything but 'groovy.' It's quaint. But please, that *ponytail.* Who does he think he is, Cochise? He's cute, though, he really is. And he's nice. You could use some nice. Though he doesn't seem overly, uh, complicated." She was leaning against the sink, sipping vodka. She grinned pointedly. "And I'm afraid—you asked—I think he might be too self-centered. Too sort of . . . larger than his smallish life. Maybe a tad too much Kenny Rogers. I can't put a finger on it. . . ."

"Kenny Rogers? *Cochise?* You're so mean. And you are certainly spending the night here." I reached for her glass, but she twisted away. "Actually, I don't care what you think. I think he's sweet. And you ought to see his paintings. They are *very* complicated."

"Well, antifreeze is sweet. Dogs lick it off the road and die." She laughed loudly. "Just kidding."

"God you're a bitch."

"Hey, you're always telling me so. Must *be* so."

We both laughed, but I was faking.

Clem poured me a glass of wine. After she handed it to me, she stood staring out the window. "Poor things."

"What things?"

"Those rabbits, those birds. Victims of haute cuisine."

"Well then," I said, "poor trout."

"Not the same thing," said Clem, pointing a finger at me. "Eating *wild* animals, that's something else."

"Look, could we please not get into some Greenpeace debate, just for tonight? Things are tense enough, no thanks to you." About ecology, I am a dunce. I can hardly manage cocktail banter on the greenhouse effect. Clem is always telling me alarming things about the future, how immoral we all are, how it's too late even if (and forget it) we could change our ways. Imagine Jonathan Schell and Rachel Carson as Siamese twins: that's my sister at her worst. She'd told me, for instance, how thousands of dollars were wasted on cleaning up birds after a major oil spill off the coast of Scotland. "That relocation business? Bleeding-heart ignorance. These are birds that nest in the same place for *life*. They go back no matter what. They'll wade through the same muck all over again, die anyway." She told me this after I'd just sent money to the World Wildlife Fund. "Save the pandas? Hey, no harm in trying! And you get a free tote bag, too. How much of your money went to *that*? Rule number one, Lou: don't give a cent if they promise you a tote bag."

The trout was, as Sam declared, flawlessly awesome. I'd stuffed it with tomato, chili peppers, and cilantro from the garden. (My filet went into the freezer.) We ate on the verandah. Sam chose the music, and the first record he played was the Doobie Brothers. "We are livin' on the fault line!" he sang softly, earnestly, as he held out my chair. Clem rolled her eyes at me.

Luke seemed less miserable, in part because he was ignoring Clem. He talked about the building of the Brooklyn Bridge, aiming his narrative at Sam and me. He had tears in his eyes when he told us about everything Roebling suffered to build his masterpiece, how in the end it literally killed him.

Sam was mesmerized. "I live right *there*, man," he said. "I never knew all that. It's shameful not to know the history of where you live!" He shook his head.

Clem said very little. She ate studiously, almost eagerly, but she paid only the slimmest attention to the conversation, as if it were so dull that she preferred the diversion of nearby trees, the darkened sky, the occasional passing car.

"Come to the kitchen," I whispered. "Help me with dessert."

I needed mint, to garnish the granita. Clem followed me out to the garden. As I groped among the bushy plants, I heard her inhale sharply behind me, almost a sob. "I swear," she said, but nothing else.

I stood up and turned around. "Cut this out right now. Whatever your big fat secret is, tell it to me now."

"Now is not the time."

I shook a handful of mint in her face. "Now is *never* the time, is it? Clem, no one can help you when you're like this! Forget *me*. Luke hasn't a clue what's going on."

"This was a mistake." She went back to the house.

I found her in the stone room, sitting on the table. I saw, in the brief moment before she heard the door, that she was fingering the fringes of her scar, absently, as if reading braille. "So this is it," she said quickly, shifting her weight. "The place of culinary execution."

She looked up. I looked up. Black hooks hung on chains from the ceiling.

"Game hooks." Clem slid off the table and pointed beneath it, to the steel drain. "For the blood, what do you think?" She opened the drawer in the table, one I'd assumed would be crammed full of mittens, twine, pruning shears. It held several large sturdy knives, well used but honed. "This guy's a friend of yours?" She shrugged.

"Listen," I said, slamming the drawer, "enough of your gloom! I let you come here, ruin this, this, what might have been this incredibly romantic evening, you won't tell me what's going on, you, you . . ."

I stopped because I had never seen her look like this. She watched me, almost submissive. She reminded me of the rabbits, the way they froze in the beam of the flashlight when I checked on them at night. "Sorry," she said.

"Stop saying that. Just do something, tell me something, would you? You're driving everyone crazy. Or me. You're always so alone, such a god-damn martyr."

She leaned against the table. "I'm not alone *these* days."

"Yeah, well, there's Luke to kick around now, that's nothing new."

"I'm not talking about Luke. I happen to be pregnant." She stared at the coats hanging on the wall.

I stared at the coats as well, gaunt specters in the dim, windowless room. The only light came from the kitchen. I suppressed my dismay and said calmly, "I'm glad you called Luke."

"Lou, it's not his." She looked as if something amusing had crossed her mind. "That's the joke of it."

I looked hard at her, puzzled.

"You have your fisherman," she said, "I have mine. Though yours seems a whole lot nicer. A *whole* lot."

She had to remind me about the Labrador fisherman, Spider, the man Kurt had hired to pick up her mail. After the first letter from up there,

she'd never mentioned him again. "You don't mean, all that time . . ."
I thought of how touched I always felt by her letters—how I believed
they carried the intimate weight of a journal. I'd seen myself as her
confidante.

Clem finally looked at me. "Oh, I read your mind. Like: what a slut.
Oh poor *Luke*. And I bet you thought, I *bet* you thought I'd try to seduce
this Sam guy. It's been going through your head all evening, what a riot."
She laughed. "Well, yeah, he's kind of cute, like I said." Her voice dwindled. "He really is."

Suddenly, as if having made a decision, she lifted her short dress up to
her breasts. She was facing the light, so I saw them distinctly: three
bruises hugging her rib cage. She pulled the dress down. "And how about
this." She turned her head and held her hair away from one ear. The skin
behind it was purple. "Hey, no black eyes!"

"Jesus, Clem. None of this is funny."

She pulled herself up on the table again. "It turns out Spider's very
Catholic. I mean, here I go again, right? I can't stay away from these altar
boys, can I? So when I tell him, I get a stoic proposal of marriage. I make
the mistake of laughing. I'm nervous, that's all. *Big* mistake. But I mean,
for a minute there I think about it. I really consider it. Me, him, the baby.
Can't you see me? Knitting by the sea? Vacations hunting caribou? Wow.
The honeymoon at Niagara Falls."

"You're not actually planning to tell Luke," I said. "That's suicide."

"Oh Luke. Right. The gem I'm going to lose while I hang around
waiting for something finer. He tells me he's patient. He knows inside I
really do want him, that's what he says. He's dead wrong. I'm just selfish.
I'm just cruel." She started stroking her leg again.

"Stop that," I said gently. "You're giving me goosebumps."

She looked down. "A new and hideous habit. Sort of reassuring. Like
something outside of me that's entered and become a part of me. Like
Alien. Someday it'll burst out, have a whole life of its own." She pulled
back her hem. "Touch it. Go ahead. It's not radioactive."

I touched her leg, lightly. For the first time, I really looked at the scar.

It ran fearlessly down her thigh, an eroded ravine. Feeling it, I was amazed at how much flesh seemed to be missing, the place she'd lost the dead tissue. But I saw what she meant, about the comfort. It felt solid, like a steel cable running clear through her body, breaking the surface only here. "Some parts"—she poked at the scar—"I can't feel a thing. Is it weird to like that, having places in your body with no sensation?"

"What're you guys makin' out here, crêpes suzette?" Sam stood in the doorway, Luke behind him. Two boys grinning. "In the dark no less."

"I had a tour of the garden," said Clem without missing a beat. "The moon is huge."

Luke watched her. How well he must know all her excuses, her foils.

"You gotta see it," she told him. "I'll show you."

Sam and I ate our dessert in the living room, on the sofa. He put on Bruce Springsteen and talked about how he had just missed going to Vietnam. He talked about antinuclear art: most of it politics, he said, not art at all. Art must absolutely never become confused with politics, he said. ("Would you ever see Mantegna slapping slogans on the canvas? No way in hell.") Just like church and state: you had to keep that line distinct. He cut the air vertically with the side of a hand. He was colorful, animated, a man unburdened by gravity. Or by ambivalence of any kind. He might have inhabited one of his paintings, everything was so extreme. "Phenomenal!" he said about the chocolate granita. "A jumpin' guy!" he said about Mars as he went through the records. "The coolest, snottiest, jive-talkinest phony I ever met," he said of a very famous painter who'd come to a party on his roof, a painter sanctified in one of the essays I had just turned in to Hugh.

Sam talked, I watched. He was funny-looking and elegant all at once. His ears were sunburned and peeling. His hair gleamed marigold in the light cast by a saffron lampshade. His Hawaiian shirt, much too big, was ablaze with large purple flowers. It looked silky. I longed to press my face against his chest.

"Gale force, that sister of yours," he said after side B of Bruce Springsteen came to an end. "That's some scar she's got. A shark bite."

"She wears it like a medal," I said. I described the accident.

"She's intense. I mean, intensely intense. Like"—he laughed—"like you can see why she works with *wildlife*."

"I've got too much of an affinity for people," I said, ignoring a pun I'd heard too many times about my sister. "I couldn't live focused on animals. I think it would make me too sad. All that helplessness. Though that's the point, says Clem. The helpless need help most of all."

"Sort of ying and yang, you guys. Cool. I like that." Sam got up to find a new record. He spent a good five minutes poring through the collection, issuing sounds of approval or surprise. I realized, with an unexpected relief, that Sam was oblivious to my longings, all of them. To be fair, I was oblivious to his—or rather, I wanted only to use them. I wanted to be infected with the passion he had for his work. I wanted that passion for mine, for turning the lip on a bowl, for watching a perfect glaze emerge from the kiln. Inoculation against my doubts, that's what I wished for in Sam. At the same time, I was relieved that I liked him, relieved that he was *nice*. He really was. I would fight the disappointment, the notion of something unrequited.

Luke and Clem, I imagined, were kissing out there among Leah's flowers, making up despite the odds. If he told Clem what I'd said on the phone, she would kill me—though maybe she loved him more than she cared to admit. That would be my defense.

I walked onto the verandah and, sure enough, heard my sister's voice, just a murmur. She was somewhere near but out of sight. Already I had a plan for her: She and Luke could borrow my apartment for a few days. I knew of a clinic. I knew many things and could be fairly certain of others. Over her insistence on going it alone, that this had nothing to do with him, Luke would accompany her, sit in the waiting room holding her hand. I saw them in this clinic: the plastic ivy, the magazines, the fluorescent lights droning like bees. Absently, Clem would touch her scar while she waited, Luke beside her with nothing to say. I remembered exactly, uncomfortably, how it felt to the touch: ridged and dry, leather embossed with hieroglyphics. Conspicuously gruesome, but wasn't it also a caution?

I could be almost certain, too, and it made me both fearful and sad, that Luke would take a chance on proposing marriage yet again. And I knew how Clem would respond. *Now is not the time.* Now was never the time, not for things like that, not for her. *Don't ask for anything; just stay,* I begged him silently, selfishly. My stake in having him around seemed to be this: I saw him as Clem's one dependable link with sanity, with safety, as the proof that she was even a bit like me, that we could somehow remain joined. *Plus ça change,* however it goes: I still want to be the benevolent tyrant. I want to outshine her, I want to be the wiser, the smarter, the better loved, but I want to keep an eye on her. She is, after all, irreplaceable.

Husbandry

1986

I'm on the graveyard shift when my mother calls to tell me that ten of her prize hounds have been abducted by her kennelman and are, or so she suspects, headed clear across the country to Carmel. "Took off! Took off, the lunatic; thinks he can pull a Houdini on me! Well let me tell you, his notion of cunning is pathetic." She rants on, sharp as she always is when provoked: she has her sources, she's no idiot, she'll track him down and have his hide on toast. "Years of trust, *years*, and what? What are the man's true colors? A monster, just a crazed sadistic monster biding his time!"

I listen—all I'm permitted to do, which is fine by me. But here's what I know: Titus Goodwin, who's hung around our house for ages, fondly known to us as Tighty, hasn't one sadistic atom in his battle-weary soul. And monstrous? No way. Crazy, though, you couldn't rule out. He has a vindictive temper, an appetite for tragedy, and drinks like a camel refueling at an oasis. A bad mix. Otherwise, he's your run-of-the-mill deposed aristocrat who, if scornful of the human race, has nothing but tenderness and reverence for all living creatures, down to the prickliest sea urchin. This is why I will always love Tighty, no matter what he does to the people around him.

But I have no time for his neuroses or for my mother's fury. There's a cat due here any minute, classic urinary blockage, and it's my job to call in a vet. "Look, say they got off at dawn," I say. "They can't be any farther than, what, mid-Ohio? Indiana? Tighty'd never break fifty-five with hounds in the truck. I don't know what you think I can do, but whatever it is, I can't do it till they get here." I live in Monterey, right next to Carmel. I can't imagine how you'd hide ten restless foxhounds in a town that snug, but Tighty's never been rational. Nor has my mother, which may help explain how they've gotten along all these years—parallel lines that kiss at infinity. Mom is master of the Figtree Domain Foxhunt. Tighty is her kennelman.

"Go to the police is what you can do!" she says. I look at the clock; her time, it's two in the morning. My father will be upstairs, long asleep, head clamped under a pillow. Mom will be pacing the kitchen: talking, smoking, sipping vodka, her reflection over the sink goading her on.

"Mom, listen, I'm afraid we've got an emergency here."

"Honey, we certainly do. He took Tallulah—she's whelping in less than two weeks!" Tallulah, a sublimely marked blanket-back crossbred, symmetrical as a Rorschach blot, took Best in Show last year at Bryn Mawr and gives incomparable tongue. She's my mother's number one brood bitch.

Bench queen or mutt, a dog in whelp on the road is bad news, but I tell Mom I have to go. I don't tell her I have no intention of calling the police before I talk to Tighty—that is, if he gets this far. Because where would he stay? Your average Motel 6 isn't likely to let a pack of dogs cozy up in their massage-o-matic bed. (Nor do I tell her that Louisa will be arriving here tomorrow, having informed my machine four hours ago, in a voice jagged with tears, that she's catching a dawn flight from New York, that she's had it with Hugh's inertia and thinks she might leave him.)

Headlights sweep the parking lot. A car door slams, and then I hear the unmistakable yowling of feline pain. I speed-dial the night vet and yank on clean scrubs as I hopscotch my way to the stairs, cordless in hand. I'm halfway down when he answers. "Poosepoose Simonson's here," I tell him. "Roto-Rooter, major league." I hold out the phone to share the cat's distress, echoing off the tiled floor of our waiting room. Poosepoose, a massive fur-bound coon cat, writhes in Mrs. Simonson's arms. Mrs. Simonson begins to cry. I suggest gently that Poosepoose might prefer his carrier, and she bawls, "When this may be his last hour on earth?"

Are the planets out to spite me? Why is everyone suddenly indulging in hysterics? I put my hand on Mrs. Simonson's shoulder and say, very softly, "It's okay. Dr. John will be here any minute. Everything's going to be fine, I promise." This calms her down instantly. I don't know why, but people trust me.

I've got two part-time jobs and am supposed to be finishing my thesis. Four evenings and two overnights a week, I work at the Monterey Ark. I pin down hostile Dobermans, unwrap and fill syringes, give worming instructions, clip wings, prepare anesthetics, sort true emergencies from episodes of hypochondriacal projection. Three afternoons I'm an underwater guide at the aquarium. I dive down into the kelp forest, feed the fish, and answer silly questions from the tourists who swarm beyond the glass wall.

My thesis is a proposed compromise between conservationists protecting West Coast seals and the increasingly hostile fishing merchants, who, like Republicans on the subject of welfare, slander their marine foes as slothful, greedy, unproductive citizens who ought to have had their tubes tied long ago. If my disingenuously optimistic theories are coalescing at the speed of a slug, and if there's anything to blame outside my native lethargy and my brooding struggles with pointlessness, it's Zip. I met Zip at Miso Magic, where he is a regular. I go there once in a while, when I long for virtue, and I ought to have known better—realized that a man so free of toxins would make me feel doubly poisonous by comparison.

Zip says I'm too much Of The World. He frowns on my lust for tequila, my sarcasm, my secrecy, my habit of dancing with strange men in bars (just dancing, that's all!). He says I eat too much yin food, and he suspects I don't go deep enough when I meditate. I wouldn't tell him that I don't really meditate at all; I go through the motions sometimes, just for him, and I've tried, I really have, to let go of the world—but I can't. The world weighs so much, and it bears down so hard. We've been seeing each other for three months and he's sort of moved in. Not that he's a freeloader. Speaking of productive citizens, in fact, Zip is the county's social services director. I like his idealism. Would that it were contagious.

He stays over most nights and always does the cooking. He bought a set of Japanese knives for my kitchen and treats them like holy relics. They are the sharpest knives I've ever touched, sharper than hunting knives, sharper than envy. The night he brought them over, I ran one lightly across my palm—the one time I've seen him lose his cool. "For God's sake!" he shouted; the knife sliced my skin like the easy flesh of a melon. A lot of blood for so shallow a cut, and I laughed as Zip wrapped my hand in a dish towel. "Hey," I joked, "life is never dull." Zip was not amused.

He moves around my kitchen with the grace of a priest; just to watch him is reassuring. But lately I'm sick of hijiki salads, brown rice breakfasts, and daikon root stews, even if I do gaze across my chopsticks at a face akin to Rob Lowe's (better: less of the chipmunk). There's the mental brown rice, too, of which I've had my fill and said so. I may lie about meditating, but I let him know when I've had enough woo-woo talk. But Zip's a crusader, a member of the spiritual-health gestapo. My resistance seems only to make him more ardent. He is determined to save me.

I drive to San Francisco on two hours' sleep. My sister waits on the United sidewalk looking like she cried across all four time zones, but even if she is a wreck, she's composed: a proud wreck, as befits the Confederate trunk of our lineage. As I get out to greet her, I say, "Guess they don't call it the red-eye for nothing." Right away, I realize how stupid and mean this sounds, but adjusting to Louisa's presence is always a tricky business for me.

"Is that your best shot at sympathy?" she says.

"Bad joke. Sorry." I hug her; briefly, she lets me. "But I warn you, you're looking at a walking, talking stingray."

"Better than a soon-to-be-ex-husband deep in an emotional coma."

"So what did he do?"

"You mean what didn't he do, what doesn't he *ever* do."

"Okay, what doesn't he ever do?"

"Pay attention! React to the emotions around him! Live life!"

I heave her suitcase into the trunk. I can't tell if she's planning to stay a month or has simply overpacked as usual. I've come to the conclusion that there's some innate melodrama in my sister's soul, something that leads her to travel anywhere, no matter how temperate, as if she must be prepared for every natural catastrophe ever leveled at the planet. Years ago, when we'd pack for summer camp, I'd watch her fill a trunk with everything from flannel pajamas to party shoes.

"Those are pretty serious charges," I say as we get in. "But it's not like Hugh's a very, well, emotive kind of guy." I think of the first time I met him, a couple years ago, when Louisa brought him to Maine for a visit. It was summer, I was still in grad school, still with Luke, the guy almost everybody thinks I was stupid not to marry. One night a whole bunch of us made roast beef with Yorkshire pudding, smoked a little ganja, and danced in Luke's living room to quadraphonic soul. Hugh was friendly but held back on all the excess; no drugs, no dancing, not even much roast beef. He'd brought along a huge book—a biography of the artist John Singleton Copley, such a weird book to carry around that I have never forgotten it—and vanished in the middle of the meal (not that most of us noticed, I have to confess). Later, we found him asleep on Luke's bed, the big book splayed on his tweed lapels. Soon after that, Louisa broke it off with Hugh because, she said, he had no wild side; a touch of true wildness was crucial. I agreed heartily with that, though the guy had seemed perfectly nice. Then, last year, almost out of the blue, they got married. Not like they had the mercy to elope. No; I had to wear one of those poufy satin dresses, get up at my parents' beach club and make a toast.

"He's never been the kind of guy," I say now, "to revel in things—to, like, take up flamingo dancing. You know that. But then, he's never impulsive, he's . . . dependable." I choose my words carefully—but not carefully enough for my sister the word nerd.

"Flamenco," she enunciates quietly.

"What?"

"It's *flamenco* dancing."

"I knew that." (Did I? I need to stop counting the lies that don't matter.) I reach over to jostle Louisa's shoulder, trying to calm her down the way I did Mrs. Simonson. She is clearly all wound up. I say, "So, hey, looks like we've got a new dance to invent."

It doesn't work. She says impatiently, "No more jokes. Please. I don't mean to be rude. I'm just . . . I've lost my sense of humor."

I try to imagine what she wants to hear, why she came all this way. I say, "I'll drive, you ride. Talk if you want. Or don't. Just have a vacation." *Just be here,* Zip would say. *Be here in the I Don't Know.*

I take the scenic route, through artichoke country, striped green fields ending at cliffs on the ocean. No trees; just fields, rocks, water, and this one endless ribbon of road, rippling with the tentative heat of late May. "Incredible, isn't it?" I say. At last, she agrees with something. Where we come from, you'd see fancy houses, not vegetables, sprouting left and right—hidden by tall dense hedges.

Louisa is four years older than I am; also nearly four inches shorter and about four decades more full of opinions. Sometimes when she enters a room, it feels like half the air's been sucked out. I know a lot, but around her, it's never enough.

We are as different as white chocolate and seaweed, the Milky Way and a tropical reef. For one thing, I do not know how she, or anyone, lives in New York City. For another, I do not know how she, or anyone, can suspend disbelief long enough to turn up married. The first thing, Louisa says, she understands perfectly; the second she says I'll grow out of. I'm certain she's wrong there, and this is how I see it. The world evolved, the only way it could, as a place of competition and loneliness. Everything natural or invented that we see as beautiful or remarkable—from Japanese maples to bone scans—was nurtured by one or both of these forces.

You might see marriage that way, I guess, but I'm convinced it's just a major form of self-delusion, a wrench in the Darwinian works, the grandest of grand illusions.

So I am surprised at none of Louisa's accusations: Hugh's sleepy silence over candlelit dinners, his tortoiselike retreat in the face of her anger, the Jeevesy routines that drive her nuts. And it's not that I don't like Hugh: he's a stately, rock-of-ages kind of guy, if not too ambitious. Prince Charles, Gerald Ford, and Morris the Cat all rolled into one. Our mother likes him because he always shows up in a tie and, more important, descends from Cotton Mather or some other famous stuffed shirt. ("Blood will tell," she's always saying; perhaps, but I don't think she *listens*.) Dad likes Hugh because even though he's smart (he teaches history at an all-boys prep school), he's happy to let everyone else do the talking. He's also—a bonus—patriotic. He teaches mainly American history and gets teary-eyed at places like the Old North Bridge. Parents go for that. And then, on top of those virtues, what Hugh does makes sense to them. Louisa writes for an art magazine, and while our parents are hardly philistines, they never know what to ask her. You can always ask Hugh what he thinks about Ollie North or *Roe versus Wade;* he'll never offend anyone. Ask Louisa what she's up to and chances are she's reviewing some show where two women with shaved heads slip into giant condoms and fence with dildos.

When I see the Monterey County Social Services van in my driveway, I say, "There's two things I have to tell you right now. One, that van belongs to a guy I'm seeing, and please don't give me shit about how eccentric he is, because I don't think it's going to last much longer. Two, we might have a mission from Mom. Poor Tighty's flipped."

"Now that, that is exactly what I need right now. Mom and her drama."

I resist the urge to say, *Look who's talking.* "Lighten up, Lou. You're in the Sunshine State."

"Clem," she says, "the Sunshine State is Florida."

"Now there you are wrong," I say, gleeful because this turnabout is a rarity. "Florida is the Gator State."

Louisa shakes her head and smiles at me, rueful with a dash of haughty. "California is the Golden State, and the creature that lives in the Everglades—as you of all people should know—is the crocodile. I'm sorry."

"Boy, you *are* in a bad mood," I say. "And for your information, both crocodiles and alligators inhabit the state of Florida. *Alligator mississipiensis* is the genus native to the Southeast. We ever make it to *Jeopardy*, you'll never beat me in anything scientific, I promise."

"I'll just study my pants off, I've always been better at that," says Louisa.

"*God* you are smug," I say, but at least we are laughing.

She's standing by the trunk as I open it, hands on her hips, wearing a bossy smile. "I came to just the right place, I see, for unconditional love, free of hostility."

"Yeah, and to just the right place for other people to carry your ten tons of stuff." I'm lugging her grand-tour suitcase, and despite the awkwardness, she puts an arm around my shoulders. We're not the world's most affectionate family, the four of us, so this is something. I look up just then and see Zip, so handsome, so serene, watching us from my first-floor apartment.

Since moving to California last year, I've stopped telling people that my mother is a master of foxhounds. I could explain, as I always have, how at Figtree the hounds never taste blood, how it's a drag hunt—someone goes out and lays a phony trail by dragging a mop soaked in fox urine and a lot of secret odious dilutants through the countryside—but even bird-watching is a violation to the people I've met through Zip. (To them, animals treasure privacy as much as they do freedom.) And blood sports—even soft-core bloodless blood sports—well, you'd better not breathe a word unless you're out there stretching the piano wire. I'd never confess I was once a participant, dressing up in horsey attire and cantering around behind my mother and her exuberantly baying hounds.

Louisa steered clear of all that; she liked reading, modern dance, bad-
minton. She did homework. I did everything else.

We grew up near the Rhode Island coast (the Ocean State, that one I
do know), respectably well off in a town of solid if covert wealth, our
house small but charming, two miles from the beach. The hunt club
ought to have died a dignified death decades ago, but Mom and her richer
compatriots persevere in carving out a patch of ersatz country. Tuesdays
and Saturdays, fall and spring, three dozen riders thread their way
through woods and fields endangered on all sides by grandiose housing
developments and gratuitously straightened roads. Long before the
dawn fog evaporates, our mother's oversize "Tallyho!" can be heard at
the self-service Mobil on Route 14, the Windjammer Clam Hut on
Pemiquisset Point, and even, I bet, if the wind is from the east, as far
inland as the Pilgrim's Pride Mall near the overpass on the Roger
Williams Turnpike.

Until I was rudely awakened by nursery school, I thought I was a fox-
hound puppy. I was pack-trained, deer-proofed, taught to shun cur
dogs—the works. I looked to my mother for biscuits and praise, forth-
coming whenever deserved. The Figtree kennel was across the road,
down a long elm-shaded drive, but even so there were always hounds in
our house—recuperating from wounds (barbed wire, surgery, rivalry
over a bitch) or whelping litters (for which we kept a wide wooden box,
with a heat lamp, in a corner of the mudroom over the furnace). Our
mother attended these births with a mesmerized devotion we seldom saw
elsewhere. Afterward, she watched those puppies like a batch of lottery
tickets. She made sure they were all kept clean as new snow and would
rearrange them while nursing, to keep the sly fat ones from hogging the
most bountiful spigots. She shredded newspaper twice a day, Q-tipped
ears as tiny as limpets, made sure the mother had time out to laze in the
sun. She never put the runts to sleep. Once, ringside at a hound show, I
heard another master challenge her on this point. "You're defying the
will of nature," he said, and she said, "I don't know about you, but in my
house nature's not the boss."

Nor, for that matter, is Dad. Our father's work is seasonal; for most of the summer, he practically disappears. He owns and runs three boatyards in different crannies along our home state's convoluted shoreline. In his work, nature *is* the boss. And if he's not preoccupied with dry-dock line-ups or battening down for a storm, he's in his rose garden, kneeling at the foot of a Mademoiselle Franziska Krüger, or submerged in an arm-chair, reading five-pound biographies of the world's imperial pillagers. One thing I've noticed is that patient, good-natured men often worship Cortez and Napoleon—apparently, even those who also worship the beauty of nature.

Zip opens the back door. "The sister. Yes," he says to Louisa, smiling his enlightened smile.

"For better or worse," she says. We stand together in the kitchen, all silent. I see her sizing him up; I shouldn't have told her a thing.

"Take this onto the sun porch, would you?" I hand Zip the suitcase. He takes it but continues to study Louisa, sizing her up in return, though it's probably something to do with her karma or chakras. "Wheatgrass? Just made a fresh batch," he says brightly.

I open the refrigerator and scan its alarmingly wholesome contents. "She'd like a beer, and so would I." Aiming for a pair of Coronas, I snake my hand past a head of bok choy and a picnic thermos of Swiss chard broth.

"I'll try some, sure," Louisa says to Zip. "I feel kind of dried out."

"Sun. That's what you need," he tells her. "Whenever you change time zones, either direction, you should be in the sun as soon as you can. It tells your body where you are."

"Okay, so we'll stand around in the driveway and find out where we are." I'm annoyed at Zip because he's part of the reason I got so little sleep: I got home at 5:00 a.m. to be greeted by a boyfriend wide awake with lust.

"Didn't I see a little lawn out there?" asks Louisa.

"Our crabgrass welcome mat? I guess that's a lawn if you come from New York."

Zip and I take the front steps, Louisa sits on the grass. "This does feel nice, I'm sure you're right," she says, slanting her face to the sky, sipping her juice.

Zip begins to expound on our inner sun compass and his solar-therapy program for shut-ins. Through the open window above us, the phone rings.

My voice clicks on, backed by Charles Mingus. Mom tackles that beep like an otter swatting a fish onto dry land. "I've been trying to reach you all morning, honey, you are never in! Shouldn't you be working on that paper of yours? Are you at the library? Are you there but *hiding?*" Crackling pause. "Well, I am beside myself here, beside myself! Call me right away, please, the minute you get this, and tell me what the police have to say. Time is of the essence. The FBI practically laughed in my face, and your father says we'll never be able to extradite on dognapping charges, but so help me, if I have to fly out myself, that man will pay with his skin. I will flay him alive with a bread knife. I've already changed the locks on the carriage house. I don't care if his great-great-grandfather did build the First Presbyterian."

The three of us listen for another long minute, as if to a radio play. Finally, the machine puts an end to her tirade. I feel guilty and decide that if she calls right back, which she often does when she's cut off, I'll run inside and pick up the phone, but she doesn't.

"Tomatoes. She should cut down on nightshades," Zip says with compassion. This is his routine diagnosis of people who lose their temper, and he may be right; he never eats tomatoes or eggplant, and he never gets mad.

Louisa's travel pallor has vanished. "Do you think it ever occurs to her that people have problems all their own?" Nothing and no one raises her temperature faster than Mom. "And what's all this stuff about extradition?"

Zip shakes his head with his typical air of omniscience. "Dogs.

According to the law, they're mere property. The police will treat them like stolen appliances. Worse." His tone is ominous.

"Will somebody please tell me what's going on?"

"Well, Lou, while you're flipping out about Hugh, Mom is flipping out about Tighty, who's also clearly flipping out, though I'm not sure about what." I tell my sister what I know.

"A plan. You'll need a plan," says Zip, who doesn't question the wisdom of getting involved. Zip believes in loyalty to family against all logic. That's fine for him, since his parents have passed away and his only brother is well employed, happily married, and lives in Montreal.

"What I need is a good long nap," I say. "Then dinner. I have a craving for greasy nachos; sorry, Zip. A margarita, big and salty. Otis Redding."

Louisa says to Zip, "I like the way Clem always knows what she wants."

Louisa's so smart about some things, so gullible about others. And a master of double-edged praise—both sides sharp as those Japanese knives.

She never lets me forget this one ridiculous summer: the summer after she'd graduated from Harvard, the summer after I found out I didn't get in, that I'd be shipping out to Michigan instead (deep down I was glad). She was commuting to a job at the art museum in Providence, but she'd flipped for this guy up the road who restored vintage motorcycles. I didn't notice. Honest. In general, I ignored her. We had so little in common. (That's still mostly true, except for family, which sometimes—like right now—looms a little too large.)

I was a lifeguard at the beach club. Evenings, I volunteered at the bird sanctuary: pinned wings, fed displaced nestlings. I'd learned to ride a unicycle and rode it to both of my jobs because they were near. Some mornings, Louisa would pass me in her frumpy little Dodge; she'd wave without looking, then head for the highway, hands on the wheel at ten and two.

When Louisa's car broke down, the motorcycle man came by with his tools. They were drinking beer on the porch when I soared around the corner on my single wheel, holding a cardboard box. "Are you crazy? Poor thing," said Louisa after peering down into the box. The box held a baby osprey. The motorcycle man—Mike was his name—asked a million questions that night about birds, but the osprey wasn't the magnet. There's something about unicycles, I learned: the subtle way you swivel your hips to stay balanced.

After two weeks of my polishing chrome in his garage, of his helping me feed that ravenous osprey, I invited Mike to our family's Fourth of July cookout. Louisa had this fabulous dress: blue silk, low neck, tight hips—on me, outrageously short. I'd borrowed it before, so I figured she wouldn't care. So there we were dancing, Mike and me, not even close or romantic, just flinging ourselves around and laughing, when Louisa comes right over and throws her wine in my face. How was I to know that, weeks before, she'd taken Mike to her museum, come back to tour his collection, crept home from his house at dawn, certain this was true love? He hadn't told me, nor had she, but all Louisa saw was revenge. She screamed at me the next morning that it wasn't her fault if Harvard didn't take me. I laughed at her and said, "You think I'm getting back at you for better SAT scores? How big is *your* universe?" Needlessly cruel, okay, but my hair still smelled like wine.

"He has such beautiful skin. I couldn't stop staring."

"Yeah, well, no booze, no butts, and if you can believe it, no caffeine. That'll do it."

"Or genes. I'm convinced more and more these things are genes," Louisa says.

"The Gospel According to Mom."

Louisa flinches. "I'm admiring his complexion, Clem. I'm not asking if he's up for stud."

We are sitting in Jorge's Cocina, a café out on a wharf. Half a mile down the coast, the aquarium looks like a ship that yearns toward open sea. Sometimes I stop here after work and watch the sea lions below. They lurk around the barnacled pilings or sun on the rocks, their Goodyear hides gleaming blue and cinnamon brown. Call down and they squint up, their noses pointing out precisely *you*, sniffing you out long distance, benignly condescending. Throw them something to eat, they chortle and bark. I throw down chum I swipe from the otter station, a ziplock Baggie stuffed in my knapsack before I leave work. And if I've been writing, sifting through stats on the poaching up north, I look at these guys and feel better, just a little. I like to think they're safe here, protected by tourism kitsch. They tolerate heckling, broken bottles, plastic debris, they eat Mallomars and Slim Jims, but nobody's out to shoot them. The best I can wish for them is safety.

"Does he have a sense of humor? I can't tell," Louisa's saying. "Maybe not—but he seems almost wise. He knew so much about me."

"Excuse me," I say, "but do you think I never mention your existence?"

"Inner things, things about who I am at the core."

"Let me guess. He gave you that book. Wow, Lou, this is *so* not you."

Zip carries around extra copies of the book that changed his life. It's called *Inner Aura: Gem of Nine Facets*. Not a stupid book, pretty eloquent in fact, but it's one of those if-you-don't-go-Zen-you'll-never-get-your-shit-together sermons that tempt me because they're so sure and then bug me because they're so naïve. I tried yoga once, but every time I looked in the mirror and saw myself as a spandex pretzel, I thought, Who's this meant to fool? I'm anything but pure. When we argue, I tell Zip the human race is evolving apart, not together. There are many paths, okay, but they do not lead to one truth. And unless you lose a few million brain cells en route, they do not lead to some all-infusing serenity. Serenity is one thing we're always leaving behind. We watch it recede as fast as an oil truck crossing Nevada. Nothing but a cloud of dust.

"You're right," says Louisa. "I never go for these packaged wisdoms, but I felt as if he really cared about helping me."

"Unlike Hugh."

"That's not the point." She looks hurt.

"So what did Zip prescribe? He likes to prescribe."

"Well, he says I need camping."

"Oh Lou." Now I'm cracking up. "You? Camp?"

"He *says*," she continues, defying my ridicule, "that the only cure for city living—which he says is deeply toxic, and who can disagree with that?—the only cure is sleeping outdoors whenever you can. Roofs compress the spirit, he says. So do mattresses. Marriage, he says, is like an old carpet. No matter how beautiful or priceless, no matter how familiar, it needs airing out, needs to rest from being trampled on. He says I did the right thing by coming here."

I am thinking that Zip should run for governor. "You're right that he cares, Lou, but the trouble with Zip is that to him everyone is a problem waiting for a solution. His solution. *The* solution."

"Everyone has problems, Clem. He's trying to help. But you—I suppose you don't have problems."

"Oh, by the score," I say. "Please. But nobody else has the solutions that suit *me*. Certainly not in some list of noble platitudes."

Our skillet of fajitas arrives, lots of fussy little dishes on the side. Right away, Louisa takes most of the sour cream. She does that when we share something, takes the bigger half. Like she's letting me know she deserves more because she came first.

"Don't you like the guy?" she says.

"Yes, sure!" I say, nearly choking on my first bite. "But sometimes I wonder if it's possible to *move* him, to catch him off guard. He's like a cat. Everything that happens he's already seen. He's one step ahead of the world every minute."

"Have you noticed," says Louisa, "how everything he says starts with a noun? For instance, when I was describing how I yell at Hugh and Hugh says nothing—but in this utterly blank way that only enrages me more—Zip said, 'Self-awareness. Focus more on yourselves than on each other.' Like that."

"Zip's a noun kind of guy. Very concrete. That's what I mean. He has no doubts. It's admirable, but it's also a little creepy."

"That's certainly not our problem," Louisa says morosely.

"Listen," I warn her. "Don't drag me down, okay?" Because I feel it begin to happen, the air starting to thin.

For a while we just eat, glancing out the window, as if each of us were alone. There's no moon, so the ocean looks dark and dense, like moss. I like to picture the life underneath. I've been to Alaska, to the Amazon— I've seen and heard wildness, true wildness—but under the ocean moves me the most, because it's so strange, so out of time. In Barrow, I got to listen to whales, the crazy-fabulous sounds they make, calling to one another as they swim along, staying in touch as they migrate north. It sounded like a jungle or a space-age orchestra. Listen to that for hours on end and human voices, when you hear them again, sound pointless.

When I go to work at the aquarium, when I dive down into the kelp forest that's fed by the bay, by its tides, I love that moment when the water takes the weight of the tank, how I feel the cold but it's somewhere else, benignly removed from my skin. The wet suit holds me tight all over, dependable as the ideal mate. It deflects the bite of the world, fills me with a fearless cocaine shimmer. Everything I see sways to the sound of my breath—swarming bubbles, schools of flashing fish—and I hear just how alive I am.

I fantasize about sneaking into the aquarium at night, diving down among the sleepy creatures—the petticoated cuttlefish; the nurse sharks; the rays, soft as velour. During the day, when I come bearing food, the sharks and the rays are the most aggressive, nudging and skimming my body over and over. But in the night world I long for, we are equals. We drift together between rocking ribbons of seaweed, no one watching, no one asking questions. No crises to solve, no talk of any kind. Everything drugged and blue as a dream, under the skin of the sea.

"Time for music," I say. I head for the jukebox, but I decide against Otis. Too risky; too sad. "I've Been Loving You Too Long" is what I almost always play. Zip likes it, too. The one time I dragged him here, we put it on, closed our eyes, and held hands, just sitting at the bar. It felt intense the way it feels intense locking eyes with a tiger. (Zip's an intensity artist, one reason I can't let him go.) So tonight I pick Bob Marley.

"Lively Up Yourself." "Love Is the Only Law." For Louisa I punch in "Respect," dependable, wise Aretha. Because of the numbers, it's already playing when I get back. Louisa's smiling, a nice reward.

"Corny," I say. "But true, right?" I'm not referring to Hugh, but she takes it that way.

"Well, the issue's not respect." She dips into my guacamole, having finished hers. "It's more like . . . apathy. The other night we were walking home after a movie. It was the first really warm night. We were walking by the planetarium and the park. You could smell the new leaves, rainy without the rain, you know? And I thought about . . ." She plays with her silverware.

"What? Thought about what?"

"The future. Us, our future. I was in a great mood, and I wanted to talk about it, like where would we be in five years? Would we have children? What would we be doing? You know."

I could say, *In fact, no, I do not,* but I nod.

"I tell him how maybe it's time to start thinking about a baby. I ask if he wants to stay in the city forever. I tell him I've been thinking about our moving up to New England, maybe Boston if I could get a museum job—just thinking. He walks along, not a single word. I'm doing one of my monologues, but he could nod or smile or look at me, *something.* For all I know, he's planning tomorrow's lesson, thinking about Bronson Alcott or the Bay of Pigs while I'm talking to the air. So I stop. Just stop. And of course he walks on a ways before he notices I've stopped. 'Where *are* you?' I say when he turns around. 'I'm right here,' he says in that bland voice I hate. I ask him what he thinks about the things I've said. He says, 'Sounds good to me.' I say, 'What, which things, *what* sounds good?' He just looks at me, oblivious and fearful at the same time. I say, 'I guess I'm asking, what do you want from life?' We've been married one whole year and we've never had this kind of conversation and I'm horrified. It's my fault, too, I realize. But do you know what he says?"

"What?"

" 'To be comfortable.' That's it! What he wants out of life!"

"That doesn't seem like an unreasonable goal," I say. "A more honest answer than most."

"But it's so aimless!"

"What are you, full of a million aims?"

"And when we went home," Louisa says, "I lost it. I cried and cried. Hugh went into the bedroom and read. *Read.* He got up in the morning, shaved, read the paper, and went to *work.*" She looks down at her empty plate. "And to think I was thinking about getting pregnant."

"You wouldn't be so stupid," I say. I'm feeling irritated because some idiot's Neil Diamond appears to have bumped my Bob Marley. Actually, Louisa probably should have a baby. For Louisa, that makes sense.

"It would be, wouldn't it, things the way they are," she says sadly.

"Well, if you want to talk *rationally* about having babies, no time would be a good time." I can't seem to shut up.

Louisa rolls her eyes. "Oh, right, the world's too awful a place to inflict on a child. Spare me."

"No, not exactly. It's more like, sometimes I think, people are too awful to inflict more of them on the world." This leaves Louisa speechless, which is rare. "And say you did have a kid. If it's a girl, she'll grow up to despise her mother no matter what, because that's what daughters do. A boy? He could end up gay, get AIDS, and die. Break your heart, either way."

Louisa gasps. "What a horrid thing to say, what's the matter with you? They're going to cure AIDS, they're getting nearer all the time."

"No, they won't—and it's so incredibly tragic. I'm not a bigot. Listen. No one's ever cured a virus. The media's full of treacherous wishful hogwash. A vaccine, maybe, but who'd take it?" I explain carefully and coldly how a virus works, how this one mutates like nothing they've ever seen. Bob Marley kicks in at last with "Lively Up Yourself." Louisa looks both appalled and demoralized, and it's all my fault. How can I laugh at Zip? At least he knows how to console. I say, "Hey. Do like the man says."

Now she's almost in tears. "You are an utter nihilist."

"I'd rather be pleasantly surprised than fatally disappointed." And then I do shut up. As always, too late.

For the next three days, we hardly see each other. I'm buried in the library—disciplined by Louisa's mere presence—and two nights I'm on at the clinic. I haven't asked how long she plans to stay, and she hasn't said.

She sits on my couch, drinks mug after mug of Zip's mint tea, and reads a bunch of books she's supposed to review. I realize now why her suitcase weighed so much.

Tuesday night when I get back, she's on the phone. Zip's out, running his soup kitchen. Louisa smiles quickly when I walk in, turns her back, and lowers her voice. She murmurs, "Yes, I will, I know, I promise. I have to go but yes, of course, I will, don't worry, me too, I will, soon," things like that, so I know it's Hugh and I'm glad, but when she gets off, she looks sheepish, as if jilting him would please me. She asks how things went at the clinic.

"This Rottweiler swallowed a tennis ball. That caused a little excitement. One of those neon pink ones." I describe the owner's hysteria, the surgery, tell her all about Rottweilers' oral compulsions, about the things I've seen emerge almost unscathed from their stomachs: balls of tinfoil, rubber spatulas, spiky toy dinosaurs, a pair of fuzzy dice. Last month we x-rayed a dog who'd been vomiting for days and wouldn't eat. We saw a long straight line all the way from the esophagus down to the upper intestinal tract, a total mystery. What we removed was the rubber-coated telephone antenna from the owner's Jaguar, nearly as good as new (as was the dog after surgery). I took the antenna into the waiting room and waved it in the guy's face. "Missing something?" He wasn't amused.

Louisa nods at the phone, which blinks double time. "Guess who," she says. "First, to say she's certain he's here. Second, she's decided to forget the police. She had an argument with a desk sergeant in Carmel who she describes as an 'animal-rights fundamentalist.' "

"You didn't pick up?"

"I don't want her knowing I'm here. How do I explain?"

"Say you're reviewing a show for your magazine! You're the creative one. I hate dealing with this all alone."

"You took it on. I'd have refused."

"Easy for you to say." I sigh. It's ten o'clock here, too late to call back. I see, too, that any hope I had for my sister's willing help was a delusion. Though Louisa, I'll admit, sees the harshest side of our mother. Because she's too smart? Because she interrupted something? I don't know. But I know this: when Louisa got into Harvard, how proud was our mother? The first words out of her mouth were "Cambridge? Hotbed of political heretics and whining overgrown hippies. If you ask my opinion, it ought to be designated a nuclear-waste dump. Drown the bastards in PCBs." When Louisa became engaged, she said, "Now don't you let that boy down. The ring alone must have cost him a fortune!" Louisa never challenges these insults. She's been hearing them forever, I guess.

"I have an idea," I say. "Let's go for a drive."

"At this hour? Where?"

"We'll look for the hound truck," I say, pleased at my ingenuity.

Part of me wonders what the hell Tighty could possibly be *thinking*—and part of me is shaking its head like a parent, muttering, Great. Just great. He's fucking up all over again.

Tighty is fifty, almost a decade younger than Mom. He doesn't rate as a lost soul—he's not quite derailed—but his bitterness, his sense of never having found a way to make an upper-class living, comes across loud and clear. He dropped out of Yale in the late fifties and liquidated his fledgling trust fund to travel around the world. Batiked and bearded, he returned to Rhode Island to find that his father was divorcing his mother, selling the family homestead, and heading south in pursuit of an equestrian debutante fresh out of Vassar. He spent half of Tighty's would-be inheritance roping her into a three-year marriage. Poor, bewildered

Tighty took a job at the local stable in our hometown and stayed there till it closed ten years later. Enter my mother, May Jardine. She had just revived Figtree Domain and needed a chaperon for the hunt's forty foxhounds. Tighty happily seized the job, which didn't pay much though it gave him a small but classy place to live: the carriage house next to the kennels.

When Tighty isn't mucking out the runs, leash-breaking puppies, or currycombing his mare, he likes to paint nudes. Even Louisa says he has talent, of an old-fashioned sort. In the second bedroom of the carriage house, store-bought canvases are stacked against the walls. Tighty covers them with generously built women, young and not so young: models he hires from bars in Fall River or sometimes, after a rowdy hunt breakfast, horsey forlorn divorcées. I don't think he's ever shown his paintings in public; maybe he doesn't even want to. He wishes he'd been born Degas—no, Louisa corrects me, Rubens.

Tighty has frazzled graying red hair and is built like a Percheron, pure heft, but he has soulful green eyes and a purple velvet voice that, when he wants, do the seducing for him. As far as I could tell, growing up, he had a different girlfriend every week. We're the boss's daughters, so we were always safe, and when I hung around the kennels after school, he was kind and businesslike, showed me a hundred ways to watch over animals. He taught me how to pill a mean tomcat, drain a bad boil, peroxide the gums of a hound with bad breath. One winter morning he taught me how to save a colicky horse's life with an enema, a task involving ginger ale, a garden hose, a funnel, and expendable clothing.

Whenever he and my mother set forth with their gay obedient brood, forty white tails alert as quills, the world is a luminous place. Maybe this is the closest he'll ever come to a marriage, to having kids. Did reality suddenly hit him? Is that what's going on?

One thing is clear: Tighty's crime reeks of passion and folly, not stealth. According to Mom, his mother lives in Carmel, yet she managed never to tell me why she's so sure he'd bring the hounds out here. Apparently the woman's remarried so many times that the phone book is totally

useless. Yet, as I suspected, it takes us only twenty minutes of cruising
Carmel to find the truck, parked in front of a stockade fence on a street
hooded with luxurious trees. It's a four-door pickup with fencing and a
wooden roof over the back. The hunt insignia, a circular design in which
a fox head crowns a lighthouse, decorates the driver's door; in the leafy
dark, it stands out bright as a moon. "A genius or what?" I say as I pull up
behind the truck. Between the slats of the fence, light shines from the
cloistered house, so I close my door gently.

Louisa gets out, too, when she sees me trying the doors on the cab.
"What are you doing?" she hisses.

"Investigating!" I hiss back. The doors are locked. Strewn across the
front seat are half a dozen disposable coffee cups, a pair of leather gloves,
and a pile of maps spilling onto the floor. The backseat is a snarled mayhem of tarps, dog couplings, sweaters, and socks, but I can make out a
saddle, a fifty-pound bag of dog food, a sleeping bag, the glint of Tighty's
hunting horn.

From the back bumper, I hoist myself onto the roof. Louisa is standing
in the middle of the street having a pantomimed fit. "Get up here," I
whisper.

Behind the fence is a modern house, all glass, and a yard. A sliding
door leads into a turquoise kitchen. Outside, on a patio table, a wine bottle and a glass. No one in sight. Standing together on top of the truck,
our heads in the swaying branches, we can hear the ocean clearly, a dozen
blocks away. It growls and sizzles, sucking pebbles away, herding them
back.

"This is where his mother lives?" Louisa whispers.

"Beats me," I whisper back. "But it stands to reason."

"Beautiful town."

"Clint Eastwood's mayor," I tell her.

"I know that!" she hisses.

Then we hear it, from the garage, and instantly I know the voice, deep
to begin with, then mournful and tremulous as it spins out, bell curve in
a minor key. It's Juno: a bitch from one of the last litters I helped raise

before going to college. A canine dowager now. Then Tighty's voice, soothing her.

Along with the usual virtues—intelligence, nose, conformation—my mother breeds for tongue, for the melodious strength of a hound's voice. In hunt circles, she's famous for that. At field trials, the Figtree pack is the one that sounds like a small intense concerto. It isn't a quality judged; the scores are on speed and faithfulness to the line. But it's a masterpiece, that sound. My mother knows the voice of every hound, can pick out each one from the distant jumbled thrill of thirty dogs in hot pursuit of a phantom. "There's Cicero, he's up front, having a heck of a day," she might say, "and Jazzman's right behind Garbo, good boy. Apollo's pluggin' away; hear that *nork nork nork*? But Barrister, where's he? Barrister, you layabout!" And then she'd raise her own powerful voice: "Try on, try on, *hoowee!*" Following, listening, I couldn't help learning the best ones myself.

Tighty emerges from the garage. Curiously proper, he wears a long white kennel coat over his clothes. The hounds spill into the yard behind him, joyously sniffing the night air, relishing their adventure. Tighty talks in a low playful voice, reassuring them, keeping them quiet. From a deep pocket, he hands each one a biscuit. When he sits at the patio table, they settle in an untidy crowd at his feet, scratching and grooming themselves, bickering lightly over who'll get the spots next to Tighty.

He bends to stroke the heads of the nearest hounds, then pours a glass of wine and downs it like medicine.

"Don't care if she does!" he says with belligerent abandon.

A few of his companions thrash their tails, as if to second his righteousness.

"But watch her try to fix it. Ha!" He sighs loudly and hugs himself, rocking to and fro. Behind him, the kitchen glows cleanly, bright as a swimming pool. He covers his face with his hands.

Louisa whispers, "Now what? This is completely bizarre."

"Now nothing. He's too drunk. Too sad. We'll come back tomorrow," I decide. "The hounds are safe, that's what counts."

"You think he looks sad?"

"Sad disguised as really pissed off." I'm surprised Louisa doesn't see this.

"What if he up and leaves?" she says.

"Just look at him." I look again myself, and it sort of breaks my heart. Whatever made him lose his grip, this fifty-year-old guy had nowhere to go but his rich mother's house, three thousand miles away.

Carefully, we climb down from the truck; I get down first and help Louisa. Tighty's beyond noticing even a major earthquake, but we don't want to alert the hounds. As we follow the fence to my car, Tighty groans. "May, you bitch," he says and then, in case the neighborhood didn't quite catch it, enunciates loudly, "You royal everlasting bitch! Untie *this* knot!" A hound whines in sympathy.

As we drive away, Louisa gives me that censorious big-sister look and says, "If I were me, I'd stay a million miles away from this one."

"Well, go ahead and take the next plane out," I say, and when she's silent, I know things must be pretty bad with Hugh. *Oh Louisa, don't go proving me right about marriage.* That's what I think but don't say.

In 1950, our mother left her parents' Minnesota farm when she won a scholarship to the school of agriculture in Montana. She won it for her celebrity record at state fairs, exhibiting cows from Topeka to Lansing. There were so many trophies and blue rosettes, my grandparents' house looked like a bovine hall of fame. After school, she figured, maybe she'd work in cattle feed. She could be a nutrition consultant. She knew all about how this grass or that, this grain or that, affected production and flavor of milk, sleekness of coat. In the spring of her senior year, she flew east to represent her school at a Budding Businesswomen of America symposium, held in Cambridge. She'd never been on the right bank of the Mississippi, and when she stood in Radcliffe Yard, a trembling hand splashed with chablis, surrounded by stiletto sandals and gleaming French twists, she might as well have crossed an ocean. All the young women wore badges: SUMMER CAMP ADMINISTRATOR, SMITH; GAL FRIDAY AT MORGAN GUARANTY, BARNARD; VACATION PLANNER, FLORIDA AT TALLAHASSEE. People couldn't help giggling, however kindly, whenever they spotted May's. It read, BREEDER AND HANDLER OF BROWN SWISS COWS, MONTANA AT BOZEMAN.

The wine was risky, but she drank to keep her hands busy. Not long and she found herself teetering carefully down a rugged brick sidewalk, lost but relieved. She went into a coffee shop, sat at the counter, and ordered an ice-cream soda. Beside her, a young man was reading a seed catalog as if it were an Agatha Christie whodunit. His white shirt was pressed, his black hair combed and glossed, but his fingernails were haloed with dirt. When she stood up to pay, the young man turned and found himself staring straight at May's badge, perched on her well-rounded chest. He said, "Oh, are they the ones that turn out the luxury chocolate?" She says he was perfectly serious, didn't even crack a smile. She was about to slap him when she realized that she was still wearing her name tag.

He told her he was studying horticulture. He took her to see the glass flowers at the Peabody Museum. Next day, at Arnold Arboretum, he actually dared to kiss her. I can't imagine daring to kiss my mother.

She married our father, she likes to say, for his excellent teeth, good posture, and pedigree: descent on his mother's side from the *Mayflower*, on his father's side from Huguenots who settled New Orleans. Lots of generals, lots of muscular prolific wives. "You may buy education," our mother says, "but class flows in your veins." Those French twists no longer faze her.

Louisa agrees with me that we should leave our mother in the dark until we figure out what we've got on our hands. So I call Mom next morning and tell her to sit tight; no concrete leads but I'm on the job.

"So help me, I will sell every stick of his furniture, every heirloom antique," she says, "to pay for shipping those poor creatures back.

They'll travel like stars. I'm going to give his car to the first college dropout who wanders by. Blacklist him with the Humane Society of the United States."

"Hey, you can do that?" I ask, thinking of all my daydreams about certain corrupt harbormasters, fishing inspectors, seal-bashing senators who pose for the papers chucking their golden retrievers under the chin.

She sighs. "There's a first time for everything, honey."

I'll be at the aquarium in the afternoon, so we plan to head over once I'm through diving. The plan is to take Zip's van, with Zip as our driver and strongman (though I doubt we'll be exerting any muscle).

Late last night, I took another stab, feeble as ever, at breaking it off.

He'd picked me up at the Ark, where we had a slow day. Reading papers from a wildlife conference, I'd let my attention stray to a talk on black rhinos. *Endangered* becomes quite the soft sell. So when I climbed up into Zip's van, doom hooded me, damp and meddlesome as fog. We sat high above the traffic—which as a rule makes me irrationally happy, like a small hit of endorphins—and Zip told me about visiting a farm where autistic children ride horses. "Miracles," he said. "Miracles begin to look possible."

But his reasonable virtue just pushed the gloom deeper, right into my pores. I made trite sounds of encouragement, but all I could think was, What is the *point*?

Louisa made us dinner. Smoked-pepper soup, curried lentils, and garlic bread; she appointed Zip her sous-chef, and the two of them danced up my kitchen like a couple of courting woodcocks. "You're not to lift a finger," she told me. I should have felt like a princess, but I felt like an unwanted guest in my own home. After kiwi sorbet, green as new grass, she insisted on washing up by herself, so Zip and I went for a walk.

After a long strolling silence, I said, "I can't figure out what you want—from this, from me. Besides the sex, okay, and maybe my fridge, which is bigger than yours, and my oven, which does better bread."

"Entrance to your heart," he said. "That's what I want. The hinges are rusty, I know."

"Zip, what do we have in *common*?" I was fending off his let-yourself-be-loved speech, which I'd heard before. But I wondered, too, what the hell I was doing. Was I really ousting this beautiful, smart guy from my life? This guy with a responsible job, two vehicles, no shortage of patience; and hey, no family baggage?

"Common," Zip said, perusing the word like a bite of fruit. "No. It's the *un*common that concerns me, that draws me in."

"Well, I'm an uncommon pain in the ass, sure."

"Uncommon souls, that's what I'm talking about. Uncommon communion. Uncommon sense of justice."

"Stop acting like a guru. I mean, raise your voice now and then! Snort when you laugh! Swear in your sleep! Have a single *vice*! Do you remember the first time you came over, how we talked about the World Series? About antiwhaling sanctions? About the Kitty Dukakis factor and the bow-tie factor and whether Gephardt was dyeing his lashes? About *life*?"

"The debates." Zip smiled. "You made me laugh. That was fun."

"Fun, yes. That prehistoric conceit, shallow though it may be."

"You don't think we have enough fun," he said gravely.

I thought of how we'd cycled the rim of Big Sur. I thought of our Otis Redding connection. I thought of his black-bean chili with tiny cubes of roasted tofu glazed with cayenne. "Oh what do I know, what do *I* know? Except, I'd like to see you unprepared just once. Is this nuts? Am I a bitch? You're like this Boy Scout, you know—always so damn *prepared*."

We had circled the block and were back in front of my driveway, under a cypress that whispered and creaked. I tilted my forehead toward his.

"You're so tall," he said. His smile was too close to see, but I heard it. "I've always liked how tall you are." He weaseled a hand deep in my heat-tangled hair. "Clem."

"Let's go to bed," I said, because I love the way he makes my name sound holy, because his fingers had crept to that tingling furrow under my skull, and because when you get there with Zip, in bed, you would never call him a guru.

⁓

"Tighty," I say when he opens the gate. "Tighty, Tighty, Tighty." I'm shaking my head and carping like a headmistress. *Higher ground,* Zip advised me in the car. *Claim the higher ground.*

"Jesus Christ," says Tighty, and then, when he spots Louisa behind me, "Jesus Double H. Fucking Christ." But he lets us in. The hounds, basking in the yard, are thrilled to have guests. Well mannered as ever, they sniff us demurely but never jump up. No one barks. I recognize nearly all of them, acknowledge the ones I know by name. Louisa hangs back by the gate.

"Both of you? Oh Jesus. What did she do, hire Jeane Dixon?"

"Face it, Tighty, you did nothing to hide your tracks." I can't help smiling. "Should I ask why? Or can we just turn this whole thing around somehow, U-turn, no questions asked? Because I haven't called the police—like I've been ordered to do, by the way."

Relieved but cautious, he smiles back. "You are anything but your mother's daughters," he says. "Take it from the loyal retainer."

"Loyal you've always been, but *Tighty.*" I cock my head toward the trusting, far more loyal creatures around us, oblivious to why they're in this strange place, yet loving every minute. Like a quiz-show audience, they gaze at us in gleeful suspense.

I introduce the two men; they shake hands without a word. For a few seconds we hover in a sheepish trapezoid, hounds milling everywhere, rubbing against our legs, panting and shimmying. *Oh wonderful, a party!* they seem to be saying. One thing they need is a good long hike.

"This calls for a toast," Tighty says drily. "Everything does these days." He goes into the kitchen and brings out an expensive-looking chardonnay, doubles back and retrieves a clutch of stemmed glasses. "This house belongs to my mother," he says, addressing our nosy appraisal of the surroundings.

"Where *is* your mother?" I ask.

"Europe. Stepdad Rolf prefers London." Tighty shrugs. "But he likes

his California wines. Cellar's stocked to the gunnels. Thank you, Rolf."
He salutes vaguely toward the sky with his left hand while pouring with
his right.

Zip declines, but Louisa and I accept, to humor Tighty. He raises his
glass. "To love. To foolish love. To foolish, doglike, dirt-blind love."

Louisa throws me a missile of a glance: You got us into this, you get
us out.

I clear my throat and say, "To passion. To impulse. To letting the chips
fall where they may." In turn, I throw my own piercing glance at Zip, but
he is enthralled by the sea of dogs gently engulfing our ankles.

It feels like a parody of so many evenings when we were small: our parents and their friends outtoasting one another beneath our bedrooms.
Catching on, Louisa jumps in. "To cutting a deal. To getting the hell out
of hot water." Hers the practical toast.

"To the wages of blood sport," rejoins Tighty, and oh, if looks could
gut a fallen elk.

Whatever tatters of sanity lurk in our midst, someone, I decide, had
better start patching. "Right. Okay," I say. "No harm done—except
maybe mileage on the truck—but Tighty, we've got to get these guys
home. And look, unless you've made other plans, we've got to get you
back in May's graces."

"You think this was a joyride? A lark?" Tighty snorts loudly. "No way
I'm driving them back, I'll tell you that much. No way I'm giving anything back to that mother of yours. No way she'd take *me* back. No lousy
way. I'm through with being a serf in her kingdom. Her Majesty Queen
May." He makes a mocking flourish with his wineglass, then sets it down
and crosses his arms. I look at Zip, wishing for once that he would
unleash a few of his effortless wisdoms, but he is petting Cicero and
Rhapsody, intent on doling out equal affection.

"Besides, it's too late," says Tighty. He smiles triumphantly, stands
up, slides back the glass door, and waves me into the house. Zip stays
with his newfound friends. Louisa sulks in her lawn chair.

The house is a lair of aquatic chintzes. Tighty leads me down a dusky
blue hall, a lavender carpet muting our steps, to a bedroom like a honey-

moon suite on Barbados: king-size bed canopied in pistachio gauze, basket of pink-bellied conches, teak ceiling fan, Winslow Homer palms. But even out of context, there's no missing her: in a corner, lying on a thick pad of newspapers fenced off with ladder-back chairs, here's Tallulah. It's clear, from her fervent panting in this shady retreat, that she's in labor.

"This," I say, "now this was foolish, bringing her. You know that."

Tighty looks at me darkly. "I raised her, I made her the perfect creature, the good dog she is. She's mine." He kneels beside her then and, as he feels her nose for fever, says quietly, "She rode in front with me all the way. I never let her out of my sight." He strokes her head and, for several minutes, coaches her with the words of a lover. He spreads one hand like a starfish across her abdomen. "Damn," he says. "Sideways."

From the kitchen, I hear the sound of the sliding door and Louisa's voice, impatiently calling my name. But the first face in the doorway is Zip's. "Oh!" he gasps. "What—oh."

Louisa pushes past him. "This is a farce," she says. "This is pathetic. This is just ridiculous."

"Quit complaining," I say. "Quit acting so Ivy League above it all."

Tighty couldn't care less about what Louisa thinks. He says to me tersely, "Gloves. There are latex gloves in my shaving kit." He points toward the bathroom.

As I look around the bathroom, I notice—in the shower, of all places—a short stack of canvases facing the tile wall. But there's no time to snoop. I see Tighty's kit on the counter by the sink.

When I return, he's wrapped himself around Tallulah, his arms and legs a cradle. He performs a complicated massage on her belly. Tallulah whines, but she tolerates his meddling, trusts him like a father. "Down you go," he whispers, "easy and over. . . . Just turning the little guy over, babe, just a hair more—this way, sweetheart, here we go . . . I'm right here." He mutters amorously on, sometimes grunting, sometimes pausing to kiss Tallulah's left ear. With long patient fingers, he steers the unborn puppy.

"How about calling your clinic?" Louisa says to me. Zip, kneeling behind Tighty, is transfixed, mute as a mannequin. For once, he has no prescriptions.

"How about you mind your own business and let Tighty do what he's done for years?" I say to Louisa.

"Three, two—good girl!" says Tighty, and the first puppy slides out, slippery and smooth, pink as rhubarb in its opalescent casing. Talullah nudges Tighty's arm aside, stretches down and roughly, gently, roughly, licks this still object into a struggling four-legged creature: blind, okay, but ready to tackle the planet.

"Now *that* calls for a toast," I say. "I mean, wow. Canine Lamaze."

Tighty lies back on the lavender carpet, eyes closed, face flushed and gleaming with sweat. He sighs. "Business as usual." That's when Zip, still kneeling, utters a small sob.

"Hey." I reach toward him, alarmed.

"Birth," he says. "The first one I've ever seen. Actually *seen*." I put an arm around him. It's clear that for once the world has caught him completely by surprise.

Back on the patio, Zip opens a bottle of pinot gris. The ocean murmurs complacently. The stars are so bright they flicker.

Louisa sits across from me but talks only to the men. She leans her shoulder against Zip's. "What do you want out of life, do you know?"

I expect to hear something about cosmic understanding, worldwide forgiveness, but Zip says loudly, "A dog. Right now, what I want is a dog!" He looks at me sadly. "We never had animals when I was a kid. My mom said she was allergic. Now I think she might have made that up."

"Well," I say, "there's something else we do not have in common." He's heard about the foxhunting, the horses and hounds, the countless barn cats, but tonight I tell him how, when Louisa and I were Girl Scouts, Mom enlisted Tighty to teach the classes for earning an "animal hus-bandry" badge—as if any of us, in suburban Rhode Island, would grow up to breed hogs or harvest eggs. Those who had dogs learned to teach their pets some manners, those who had ponies learned the finer points of grooming, and those who had cats learned all about clipping nails and warding off fleas. Tighty gave lectures in our living room: about responsibility and respect for fellow citizens of other species. We cut wild animals from magazines and made a book called *Family Album: Planet Earth.* The year he taught my troop, Hurricane Agnes ransacked the coast. Dad was gone for three days, salvaging smithereened yachts. A heartsick elm fell through Tighty's roof, so he stayed at our house. He and Mom were up till all hours at the piano. I remember lying awake at two in the morning, unable to sleep through the endless renditions of "John Peel," complete with live hunting horn. A brutal song if you listen.

When I get to this part of the story, Tighty looks grim and goes into the house. He has refused to tell us what drove him to flee. When he re-emerges, he dumps half a dozen boxes onto the table. "Hungry? Speaking of Girl Scouts. A little green delivery person stopped by today. Seems my mother placed an order."

I paw through the packages. "Samosas? Nothing but Samosas? No mints, no butter cookies?"

"I guess she's crazy for coconut," says Tighty.

Out of Tighty's view, Zip slips a Girl Scout cookie to Hero.

"Samosas," says Louisa. "Where did they get that name? Not to be confused with mimosas. Or with Samoans, natives of Samoa. Or Minoans, builders of Knossos, lovers of bulls."

"Lovers of *bull*? Louisa, you need a call-in trivia show. You're like The Source," I say. "You're shameless."

Zip leans across the table and says to me, "You are just as smart. You could show off a little more."

"Believe me, I'm not in a league with you two—you two were made for each other. Me, maybe I belong with Hugh, the guy who keeps his emotions in mothballs."

Louisa stares at me. "I didn't come out here to make you mad."

"Well, what did you come out for? I mean, you really came all this way, spent all that money, because your husband wants a little indulgence from life? How big is *your* universe?"

"You're right. Why would I come here when you're just like him? What kind of cloud am I living on anyway?"

"A cloud of your own making, no doubt about that."

Louisa stands up and says primly, "Fuck you. Fuck you and your nihilist, amoral, homophobic, fuck-the-world attitude."

Tighty goes around the table and stands behind Louisa. He wraps his arms around her from behind and presses his cheek against the top of her head. "Girls." His voice is mournful. "Girls, if I told you your mother would love this, could you please stay friends?"

Louisa sits down and looks up into the trees. She's trying not to cry.

"Listen," says Tighty, "I'm the one in the hot seat here. I'm the one with music to face. And it sure ain't Brahms." Despite the bravado, he looks deflated. The whelping took a lot out of him, but it's more than that. After nearly a week of pure rage, he can't keep it up any longer.

"We'll get you out of this fix," I say. "We have to."

Tighty touches my hand. "Clement, sweetie, I haven't a single excuse."

Louisa rubs her hands over her face as if to wake herself up from a dream. She sighs with determination. "Now this," she says, "is a ridiculous plan. But here goes."

It's Louisa's idea that since our mother has such awe for genetics, we tell her there's manic depression in Tighty's mother's family and he may just have had what Louisa calls his first "break."

"Lou, you're a mad genius," I have to admit.

"He promises to pursue treatment," she says.

"Are you out of your minds?" says Tighty.

"Well, you've certainly behaved as if *you* are," I say, "and do you have anything better to offer? Do you really want Mom to fire you? Or, as she keeps saying, to skin you and serve it on toast?"

"That's a repulsive image," says Louisa.

And then Zip, who's usually immune to anything other than the truth, whole and nothing but, supplies a few textbook symptoms of manic depression that he recalls from his social-work training. It begins to feel as if we're all back in high school, planning some outlandish prank.

All of a sudden, Tighty leans down, hands on his knees, face toward the ground. At first I think he's going to be sick, and then I realize it's more like he's caving in. He gasps "Oh God" several times, and then I hear him breathing deeply, regaining control of himself. Zip stands beside him, stroking his broad back. And then, just like that, Tighty straightens up and goes into the kitchen. He comes back with a phone on a very long cord. His face crazes into a grin. "Speakerphone, shall we?" He punches the buttons with cavalier glee.

My mother's voice is painfully loud in the clear, quiet air. Tighty barks, "Hello, love!" and chews loudly on another Samosa.

The icy silence is no surprise, but then out flows a torrent of insults, and as my mother carries on, the hounds grow rapt, harking to the disembodied voice of their leader, their alpha. Tails slap the flagstones around us.

Then her voice turns cold. "Titus, you are more than fired. You are blackballed. You will never work in an organized foxhunt on this continent again, so help me. You will never again dare to show your face in respectable sporting society."

"Well," he retorts, "guess I'll learn to train Seeing Eye dogs or bomb-squad beagles. Bet the benefits aren't so stingy."

I shake my head at him, but he won't look at me.

"You'll be mucking out stalls again if you're lucky," Mom says. "That's all you were ever cut out to do in the first place."

Belligerent tears hover in Tighty's eyes. I wave a hand in front of his face and maneuver myself closer to the phone just as my mother starts in with empty threats involving the Providence mafia. "Mom! Hello, Mom, it's me. Listen. You don't understand. I've just had a long talk with Tighty. He's in a terrible crisis. He's been in this awful state. He needs your help." The mental illness defense, which I deliver astutely, broadsides her anger.

"Well," she says, "no matter what, honey, there's going to be a hearing. I don't own this hunt, you know, or those mistreated hounds. I do not make all the decisions."

"Let's be philosophical, Mom. The hounds are having a blast. They got to see America. They got, like, a joyride. They look great."

"I'll give him philosophy. Socrates! Arsenic! . . . What is that echo? I feel like I'm talking to Rhodesia. And listen, that sister of yours, is she there? I just talked to Hugh. Poor Hugh."

Louisa recoils, but I motion her over. "Quit hiding," I whisper.

"Have you jumped ship, honey?" Mom barks at Louisa. "You've broken Hugh's heart. Running off like a lunatic. Everyone is AWOL! What's going on? I feel like we've collided with a comet but nobody's told me!"

"What's going on with me and Hugh is going on between us," says Louisa.

"I'm your mother," says Mom. "I know all about marriage."

"All about yours," says Louisa. "Leave mine to me. Please."

"Running away never solved anything, honey, believe me."

"I'm not running away. I'm . . . resting."

"Resting! Resting! Marriages have been annulled for less!"

"Last time I checked, we weren't Catholic," Louisa says sharply. "And Socrates poisoned himself with hemlock, in case you forgot. Rhodesia's been Zimbabwe for years."

The look on her face is pure murder, so I intervene again. "Mom, hello Mom, time out here, okay? Now listen, you'll like this. This makes sense. Louisa will help Tighty drive the hounds back, okay? She's volunteered. It's very generous. Everything's going to work out fine." I avoid looking at Louisa, who's performing frantic semaphore.

Mom sighs angrily. "Well, I suppose it makes as much sense as anything can right now." Then she asks about Tallulah.

I take a deep breath and say, "Six future Bryn Mawr champions, all normal, I promise." For one sweet moment, I hear only the clockwork drone of the ocean.

We order pizza and stay up till all hours naming the puppies. We are drunk, silly-drunk, not so much on the wine as on pure oxygenated relief. Punchy as robbers dividing their loot after the perfect heist.

At Figtree Domain, names are all-important. Leaf through the national foxhunting stud book and you will find pedigree listings for Plumber, Bozo, Crabcake, and Tootsie, but Mom finds such names belittling. Even risky. A name is a prophecy, a talisman. A hound should be named with panache, dignity, romance.

"May wants the litter named for their mom," says Tighty. "So think *T*, everyone."

We sit around his mother's table, reciting hundreds of bad names to come up with six that will make the grade. In poetic parody, we call out *Tarnish! Turpentine! Trainwreck! Tarantula! Tarmac! Toupee!*

Breaking a rare silence, Zip says, "Tutu."

Renewed hilarity.

"I'm serious. For Desmond," he says.

But the rest of us are ruthless. He shrugs. We're all, for just a few hours, happy.

In the end, Tighty writes down *Talleyrand, Troubadour, Tremolo,* and *Troy*; for the two little bitches, *Tahiti* and *Tosca*.

I slip inside to check on Tallulah's nest and use the bathroom. I tiptoe through the dim, cool bedroom. Tallulah's sleeping now, the puppies against her belly.

I close the door to the bathroom before I turn on the light. The paintings stashed in the shower had slipped my mind. I can't say I'm really surprised—shocked, but not surprised—when they turn out to be a series of nudes depicting my mother. The dates penciled on the stretcher bars span the last fourteen years; maybe that part surprises me. I don't look for long. *Poor Tighty,* I'm always saying, and now I know why: because Tighty will never see the talents he's blessed with, only the ones that he yearns for.

"What will you name your puppy?" I ask Zip when I return to the patio.

Before speaking to Mom, I decided that the seventh puppy—or the

first one; the reluctant sideways leader—would go to Zip. It's a male with
a knuckled crook in his tail and a round black spot on his head resembling
a rakish beret.

Zip looks at Tighty, who's falling asleep in his chair.

"Titus," he says.

I say, "Well, of course."

At the end of a yawn, Louisa smiles. "That's perfect."

A Door to the Sky

1989

"Why are you sleeping so much?"

"How much am I sleeping?"

"Too much, that's how much. Nearly twelve hours." I point to the alarm clock on the table between the beds. I watch my husband's legs, the legs of a human stork, straighten beneath the quilt; he's in no hurry. He's never in a hurry. I now see this quality as a kind of resistance, though I used to name it as one of his virtues.

He yawns. "It's the weekend."

I am standing in the doorway of the room that was mine for so many years that the words *my room* will always, till I'm a fetal hunchback and have forgotten nearly everything else, signify this room and no other. Even if my parents now call it the guest room. Even if my desk was banished to a consignment shop, my high-minded posters to landfill. The place where I wrote all the clever compositions that earned me a fancy, mostly underutilized education is occupied now by a television set, and on the wall where I tacked up self-portraits by Modigliani, Foujita, van Gogh, and Rembrandt, my mother's hung "real art": two watercolor seascapes bartered by a local painter for her daughter's riding lessons. These paintings are upstaged, however, by a very large photograph that recently took the place of the mirror in which I struggled with hair and fashion woes, scrutinized my body in all its thrilling betrayals. It's a portrait of my mother on Kingsley, her all-time favorite horse, a Thoroughbred gelding who flunked out at the track. They are perfectly groomed for a foxhunt on Thanksgiving Day, the foliage behind them bold as gossip.

Hugh lies in one of the creaky twin beds, the one in which my girlfriends slept when they stayed overnight, when we whispered and giggled till dawn, discussing our crushes on movie stars and our crisply focused plans for an independent, productive, uplifting future. Now, in a smudged version of that future, it is eleven o'clock on the Saturday of Labor Day weekend, and I have been up for hours, awakened by my parents' heedless chatter in the kitchen.

Hugh sits on the edge of the bed and knuckles the sleep from his eyes. He seems to be ignoring my presence. These days, nearly everything about Hugh strikes me as a matter of *seeming*, requiring emotional guesswork. Last week, a friend asked me if Hugh likes his job, and I heard myself say, "He seems to." Just as he seems to be happy with me or seems to enjoy walking on the beach. People who meet Hugh for the first time assume he's shy, but it's more that he's clandestine. Whatever feelings he has, he keeps them in the shade. Or so it seems. Seems!

"You know, I really wonder about you," I say. What I really wonder, for an instant, is why I didn't say *worry about you*. I wonder if, when it comes to Hugh, I am past worrying. That in itself is a worry.

Hugh looks at me for a moment as if he's waiting for an answer. At last he says quietly, "So what exactly do you wonder?"

"Stop throwing my questions back at me. Please get dressed. Dad left for work ages ago, and Mom expects us to meet her at the beach club for lunch in an hour."

"That's fine," says Hugh. "I don't need breakfast."

"I'm going back to the hayloft. Your striped shirt is on a hanger in the closet. Mom says to please keep the showers short. It's barn laundry day." I resist the temptation to tell him that the day's events do not revolve around him and his need for meals. The truth is, I'd be a lot happier if the day, or anything—like my heart or my soul—did revolve around Hugh.

My parents' barn is twice the size of their house. This is why they bought the place thirty years ago. With room to spare, it currently shelters two horses; a makeshift greenhouse for my father's floral pursuits (his dream is to graft and name a rose of his own); a large, accidental population of cats; and, in the hayloft, two facing fortresses, one of baled hay, the other of boxes containing ancestral photographs, old clothing and uniforms, sabers and medals, books, toys, school papers spanning at least three generations, stuffed animals, outmoded polyester curtains, outmoded stereo equipment, glassware too delicate for everyday use, screws and doorknobs and tools of indeterminate provenance and utility. The good thing about their being up here, out of sight and mind, is that for decades it has prevented a war between my mother, who is practical and unsentimental, and my father, whose family motto must surely be whatever's Latin for *You never know when it will come in handy!* Not that you could find it if it ever did—or remember you had it, whatever it was.

The only direct ventilation in this space is a wide double door at one end, under the peaked roof, that opens into thin air one story up from the driveway. My sister, when we were little, called it the door to the sky. As a guardrail, Dad nailed a pair of two-by-fours across the inner frame, but still I see it as a treacherous maw. If I have to open the doors, I unlatch them, step back, and push them ajar from a distance, using a broom. The breeze smells strongly of ocean. The warmer the day, the stronger the smell. For that reason alone, high summer is my favorite time of year in this place.

It is not, however, an ideal time of year to be ordered by your mother to "please clear out all your old moth-eaten stuff or prepare to have it cleared out for you." Especially when you live in a New York apartment with no storage space whatsoever, let alone a hayloft the size of Bryant Park. Especially when you are not sure about the state of your marriage, and your husband is the one with the lease.

It's not as if my parents are moving or remodeling or doing anything for which they need that extra space, the modest corners occupied by my two dozen boxes of life souvenirs. It's more like they're sending me a message.

You're a grown-up, Louisa, did you know that?
The thing is, I do know that, and the knowledge is weighing me down.

Four years ago, I married Hugh on the lawn I'd be able to see from up
here if I weren't afraid of standing anywhere near the door to the view.
My dad's roses were in high, plush bloom, brandishing their fragrance in
the soft humidity of June. Also present in colorful abundance were my
dozens of aunts, uncles, and cousins from down south, the clan my father
left behind when he came north to college. They crank up any occasion
till it feels like an affair of state.

I married Hugh less than a year after taking over his job. It's a family
joke: *She got Hugh's job and then she got Hugh.* He was a good boss, and
when he left the magazine to teach at a private school, I stepped into his
shoes. Almost instantly I missed him. I understood why he'd been such a
good managing editor, and I understood just what "managing" really
meant. Hugh knew how to keep people calm and efficient in the face of
contention (and we are talking art people, people with absurdly towering
egos, with short tempers that someone's decided are justified by so-
called creativity). This retrospective admiration of Hugh's diplomacy
and patience made me ponder what a good husband and father he'd
make. I was thinking about my girlfriends, the ones who were panicking
about not being married as we all closed in on thirty. I did that thing
where you fix the guy up with the woman you see as his ideal match and
then, the morning after their first date, she phones you to say that you're
right about the ideal part, but he's ideal for *you.* Other friends meet him
and volunteer parallel opinions; they consult with more of your friends
and come to a joint conclusion. The conclusion is, Don't blow it! Then,
weirdly, you find out somehow that all of *his* friends who've met you at *his*
parties arrived at that conclusion, too.

One day you look at each other and you know. You might even laugh
out loud. It's obvious, it's *easy.* How silly that you didn't notice before the
rest of the world around you.

Parties are thrown in your honor; the circle of approval grows; the toasts (many about your adorable, shared obtuseness) evolve toward an eloquence that makes you feel as if you are in the benevolent presence of Destiny itself. (Hugh's best man wrote a comic ballad called "Much Ado About Lou and Hugh." No one but my sister is allowed to call me Lou. Still, it drew a standing ovation at the rehearsal dinner. My Confederate cousins whistled and stamped.)

Your parents like one another; my goodness, they drive the same car! Same year, same *color*! Turns out you went to his father's alma mater. Like your dad, the other dad played lacrosse. (Is it conceivable the two men actually crossed sticks back in 1951?) The whole thing comes together like a jigsaw puzzle, just the way my mother insists you proceed: Put the edge together first, then work your way toward the center, organizing the pieces into groups by color and, within color, by shape. A few rows in, you see that it's going to get much easier—it has to—because you're finding the right place for each piece faster and faster. The picture will be finished and perfect in no time. (Never mind that after all your hard work, it will go back in the box.)

My mother buys our family a puzzle every Christmas—not too hard, not too easy, always intricate with color; an opulent Dutch bouquet or a clamorous sporting print—so I know the routine. In fact, I'm incapable of having fun with a puzzle that's put together any other way. I'm that well trained.

Today is like the opposite of Christmas. I'm opening all these boxes, their contents often a mystery even though they're already mine, but what I need to do (as sweat pours down my spine and soaks the waistband of my shorts) is to make myself discard things, not add them to my already cluttered life. So far this weekend, I've saved a few of my favorite reports from grade school (one on volcanoes, one on the ritual sun dance of the Sioux, one on photosynthesis), a few precociously detailed still-life drawings (seashells, daffodils, a taxidermied wood duck, a kerosene lantern), and the only Barbie doll whose hair wasn't harvested for nesting by a family of mice that must have eluded the cat patrol. Steeling myself against sentiment, I've stuffed mounds of brittle composition paper and limp stuffed animals into garbage bags.

I am working my way toward a stack of wooden crates I would give anything not to open. They contain the last vases and bowls I made before I gave up on pottery, before I moved in with Hugh, even before I became the managing editor of *Artbeat*. (I can't blame the surrender of my own art on Hugh.) They are not supposed to be here, in my parents' barn, but I sneaked them in on one of our visits when, as usual, my mother was so busy fussing over Hugh's arrival that she didn't notice me open the trunk and stagger into the barn with my loot.

But here is a cardboard carton of childhood books: Dr. Seuss, Mike Mulligan, Mr. and Mrs. Mallard, Ferdinand, Charlotte. Classics all— saved, presumably, for children of my own, though they smell so un- speakably musty that the concept of holding them anywhere near a child's face seems laughably perilous. Hugh owns a box containing almost exactly the same collection of books; I know this because it's in the back of our bedroom closet. Probably, I think with irrational resentment, they are in much better shape for having received this preferential treat- ment. If I believe we will honor our vows and stay together forever, the choice here is obvious, isn't it? (Though I've made the excuse to myself that if we have two children, why not have two copies of all our favorite childhood stories for them to inherit?)

I close this box and drag it toward the steep wooden stairs. I scare a cat from behind a rusty sled; it darts down the stairs and out of sight. When my sister and I lived here, the cats were friendly because we played in this loft with our friends. It was more than a warehouse; it was a catacomb, an imaginary village, a lesser Narnia. My mother feeds and worms the cats, she has them fixed and takes them to the vet if they're injured, but they no longer get much human affection. Their residence here is a business deal: Friskies and shelter for mice. A dead rodent on the doorstep is as good as a rent check.

I suppose, in retrospect, that once we'd passed the Narnia stage, Clem met boys up here. More than a few, I suspect. Hugh and I, after we were engaged, had one literal roll in the hay. It seemed like something we had to check off the list of courtship rites, something permissibly naughty.

After I've finished with the books, four boxes in all (from which I salvage a dozen yellowed art books and a copy of *Moby-Dick* filled with endearingly naïve notations, made for the soulful eyes of the teacher on whom I had the biggest crush of all time), I head back to the house.

My mother is in the paddock with two of her students, lithe freckled girls who, if they lived in New York, would be loitering about Lincoln Center in leotards and metallic ballet flats. Here, in semirural Rhode Island, they wear black leather boots, skintight buttermilk jodhpurs, and velvet hard hats. Their faces are pink from the heat, but they look happy. Their horses are having a water break, drinking deeply at the trough.

"Never clutch the pommel," my mother is saying to one girl. "Have confidence in the reins and in your seat; hold on to the mane when you gallop. But hands off that saddle, young lady!"

I never took to riding, not in any daring way. I liked our horses, but they were big dogs to me. To pet them, feed them, watch them roll in the grass, that was enough. I did not like cantering or jumping fences any more than I like heights. My sister got the horse gene, along with the daring gene. She rode for most of her childhood. Now she skis and scuba dives. She marches fearlessly into forests where predators lurk.

I am sitting alone at a table overlooking the club pool and, beyond it, the beach. I decided to walk here on my own, to get some exercise; I expected Mom and Hugh to pass me in the car. They are already ten minutes late, and I've made the mistake of ordering a glass of wine, which is going straight to my head. The lifeguard is half my age and very, very cute. I think of Clem, who would be chatting him up right now if she were here. She would not be sitting here so passively: bored, annoyed, separating the lamination from the menu.

"Hugh is one strong fellow!" my mother calls out, startling me from my funk. She's exchanged her riding clothes for a light blue linen dress, tapered and sleeveless, that shows off her impressively solid curves and her athletic limbs.

Hugh smiles at me over her shoulder; it's too vague a smile for me to interpret. I don't expect Mom to apologize for being late, but Hugh has manners (here he is now, pulling out a chair for her). That's one thing he's got in spades. A few twigs of hay cling to his shirt. I reach across the table and brush them off.

"I'm glad he was helpful," I say.

"Helpful and *strong*," she insists. "Do you know how strong your husband is?" She is waving at the waiter. "Chip! My son-in-law would love to try that local brew. He's earned it!" Chip will already know what to bring her.

"Did your father call? I left him a message. Is he joining us?" Mom glances at the menu and sets it down. "Chip," she says when the drinks arrive, "the chicken salad special: is that white meat? Yes? Then that's what I'll have, but regular lettuce, please, instead of spinach. Raw spinach makes my tongue feel furry." She turns to Hugh and touches his arm. "Order whatever you want. If you like lobster, the bisque is tops."

I wedge myself into the sphere of her attention. "Dad's caught up with the harbormaster. Something about fireworks for a wedding on the bluff tonight."

"He volunteered for that boating safety committee again. Glutton for punishment, that's your father." Mom smiles at Hugh. "Have my roll, please." She puts her roll on his bread plate, giving it a brief pat as if it might fly away.

Hugh hasn't said a word. This is typical, my mother's domination notwithstanding. I'm not even sure what lifting or dragging job she enlisted him for—something in the barn, obviously, and though I'm curious, I don't want to ask, because it will draw out an endless story involving people from the foxhunt or the 4-H or her spoiled-princess riding pupils, someone who let her down so that Hugh could stand in as last-minute hero.

Mom asks Hugh about his parents. He tells her about their recent vacation in Scandinavia, a Harvard-sponsored cruise with expert lecturers and a gourmet chef from Sweden.

"You could do that," Mom tells Hugh.

We look at her blankly.

"Be the professor type on one of those cruises! Louisa could go along and paint the scenery. I miss your paintings, Louisa."

"Mom, Hugh teaches mostly American history." He does teach modern European, too, and a senior seminar in twentieth-century art, but I'm annoyed that she suffers from a chronic refusal to accept that I haven't painted since college, more than ten years ago.

"He could do one of those riverboat tours on the Mississippi. Or an Alaskan cruise. Or Chesapeake Bay! Your father wants us to sail the Inland Waterway when he retires, just the two of us." She adds gaily, "Maybe with his *second* wife he will."

Having grown up on a farm, my mother claims that she still yearns for a landscape far from the sea, somewhere the soil yields more than stones for building walls, but long ago she resigned herself to life in New England. She gets a lot of martyr mileage out of the sacrifice she made. And she translated her talent with livestock into her knack with horses and hounds. She gives riding lessons in the summer only; for the rest of the year, she devotes herself to the hunt and its artificial yet creaturely occupations, filling the nearby woods (what's left of them) with the tumult of hooves and the voices of dogs in joyful, throaty abandon. The phony fox scent is laid down ahead of time by local high school boys trained by Mom to simulate the cunning maneuvers of foxes.

"Speaking of Europe," I say, "I'm thinking of applying to a graduate program in England. For a year from now."

She eyes me over the rim of her sherry glass. She sets it down. "England!"

"It's a fellowship for writing about fine art, a master's degree."

"Why England? What's New York for if not studying art?"

"It's a special program, at the Tate. There's nothing like it anywhere else."

"What would Hugh be doing there?"

I look at Hugh, who is looking at the pool. "Hugh would be taking a leave from his school," I say when he doesn't say it.

"Won't he lose his job?"

"They have sabbaticals." I glare at Hugh, trying to rope him in, even just get his attention back to the table. "He's been teaching there just long enough to take one, at least for a semester."

"Hugh!" Mom exclaims. "Do you like this idea?"

"England would be interesting," he says. There's that vague smile again.

" 'Interesting'?" my mother scoffs, and I'm thinking the same thing. Whatever happened to *incredible*? *an adventure*? *a blast*?

"Fascinating, I mean," he says. "I could take classes, too."

Or lie around in bed all day.

"Louisa and I could be students together," says Hugh. I feel a tug at the sound of his voice. Does he mean to sound romantic?

"It's all the rage these days, isn't it? Going to school forever," says my mother, and her tone is no longer flirtatious. She looks accusingly at me. "Have you been in cahoots with your sister? She's on that bandwagon, too. Now she's decided she needs to get some sort of extra degree in extinction management or something even more specialized and impractical than what she's already studying. How many degrees does a person need? College was enough in my day, then you plunged into the experience of *life*. And look at your father's fancy degree. Botany! Beau tells me 'botany' doesn't even really exist anymore! And is that how he makes his money now? Plenty of hugely successful people have been to college, period. Now education is like an elastic band. You just keep on stretching it and stretching it. A bungee cord, that's what it's like! You two young people have jobs, good jobs! Who's to say that Hugh's teaching position will be waiting for him when you return?"

I say sharply, "A contract, that's what." But I'm distracted by the pernicious thought that my sister's probably wheedling money out of our father. And the wounded feeling that she's told them about her plans before she's told me. Not that we're the best of friends, but we respect each other. It's not as if I'm planning to ask for money from them myself—I'm applying for a grant—but I know the power Clem has over Dad. He glows when she tells her stories, all about her Darwinesque adventures in Brazil, Labrador, Alaska; she makes him nostalgic for science. I can't even keep straight what animals she's working to save, though mostly they're animals who live in the water. She's always said that school, to her, is nothing more than a necessary evil, so my mother's news is startling.

"Well, whatever you say," says Mom. She sighs the sigh of someone wronged and eats a bite of her chicken salad. "Your sister has a mind of her own, and I can't argue with that, can I? I raised you girls to be independent, and independent you are."

Hugh is staring toward the pool again, and I get the creepy, panicky notion that he's staring at the lifeguard. I tell myself that just because we now sleep together like friends—just because all he can do in bed these days is sleep, then sleep some more—doesn't mean he's gay.

"What about babies?" my mother says then, as if she's reading my mind. She's scary that way.

"What *about* babies?" I say. This tears Hugh's gaze away from the pool.

"I don't mean to be pushy, but Louisa—and Hugh—isn't it time? We're coming up on what—your fifth anniversary?"

"This isn't lunchtime conversation."

"What is it, honey, breakfast conversation? Bedtime conversation?" She laughs lightly at her unintentional quip. "Or do you mean it's none of my business?"

Hugh laughs appreciatively. Whose side is he on?

I say, "Actually, that's precisely what I mean," making sure there is no humor in my tone.

"Chip?" My mother touches the waiter's sleeve as he passes our table,

and for a minute I think she's going to ask him whether he thinks my having a baby is her business or not. "Chip, can we please get more rolls? I
worked my son-in-law hard this morning."

As sun encroaches on the terrace where we sit, I notice that bees are
feasting on the border of blue hydrangea. The blossoms are as large as
melons. Mom, whose dress precisely matches the flowers, hasn't noticed
that a few of the bees hover near her shoulders. She is on a mission.

"Can I tell you both one thing, just one thing?" She doesn't wait for
permission. "Don't wait to have children until you are ready. You are
never ready. Never. Ready is irrelevant. And I understand the health care
system in England is perfectly fine. And *free.* How about that?"

I want to tell her that nothing's free, but I'd rather change the subject.

I come upon the box that contains my specially preserved, freeze-dried
or mummified or vacuum-packed, wedding dress. There's a little peeka-
boo window, a glimpse of the embroidered bodice, worn once, perhaps
never to be worn again. Certainly not by me. But it was my understanding that this item had earned storage in the house, away from the radical
temperature changes of the barn. Last time I looked, it was in the top of
my— of the guest-room closet. Panting from the afternoon heat, I allow
myself a moment of idle stupor. I wonder if I'm going to carry it down
and confront my mother. I hear her outside right now, talking to someone
in the driveway below the window. There won't be lessons now; it's too
hot. Mom is compassionate toward her horses; most summer afternoons
they spend snoozing under the maple trees at the edge of the pasture,
swishing their tails at flies.

I can't hear what she's saying because I've plugged in a fan to keep
from getting heatstroke. Thanks to the wine at lunch, which I regret, the
stifling air up here is making me dizzy. I throw the box aside in disgust;
it's large but very light, its contents all gossamer and tulle. I slice open a
box labeled only 1970–74. The box contains letters. Letters I received
from friends during high school, most of them written in the summers

we spent apart, most of those during the months before I left for Radcliffe, when several friends had jobs away from home. That summer I was living right here, commuting to a secretarial job at a nearby community college. I answered a phone that rarely rang and typed a few insignificant letters for the dean of admissions, who came in only two or three days a week. The campus had been more or less abandoned. I felt like I was living in a future, Ray Bradbury kind of time when education had ceased to matter; when books, rather than being burned, simply gathered dust.

I pull out a rubber-banded clutch of lime-green envelopes. Oh, Eliza. Dear Eliza, with whom I lost touch for no better motive than sloth. Or maybe, I'm ashamed to say, I felt superior going to Harvard when Eliza was going to Hollins.

Eliza was madly in love that summer; really, except for me, who wasn't? When you're seventeen, love is constitutional. It's oxygen. I open one of the letters. It begins:

Dear Louisa, God I know what you mean. My sister drives me totally crazy too. She steals EVERYTHING from me and lies about it all the time. But Jeremy says not to let it get to me. Jeremy has 3 little brothers who are spoiled rotten. He's like a third parent, held to a different standard. He is going to go so far, and he's going to do something that makes a difference, not be a slave to the Money Tree like his father. Have you ever heard of Médecins sans Frontieres? It's so AMAZING. . . .

The rest of the letter was about Jeremy, his golden muscles, his eyelashes, his noble ambitions, his way of somersaulting backward off the pier. He was another counselor at the camp in New Hampshire where Eliza was working that summer. She was about to let him be the first guy she'd have sex with.

God he's driving me totally crazy with LUST, I just know I'm going to break down! He's so polite and so persistent all at the very same time!!! And he's really serious about me. I know, I know, but REALLY. Every

night after lights out, after our kids go to sleep (it's like we're playing
HOUSE!!), we sneak out to the lake and swim. We're never the only
ones, which is probably good. We take off our suits like everybody else
and I dive in really fast so he won't really see me naked but then he swims
over to me and OH GOD I can't stand how sexy he is underwater. The
invisibility is practically fatal, if you know what I mean! How much will
you hate me if I do it first? And GOD, Louisa, don't show this letter to
ANYBODY, EVER!!!!!

I sit down and read the entire letter. It's eight pages long. The whole
Ray Bradbury feeling comes over me again, but in reverse. *Now* is the
time that's strange; we've just been brainwashed to live the way we do.
We are not enlightened. We've gone astray. I think about skinny-dipping
at midnight with friends, in the ocean just down the road: naked bodies
slipping against one another as amicably as if we were dolphins. It's
something I've practically forgotten and will probably never do again.
Why doesn't anybody write letters anymore, handwritten letters that go
on and on for neon pages, inscribed with a torrent of exclamation points
(the top of each one a meticulously inverted teardrop)? These are emotions you can hold in your hands. You tell each other every little thing,
things like the fatality of what you can feel but can't see. Suddenly I am
remembering the excitement, the anticipatory thrill, of opening our mail-
box that summer and looking for that particular flash of green. As if Eliza
were my lover. I ate up her news, her news from the world abroad, dip-
ping into that girl talk like chocolate fondue. I'm eating it up, now, all
over again. You'd think it would embarrass me, but it moves me. When
was the last time anything seemed AMAZING to me?

I turn at the sound of footsteps on the hayloft stairs.

"Hello there, you there."

Dad is just back from work, earlier than usual because I'm here. He's
wearing a khaki hat with a wide floppy brim, but still his nose glows like a
poppy. I envy him his grown-up job that permits him to spend all summer out in the sun. I'm lucky to have the job I do, but there are long days
when I go without breathing a mote of fresh, sunlit air.

I stand up and kiss him on the cheek. "I'm trying to throw stuff away. Trying."

Dad gestures at the Everest of boxes—his—that dwarfs my stash. "Allegedly," he says, "all things must pass."

Allegedly is code for "according to your mother." We share the conspiratorial laugh of the family pack rats.

He asks if the two large plastic sacks are garbage. When I say they are, he drags them to the loft door and tosses them out.

"Watch out belooooow!" he bellows. I hear two loud metallic thuds.

"Dad!"

"Louisa, I've got the truck out there." He tells me I've made admirable progress. "I order you to quit. Or your mother does. Clemency from on high—or down below. She's opening a bottle of champagne."

Only as we cross the driveway do I realize that I'm still holding Eliza's letters. My mother's in the kitchen now, back in barnworthy clothes (jeans and a threadbare cotton shirt that my father's paunch outgrew some years ago). She's pushing cherry tomatoes and chunks of oily meat onto skewers. "Aha!" she says when she sees me. "Time for a toast!"

"Where's Hugh?" I ask.

"Reading, I think. He came back from the beach two hours ago."

Upstairs, I find him in bed—or on the bed, in his bathing suit and a boyish plain white T-shirt, asleep on one of the quilts made long ago by one of my father's dowager aunts. There's sand in his dark curly hair. "Jesus," I whisper.

I have the urge to tell him he shouldn't be lying on that antique quilt with sunblock and sand all over his body. But I decide, right now, that I have to stop being rude to him. I think of a time, only a year or two in the past, when I would have lain down beside him and kissed him, face-to-face. *Hello there, you there,* I would have said.

He opens his eyes. "I know. I'm sleeping too much."

I sit on the opposite bed. "Are you sick, do you think? Do you need to make an appointment with Dr. Breen?"

"No," he says firmly, with a trace of belligerence. "I'm storing up, like a solar panel. School starts in three days, you know."

"Of course I know." But then I say, more gently, "So get dressed, okay? We're having champagne for some reason."

"Your father's just made a lucrative deal with somebody like Ted Turner, only not Ted Turner."

"How do you know?"

"She told me while I was carrying hay."

"Why didn't she mention it at lunch? Why did she tell you and not me?"

"He phoned while I was with her, I guess." Hugh opens the closet to pull out the same striped Brooks Brothers shirt he wore to lunch. I glance at the shelf above the hangers. Before Hugh closes the door, I see two cardboard boxes. On one, in Mom's handwriting, is written XMAS DECO. Glass baubles displaced my wedding gown?

"What's for dinner?" asks Hugh.

"Shish kebabs. Marinated in Ken's Steak House dressing."

He makes a noise of amused contempt.

"Actually, they're pretty good." I leave the room. My goodwill has vaporized. I would never, in a million years, be saintly enough for Doctors Without Borders. I wonder what became of Dreamboat Jeremy. Probably high on the Money Tree by now. I've probably passed him in Midtown.

My mother's poured four glasses of Codorníu, the Spanish stuff in the bottle shaped like it's melting. "Aha! Where's Hercules?"

"Resting from his labors. Holding up the world is hard," I say. I announce that I need a shower before I can drink champagne. I am a sweaty, dusty mess.

"There won't be much hot!" warns Mom. "I just washed the saddle pads!"

"But I *love* cold showers." I am now a full-fledged grouch. "And I love being married to a guy who does nothing but sleep."

"Honey, it's the sea air," says Mom. "It does that to people."

"Sleep is good medicine," says Dad, who's leaning on the counter, paging through a magazine. "People who sleep a lot live longer. Did you know that?" They're aligning themselves against my doubts. Or that's my paranoid impression.

"You look like a salt lick," Mom says to Dad. "Go comb your hair."

"Aye-aye, commodore," he answers.

I hear her say, as I head back upstairs, "Commodor*ess* to you."

When I come out of the bathroom, out of my brief, tepid shower, Hugh is still in the bedroom, though he's dressed. He is reading one of Eliza's letters, which I left on my bed after waking him up. I snatch it away from him.

"What?" he says.

"That's private."

"It's about two decades old," he says. "I didn't even know you then."

"It's not about me; it's about someone else." The rubber band around the letters has disintegrated; I hold them tightly in one hand, searching the room for something to bind them together again. I look instinctively to where my desk once stood.

"Lovebirds!" my mother calls up the stairs. "The bubbles are escaping!"

I push the letters under my pillow, which makes Hugh laugh at me. "I don't see what you have to hide, Louisa."

I don't, either. My keeping the letters to myself seems like a matter of principle, though I know it's utterly silly.

When we get downstairs, Mom is pouring another glass for Tighty, who's materialized, as he often did at this hour through my teenage years. I guess nothing's changed. Though I feel almost traitorous, since he's practically a member of the family, I can't help seeing Tighty as a walking, talking cautionary lesson, a brilliant guy who can't seem to put together a life worthy of his talents. I notice that he's gained even more weight since I last saw him, yet I suspect that's made him no less alluring to the horsey women who giggle like teenagers when he's around. Clem says Tighty has top-notch pheromones. She says they're the glandular equivalent of high EQ.

"Yo," he says to me, a new greeting he must believe makes him sound younger. He raises the glass in a toast and takes a generous sip.

"Hey," I answer. "How are you, Tighty?'

"I am stupendous, *comme toujours*," he says in his perpetually sardonic manner. With his free hand, he reaches into a large square pocket on the side of his loose grimy pants. He pulls out two plastic packages and lays them on the kitchen counter. "Dr. Feelgood, at your service."

The packages contain syringes. The fancy wedding; the fireworks. My mother's horses would go nuts with fear if they had to endure the fireworks fully conscious, galloping and snorting around the pasture. Closing them in the barn would only compress their panic. One Fourth of July ritual that goes back almost as far as I can remember involves making sure the horses are tranquilized at just the right time and that someone's over at the kennel to babysit the hounds, pill the ones who get anxious. They get Valium in a meatball.

Tighty is staying for dinner. This is good, in that it will subvert any Serious Conversation about things like whether Hugh and I ever plan to have babies (or why Mom banished my wedding dress to the barn), and it's difficult, in that Tighty and Hugh have zero chemistry. They go through an awkward guy-dance of pretending to care passionately about baseball (which neither does) or President Bush's foreign policy (about which Tighty will know nothing, as he lives in a political vacuum) or the art world (which, actually, they both know about, though art talk leaves my parents in the cold, and Mom won't tolerate that).

They shake hands. "What's up with the teaching?" asks Tighty.

"Well, it's still summer," says Hugh. "For a few more days, at least."

"Oh," says Tighty. "No summer school for you."

"No," says Hugh.

"Right," says Tighty.

Dad, who might rescue them, is on the phone; he gets so many calls during high boating season that Mom forced him to get a separate line, on a cordless phone, mostly so she can chase him out of the room when she's sick of hearing nautical talk. He paces around the house with his free hand pressed against his open ear, carrying on loud conversations related to weather forecasts, sailing regattas, mooring disputes, and the health of local shellfish.

"Out, Beau. Scram," says Mom, steering him away from the kitchen, her palms on his shoulder blades. She asks me to set the table, and she asks Hugh if he can take over the grilling. She likes dinner on the table at seven sharp.

When I open the cupboards, I see an unfamiliar set of plates.

I hold one up toward my mother. "Mom, where are mine?"

"Yours?"

"The plates I gave you and Dad for your anniversary?"

"Oh." She refills Tighty's champagne glass. "Well. We got a new dishwasher—you remember that flood we had at Christmas?—and I'm afraid your plates just don't fit in the dish rack."

"But where are they?"

"I put them away for now," Mom says. "Don't fret about it, honey."

Tighty watches me closely. He's seen knock-down verbal melees in the kitchen, one adolescent daughter after the next. "Yo. How's Clem? I miss that girl." Tighty and Clem were close when she was younger; sometimes I wonder how close, but I've never dared to ask, not even when she saved his ass out in California. That whole farce—from Tighty's cross-country dognapping to my cross-country marital tantrum—is so excruciating to recall, for both of us, that we have never mentioned it since. Sometimes I can almost believe it never happened. You'd think we might have bonded on our shared retreat in that truck, across a dozen states over nearly a week; hardly. We got along fine, but our embarrassment only increased with the mileage. I still don't know why Mom didn't fire him, but I think she regards him like one of her animals, and that's a compliment. She will never give up on an animal.

The subject of Clem sends Mom into her tirade about education as a bungee cord. With which Tighty, whose three years at Yale led him nowhere, opts to agree. "Education," he says, "is one very pricey form of procrastination."

If I were Hugh—if education were the source of my income—I'd jump down Tighty's throat, but right now Hugh simply looks bemused. Perhaps, unlike me, he knows a pointless struggle when he sees one. I ready myself for conversational combat, but Mom starts handing us dishes, sending us out to the porch. The horses watch from the pasture.

When the four of us are seated (Dad is somewhere else, still on the phone), Tighty declares, "So. Speaking of education as a farce, rumor has it that Millie's writing a book."

"Millie who?" I say.

"Millie the White House springer spaniel. What other Millie is there?"

Mom snorts with laughter. "Tighty, you'd better start taking notes over at the kennel. I'll bet *our* guys have much better tales to tell than some oversize sissy lapdog whose breed has been hopelessly corrupted."

This leads Mom and Tighty into a spirited condemnation of the AKC and how its narrow guidelines for canine beauty have led to the proliferation of congenital tragedies like sudden rage syndrome and an epidemic of hip dysplasia. I notice that Mom has covered my father's plate to keep his food warm and doesn't seem bothered that he's still absent from the table. I glance at Hugh. He glances back at me and smiles, perhaps at the eccentric turn of conversation, perhaps out of fondness. Why do I need to know why? I return his smile.

"News bulletin!" Dad announces as he joins us. He's just finalized the lease of his smallest boatyard, starting next summer, to a Texan who's taken up yachting in Newport. "Your mother should've bought the real thing," he says as he opens a second bottle of Codorníu. "For about fifteen minutes, we'll be feeling very rich."

Mom glows with delight. She says to me, "How much would I bet that your father is scheming to buy the boat of his dreams?"

"May, your imagination sometimes fails you," says Dad.

"We'll see," she says. "We will just wait and see." She winks at Hugh.

Outside, the sun has set and the crickets are revving up. Tighty looks at his watch and excuses himself to drug the horses. As soon as I've cleared the unfamiliar, mass-produced plates, I beg off to continue the parsing of my childhood belongings.

"Tighty!" my mother is calling toward the barn as I go upstairs to change for the fourth time today. "Take the rest of that pie when you go, will you?"

Fortified by cheap champagne, I face the crates containing the pottery I neither sold nor gave away, nor continue to use in my everyday life. And there I find, sure enough, a new box—smaller, as if to apologize for its insignificance (or as if to hunker down in hiding)—containing the twelve plates, blue as the ocean in August, their glaze crackled to a dragonfly shimmer, that I gave my parents for their twenty-fifth wedding anniversary. I was proud of these plates when I made them; they look both ancient and new, each a little different from the rest. They are much nicer than the dark raku plates Hugh and I use every day in New York.

I've switched on the barn lights, spooking a dozen cats from their lairs in the ramparts of hay. Two bats zigzag through the rafters and out the door to the sky, now the pure blue of twilight (a blue I once yearned to mimic in glaze).

Several mundane thoughts convene around my indignation.

The plates should never have gone in the dishwasher to begin with. I did not expect them to be saved for special occasions—those are reserved for my grandmother's china—but I did expect them to be washed, lovingly, by hand.

My mother apparently knew about this stash of boxes, which leads me to wonder what else she knows about my things. I picture her snooping through the boxes, including all my teenage letters, resealing them carefully so I'll never know. This is absurd, of course. She has neither the time nor the inclination for such deceit. For better or worse, she lives life out in the open.

What makes my parents so compatible when it seems they are anything but? Is it just a matter of sticking it out, the never-ending aggravations, till all the habits you have, good and bad, are simply all you know, easy because they're familiar? Yet my parents make a happy marriage look real.

Here, in the next crate, are my teapots, elongated vessels with serpentine spouts, green with flares of orange and violet across the surface. I remember the sensation of blowing the glaze through a narrow straw, taking care not to draw it up into my mouth, yet tasting chalk and metal for hours. Some of the pigments smelled like spices: cinnamon, turmeric, mace. I called this my Arabian Nights phase. Though I didn't know it at the time, this was my last phase, during which I started working at the magazine, during which I met Hugh. "I must be looking for a sultan," I said, self-consciously, the first time I took him to my studio and showed him these pots. "No, not a ceramicist," I corrected him. "A potter. I'm a potter." Words, in the end, came to matter more. Now I shape words, not clay.

A loud crackling noise stuns me with fear for an instant. It comes from outside the barn, yet it's close. Beyond the door I see only dark sky, the tops of trees around the house. Then comes a long sharp whistling, a war-movie sound, followed by a soft, thunderous echo. A small string of explosions. I'd forgotten all about the fireworks.

At the next fusillade, I walk over to the door, edging carefully toward it, holding on to the top rail with both hands, leaning forward so that my feet remain a good ten inches from the threshold leading to open air. Though it doesn't include the fireworks—which I realize now would be visible only in the opposite direction—the view of my childhood house, in the dark, holds me there for a moment despite my fear of heights. (If I were to fall, I'd land in the bed of Dad's truck, on the bags of memorabilia with which I've reluctantly parted.)

Nearly all the windows are alight. In the kitchen, my mother is at the sink, rinsing her nonexotic dishes, talking on the phone, probably with Tighty, checking in at the kennel to make sure the hounds aren't panicking at the inexplicable clamor from above. On the porch, Dad's pacing and talking on his phone. I hear him laughing. I hear him say *rich for about fifteen minutes.* Upstairs, the light is on in my room, too. Is Hugh reading? Has he defiantly taken Eliza's letters from under my pillow (do I really care?) or is he in the middle of that book on Vietnam, the one that puts such a dark scowl on his smooth, kind face?

I look back at my parents, each involved in a separate conversation. Or what if they are talking to each other? What if they phone each other all day long, because that's where they talk best, even when they're steps away from each other? Is that their secret? Do they even have one?

When Clem talks about how crazy she thinks it is to get married, she claims that it's like making a decision based on geologic time— antithetical to human nature, she says. To mortality. The first time I heard this little sermon of hers, I told her she'd lost me. "Like, come on," she said. "All that talk about *forever*?"

I asked her, "What about our parents? They seem to go on and on."

"Well," she said, "they have an *arrangement*. I don't want an arrangement. Do you?"

But what is a marriage, I think, if not an arrangement? Is that so bad?

I walk back to the safety of the loft interior. I will finish my difficult task tomorrow. I turn off the fan. I leave the door to the sky wide open; I don't have the courage to close it myself. I'll ask Dad to do it tomorrow. I find the box, tape it up again, and carefully hoist it onto a hip. I take the stairs slowly, one at a time.

In the driveway, I set the box down and move to where I imagine I will be able to see the fireworks, over the trees at the back of the pasture. But all I can see is the varicolored glow; the spectacle itself is out of sight. I watch anyway, until the orgasmic crescendo comes at the end of the show. A couple of long, cometlike flares rise high enough that I can see them. I hear one of the horses snort. The bride and groom will be climbing into a long white limo, blazing off toward a honeymoon somewhere classy and expensive. Tuscany. The fjords of Norway.

I open the trunk of our car and lift into it the box containing the beautiful plates I made for my parents that they are never going to use. As quietly as I can, I close the trunk, pushing down until I hear it click.

I enter the house with a purpose, so that no one will stop me—but both of my parents are still on the phone. As I pass through the porch and then the kitchen, I wave at my father and then my mother. They wave back but do not interrupt their conversations. I was right: Mom's talking to Tighty, though it sounds as if the hounds are fine.

I head upstairs resolved to have it out, to unbox Hugh the way I've been unboxing everything else. I am going to say, *I love you, but we are in trouble.*

He's asleep, of course, the Vietnam book askew at his hip. It's nine-thirty and he's asleep.

I sit on the edge of my bed and stare at him. I could wake him up. What if this is the moment that will be the turning point, the one that determines whether or not we stay together? Which is the right choice, to wake him or let him sleep? In the scheme of things, in geologic time, how can it be urgent?

Two years ago I was pregnant—briefly. It pleased us, even amused us, because it had been so completely unplanned. Before we'd decided whether or not to tell anyone, but not before we'd begun to talk about names, I miscarried. I had just turned thirty-one. My doctor said, "Don't worry! This is normal. Take a break for a couple of months and then you'll get right back up on that horse."

I did not appreciate the equestrian analogy. I was relieved when, because of a glitch in my health insurance, I had to change doctors soon after. I did not ask the new doctor about getting pregnant again, and she has never pried.

Hugh didn't say much about the subject, either. Several months went by. The time to get right back up on that horse came and went. We let it slip farther and farther behind us. As if losing the baby, or even being pregnant at all, had been an embarrassment. We never told our friends; by then, too many of them were desperate to be pregnant or desperate simply to be coupled off. We were at least half lucky that way.

Hugh sleeps quietly, looking every bit the reasonable, patient, likable guy I married. The air from the fan in the window ruffles his hair, still sandy from the beach. "Where are we?" I say quietly, experimentally, to see if he will wake. He stirs, but only to turn around in his sleep and face the other way. The Vietnam book begins to slide, slowly at first, then tumbles onto the rug. I think about leaving it there, its paper innards bent and curled. But that would be childish. I pick it up, straighten the pages, close it, and set it on the table between the two beds.

Now I am looking at the back of his head. This means nothing, I tell myself. I am tempted to touch the roiled, humid curls, Hugh's boyishly ungraying hair. Just that I'm tempted seems hopeful.

I take off my clothes and put on my nightgown. When I pull back the quilt on my bed, I see that familiar, livid green poking from under the edge of my pillow. I make myself comfortable and, in my lap, arrange the envelopes in order by postmark. There are twelve. As I read them, I realize why it thrilled me so much that summer to get them. They are love letters: letters all about love, at least how it begins.

I See You Everywhere

1990

Safety-pinned to my blanket is a pink WHILE YOU WERE OUT slip. An OUT, I'm to learn, of titanic proportion. *Your sister called. Loves you very much. Coming by train tmw.* I puzzle thickly over those three letters. Tramway? Tomahawk? Tunisian Motor Works? My mind feels like a fly-mobbed garbage barge plowing through a sea of tar. At the foot of a strange bed, a strange window: leafy branches, bright sky, parking lot of blinding glitter. Pin-striped curtains wall me in.

My right arm is in a cast. From my left hand, an IV snakes its way up to a large crystalline prune. HYDRATION, my brain remarks, the word flashing out, a lighthouse on my sea of tar. I turn my head—to another flash, this one exuberant pain—and there's an electrocardiograph showing the placid skip-to-my-Lou of a healthy heartbeat. E K G, my brain instructs, each letter another beacon, a tiny gem in the murk.

Wow, so this is amnesia. But now I recognize the woman asleep in the strange chair by the strange window. My name, my profession, the goings-on in my life: I seem to know all these things and am vaguely disappointed that I do—except for Jerry, hot-as-a-short-order-skillet Jerry.

The pink note still clings to my thigh. "Oh, *tomorrow*. Shit." A whisper but, against the white noise of life support, stunning.

In a flash, my mother's awake and pressing a hand to my forehead. "Honey, honey, it's *you*."

"Like I'd be, who, Mick Jagger?" I sound like wheels on gravel.

"Don't talk! Save your energy, sweetheart." She pulls back the curtain and calls out, "Gwen! She's with us at last, she's here!" Someone shushes her gently. Before she lets the curtain fall, I see half a dozen beds in a long arc, some tented, all flanked by machines.

Mom scrapes her chair up beside me. She clearly wants to take my hand, but both are already taken—one by the IV, the other by a sling.

"You're in the hospital," says Mom. As if I might think we're in a pool hall or carwash. "You've had an accident, but you're going to be fine." I am about to say, *Jesus, Mom,* what *hospital,* what *accident?* when she puts a finger to my lips. "Please, sweetheart. In a minute, I'll call Dad. He had to go home to dry-dock a Friendship and feed the horses." Again I take stock: My father runs three boatyards. My mother is an accomplished rider, a master of foxhounds. They live on Pemiquisset Point in Rhode Island, where I grew up. These swatches of knowledge are safely intact, that part of my cerebral quilt unfrayed. But the NOW of my life as I know it takes place largely in Portsmouth, New Hampshire, where I am staying with Jerry while I figure out where my next job's going to be. Jerry says that maybe I should figure out, first, why I change jobs so often, especially since I never get fired.

A nurse enters my tiny lair. "Well, well. Forty winks and then some." She wrangles a pressure cuff onto my cast-free arm. As she leans across me, I see her badge. Her name is Gwendolyn Treeble, she is a blizzard of freckles (in person; the flash of her ID photo bleached them all out), and we are at the hospital in Boston that my father, who went to Harvard and had a broken femur set in this place, calls Poobah General. My brain flings out the weirdest details.

" 'Scuse me," I say, figuring she will be more helpful than my mother, but then a man in a white coat pops in behind her. "Well, well," I hear again, as if it's the password. "And how do *you* feel?"

"Caved in," I say, straining to enunciate. "Kicked by a Clydesdale."

He laughs, a small mannerly laugh. "Vocabulary an excellent sign." He leans in from the foot of my bed and holds out a pen, moves it back and forth before my eyes. Then he untucks the bedding, pulls it up to my ankles, and uses his all-purpose pen to stroke the soles of my feet. When

I flinch, he winks. "Guess we'll forgo amputation." Finally, he puts his hands around my neck, hands as cool and dry as a lizard. He seems to be making sure my skull is still attached to my spine. His badge tells me he is Eric Slocum, Chief Res., Emerg. Med. His clipboard, now on the table beside my bed, tells me today is July 28. But wait. That date is more than a month in the future. Isn't it?

"Doctor, excuse me, but have I been out cold for a month?"

He watches the ceiling while taking my pulse. "We don't know why you aren't a lot worse off. You are a very lucky young lady with a noggin of grade-A granite and a pair of very resilient lungs."

Real conversations with these people are going to be difficult. But then, I've been at the mercy of doctors before. I know their game of bait and switch.

Mom's eyes are swollen. Weeping isn't her style, so something serious happened here. She is a woman made of gristle, pumice, and more than the customary dash of testosterone. If my noggin's made of granite, her genes are to thank. She believes in the supremacy of genes; that gene I got from her, too.

Jerry is in the business of genes. I had never wanted a guy the way I wanted Jerry, almost the minute I met him. I was feverish, crazy, jealous of everything he touched, from his cat to his phone to the steering wheel in his jeep. By nature (genes again!), I am far too skeptical, too bound by gravity to ever get swept off my feet, but if anyone's come near, it's Jerry. Jerry is a high-tech veterinarian. He flies around the country and orchestrates in-vitro breeding of pedigreed cattle and horses, from genetic counseling to the carefully engineered reproductive moment of truth. (His dream is to do the same for lions on the Serengeti.)

I met Jerry last winter in Augusta, Maine. I was alone in a bar, consoling myself after a disastrous interview for a job I might have had tagging moose. Till now, my work has taken place on the ocean, but lately I've been restless for the reassuring enclosure of mountains and lakes. And the ocean is becoming too politically charged. Overfishing, nuclear testing, PCBs, and a mulish nostalgia for whaling have all conspired to make the practice of Darwin-style biology next to impossible.

We got talking about something predictably high-minded like the dawning obsolescence of wilderness. He was wearing a bolo tie, a ridley sea turtle treading water at the throat of his denim shirt, under the reef of a coral-red beard. I remember wanting desperately to impress him. That's not like me, so I was partly hooked, partly annoyed. We'd been talking less than an hour, had moved on to Richard Dawkins and selfish genes, when Jerry admired my earrings, tear-shaped slabs of turquoise hanging from silver studs.

"How'd I look in one of those?" he said. He reached out and gently unfastened my right earring. I was acutely aware of his callused fingertips; of his beard, like fiery sagebrush, grazing my face. Not a soft square inch on the man except this pair of blue eyes, a blue like bridesmaid satin. I expected him to turn toward the mirror behind the bottles and hold the earring up for show, but instead he set it down. When he took an ice cube out of his scotch and held it to his right earlobe, I laughed and said, "You are bluffing."

Merely smiling, he put the ice cube on the bar, where it slid aimlessly away. He took the earring and, just like that, pushed it through. The noise was faint but excruciating, a cell of bubble wrap popping. He did not blink.

"Now we're a package," he said, pressing our naked ears together and facing us toward the mirror. "Siamese, inseparable."

"Get away!" I shoved him, but I was laughing hysterically. The part of me that was hooked had just won me over against all survivalist caution, of which I've been told I possess next to none.

Just like that, I've lost a month of my life. Sloughed off my frontal lobe like snow shearing off an ice floe in May. Other people fill in the details, but what do you believe? One incidental thing I'd like to remember: the helicopter ride to the hospital. A chopper careening up the muscleman arm of the Cape: Ride 'em, cowboy! Woo *hah*! My mother says, "No you would not want to remember, honey, believe you me. You were in a lot of pain. Sometimes God is merciful. God or whoever. *What*ever." She is a

Minnesota-born Presbyterian and goes to church only on Easter and Christmas Eve. She went a lot more often when Louisa and I were small, to make sure we had our full dose of Sunday school—like a course of antibiotics—but she could never drag our father along, not even for the "Hallelujah Chorus" by candlelight. (He is not swayed by bravura or sentiment, least of all by a merger. In this way, at least, I am his daughter.)

The afternoon is ruthlessly long. There is no conversation around me, and the fading light outside has no impact on the homogenized glare within. Dinner, equally dull, might as well be intravenous, and afterward, every time I drift toward sleep, Gwen or some resident pokes me. Or I hear another patient in distress. Even if I had the energy to complain, I'd feel like a brat. It's no secret that some of my companions here, just beyond my curtain, are going to die—die right here and soon. That's why they're here. They're like planes in a holding pattern over an airport, waiting their turn to land. This doesn't spook me—I think about death sometimes as a state of respite—but I know that I'm moving away from them, that I'll make it out of here. At which point I'll face another struggle. Best not to think about that now.

In my jackknifed bed, subdued by a pill whose name I've forgotten, I assign myself a mental calisthenic: to configure my life as a timeline of medical crises—of which there have been quite a few.

1 year old: rolled off the changing table while my mother answered the phone, landed on my chin, and bit through my tongue. The scar's still there: a tiny crescent, like the nail shard clipped off a pinkie.

2 years: while visiting my father's cousin, an antiquities dealer in Charleston who thought she put everything I could destroy out of reach, meandered into an empty room and found, on a low table, a primitive stone head as big as a melon. Carried it all the way to the kitchen, to show the grown-ups, before dropping it on my right foot. Stone head unharmed, middle metatarsal cracked.

4: bitten in our barn by a rat I was determined to befriend. I wasn't angry; I understood his fear. He was cornered in the grain bin and I'd been too pushy. Winced through the ministrations of the cardiologist who lived next door, but couldn't comprehend my mother's hysteria or the grim aggression with which my father trapped the rat in a shoe box and marched him to the car. A scalding July afternoon of beach traffic; it took us (all four of us—Louisa hissing in my ear, over and over, "Boy are you gonna *get it*") three sticky hours to reach a sterile, stingy-windowed building up in Boston. Dad said we were taking the rat for a checkup but emerged from the building without the shoe box. The ride back mostly silent, my questions dodged. That night, overheard Dad describing to Mom how beheading was the only test for rabies (still true; when I worked one summer for a wildlife refuge, I hated that part of my job— raccoons and foxes, loitering like drunks on somebody's lawn, that I had to corral and deliver for decapitation). Mourned my lost friend all night in secret. Next day, made a shrine under our privet hedge: a cross of twigs beneath which I buried a matchbox holding two cashews, a morsel of cinnamon Pop-Tart, a zebra shoelace, a snip of my hair. That same week, Mom came home from the animal shelter with four scrawny cats and moved them into the barn.

7: a violent allergic reaction to blue cheese dip, which made my throat swell up so tight the doctors threatened tracheotomy; I still remember the terror in that one alien word. Having never liked blue cheese, can't imagine why I'd touch it. Forced by Louisa, I bet. For a year or so there, she'd trick me into eating disgusting foods by promising favors that she rarely fulfilled. A sandwich of dill pickles, Marshmallow Fluff, and paprika stands out in my mind.

10: on a Girl Scout camping trip, heading off to find firewood, trampled a nest of yellow jackets. Luckily, this is one allergy I don't have. Stung twice on one arm, once each on lower lip, left eyelid, left ear. The ear hurt most, throbbing to the core of my brain. Eye swelled shut for two days. The perfect excuse to drop out of Scouts. I was tone-deaf to that kind of fellowship anyway.

15: to impress the boys with whom I'd broken into a public pool at one in the morning, dove off the high board completely stoned. Landed on the water like a johnnycake flipped on a griddle and was sure I had broken my nose. Mostly, I'd pulverized a slew of capillaries and bruised my left cornea. For the next week, I looked like a raccoon wearing a tea strainer over one eye.

22: on a bike in Michigan, racing with my old boyfriend Luke (we still talk on the phone: lots of silences, mostly his anger, which I often deserve), roared across what I thought was a one-way street—let the record show I was winning—and sideswiped a station wagon, plowing a foot-long gash in my thigh. Now a magnificent scar, a conversational ice-breaker when I'm in shorts.

22 again: an ectopic pregnancy that threatened to rupture while I had a plum internship on a project to record whale songs on a sailboat off Newfoundland. Completely unexpected, since I hadn't seen Luke in two months (though there was this flyboy, one sweet fly-by-night in Montreal on my way north). If I were ever to change my mind about children, I might be a little tense . . .

23: . . . though somehow, a year later—stupid, stupid, stupid—I was careless enough to get pregnant again.

Then a period of grace until now, seven years later, this. Again, at sea; so I'm told. Head trauma, fractured collarbone, assorted nicks and bruises. Two cracked ribs, three days in and out of a coma, five weeks of memory erased.

Louisa's smart, smarter than me in the report-card sense, but whenever she's nervous, she babbles. Today, day two of my renewed consciousness, she's worse than ever, as if she's burning off extra fuel. I guess she's just glad I'm alive, and if I weren't so drugged up, I hope I'd be touched. "So I get home," she's saying, "Hugh's already asleep, I've had too much wine, and what do I find on the machine but one of Mom's classic soliloquies. Something like 'Clem's been in a serious accident, honey, I'm not at home because I'm here with her and your father's back and forth because there's a hurricane off Bermuda—Ethan or Efram, I think; your father says it's a bad sign that here we are not even August and already up to E. C and D passed us by, but B was a very close call. Great for the roses, though. You can't speak to her, I'm afraid, but call this number, I'm giving you this number, just a second, hang on, it's here in my purse. Is it as hot down there as it is up here? Yes, here it is, right, so call and say you love her. Will you do that, please? She can't talk, but have them leave her a message, I'll call you later.' "

Louisa stops pacing. "So of course I have no idea where 'here' is or who 'they' are, but I call the number, I'm frantic, and this woman answers, 'I see you?' as if I'm expected to answer, 'Aha, but I see you, too!' Like a game of some kind. All I can say is 'You see me? How?' and she laughs. 'That's a new one,' she says. 'This is intensive care,' and I freak out. I can't believe she's *laughing*."

"That's cute," I say. "Like, ICU in my dreams. ICU on the Johnny Carson show. ICU everywhere."

"More like, ICU every time all hell breaks loose. For both of us."

"Yeah, well, life is never dull." I'm too slow to pick up on the second half of what she said, but later, when I'm alone, it comes back and I tell myself, *Remember to ask her.* This is like trying to leave a footprint in sludge.

"Sometimes I wish you'd let it be. Dull. Just for a change." She puts a hand on my leg. "Are you in a lot of pain? Can I get you anything from the outside world? Mom's buying books, since they say you'll be in here awhile."

"I have a concussion. You can't read with a concussion. And no, the pain is just sort of predictably there, not too much, not too little. I know what drugs to ask for. But thanks." What I want from the outside world, of course, is Jerry, Jerry, Jerry. Why isn't he here?

Because no one told him. Who would tell him? I've kept him to myself for months. Not because he's not important to me. Because there's so much at stake. That's when I clam up.

I interrupt my sister's running commentary. She's acting weirdly jumpy. "Louisa? Can you make a call for me? I can't have a phone till I'm in a regular room." Miraculously, I recite his number.

"Who's Jerry?"

"A guy I met who . . . Can you please just call him and tell him where I am?"

For once, I don't get her patent-pending look of disapproval. "Anything you need. Today, I'm your slave." She smiles and lowers her voice. "Your go-between."

I feel sorry for her, but it passes. Louisa's married, and before that, her love life was never too complex. When I see her these days, I keep waiting for her to tell me she's having a baby. It's way beyond time.

I don't think Eric Slocum's superiors would like how familiar he is, the casual way he sits on my bed, twiddling his stethoscope. He's just told me that I was in an accident during a sailboat race off Westport, Massachusetts, on July 25. "You do sail," he says coyly in response to my shock.

"Yes, I sail," I say, perhaps rudely. "But I have never been in a race. I grew up around boats, but I'm not the yachting type. I've sailed to do research."

"Research?" His eyebrows, raised, sprout tiny projectile tufts. Other than this hint of vampire, he is Ken-doll handsome, down to his patent-leather hair.

"Whales and seals. Until the money for my last job dried up. I was in California. The last place you want a state-funded job right now."

"Ah." He looks impressed, though I doubt he is. He writes something down. If doctors are impressed—a rare event—it's by artists, acrobats, athletes. Any science other than medicine has the cachet of hand-me-down clothing with perspiration stains.

I want to ask again about the race but stop myself. Best not to invite more concern than I want from this guy. Now he is telling me that I was unconscious when I came off the chopper, but talking nonstop.

"What was I saying?"

"According to the EMT who took your vitals, it was mostly nonsense but weirdly intelligible." He looks at his notes. "When I arrived, you were asking for Band-Aids and coleslaw—and there was something about 'Krishna sloughing.' " He leans closer. "Are you fond of coleslaw? Are you a Hindu?"

"What I am is tired." Is he actually flirting?

He knocks on one of my shins, as if to see who's home.

"I can feel that. In case you've reserved a wheelchair."

He laughs nervously. "Dr. A. will be through in an hour. One more night without further complications and we are copacetic. Upstairs you go." Dr. Slocum nods at the hills and valleys of my cardiograph, sound as a Sousa march. Earlier today, I flipped through the printouts on the clipboard tied to the head of my bed. They looked more like the Tetons my first day in; a solo by Max Roach.

"Gwendolyn taking good care of you? Everything to your satisfaction?"

"Just swell. I'd turn down Mar-a-Lago to be here."

"Attagirl." He knocks on my shin again and, finally, leaves.

Coleslaw is the name of Jerry's old tomcat who is missing so many teeth that he emits, when he sleeps between us, a snore as loud and jagged as a woodchipper mauling a dead Christmas tree. Krishna is the mainsail of the *Gannet*, orange like the robes of the bald guys who chant and beat tambourines. (Krishna's *luffing*, I must have said.) The *Gannet* is the sailboat on which I helped record whale songs eight years ago, the summer my uterus lost access to an ovary, the summer I fled Luke and his first proposal of marriage (two reunions, two breakups, lay ahead of us yet). Not that I wasn't working my tail off. The crew had names for everything: The galley stove was Pelée because of its volatile nature, the keel Great Whitey because the captain said it was sure as a shark. The head, my favorite, was Tricky Dick, Nix for short, because it liked to spit back at opportune moments.

I eat my entire inedible breakfast. What I am ravenous for is visiting hours. Louisa, I hope, will have spoken with Jerry. If she caught him at home last night, he should be here soon. I asked Gwen to open my curtain and turn my bed around; that way, I can see the window to the waiting room and the clock above the door. Assorted loved ones, visible from the waist up, begin to gather and mill about, like a captive school of fish. Gwen is strict, unless someone is dying. From ten to noon means just that: she unlocks the door exactly when the second hand sweeps the twelve.

At fourteen to, three short, round, Italian-looking women arrive. They try to get Gwen's attention by tapping the glass (soundlessly, from this side). At thirteen to, a stooped elderly man shuffles straight to what must be a chair and sinks out of sight. At seven to, the elevator releases a tall blond man in a crisp suit, worthy of a magazine. He wields an enormous bouquet, a *shrub*, of roses. As if it were a torch, everyone else in the waiting room steps back. The color of those roses, a chaste milky pink, is so foreign to the spectrum in here (various hues of puke) that the sight of them sends a seismic tremor across my EKG. I have to smile, wondering who the roses are for, knowing—as this drama king does not—that flowers are forbidden in the ICU. No spores, no ants or earwigs, no pollen—which means no summery pungence, no visual joy. My father's roses are the old-fashioned kind that resemble cabbages, infinitely petaled, earthy and elegant as the mistresses of kings. These pink ones, I suspect, are more like Vegas bimbos—callow, chilled beyond fragrance—but all the same, seeing them makes me long for grass and sky, for sun on my skin.

The drama king comes straight to the window and cups his free hand to block the reflections and search for someone—mother? grandmother? fiancée? . . . Right Side of Beacon Hill fiancée. I look around at my neighbors. Of the patients I can see—those without masks or tents—no one appears even potentially glamorous enough to merit this botanical fanfare.

Now he beams and waves. If I didn't know any better, I'd say he was waving at me. Just then, my sister shows up. She looks around and then actually goes up to the guy and taps him on the shoulder. They shake hands, smiling like old friends. Side by side, they wave in unison. I wave back.

~⌒

In the cattle business, they call Jerry the Fertility Wizard. In a single liai-son, he can coax more eggs from your prize cow than there are loan sharks in Providence. I wouldn't take Mel Gibson's income to put my arm where he routinely puts his, but he does it with such concentration and dignity that, to look at his face, you'd think he was a pastry chef at the White House.

In March I flew with him to Milwaukee and watched him harvest eggs from a Holstein cow who milks the world record. One of her test-tube calves costs more than a brand-new sports car.

We checked into the best hotel overlooking Lake Michigan. We had lunch with a handful of dairy hotshots, big sweaty guys who love their bourbon and steak followed by ice cream in flavors out of a time warp (black raspberry, butter pecan, peppermint stick). I would have been happy to play Miss Ornamental, but Jerry wanted me there as Ms. Accomplished. A woman doing what I do would be, in that circle, a cap-tivating eccentric. Maybe he figured a little extra brainy hauteur would scare these guys off from questioning his fees. From the way their eyes traveled, though, I think they took me for a Sea World Suzy Cream Cheese, the girl in a wet bikini who tosses the Frisbees.

We went back to our room after lunch and kept ourselves naked and busy. We drank two bottles of champagne, then lay back and watched the six o'clock news, Jerry's head on my ribs, his rough hair pricking my belly. When they flashed the picture of a missing schoolgirl, he said, "The worst thing that could possibly happen to you. To a parent."

"And if you're not, what's the worst thing then?" I said.

"That you'd be conscious of? AIDS. Watching helplessly while your body's colonized by a kamikaze virus. Or genocide. Watching your fam-ily get slaughtered by your neighbors."

"What a nice imagination you have. But what do you mean, 'conscious of'? What's the biggest tragedy you *wouldn't* be conscious of?"

"Letting life pass you by. Living like a starfish, clinging to your one unchanging colorless rock."

"Don't scare me."

"But you wouldn't. *We* wouldn't." With his neck pulled up short on my belly, his laugh came out a contemptuous snort.

"Well, aren't we superior. Living our lives like the glorious vertebrates we are." On TV, another borrowed snapshot: a fireman, younger than I am, killed in the line of duty.

"But some people," said Jerry, "say life passes you by if you don't have children. Having children *is* life. Being a parent."

"Is that what you want?"

He tilted his head back to see my upside-down face. "A few years from now. Sure." Unspoken was a clear *And you?*

Was this a potential invitation? An early appraisal, like the first vetting on a thoroughbred? I looked at the TV. I didn't say, *Not on your life* or *Scares the bejesus out of me.* I said, "Guess I've yet to meet a gene pool worthy of mine."

He laughed. "Or you're afraid of your animal self. That's the danger of living too close to the beasts. When the idea seems repulsive to me, the idea of kids, that's what I suspect. Like, all this education, all this cerebral honing, and I'm going to what? Fritter away my time sniffing small butts? Aiming spoonfuls of mush at drooling mouths? But even more, I think, will I let myself knuckle under to my instincts, with no more control than my ancestors down in Olduvai Gorge?"

"Victim of your own biology," I said, relieved. I frisked his hair.

"But, *but.*" He twisted around and sat cross-legged, looking at me. "I'll always be a Catholic, at root."

My turn to laugh. "Doesn't mean you have to reproduce like one."

"I want a wild and freewheeling life, a life of pick up and go," he said. "I believe anything can happen; there's no individual ration of good and bad. But I can't lose sight of God's purpose—it's sort of there all the time, just outside my peripheral vision. Embracing us everywhere, a grand invisible womb." I listened to his voice slide away. I let that be the end of it, and so did he. He straddled my thighs and began to massage them, smiling.

I wanted him too much to laugh at the notion of a grand womb (why did I see a circus tent?). Before we let go again, I made him promise we'd drive to Chicago for dinner and dancing. Then I said, "Prove you want it wild." Four hours later, we stood at the top of the Sears Tower, the image of my sequined dress, bought just for this trip, confounding the lights of the city. We talked about Africa, and I remember not saying *Take me with you* but teasing him instead, singing "Born Free" to the lasso of shoreline below us. Even his ambitions made me jealous when I saw how tightly they held him.

The drama king is the first to reach my bed. "Honeybee, they confiscated your flowers!" He saves me the difficulty of a reply when he kisses me, long and tender, on my mouth. I gasp, not just at the shock of being kissed like that by a stranger but because I've grown so used to Jerry's beard, its prickle and rasp against my mouth. I feel like I've just been kissed by a Victoria's Secret model.

Behind the guy who kissed me, Louisa gloats like a yenta, and behind her, Dr. Athanassiou makes his typically fragrant entrance. Dr. A. (which is what the other doctors and nurses call him) smells like what I imagine backyards must smell like in Greece, like plants that are green but frugal and thorny, thirst-proof succulents. Ordinarily, I find perfumed men repulsive, just as, ordinarily, I find doctors tedious. To both rules, this man is an exception. Yesterday he came to see me three times. Whenever he arrives, he stands very still for a moment at the edge of my curtain, an unspoken request for permission to enter. He never barges in or bustles around. He's no Dr. Slocum. He asks me strange and amusing questions, like "Can you name for me the capital of France?" "The vice president of your country?" "Your favorite fruit?" "Do you habitually wear pyjamas?" "How many first cousins have you, maternal and paternal respectively?" My favorite so far: "What is chivalry?" He has a regal posture, a thicket of a black mustache, slightly salted, and an accent that I like to imagine comes from Athens by way of upper-crust Nairobi or somewhere equally dashing. He makes me feel like the winning guest on a game show. I don't think I've flubbed an answer yet—but he's still being cautious. Otherwise, he'd have released me to the upstairs world of flowers and phones. And there's the gash under the bandage on the back of my head. When I asked him how much they shaved, he frowned at me and said, "Would not a touch of baldness be but a trivial price for your life?"

The first thing he does today is wheel my bed around, so once again I'm looking out the window at the parking lot. "I prefer that patients face the light," he says.

After I introduce him to Louisa, the drama king grabs his hand. "Larney Poole. I'm the one who got her into this pickle, I fear." Pickle? Is this guy related to the Dr. Slocum of *copacetic* and *noggin?*

Dr. A. pats him on the shoulder and says, "I am quite sure your young woman does not believe sailing is checkers."

We chuckle politely.

He turns to me and says, "It is what day today?"

Thursday, I tell him.

"Who are your visitors today? Tell me of your companions here."

I try to draw out a speech on Louisa—how she lives in New York, she's four years older, she's an art critic at a magazine, her husband is a guy named Hugh who teaches American history at a prep school. . . .

Dr. A. interrupts graciously. "And this young man?"

"Barney," I say quickly, pleased that I've remembered his name. "He tried to bring me roses, but roses are taboo. Well, I guess you know that." I crane my neck, which hurts like hell, but I need to see the waiting-room window. Still no Jerry. Instead, Mom. She waves a shopping bag in the air and grins. She'll have to wait for someone to leave, since Gwen never bends the two-guests-only rule. "And hey, there's our mom." I point.

I can't tell what Dr. A. is thinking. His tone is always so calm and professional. He says, "We know that you do not remember the accident which placed you here. This is not unusual." He explains to Louisa and Barney what he has already told me. "The memory is not there to retrieve because it was never encoded in the primary instance. The trauma of the moment precluded any recording of events as they had come to pass. The tape, you may say, is not erased but blank. However, your actual memory loss of the entire preceding month—that you believe we are still in the month of June—this is of greater concern. . . . Possibly it is a vestige of shock or of oxygen deprivation." He turns back to me. "But if this young man was a vector in the accident, it is to my great curiosity whether you remember *him*."

I take a good look at my admirer. The passion that gleams from every microscopic pore in his patrician face is way beyond flattering; anyone could see it's been requited. Other than his madras bow tie, I guess I could see myself not turning him down. He is Newport handsome, with eyes not Jerry's wild-yonder blue but the earnest blue of Lake Michigan as seen from that Milwaukee suite. My heart sinks; he is the inverse of Jerry. He is rebound material par excellence.

"You don't, honeybee, do you?" he says. "Remember me." He looks more amused than offended, even touched.

"I don't. I'm sorry, but I don't know you from Adam."

I wait for him to look wounded or angry. But his expression remains bright, and then he actually laughs. As if I've just confessed undying love. He comes over and kisses me again, this time on the hand snagged by the IV. "Then you'll be my Eve. I'll have to convince you what a fine time we've been having, win you all over again. What a challenge—what a pleasure!"

Louisa says she has to make a phone call. Dr. A.'s beeper goes off. He says he has grand rounds but will return after lunch. This leaves me alone with the stranger who thinks he's my boyfriend. Or the boyfriend I've mistaken for a stranger.

"Barney, I'm sorry, but who *are* you?"

"Larney," he says. "I'm the guy who was lucky enough to offer you a ride before the rest of the world had a chance."

I am trying to frame a question to this alarming statement when Mom joins us.

"Hello there, you dapper young man."

"Hi, May." He kisses her on the cheek.

"Did my daughter dent your uncle's boat? Clement's made of tougher steel than the hull of the *Intrepid*. Don't you mess with her."

"Mom, I'm right here. In case you hadn't noticed."

She reaches into her shopping bag. "Yes you are, sweetheart, and we have never been so grateful to know it, believe you me." Mom wears large gold fox heads on her ears and a scarlet knit dress that few women her age could pull off. She'd never dream of a face-lift or color her silver hair, but years of posting in a saddle have preserved her tight hips and legs.

She sets on the chair a racehorse mystery by Dick Francis and a hot-off-the-presses book about the *Exxon Valdez* disaster. "But wait till you see this," she says triumphantly. She plunks a book on my lap called *Why the Reckless Survive*. "I was relieved to see someone thinks that they do! A scientist, no less." She points to the Ph.D. after the author's name.

Larney laughs. He seems to laugh as readily as most people blink.

Mom points back at the shopping bag. "Bananas and grapes, clean undies, Jergens lotion. Am I a good mother?"

"Yes, but you're making me nervous rushing around. Sit."

"That's because I'm temporary." In her maddeningly androcentric way, she addresses herself to the man in the room. "I'm going to wash the grapes, and then I'm leaving you two alone and heading off for lunch at the Chilton Club. I talk too loud for the place, but they'll just have to squirm their way through it. I give the maître d' a naughty thrill. He loves me. He's from Duluth; we talk about the Vikings between courses."

After she leaves, Larney puts the books back in the bag and pulls the chair to the bed. He leans an elbow against my hip. "I'm not going to take advantage of your forgetfulness. I know I'm just a vacation in Bermuda. I know about your animal self. I know about the sperm king. But we were having a fabulous time. You'll have to take my word on that."

"What *about* my animal self?" (Though I want to ask, "What *about* the sperm king?")

"How you're giving in to it, letting it rule; those were your words."

I sigh. Would he mind just telling me how we met? He attacks the task with pleasure. I was hitchhiking south of Boston. The sun was setting. When I got into his car, he could tell I was very upset: heartbroken, angry, or both. When I told him where I was headed—to my parents', God knows why—he said his destination was just ten minutes from there. He got me to talk about my policy work on conserving seals in the Northwest and convinced me to go to a cocktail party the next night (at the home of his uncle, skipper of the fateful boat). I showed up at the party in what Larney describes as a Minuteman missile of a sequined dress, a dress intended, in his opinion, for tearing off. I agreed to go home with him if he understood one thing. "You said, I remember exactly, 'I'm in the market for a little amnesia.' "

"Well hey, if I'm in the 'Be careful what you wish for' sweepstakes, I just won. So, did you tear it off—my dress?"

He closes his eyes. "I came close. I pictured all those popped sequins like shooting stars. But no."

"Thank you. That dress is one thing I do remember. I got a third Visa card to buy it." It was the dress I'd bought for my Ms. Accomplished weekend with Jerry. We laugh together as Larney holds the hand that emerges from my sling. He is smitten, and I know a good drug when I see it. The pleasure is surprisingly real.

"May I take you wherever you're going, whenever they let you out?" he says. Because he sounds as if he's sure I'll say no, I tell him of course.

"What do you drive?" I ask, because cars so readily seduce me. Maybe I will remember his car.

"A blue SL convertible. You liked how it matched your dress. You told me what you needed right then was an expensive car and, if possible, a large cock. Again, I quote you verbatim. I'm nothing if not honest. You told me honest was just what the doctor ordered. You took my breath away."

This is making me feel ill, but I press on. "One more question. This is important. Do I have a job yet?"

"No," he says, "but you're closing in on a good one, and damn it, it's going to take you miles from me, way the hell out to the Rocky Mountains."

This is when Louisa returns. Larney says he's sorry but he has to get back to "the firm." (Law or brokerage, I assume, though his fanciful image of flying sequins makes me think interior design. He's too sweet to be a lawyer.)

Louisa's mood has cooled; she seems agitated, impatient, no longer my willing slave. She picks up one of the books and pages through it. She doesn't sit down.

"Don't stay if you need to get back home," I say. "I'm not going to be a vegetable."

She snaps the book shut. "I'm sorry."

"Sorry for what?" Looking at her in profile, I notice (not meaning to, not out of spite) that her chin is beginning to sag, just barely. The four years between us once seemed like an eon. Now the gap feels uncomfortably slim.

"Sorry, but yes, I have to go back tonight. Sorry I'm so spacey. It's just . . . a hospital's not the most festive place to hang out." As if she's sensed my scrutiny, she unclips her hair, letting it fall around her face.

"Lou—did you ever talk to Jerry?"

"I spoke to someone named Sheryl and left a message. I'll try again if you want."

"At his house? This . . . Sheryl?"

"I called the number you gave me."

"Did she know me?"

Louisa looks unambivalently irritated now. "She wasn't extremely friendly. I assumed she would pass on the message. I said it was urgent."

The neighbor who feeds Coleslaw? I'm leafing through the women I remember in his life.

"So," Louisa says abruptly, "how many do you have in mothballs?"

"How many what?"

"Men."

I'm about to ask why she's picking a fight when suddenly I get it. Her nervous comings and goings? Nausea. Her instinct for combat? Hormones. Now she's saying—in a kind of hiss, because we have to keep our voices down—"What I can't believe is this guy Larney—this, in case you hadn't noticed, outgoing, funny, gorgeous guy—how he doesn't *mind* about . . . what did he call him? 'The sperm czar'? Who I assume has got to be this Jerry I'm chasing down. Last I heard, you were still talking to Luke, still on the fence about Zip—whom I liked, you know, despite all his talk about inner power and yin food. . . ."

I wait to be sure she's wound down. "Last I checked, 'talking' and 'on the fence' aren't fucking."

"Did I say anything about fucking? I don't care if you're fucking them all. I'd just love to know how you keep them in tow."

"Louisa, we're not all blissfully married like you." I don't mean to insult her, but the look on her face tells me plainly that I did.

Gwen pokes her head in. "Ten minutes, you two."

The minute Gwen's gone, I say, "Lou, are you having a baby?"

I do a lot of reckless things, my mother is right, but I don't hitchhike (mainly because it's so boring and inefficient). If I was in fact hitching a ride—close to dark, on a highway—and if I looked heartbroken, angry, or both, I dread to think what it means. Years ago, in the rain, I hitched away from my very last breakup with Luke. He was devastated; I walked out like a guy, like a cad. No one will ever watch me weep from a broken heart. At my worst moments, I wonder if I know what a broken heart is— or a heart before it's broken. Maybe broken is all I know.

When we were little, I was sick all the time. Not sick in bed or withering away, but I had a lot of violent allergies, as if life were constant provocation, my body itching for a fight. So I got just about all the attention, deserved or not. Anxious, most of it. The anxious devotion of my mother. Which grew, eventually, into proprietary devotion, because I liked the same things she liked: horses, dogs, working up a good sweat. Later, holding the fascination of men. People talk about "matches" between parents and children, the luck of the cosmic draw. Mom and I are a pretty good match.

One year at our annual Fourth of July cookout (I was in high school, Louisa in college), Mom was telling a bunch of our neighbors how I'd broken into the town pool. (I was still wearing that tea strainer over my eye.) She'd had a decent amount of gin, and her voice carried across the lawn: "When I answered my front door and saw Officer Graves, his ground-chuck nose on the other side of that screen, I remember thinking, Oh my God, my darling baby, my favorite child—don't tell me what I can't bear to hear, you son of a bitch! I would have ripped the man's tonsils out with my bare hands, believe you me, if the words I feared had come out of his mouth."

I looked myopically up from wherever I was in the crowd and happened to see Louisa's face, wherever she was. Completely tuned in to our mother's words, she was staring me down, the look on her face triumphantly sour. She'd always said I was our mother's favorite, and I would deny what I knew to be true, because until then she never had proof. *Here it is at last,* said her look, what she'd been waiting for: justification she could bank against any future family injustice. Funny, though, how then we were free to be friends—carefully, but still. It was like the end of a game of musical chairs: over, all that wondering who'd get the seat; win or lose, the same relief.

Louisa's still angry, but I've made a dent, because she laughs for about ten seconds. "Oh, I am anything but having a baby."

"Well you are *something.* I don't know what, but something."

She hides her face again. "Something. Yes, I am something."

I wait. "Well?"

"Clem, can I ask you a question?" She looks serious. "Do our lives, I mean ours in particular, revolve around men?"

"Pardon my intrusion."

Louisa and I look over, startled. It's Dr. A. "I had meant to observe the back of your head, Miss Jardine. Then I will entrust you again to your sister."

As he snips gently at the bandage, he asks me random questions. His smell is so overwhelming, so lovely, that it takes me nearly a minute to recall how many playing cards there are in a deck, sides to a stop sign, states in the Union. His fingers touch my bare scalp. I tell him Tangier is a city or maybe a country, tangelo a fruit, tangent a geometric divergence. When he leaves, I say to Louisa, "What does that man smell like? It's beautiful."

"That's vetiver," says Louisa. "It's nice, you're right."

Gwen pulls back my curtain. She taps her watch. "Time, girls."

Larney's roses await me. They are nicer than I thought—pungent and meaty, flowers of pedigree and substance. The card reads, *With profound apologies & unswervingly tropical affections, Yours and yours only, L.* At the top, a deft slash through J. LARNED QUINCY POOLE, indigo on ivory.

Thanks to Dr. Slocum, I have a private room at dormitory cost. After two sessions of dramatic pleading, the day nurse finally agreed to turn off the fluorescent light that runs like a racing stripe around the upper walls. So the light in my room is now sun, which swells and fades as the clouds come and go, the way a pupil widens and constricts. In a week, it's the closest I've come to open air, which I desperately crave. I nap erratically, black holes of dreamless sleep that quench like rationed swigs of cold spring water. Each time I wake, my head aches with the labor of healing.

Dad is my first visitor here, exhausted from hurricane vigil. For half of every summer, hurricanes are to my father what national economists are to CEOs: whispering *Disaster, disaster* right in your ear, then half the time saying *No, sorry, just joshing!*

It's the first time I've seen him since coming to, but Dr. Slocum tells me he was here on the second day of my delirium. Between tests, he sat by my gurney while Mom paced and cursed and bargained with my absent self. Now he carries a rose—a Mrs. Anthony Waterer—red as a cherry sno-cone. He loves reciting the names of his roses, most of them Baroness This, Comtesse That, Principessa Hooha. He carries my rose in a mason jar with a punctured lid, which he will have packed in a picnic cooler to keep it fresh for the two-hour drive.

It's Dad who tells me exactly what happened, and the story seems to give a purpose to his presence that makes him less uncomfortable in mine.

The uncle had a crew member cancel before an important race, and Larney recruited me. Entering the last leg, a strong wind at our stern, we were neck and neck with another boat to port. When their bow began to veer toward ours, the skipper panicked: He tacked before us when we had the right of way. I was on the foredeck, raising the spinnaker, which unfurled against my face and snapped in the wind like gunfire, leaving me blind and deaf to all warnings. When the two boats collided and our bow rode up over theirs, I was smacked in the chest by their boom and hurled backward into the water. As I went in, the jib sheet snared my right arm, snapping the ulna; then my head slammed against the side of our boat. Larney dove in and passed me up to the other crew members. Somebody radioed for an ambulance. The paramedics, en route to the nearest ER, called in the medevac from Boston.

Though Dad inhabits the sailing world and lives a life many would kill for, in his dreams he's just the plantsman he was schooled to be, pruning vines, cataloging spores, protecting fragile blooms from extinction. This old longing gives him a professorial tone when he tells tales, not the blow-me-down air of your average nautical windbag. As I eat my dinner, he reenacts methodically the way in which his youngest daughter almost died.

"But here you are, safe," he says at last. His tone is so reverent, it makes me nervous.

"After a fashion!" I say, to lighten him up, but he doesn't smile.

"I would like to impress upon you that your mother and I were terrified. Please realize, this is the third time our town police chief has materialized at our front door on your behalf. Clem, honey, it is my sincerest, most heartfelt wish that this time will have been the last. The very arrival of this man's car in our driveway again would do us in." He's still holding on to his flower, as if he's not sure I deserve it. Condensation from the jar drips onto the floor and one of his boat moccasins (a new pair).

"Dad, it's my wish, too," I say, but I have to suppress the urge to giggle at his solemnity. Apology is no more my style than gushing about grief, love, and mortality is his.

He kisses me on the cheek and sets Mrs. Waterer beside Larney's bouquet. He stops to finger one of the pink blooms, now fully open. "*Souvenir d'un ami.* Your young man is not undiscerning."

Before leaving, he reaches inside his jacket. "This looks important," he says. The envelope is addressed to me at Jerry's, forwarded in his scrawl to Rhode Island, and I wonder if Dad saw the irony: his daughter bashed up in an ICU while there's her name, *Clement Jardine,* typed on a clean white surface, placid as a stormless sea, *c/o Mr. Beau Jardine,* in whose care she has not been for some time. I'll bet it made him feel awful, that *c/o.* It makes me want to say something reassuring, but I fail again, because he is out the door, with a taut wave, before I can think of a thing.

The return address is Jackson, Wyoming, and the letter inside—from someone whose name means nothing to me, Department of Game and Fish—tells me that he and his colleagues were "more than impressed" by our meeting and hope I will, taking into account the funding constraints we discussed, accept a position as research biologist on the Interagency Grizzly Bear Study Team and move myself out west by September. I concentrate hard, but no bells go off, no boards light up, no fireworks fill that dense black sky. I have flown across the country, seen a place I've always yearned to see, landed myself an impressive if poorly paid job, and right now I can't remember a bit of it. I am not going to tell this to Dr. A. I can only hope dependable Larney will tell me about the sights I saw and, if I told him enough, about the people I more than impressed.

The sky matches Larney's roses when the nurse shows up to take my tray. I tell her not to turn on the lights just yet.

Jerry answers the phone, like he always does, "Heya."

"Hey yourself." My fingers burn on the receiver, as if I've just come inside from a bitter cold day. I trample right over the pause: "Just us lately comatose invalids here, don't mind us." I stare at my laid-up wrist, at the bruise seeping from under the cast. I apply what I know about healing to its spectrum of yellows and blues.

"I heard you're in the hospital. I'm sorry." This is the voice I've heard, deep and careful, when he's talking with difficult but wealthy clients.

" 'Sorry.' Ah." I look up; my room is nearly dark. When I switch on the reading lamp beside the bed, I switch on my reflection in the window. I'm a mess, except for the ivory satin pajamas that Larney brought when they let me out of purgatory. "Listen, Jerry, just tell me this. Back in, oh, late June, why would I have been hitchhiking outside Boston, madder than Croesus?"

He laughs briefly. "I think it's 'richer.' "

"What's richer?"

"Never mind." He says gently, almost playfully, "Are you drinking?"

"Jerry, I have amnesia. I'm in the hospital. Cocktails are not one of the amenities offered. So help me out here. The last thing I know, I'm maybe moving in with you. Then it's five weeks later, I'm at death's door in the ICU, and you are nowhere in sight."

"ICU . . . my God, the ICU—"

"As in, I see you dumped me when I wasn't looking. Yes?"

"Bad timing, Clem. I'm sorry. I don't know what else to say."

"Bad timing?"

"Your forgetting, I mean. This is . . ." He sighs loudly. "What a mess."

My reflection grows more and more insistent. A winking jet soars through my bedridden self.

"Would it be a good idea or not for me to come right out and beg you to tell me what happened? Did I make too big an ass of myself? Or do I just pretend, oh well, oops, a chapter got ripped from my book."

I get a second laugh from Jerry, still far from warm, but he tells me. Because he wants us to be friends. I glare at my reflection: Cold day in hell.

We were out to dinner in Boston, eating at a sidewalk table, when a panhandling gypsy offered to read my palm. Jerry had been waiting all week—a coward, he admits—to tell me about this woman he ran into, someone he knew in college. The gypsy gave him the only chance he saw. And you know what's weird? Unlike all the things about my lost month that I have to fish from other people, the encounter with the gypsy I reel back in, here and now, on my own. Like some archetype who's shown up in too many dreams, she wore the gold hoops, the garish peasant textiles, smelled too perfectly of garlic—the only glitch her local, car salesman accent. "A world explora" were her first words. "I see you in Africa, hon, I see you in Java, I see you with the Eskimos way up nawth. I see you everywaya." She didn't say how she could draw this travelogue from my cupped hand in hers, but I didn't mind.

"And love, love, love. Hon, I see a tapestry of love. Hahtbreak, flirtations, wild lee-ay-zones, marriage, the gamut." I smiled at Jerry when she said this. "See any offspring?" I asked, and I can imagine the goading edge to my voice. The gypsy shook her head. "Can't see it clearly, hon. A toss-up. But see heeya?" She twisted my hand toward the candle and jabbed my palm with a long sharp nail. "Middla the life line, a break." I leaned in, my hair mingling with hers. She was right. A miniature chasm, bisecting the line.

"What does it mean?"

She shrugged. "Could be a crisis, I nevva lie. A serious accident. Loss of a deeya one. Your house burnin' down. But see heeya, the line goes on? Resurrection. A second wind." She stood up and readjusted her shawl. "Time waits for no man. No woman neitha." Without a wave or a nod, as if the prophecies ticked like minutes off a meter and my dime had run out, she walked on down the street, turning the nearest corner.

"A big crisis? That's easy," I said to Jerry. "The day you leave me." The copper light from the candle made me happy, the way it flickered so fondly through his red beard. I was feeling romantic, smiling like a fool. I was a fool.

Jerry stared into the candle as well, but the glow it cast on his face did not illuminate a look of romance. "I'm sorry to be such an ass," he said, "but I've got to put this on hold."

"This? What do you mean by 'this'?"

"Us," he said sheepishly.

That's when he told me about the woman, and that's when I told him no one was putting me "on hold," like some alternative phone call. I don't remember that whole conversation (who'd want to?), but now, as he tells me his side of the story, I do remember the wildfire racing through my limbs as I fled down the sidewalk and, not long after, the even hotter rage when I discovered, clamoring through my purse in South Station, that the gypsy, that bitch, had lifted my wallet.

"So, is it back to California?" Dr. Slocum sits, as he does too often, on my bed. He visits at least twice a day, claims he's writing me up as a special case of retrograde amnesia. The thing is, he's stopped taking notes.

"Rhode Island for a little while. Till I get my head together." I touch my bandage. "So to speak."

He twiddles his stethoscope and nods. He shifts his weight toward me and clears his throat.

"Listen, don't do it," I say, as nicely as I can.

"Do what?"

"Ask me out to dinner, say you want to see me again, whatever. No matter what you have in mind, you'd be disappointed."

When he says nothing (what would he say?), I say, "Not good timing."

He stands. "Well. Say it like it is." He fingers his beeper, willing it to save his pride.

"You need a nap; go. I'm sorry to be such a jerk. I'll see you later." We both know I won't.

"Got everything you need?" he asks.

"Within reason."

"Sayonara," with a smirk, is how he tells me good-bye.

I turn on my TV. Out blazes a football montage, men colliding over and over. Everywhere, everywhere: men, men. I leave it on but mute. Football in July? I feel more disoriented than ever.

I jump when the phone rings. *Oh Jerry, change your mind* roars to the front of my brain like a projection onto a movie screen. But it's Louisa, calling from New York. She tells me, in a breathtaking rush, that not only is she not having a baby; she's fallen in love and doesn't know what to do. She wanted to tell me in person, but she chickened out. If you want advice, I tell her, take anyone's but mine.

"I *know* what your advice would be," she says. " 'Burn those bridges! Choose hellfire over tundra!' "

"I guess that's how well you know me. You think I like hearing this news."

"I'm sorry. This is selfish. I just need to tell someone . . . outside my life. Get it out of my head, to keep from going nuts, but somewhere safe."

She sees me as safe? This brings tears to my eyes.

"I trust you, Clem. Are you pissed?"

"Come on, Lou. I'm flattered. But Lou—what a mess." Isn't that what Jerry said? Then she does what I guess she intended to do from the start, no matter what my reaction. She tells me about the guy, eyelash by eyelash, cuticle by cuticle (a man every inch the animal her husband is not). Gutless, I listen. I wonder if the gypsy put a curse on me, too—just in case I canceled all three of my Visas.

"I think I'm moving out," she says.

"Oh no," I say. "Don't do that. That's crazy!"

"I have to!"

I take a deep breath. "I thought you wanted my advice."

I have to wait a few seconds before she says, "I thought I knew what you would tell me. I guess I was wrong. It's okay."

Everyone seems to know who I am, and what I think, but me. After Louisa hangs up, I think instantly of her husband. I feel more sorrow for him than I do for Louisa, which isn't right—not morally, but because I have no real bond with Hugh. Am I suddenly the queen of empathy? No. It's more that I need Louisa to be with this placid, loyal man. I needed

her to make that choice in the first place—and I need her now, though it's
none of my business, not to unmake it. *Please stay married and have that
baby*, I'm thinking. *Please have several.* I wish I could blame all this crazi-
ness on drugs, yet my head, however sore, is clearer than I want to admit.

Dr. A. examines me one last time. When he comes in, I am as thrilled to
see him as if this were a date—even though, after so many meetings, he's
still immune to chat. "Miss Jardine," he greets me. "I know you are
expectant to depart, but will you please take your seat on the bed?"

His hands close around the back of my skull as usual. As usual, I'm
surprised how little I resent the confinement. The heels of his hands,
resting on my cheekbones, smell as green as ever, but today a little less
arid, as if they've come straight from pruning young trees. Ah, horticulture. Perhaps that explains why I'm charmed by this fusty man who I'm
guessing drives a dog-eared Civic and, come winter, wears wool socks in
bed to console his Mediterranean feet. It's Freudian after all.

He asks me to define *archipelago, estuary, fjord.* Piece of cake. Then he
asks for the names of the oceans and the Great Lakes. I leave out Ontario.
"Listen, doctor, you'll never discharge anyone with tests like this," I say.
"Schools over here haven't taught geography in years."

He jots on his clipboard. "Dr. Slocum has told me you are a scholar
of the water." He rips off a form and hands it to me. "Your father, how
is he?"

"Dad? Dad's fine. You met Dad?"

"Oh, you will not remember, of course," he says. "The day he was here
with you—a long day—he was massaging your feet while we attended to
your head. At one moment, I was resolute that he thought you were to
die. I could not say otherwise, though I felt your case to be hopeful.
Before he drove that long way home, I asked him to languish in my office
and take a little drink. He told me you were so very small when you were
born. He said it was the first time he ever prayed since he himself was a
child. This day, he said, was the second. He said prayer is—I remember

exactly—pointless but indispensable. The membrane of sanity. I told him that a doctor would be obliged to agree. It made a strike upon me." He taps his head with a finger. He gives me one of his rare smiles. "You will please thank him for the beneficent roses."

I wait for him to go on, but he looks at his watch and hands me his card. He says that if I have any unusual headaches, I am please to call. Without hesitancy. His first name, which did not fit on his badge, is Anastasias. Anastasias Athanassiou. *Live forever:* that's what his last name means, according to Dr. Slocum.

Larney has brought me a silk scarf to wrap my patchy head in, a dowdy yet sumptuous thing printed with sailor's knots. Probably his mother's. It looks silly with the jeans and Peter Tosh T-shirt he's fetched from my parents' house, but I am too touched to refuse. In the parking lot, I get a few stares.

He helps me into his car. "You are something, honeybee, you are a tough one," he says when he gets in beside me. (You might wonder how it is that I let him go on using his silly endearment. I let him because it's true. Yes I carry sweet stuff, but yes I wander far afield, and yes I sting.)

I smile. Am I something? What is that something? Why does everyone insist all the time on my toughness? How blind can they be? I take one of the inventories that have become second nature in the past week: I am confused, weary, ashamed of things I will never recall, but I am glad to feel the sun, then glad to be riding in a fast expensive car, top down, along a shining river. Though ultimately I will be in no one's care but my own, and that's just as well, today I find myself c/o J. Larned Quincy Poole and glad about that, too.

After a mile or so, I say, "Larney, what does the *J* stand for?"

"Jephthah. A great-great-grandfather. Name like a mouthful of gauze."

"Well, Jephthah, you are one charming guy. You know what? In the hospital, I got asked the definition of *chivalry*—long story. But it's you:

you're the definition. And I have a feeling you saved my life." I can tell he knows my honest praise is the beginning of a respectful letdown, fair and square. It's my way of saying that he's made, as Dr. A. would put it, a strike upon me.

When we turn south, he reaches across the rearview mirror and lowers the visor, to shield me from the sun. After I thank him, he says, "You're welcome," both reflexively and with a bottomless heart. I pretend that dust has blown in my eyes.

He says, "If you're tired, just sleep. Please."

At the touch of a chrome toggle, my seat swoons slowly back. How sweet such tiny empirical pleasures feel at a moment like this. As I turn on my good side to search for a semblance of comfort, my cheek soothed by the warm leather, I see on the backseat a blue plastic bag labeled PERSONAL BELONGINGS. It contains, I imagine, nothing I owned before the accident: just the books, underwear, and lotion my mother bought me; the satin pajamas from Larney, now flecked with coffee and saline. Stowed there as well are my sister's secret longing, my father's fears, and this stranger's curious devotion, so worthy it pains me. I close my eyes and relabel the bag THINGS ENTRUSTED TO ME . . . WE WILL SEE HOW WISELY. Then I'm off, scholar of the water winging toward a lofty, land-locked retreat.

Coat of Many Colors

FEBRUARY 1993

My machine has a name. Right up there on his brow, flashy chrome on T-bird turquoise, as if he were some kind of potentate: Theratek 9. I've dreamed up nicknames, to make our appointments feel like liaisons. On good days I call him Nine, Lucky Nine, Big Blue. When we're alone together in his underground vault, I lie beneath his single square unblinking eye, my reflection submerged in his gaze, and I tease him: *Hey Nine, what time do you get off? Do you get off, big man? Don't you crave the sunshine, the trees, the open sky? Haven't you earned at least a window, Lucky, a view of the park?*

He's the still-waters type, so I don't expect answers.

On bleak days I think of him as Thanatek, death to fend off death. I don't speak to him then. I submit, paralyzed, sometimes forgetting to breathe. A rabbit under a hedge, crisscrossed by the shadow of a spiraling hawk.

And then there are days when his rapt presence transcends the mechanism, when all its rude, ragged noises fade away. He becomes a titanic blue swan, and when the lights go out and he arcs his musclebound neck over and around me, I close my eyes and surrender, ripe as a jet-age Leda.

Be good to yourself. Take it easy. Savor small moments of joy. People are full of advice. If I had my choice, easy is definitely how I would take it. I would wear a deep groove from my apartment to my office to the hospital, then back home. A simple triangular path, no detours. But life must do what it does—go on—so today, between lunch and radiation, I take the subway to Queens to interview Esteban for the "New Talent" issue. This is our annual fanfare, photo finish to one more season in the art world. As one of my colleagues likes to say, we spend the entire winter mowing down swaths of ambition, naïve and bitter alike. Preston, our publisher, calls them the hatchlings, those two dozen souls lucky enough to make the last cut. Ray, the man I live with, called them lambs to the slaughter, loudly declaring how happy he is not to have pursued a career in the arts, how arbitrary success can be. This is funny, since he works in a business that considers itself very much an art, and it's one where success is decidedly skewed: the movies. "Yes, but I am not an artist," said Ray. "I'm a grunt. I just follow directions." Ray is a stuntman.

Of the artists who made it this year, I am proud to claim Esteban as mine: my discovery, my favorite, my (though I wouldn't say this out loud to anyone) protégé. I will write about other artists I admire, but Esteban is the one I'd stick out my neck for. He is not like most of those who make it through the gauntlet; most of these artists, however gifted they are at the work they make, have to be even more gifted at self-promotion. In this cosmos, it's true that if you cannot make yourself glow, you are doomed, but Esteban glows on his own, from the core of his being.

He lives behind the former loading dock of a onetime casket factory, his door a gate of ruffled steel. On the long walk from the subway, I scale several tall snowbanks, then plunge into gutters filled with puddles. The snowfall this year is relentless; we've outsnowed Montana, Utah, and parts of Alaska. We've had thirteen storms so far; the newly superstitious me hopes the count won't stop there.

By the time I ring Esteban's bell, my hair is slick with sweat, my boots choked with snow. I listen to the medieval clankings of half a dozen locks, hear him call out "Coming, coming, coming!" (in his Caribbean sing-song, *Combing combing combing!*). The gate clatters up, and Esteban, wearing a pressed saffron shirt and black jeans, opens his long arms to welcome me. I have met him only once before; his presence is something to bask in. He stands well over six feet, and his skin is the warm indigo brown of wet seals lazing in the sun. He gestures incessantly and has a habit of giggling every so often, a habit endearing in someone so large. If my life were not so tangled already, I'd have to fall in love. Esteban is Haitian, forty years old, and has driven a taxi for the last twelve. Hard to think of him as a hatchling.

"*Salut! Salut!* My secrets are now to be bared!"

Another thing I love: his unfashionable zeal.

"Enter, enter." He touches my back, steering me gently into a huge windowless space—an acre of garage transformed into an equatorial refuge. The ceiling is high, and in the center a cluster of thrift-shop sofas and armchairs are draped in African fabrics. Bright rugs are strewn like flags across the concrete, a woodstove roars softly, and four rubber trees, taller than Esteban, stretch toward blue lamps. In a cage, two lovebirds twitter and fuss.

"What a sanctuary."

"Muriel," he says with feeling as he pours hot water into a teapot. In French, *Mooreeyell,* it sounds like the name of a tropical storm. "My wife, *she* is the talent of the house. Talent at life, at how to *be.*"

He holds out a plate of chocolate cookies. When I reach to take one, a cunning pain flees from my left shoulder toward my heart. They come and go quickly, these jolts; I'm down to four or five a day. My surgeon says they're a natural part of the healing—nerves recharging under the scar—but each time, it feels like a piano wire has snapped in my chest.

I bite into the cookie with exaggerated relish. "Just what the doctor ordered," I say.

I sit on one of the soft, happy sofas and take a tape recorder and a pair of shoes out of my bag. When I pull off my boots, there's a high-water mark midway up my shins. Esteban insists I borrow a pair of Muriel's socks, that I take off my tights and hang them near the stove to dry. He puts my coat on a hanger and smooths away creases in the dampened wool.

He takes me through a door into another wide space, this one under skylights. His constructions fill the room, upstaging even Esteban.

Some sculptors forge and weld steel. Others find their alchemy in oil drums, feathers, rubber gloves, eviscerated computers. Whenever I think I've seen everything, someone surprises me. Like Esteban, who knits. With a pair of large wooden needles, he knits rope, baling twine, phone cord, fishing line, even vines of red sinewy licorice, into garments for some Leviathan race. In his studio, several are pinned to the wall or slump like drunks in a corner. I stand for a long time in front of *Emperor*— the first piece of Esteban's I saw. A coat as long as a bus, short in front, swallow-tailed in back, lies on the floor between two sheets of Plexiglas. Made of woven Mylar tape, the coat emits a crystalline sparkle, like a chandelier, and even without buttons or pockets or medals, it's as crisp and commanding as a uniform. It reminds me of the saintly effigies, in glass coffins, carried in Catholic processions.

I turn on my recorder. Why does Esteban knit?

He shrugs. "I just do. You write, I knit. People talk of domestic things, women's things. . . . What am I saying about their world? Am I not an impostor, a man stealing from a woman's language? But"—he giggles— "I like using my hands this way. I just do." His long legs wound through the rungs of a stool, he works while we talk, his speed unnerving. The needles ticker away, his pink fingernails like flashing petals. "In the taxi, I knit at the stoplights. I carry what I work on in a big garbage bag next to me in front. I knit in line at the airport. I knit for characters of history, I knit for imaginary characters I knew as a boy. I knit, Muriel says, to draft a private army." *Neet. Beeg. Eemageenary.* His accent has a sweet keening quality. As he talks, his hands never pause in their dance.

Blue needs cool. Blue needs space.

I think of hospitals as wasteful yet frugal places, disgorging monadnocks of garbage yet guarding every inch of floor space from frivolous use. But the room I visit each day is large: surrounding Blue is a respectful stretch of linoleum. And it's cold. If it were summer, perhaps I wouldn't mind, but I do. The first time, I told Patrice, the technician who helps me into my mummyish mold, that I was afraid I couldn't hold still because I might shiver. She patted the arm on my good side (her hand, like the room, pristine and chilly). "Sorry, hon, computers love that cool. Goosebump City, I know, but we get you through fast as we can." Patrice is slim and blond with a boy's haircut: Mary Martin as Peter Pan.

If Patrice is the handmaiden here, Juan is the high priest. After she positions me and leaves the room, Juan punches the buttons and twists the dials, inches from my face. I know the pores of his clammy, razor-nicked throat all too well. I know that though his hair is honestly black, his beard would emerge the color of scuffed ice, a bald patch along his left jaw. I know that the crucifix which sometimes brushes my cheek was made in the Czech Republic. It feels indecent, almost adulterous, to see all these details, but that's how it is.

Once Juan gets things just right, "Gantry's sixty-four!" he calls out, to no one I can see. Whatever this gantry is, it never wavers: it's always sixty-four. Each time I hear this curious mantra, an irrelevant Elmer Gantry swims across my inner screen (Burt Lancaster's face, about as handsome to me as a pot roast). Music seeps through the walls—murky retakes of Frank Sinatra, Eric Clapton, Tina Turner. One day, it dawns on me that I am hearing the Talking Heads as Muzak. To hold still, I have to resist laughter.

Nine, I say to my sober consort, *now I've heard everything.*

Above me, the ceiling's been cheerfully muralized. No slapdash job, no pizza-parlor view of Amalfi. Someone paid for a painter quite skilled at fooling the eye. Someone imagined that this view—a robin's-egg sky teeming with clouds, a sky that trills, *Life is a show tune! Dance and rejoice!*—will take your mind off the sensation that, laid out on this cold steel slab, you're already in the morgue.

Though sometimes, strapped down as I am, laser crosshairs tattooing my chest, I feel strangely secure. Secure, perhaps, the way an astronaut feels once she's readied for flight.

Count me down, Lucky, then blast me off hard.

My slot is at four o'clock, when the real sky, a frail yellow, still clings to light. By the time I leave the hospital, the sky is dark (that crisp porcelain violet of winter), and the subway overflows with people and impatience. I rarely find a seat, and if I do, there's no room to read; puffy coats and shopping bags lurch across laps whenever the train hits a curve. On the way home today, I try to think only of Esteban. Before I left his studio, he told me he's finishing his first masterpiece. A perfectly serious joke. He wouldn't let me see it because it was so new, still in need of protection. It stood in a corner, a ten-foot cone cloaked in tarps. "But soon," he assured me.

Standing, pressed between two trench coats, I remember his hands, so huge, so agile. I imagine riding behind a knitting cabdriver in a traffic jam on the way to LaGuardia. The strangest things console me.

Ray reclines on our bed, where he's crushed all four pillows into a throne. His T-shirt is speckled with beer. The soles of his red socks are black as hot tar. He lowers the sports section. "Spring training, would you believe, and these jokers have yet to buy one decent pitcher."

"When they shine, you ignore them completely," I say. "You're only a fan when they're losing their shirts." I weasel myself between his legs. Gently, he maneuvers the newspaper over my head and reads across my right shoulder. This is a new ritual, one of many. We've lived together for two years, but my invisible disease has forced us back to a courtship (minus the breathless suspense).

As Ray turns the pages, I feel his rib cage shift, rolling me like a gentle tide. "Today go all right?"

"I went out to Queens and saw the guy who knits. The man is a mystic."

"I meant the hospital." He continues to scan the paper: hockey, basketball, Davis Cup tennis.

"I'm beginning to burn. I look a little bit like pepperoni."

"But it went all right. You feel okay," he persists, speaking slowly.

"Ray, I *feel* fine. I *feel* like there's nothing wrong."

My doctors caught the tumor early and small—so early that they caught it as a concept, not a symptom, the only evidence a fuzzy blip on film. (*Nipped in the bud,* they love to repeat, as if it were some renegade pansy.) But since I didn't know it was there to begin with, how can I believe it's gone? Around Ray, though, I try not to complain. I want him to admire and stroke my strength, like the gleam of a new car; then the strength will have to be real. *Something* will be real.

From behind, he rests his chin on my collarbone. He still holds the paper before me, but he's listening. To him, silence is never a threat. I'm not like that; I want to be asked and told, praised, cajoled, or bellowed at. Where there are words, there are definitions. Definitions help contain the chaos. Ray once said that the way I lean on language makes me fascinating but also makes me uptight, ties me in knots. I take people too literally, he says.

At work, I have a reputation for getting my way. It's no big deal; I'm not approving Third World loans at Bankers Trust. But I manage to do it, most of the time, without getting shrill or losing my temper. This morning, after a meeting in which I saved two sculptors from the editorial ax, Preston whispered, "What a little shark you are." Most days, I'd have taken this as the only sort of compliment my boss knows how to give. Today, I keep seeing myself as a bloated white beast with beady, unblinking eyes and fist-size teeth. A creature that never sleeps, never has dreams. And never, according to a book recently shoved in my face, gets cancer.

"Ray, do I ever remind you of a shark?"

"When your mother calls. When all the plates are in the sink and it's my fault. Which it always is. But right now? I wouldn't blame you if you felt like mauling nearly everyone around you." He does a typically bad imitation of the music from *Jaws.*

"A ruthless predator, that's me all right." I sigh. I'm remembering that when I was little, maybe eight, I obsessed about how everything ends up on the planet in its particular shape. Why wasn't I a dogwood tree, a flagstone, a squid? I'd never heard of karma; I was just this juvenile agnostic philosopher. I had no desire to be anything else, not at all. I felt lucky and safe being human. Suddenly I don't like it so much.

"Sometimes I wish we were animals," I say. "All we'd have to do is play and sleep, hunt and eat. Have lots of sex. Roll in the grass. No plans for the future. No existential fears. No arguments. No fateful decisions."

"Animals decide things. Sure they do."

"What—hope? Calculate? Weigh options and risks? No." I twist around to see Ray's face. "So, what would we be?"

"Be?"

"Animals, what kind of animals?"

"Skunks," he says decisively.

"Thanks, Ray."

"What would you prefer—giraffes? Gazelles? Girls always want to be thought of as graceful. But I like earthy. Skunks are the essence of earthy."

"Maybe skunks don't stink all the time," I say. "Maybe when they're alone together, they smell exotic, like incense. Like those bong shops on Bleecker."

Ray squints his features into a rooting grimace and digs his face in my neck, snorting until I'm laughing out of control. He pulls away but keeps me helplessly pinned. "Since when have you, Miss Priscilla Mullins, ever so much as peeked through the door of a headshop?"

We *are* animals. And I think that's a problem for Ray.

I'm thirty-six and have always wanted children, though not fanatically— not until Ray. But Ray doesn't share my certainty. "I'm no different from anyone else," he said two months ago, back in simpler times. "I'm sure I'd be marching around telling the world it's the experience of a lifetime. The thing is, I don't *need* the experience of a lifetime. I like my life the way it is."

"You're talking like someone who's afraid of risks," I said. "But you take risks—huge risks—for a living."

"Yes, and like a lot of people, I leave my work at work."

Those were the days when we had easy, abstract debates. Now, making a family is my second obsession, what I fear most I could lose—other than my life. When I bring it up, Ray is clever or silent, no middle ground. I'm beginning to wish we could just fight it out: you can't have a truce without war.

In the evenings now, we rarely go out. I read like an addict, and Ray watches TV or listens to jazz or tackles projects: building shelves, rearranging furniture. The more restless he feels, the noisier the project. He always has something going, something physical, because he's happiest when exerting himself. His latest plan is to build a kayak. A friend in Brooklyn offered his garage, about which I am not thrilled. Ray is absent often enough.

Ray works in sprints. All together, he spends three or four months a year out west but insists on New York as home. Not long ago, there was plenty of work in all those cop-buddy features they'd film in this city. (Ray's the one who vaults off a roof into a Dumpster, rolls across the hood of a speeding patrol car, tangles with three nasty punks in a dark fogbound alley.) But now they make movies like that in Toronto, Vancouver, Seattle, cold places desperate for stardom.

Ray fell into stunts by chance. In college, he studied illustration. He wanted to be a cartoonist, but there were loans to pay off. He had a friend with a friend; somebody ruptured a disk; this was L.A. So here he is, thirty-eight and still at it, nicked around the edges but hooked on how alive it makes him feel, on the open air, on the long indulgent spaces between lucrative sessions of beating himself black and blue. At parties, I've heard him say he still draws, but all I've seen are angular ramblings in the margins of our phone pad. His old cartoons, acerbically leftist, lie in a portfolio under our bed, with tumbleweeds of city dust and out-of-season shoes.

"What a fine healer you are! So little hardening, I am impressed!" Dr. Bloom fingers the scar gently but fervently, a blind man reading Walt Whitman in braille.

His compliments embarrass me. For one thing, I've got no control over what he's praising. So I gush, "It's you who did such a good job. It's so . . . minimalist. It's nothing, really." And I mean it, since the scar is just a two-inch lavender stroke, the slip of a pen, a tiny jet trail above my left nipple. The least of my worries.

My nose is nearly touching Dr. Bloom's bald head, which looks as if it's been buffed to match the sheen of his tasseled cordovan loafers. He's young for what he does, maybe forty—Esteban's age. Not tall, but handsome if only because he's so immaculate and gleaming with health.

Ray has a grab bag of names for my surgeon: Titmaim, Razorfest, Scalpelthrust. David Coppafeel. They come to me when Dr. Bloom stands over me like this, looking so inhumanly perfect, and keep me gratefully amused. But Ray's contempt makes me nervous.

Dr. Bloom turns his attention from the breast to me. "So now. Our next step. Your radiation is, let's see . . ." He looks at his clipboard.

"Tomorrow is three weeks."

"Halftime! Good for you!"

I return his smile, but all this flattery makes me suspicious.

He folds his arms. The starch in his white coat creaks faintly. "Chances are we've cured you already. Negative nodes—the best news of all! Statistics are on your side! But"—he hugs the clipboard—"we want to give you every percentage point possible. Your tumor . . ." He sits in a chair and goes on, with incisive gestures, to portray my personal tumor as if it were one of Ma Barker's sons. He skips the jargon I've already heard—*infiltrating, aneuploid, invasive*—and springs instead for words like *angry, unpredictable, insidious, wild*. My mind bustles about like a workaholic thesaurus and offers a few more: *lawless, capricious, malicious, mean*.

"Chemotherapy, right?"

Dr. Bloom smiles without blinking. Meeting his gaze, I remember how surprisingly beautiful his brown eyes looked above his surgical mask, right before I went under. "Maybe just a little," he says.

I've read how the drugs swim straight for the fastest-growing cells. Like sharks, they aren't picky, nor do they sleep. Eggs, the delectable ova that begin to stagnate in a body this old, are among their first prey. The caviar of chemo.

He rises briskly. "You're a smart young woman, Louisa, and you're in a good place. I have faith in you." He holds out his hand.

As always, I shake it and thank him. As always, he says, "My pleasure." He said this even after what I thanked him for was cutting me open and handing me the bad news. The way he put it was "I'm afraid it's a true cancer." In the first instant, I wondered idly if others were untrue, and would that be better or worse? Was it true as an arrow, meaning fatal; or true as a love, forgiving?

Next day I meet with two hatchlings. First Garrett, a painter of arctic landscapes, vast and cryptically dark. He lives in a sunny SoHo loft drenched with old money. Yes, Ad Reinhardt is a hero, so is Munch; but when I mention Frederic Church, he's insulted. I spend the rest of the hour failing to win back his trust. It will be hard not to write about his scorn. The man is clearly spoiled. Then I head east, to Rose on Avenue C. Rose is very thin, very earnest, very young, and dresses in apologetic browns. She retrieves X-rays from the trash of a nearby animal clinic: terriers and greyhounds, cats' skulls, a boa constrictor. On the film the animals' names stand out: Tabitha, Rocky, Bilbo Baggins. Rose covers her walls with grids of these skeletons, then over them, in a squirreled white script, writes stories of love gone wrong. Through the words you see rib cages, livers, spleens.

"I copied some stuff from an article on battered wives in *Cosmo*," she says. "I can't, like, get sued, can I?" I assure her she can't. I don't tell her that Helen Gurley Brown is unlikely to come across her work.

I'm late to the hospital. On the machine, I shiver from the sweat of rushing. It pools, a salty tickling burn, behind my ears. Like a bad pop song picked up from the audio feed in a drugstore, Helen Gurley Brown is stuck in my brain. I don't read her magazine, but I've seen her on talk shows, purring away in her bouffant wigs. I remember being told that her book *Having It All* was designed to open to the page where she tells you how to give the perfect blow job. How can I think these things while my body sponges up poison? Do I wonder, spitefully, why women like Mrs. Brown seem to live forever? Do I worry that I will never have *any* of it, never mind all, except maybe a plot of Rhode Island soil a mile down the road from my parents' house?

In a flash, Blue is a mortician. I hear myself whisper, *Don't you dare leave me powerless. Don't you dare bleed me dry.*

Juan shows up to do his part and, like clockwork, Burt Lancaster makes his appearance. *Burt, have you met Helen?*

The first person I called with the terrible news was my sister. She was in her lab, packing for a field trip. Clem is a biologist who studies bears in Wyoming. She preaches the ultimate indifference of nature and can't understand why people ever have children except to submit to their bullying genes. "Fuck," she said. "Oh fuck, Lou."

"Thanks for your apparent optimism."

"No, listen, wait. It's amazing what they can do now, but you have to let them do it all. Don't fall for that macrobiotic shit, the shark cartilage, the Chinese herbs. Go for the slash and burn. It's the best they've got right now." That's my sister, blunt as a nuclear warhead. "Fuck, Louisa. I'm saying all the wrong things."

"No. I need to hear you tell me they can do it. You're a scientist, you know about cells and mutations."

"Send me your path report. I have an old boyfriend at NCI."

"You have an old boyfriend everywhere, it's incredible."

"Not at the IRS. Not in Hollywood—hey, you've got *that* boyfriend— or at the Vatican. Nowhere really influential." I knew she was trying to make me laugh, so I did.

"Louisa?" She sounded earnest, even timid, which was so peculiar for Clem. "One thing that's really important? Try to keep from flipping out."

"Thank you."

"I'm serious."

"I know." Her tone spooked me. I said, "I'd better call Mom and Dad."

"Oh no, honey," said my mother. "Oh honey."

"Mom, it might turn out okay," I said. "They won't know the whole story till they do more surgery. But they know it was small."

"These tests can be all wrong. Doctors make mistakes. They see cancer everywhere, it's the rage. For heaven's sake, people are wearing *ribbons* for that disease. Pink! The color of babies, for heaven's sake!"

I wasn't sure how to respond, so I just listened to our connection for a couple of seconds, that intercity fuzz, until she told me that my father couldn't handle bad news right then and would call me the next day. She'd decided this on her own, of course, because whether or not Dad was there, in the room with her, she hadn't consulted him. Where emotions are concerned, she makes decisions for him all the time. She started to cry.

"Clem says they can probably beat it," I said.

After crying a bit longer and assuring me that my sister was brilliant and must be right, Mom collected her Darwinian self and said, "Those've got to be your father's genes; there's no cancer on my side." She'd been picturing her family tree, no doubt, its branches groaning under the weight of all the accidents and outmoded ills that killed her forebears. I told her genetic blame wasn't the point. Before we said goodbye, she piped up, "Remember, sweetheart: it's a long way from your heart." Across a lifetime of skinned knees and injuries less physical, I'd always accepted that dismissal of pain, but this time I said, "In fact, you know what? For once, that's not a bit true." My right hand went straight to my left breast, as if the national anthem had started to play.

On my way home I shop for a frenzy of cooking. Cooking is my favorite strategy for holding panic at bay. (And if I'm to mention children again, I should do it over a good meal.) While Ray talks to his agent on the phone, I make rosemary-crusted chicken with caramelized onions, Arborio rice baked with Swiss chard, oolong-ginger soufflé.

When we sit down, Ray tells me about a possible job in Alberta, a movie about paratroopers. The happier he sounds, the more edgy I feel. He worries about his ankles—he tapes them lately when he goes running—but Alberta; Alberta is gorgeous. It sounds like he's singing the praises of another woman.

"What do you plan to do one day when your body just up and goes on strike?" I say before I can stop myself. "It's not like you're an athlete, a big name. Nobody's going to ask you to endorse their bran flakes or bunion pads. It seems a long way off, but you will hit fifty. And then?"

For a moment, Ray just chews. "Well. How was *your* day?"

"I'm serious. I have to be."

"What will I do when I'm over the hill?" He shrugs. "How about the old bag-on-the-head routine?"

It takes me a minute. "Shoot yourself? *Shoot* yourself? Don't you ever think about the future?"

"Committed vagrant, that's me." Ray stretches his mouth into an alligator smile, a pearl onion between his front teeth.

"Please stop all this mugging around. Please. It's *time,* Ray."

"Time to what? Fish or cut bait? Make babies or hit the road?" He looks out the window. In the dark, all that's visible is a nodding leafless branch. Several seconds tick by before he says, "Sometimes it feels like . . . like if I couldn't do things your way, say yes to all your desires, right now, what kind of a guy would I be?"

I fold my napkin from a square to a triangle, press it flat on the table. "What you want matters just as much." But that's not what I really think. I want to shout, *Say yes, say yes, just say* yes*!*

The soufflé, when I take it from the oven, is perfect, lofty as a delusion. Minutes later, as it sinks, the odor that fills the air—the smokiness of dark tea, the comfort of eggs—seems so wrong, I wish I could break down and cry. But not now.

When Ray came into my life, he was just that: a shaft of sunlight invading a murky room. I had been married for too long to a genteel but oblivious man whose still waters hid many things but not, after all, an undertow of passion. At first, the decorum and calm in my marriage had been such a relief that I thought, So *this* is it. But then I met Ray, and I knew, though it made me sadder than I had ever been, This is *it*. He called me Miss Fever, Miss Open Flame, Miss Hundred and Ten in the Shade—and, once, Miss Bases Loaded Tying Run on Third No Outs. One day our illicit gymnastics left his handprints in the new gray carpet of my office; that night, I locked the door so the cleaning lady couldn't remove them. Next morning, when I walked in and saw again the image of his hands, ghostly as petroglyphs, I began to shake. I locked the door for another hour. I was certain that my life as lived (so cautiously) was over.

We're an archetypal mismatch: a daughter of the *Mayflower* (my pedigree, back to the rock and beyond, sepia-inked in a leather album that my father keeps in the top drawer of an heirloom highboy) and a football star from Smelterville, Idaho (the first of seven sons, three of them cops). Ray loves to point out how pampered I've been. He put himself through USC by working summers on a desert road crew. My parents, almost but not quite rich, put me through Harvard by selling stocks.

We argue often and loudly: about garlic (whether to mince or crush), about anarchy and idealism (which is more deluded), about flowered upholstery (if it means you've sold out). I like my world baroque; Ray preaches austerity. Maybe we're so contentious because we're both oldests: argumentative and, when shoved, unyielding and abrasive as tree trunks.

Early on, I asked if I could watch him work. He told me I'd be bored, but one November day he woke me up before dawn and drove me through the Holland Tunnel to a bleak industrial lot, location for a make-believe Mafia sting. I spent hours in the car, drinking scorched coffee and wishing I'd worn thicker socks. When at last he tapped on the clouded window and I wiped it clean, the vision was a shock: Ray in a white shirt, dark suit, and tie. Ray the Fed. For an hour, I watched him make the same punishing move over and over: jump from a ladder on a water tank, roll across a stretch of tarmac, fire a gun. It thrilled me so much I was almost ashamed.

Even now, I'm consumed by the physical details. I love Ray's chaotically freckled skin, his slippery stout-brown hair. I love the way he holds his toast so primly aloft while reading the *Village Voice* or *Boatbuilding Primer,* the skeptical tilt of his eyebrows when he blows on a spoonful of chili. When we go biking, I let him lead so I can watch the muscles oscillate in his wide calves. The last girl picked for every team, I crave his solidity.

Week five and it pulls me down, a deep ice-cold weariness. Every night before dinner, I furl myself in two blankets and take a nap while Ray broods on the fate of the Yankees, his loyalty to all of us pained but unswerving. My breast is seared in blotches, and the scar has turned purple, ringed by green circles and crosses where the technicians take aim. They reapply the Sharpie whenever it fades.

A curator from the Guggenheim, someone who owes me a favor, calls me. A group show is to open in three weeks, and she's just found out that one of the sculptors was killed. Driving his work down from Vermont on a flatbed truck, he hit blizzard number fourteen—the one I'd been hoping for, to stave off a jinx. A patch of ice, a spin given surefire momentum by two tons of crafted steel, all those trees along the interstate . . . This isn't the power I hoped for, I think as I pick up the phone to call Esteban. I won't tell him why; his conscience would never let him enjoy the big break he deserves.

At the hospital, the schedule's in a shambles because of the snow, appointments backed up more than an hour. I don't like this waiting room. Nothing's private, because everyone knows why everyone else is here. There's an orgy of sharing since few of us can cope with the silence. Ordinarily, that would include me, too—me and my compulsion for

expository everything—but I've heard enough about visualization, me-
tastasis, recurrence, negligent grown children, bewildered small children,
scars, baldness, early menopause, doctors with hollow hearts. Today, though,
is different; everyone's talking about terrorism and politics. The World
Trade Center was bombed last month, and this morning there was
a scare at Kennedy, a forgotten duffel bag that led to evacuation and
mayhem.

Wise old Nine humors me, looking hard for my funny bone. Some
days, he's the only one who can find it. I tell him about the waiting room,
glad to have escaped to his dim, frigid cave. Nearly every seat was taken
out there, everyone wearing the obligatory robe. We look like a bunch of
kindergartners in smocks, waiting for our paints or a game of musical
chairs. Better, a variation of Duck Duck Goose: Breast Breast Breast
Lung, Prostate Prostate Breast Larynx Breast. Mostly breast by far.

I give Nine my litany on dying young: not having to floss, because
you'll never lose your teeth. Not having to turn down your Walkman,
because you won't get the chance to go deaf. Not living to see your parents in diapers, mistaking you for that villainous cousin who pawned the
Murano goblets to finance his golf.

As if I'm the only one who tells him these things.

Tuesdays, I'm sheltered by Science rather than Sports. Dinosaurs are on
the front page; my omen detector never shuts down.

"Clem called," says Ray. "She's in the lab till late. She wants to hear
from you."

His arms feel like a swimming pool after a subway ride in August. I say,
"Dr. Bloom recommends a little chemo. I have two weeks to decide."

The newspaper topples. "A little chemo? What, like a little night
music? A pinch of genocide? A tad of Agent Orange? He never mentioned this before the surgery, did he? It wasn't on his smug little program, excuse me if my memory fails."

"They ration the bad news. It's only humane." Anger is not what I
expected. I expected him to gang up with my sister—who called, I sus-

pect, to make sure I submit. When I tell her about the chemo, she'll tell me to beg for an extra helping or two. She will not, however, tell me to savor small moments of joy. For that I will be grateful.

"Humane as a cattle prod," says Ray.

I twist around to see his face.

"I leave for Alberta in less than a month."

"That's great. I'm glad." I think about Ray diving, over and over, out of the sky, one more fear I don't need.

We arrive late at Esteban's party because of my nap. The talk around us is half about bombs and half about babies, because in the midst of the group—radiant as a prophet, wearing a purple velvet dress and a sleeve of gold bangles—is a tall, handsome woman so enormously, tautly pregnant that she looks as if she's expecting twins, any minute.

Esteban is in raptures, sharing his good fortune with the world. As he leads us through the loft, I hear Preston—"Why we don't nuke the bejesus out of those clowns, for the life of me I don't know"—and then Mary, our photo editor: "Sweetie, you'll beg for the epidural, believe me." As I come face-to-face with the pregnant woman, Esteban says, "I have been saying, saying all the time how I cannot wait for you to meet!" and I realize as he puts an arm around each of us that this is the much-revered Muriel.

"Esteban calls you La Découvrice. His discoverer. But I say you simply lucked out," she says. "It was bound to happen, the only mystery was how."

"I'm sure you're right." I make an effort to keep my eyes on her face. When she raises her eyebrows at Ray, I realize I've forgotten he's with me.

"Nice to meet you," he says once I've introduced him. He stares down briefly and blushes. "And I guess—well hey, congratulations, I guess."

Muriel laughs. She holds her belly with both hands, as if it were a trophy.

Preston sidles up and kisses me on the neck. "Miz Looweeza, poised and fetching as ever." He toasts me with a martini. He's as overdressed as he is drunk (he drinks and dresses, after five, to unashamed extremes), in a navy-blue suit with a pink French-collared shirt and a tie with golf-ball polka dots. "I think we have ourselves a cotillion of future gods this year, a Mount Olympus in the making," he stage-whispers in my ear. Along with Esteban's friends, a dozen of the hatchlings are here.

"May I thank our glamorous hostess for bringing us all together," Preston drawls at Muriel. He spreads a hand across the expanse of velvet below her breasts. "There's testosterone humming away in there, I can feel it."

She seems delighted by his attention, or else she's a very fine actress. I'd have slapped him.

Ray has wandered away. I see him, on tiptoe, whistling into the bird-cage. Caught between Preston's sloshed preening and Muriel's radiance, I realize that a party is the last place on earth I'm ready to be. I nearly shout when I feel something damp on my hand.

"Hello, my panda king!" Muriel exclaims, reaching down. A massive black dog stands at my side, wagging his entire body. "This is Kiko. Kiko's my hottest star, aren't you, bushka?"

Kiko's arrival draws several guests in our direction, including Rose of the lovelorn X-rays and Garrett of the midnight ice floes. A large woman in an elaborate turban also joins us. She kneels beside me and hugs the dog, who licks her face. *"Mère, tu es sa favorite!"* says Muriel, making a sequence of musical gestures with her hands.

"I love dogs, but my landlord hates them," Rose says sadly.

"This is no dog. This is a pony," says Preston.

"He's a Bernese mountain dog." Muriel scratches him behind the ears. His eyes close in pleasure.

"Oh right, totes booze to marooned mountaineers."

"You're thinking of Saint Bernards." She tells us she's an animal handler. "A wrangler. Don't you love it? Picture me lassoing a steer." Muriel handles dogs and cats, plus the occasional monkey. Just now, dogs are the rage in commercials; they'll sell anything from credit cards to disposable diapers. Kiko, the only client she owns, is bringing in a nice nest egg for the baby's college tuition.

"Like, what's Kiko been in?" asks Rose.

"Next month, a TV movie about a family trapped on a houseboat in Hurricane Andrew. Kiko, as you can guess, saves their lives."

Across the room, Ray talks to Mary and Esteban. He wears a studious, tender expression and swings his arms as if directing traffic. An illustration of something grand. I forgot he could look so passionate.

The woman whom Kiko adores is standing now, all smiles, watching Muriel talk. After telling Rose about Kiko's other roles, Muriel turns to the older woman and speaks again in French, gesticulating. When the woman gesticulates back, I finally understand that she is deaf.

Preston says, "So tell us, please, what fonts of childhood fancy have shaped your son's unique imagination." Muriel translates, in French and with her hands.

Esteban's mother. I watch now as she makes a small speech with her hands. It looks so much like knitting.

"All inspiration comes from God," Muriel translates, "but Esteban was not like other boys. His favorite thing was the market in Port-au-Prince, all the beautiful cloths, helping her choose what to sew."

"Ah," says Preston. "Aha!"

"I haven't met you," I say, holding out a hand. Her name is Tatiana. She clasps my hand in both of hers and smiles, then gestures a phrase.

"She says you are the second messenger of great joy to this household," says Muriel. Her belly, of course, was the first.

"We are all together, this makes me so glad!" I feel Esteban's arm encompass my shoulders. Ray stands on my other side, and Mary glares fondly at Preston, who's filled his martini glass with red wine.

When Tatiana signs at her son, I know from her sidelong glances that she is talking about me, saying kind things.

"She wants you to tell how you found me." He giggles. "Me, the foundling!"

I tell her—Esteban translating now—how every year we go through thousands of slides, talk to hundreds of dealers, but how I saw Esteban's work in the entrance to a public school.

She nods: *Exactly as it should be.* She looks at Ray, back at me.

"Do you have children, she wants to know."

"No," I say. Tatiana sees something in my face.

"You are afraid to have children? Too many people are afraid these days, afraid of life," relays Esteban. Muriel, Preston, Mary, Rose, and Ray are watching me. I'm hoping Ray will come to my rescue, but Rose is the one who finally speaks. Like Tatiana, she's come to her own conclusion.

"So maybe you can adopt." In a nervous rush, she tells us how last month her sister adopted a lovely Chinese baby girl, how her sister says that any baby at all is a miracle, how when it's put in your arms you can't believe the love that springs from nowhere, a geyser of love, how it took two years and maybe a lot of paperwork, but what's two years? "Like, time just rushes on by, doesn't it?"

Preston jumps in with "People plan too much. I say, let the future unfold! Willy nilly! Onward the leering mazurka of life, the unknowns, tragedies, twists of fate . . ." Mary squeezes his elbow so hard he winces.

All I hear now are Kiko's nails as she trots away across the floor. "Excuse me, but I must steal Louisa," says Esteban. Like another dog, relieved to have a good master, I follow him.

He leads me back to the studio, shuts the door behind us, turns on the floodlights, and climbs a stepladder. He fusses with a fixture, aiming it at the tall tepee in the corner. Without looking down, he says, "My mother has cancer, too. It's why she stays with us." I say nothing; I'm focused on that "too." Mary and Preston are the only people I've told at work.

"She didn't want it, all this medicine. But I told her my child will have a grandmother to know and remember. Is her son selfish?" He looks over his shoulder from on high.

When he comes down, he circles the new piece, pulling off the tarps. He watches me look.

"Oh Esteban. It's really something."

"The red is not too much?"

"How could it *not* be red?" Blood, yes, on the verge of cliché, but blood as a rich, fresh force, not violation or loss.

We look together for a while. "My doctors say I'll be fine."

"The idea that *you* would be afraid of life!" He holds me to his side.

We share a cab with Preston, who can't stop talking about how we wouldn't be in the pickle we're in, we wouldn't have to live in mortal terror of some shabby abandoned satchel, if our cowering bureaucrats had refused to collude with the shah of Iran. Now we're paying through the nose. "And that boy-president we've gone and elected?" he says. "Charisma to burn, but *Arkansas*? How would a godforsaken place like that prepare you to deal with *Iran*? Well, that place is pretty godforsaken, too; ha!"

Halfway across the Williamsburg Bridge, I say, "Preston, shut up." Ray pulls his knee away from my hand. No one says a word for the rest of the ride, even when Preston gets out and hands Ray a ten. He won't remember this or much else about the evening, but that's not the point.

At home, Ray pours a scotch and spreads the plans for his kayak on the dining table. With a thick carpenter's pencil, he makes notations.

I put on a nightgown. I sit in bed and try to read, but the rustling of Ray's plans in the other room distracts me. I go in and stand beside him. "Yes?" he asks without looking up.

"I'll miss you when you go."

"Me, too." He erases a figure on the plans, writes in a new number.

I unbutton the top of my nightgown. "Ray?"

He looks up. "You all right?"

"Ray, you never look."

He sets down his pencil and turns in his chair to face me. "Show-and-tell?" He finishes opening my gown, smudging the buttonholes with graphite as he descends. He whistles. "Looks like World War Three."

"It doesn't hurt."

He tests my darkened nipple, first with a finger, then the tip of his tongue. "Crusty. Like burnt toast." He curves a whole hand over the breast. "Ground zero!" he exclaims, and, as if he were six years old, imitates the explosion of a grenade.

"Stop, Ray. It's me here," I say. I long for the days when he could bruise me with tenderness, pull me under, make me forget anything. But Ray returns to his kayak.

When I woke up after my second surgery, the real one, I lay still for an hour, dizzy, sore, so thirsty I began to hallucinate. The recovery room was noisy and chaotic. In the next bed, an older man bellowed at the nurses, lashing out at their sympathy. I resolved not to ask for a thing. I made myself small and floated away on some inner sea. Another mirage of drinking, drinking anything—Gatorade, dishwater, soy sauce—then I opened my eyes and there was Ray's face. He wore a blue gown, backward, crinkled at his throat. The look he gave me was one I didn't know. Alarm? Pity? Relief? He held a tiny ribbed cup, the kind street vendors fill with gelato. He said, as if about to ask for a favor, "They said I could give you an ice cube. One." For the next few weeks, he was full of kindnesses, small and sweet as that cup of ice.

"Are you angry with me?" I say now.

"Why would I be angry?"

"The taxi. Losing my temper at Preston."

"People lose their temper." His tone is like the night air pressing at the windows. It's starting to snow again. Number fifteen.

"Sometimes you are so cold."

"It's a chore, Louisa. Being warm all the time, just for you. I want you to be . . . happy again, but . . ."

"But you're no saint."

"Committed scoundrel, that's me."

"You like those lines. Clever little sitcom punch lines."

Slowly, Ray lifts his right hand above his plans and drops the pencil. "I'm going to bed."

I remember, at the party, watching him from a distance, his arms dancing around to illustrate something. How happy he looked. He was describing the kayak.

"Isn't it curious," I say, and it's too late to take back the meanness, "your building a boat for one. Not two. Forget about three."

Ray speaks slowly. "Louisa, everything isn't art, some precious gift-wrapped metaphor. Your life isn't a biblical flood and I am certainly not your Noah." He drains his scotch and walks around me. I follow him into our narrow kitchen with its bitter light and put my hands on his shoulder blades, my cheek against his neck. He places the empty glass in the sink, so carefully it makes not a sound.

"Nobody apologize," he says. "Everyone's going a little nuts."

In bed, Ray falls asleep right away.

Dr. Bloom says he's counting on me to make what he calls the mature decision and brave the consequences. He said it plainly, none of his usual camp-counselor verve.

Sometimes I fantasize about Dr. Bloom. Nothing sexual—though it's funny to think that he's been inside my body, his tools like scrabbling beetles right near my heart—but I do envision his other life, its ordinary details. I've imagined Dr. Bloom serving an ace, carving a roast, combing his horseshoe of otter-smooth hair. I see him in fleece-lined moccasins, reading medical journals by a crackling Manhasset fire, a chestnut boxer asleep at his feet.

I lie awake a long time, assuming Ray is fast asleep until he says, "Game of cribbage?"

I can't help laughing before I say, "Oh Ray, I could *die*."

"Louisa, we're all going to die."

"But not before . . ." Before what? Before I've gone gray? Had two children, published a book, lived by the ocean, seen Tikal?

His callused fingers brushing my cheek are a shock. "Hey," he says. Because here they are, the tears. He holds me from behind, no baseball trades to read about over my shoulder this time.

I am on a brick patio, looking across a lovely tree-filled yard at night. Dr. Bloom, barefoot and wearing white pajamas, stands beside me. Our arms touch. The air is searingly cold, and I want to ask where his shoes are, but he's talking and I mustn't interrupt. I'm paying for his time. "Look up," he says. I obey. The sky is crisp, pricked through with stars. "That one is Hurtling Treasure." He points. "There's Methotrexate, Taco Arriba, Red Grooms." I am outraged. I cut in: "Shut up. You don't know the constellations. You're a surgeon. You have to *be* a surgeon!" Dr. Bloom says, "It's just a lot of connecting the dots. Anybody who can make kimonos can be a surgeon, believe me." As he continues his ersatz tour of the heavens, he pivots like the beam from a lighthouse, always pointing. "Adopted, adopted, adopted," he says to each star. I feel a rush of love and pity. How can I expect him to know outer space? All he knows is the inside of a human body—but he can find anything there. He needs my protection to get it just right. I reach out, and he lets me hold him; in my arms, he feels like a little boy, so bony and slight.

Waking is a vortex of words: constellations, consolations, consummations. *Make it simple, Ray,* I think. Though of course he never has.

"Party shoes!"

My next to last treatment; Patrice is centering my legs.

"A work party." My red tights and black suede heels protrude brazenly from the hospital smock.

"A party's a party. . . . Off with the left shoulder, relax. Hon, you're a pro at this." Patrice has now coaxed my flesh into place, pushed my face to the side, twenty-nine times; it's become a casual yet intimate task, one girlfriend brushing another's hair. She says as she works, "My boys learned snow angels yesterday. I look out the window one minute and see them running around. Next thing, they've vanished, and lord do I have a stroke. I'm out there in my socks, freezing my butt off, calling their names, and boom! Up they pop. Yard's nearly three feet deep! You never saw New Jersey so gorgeous."

She pats my knees, and Juan comes in. As usual, no small talk from him. He handles the machine, not me.

The long loud buzzing begins. A sudden comfort, like bees browsing in a sumptuous garden. A sound I could sleep through, so different now.

After tomorrow, Blue, we won't meet anymore. Do I wish we could go on and on; am I crazy?

I remember when I met Ray for the very last time. That's what it was supposed to be. We'd been seeing each other in secret for only two months, and I thought I would die from the exhaustion of lying— or, rather, of not even having to use the lies I'd wrung myself out to invent, because my husband never mentioned my absences (long and fla-grant), my rages (at his smallest imperfections), or my culinary binges (a nonstop hysteria of bouillabaisse, lemon mousse, roast duck, lamb tajine . . . by the end, a freezer full of crepes and sorbets, duxelles and shellfish stocks). We lay on Ray's bed, fully dressed. I thought, Never ever ever again. I hadn't told him it was over, only that Hugh had finally guessed, but Ray said, "It's over," and began to sob. I had never heard a man cry so hard. "Do you want it to be over?" I said. "No," he said, and I said without thinking, "Then it won't be." Why I kept this promise before others (I exacted so much misery to keep it), I still can't say. Maybe because I'd thought he would give me up easily and I was wrong.

When the buzzing stops, I look up into that secretive eye. Nothing new, just myself in the glass, a fish beneath rain-grizzled water. I reach up and touch my machine. His skin is unexpectedly warm.

Patrice says, "Now you go have fun."

"Tomorrow's my last day."

She helps me down. "Everyone cries at the end. It's just the weirdest thing." She hands me a Kleenex.

In the changing room, I put on my red velvet dress, tight and sleeve-less. I comb my hair and twist it against my skull.

Outside, it's still light for a change, just barely. Dozens of clouds fill the sky above the park, pink as peonies. Across Fifth Avenue, Ray sits on a bench, reading his paper. I call his name and he looks up with delight. Do I give him this much pleasure, still?

But before he even steps into the street, he calls out, "Jim Abbott!"

"What?"

"The one-armed pitcher with the Angels. They bought him."

"Is that good?"

"Good enough for me."

As we start downtown, I look sideways at his clothes: black jeans, leather jacket over a tweedy sweater. The two of us mismatched as ever. I reach for his hand. He resists, but I hold on tight. Tomorrow he flies to Canada. He put it off as long as he could. Then I recognize the man heading toward us, a man in an orange turtleneck, coatless and hurrying. "Hello!" I say, blushing. I'm thinking how odd Dr. Bloom looks in such a loud color as I remember the last time I saw him—wearing pajamas.

"Louisa," he says, without hesitation. "Don't you look lovely." He turns to Ray. "Riley—yes? The Hollywood stuntman, am I right?"

Ray shakes the doctor's hand.

"Taking fine care of my star patient there. You keep that up, Riley." Dr. Bloom looks back at me and displays a pair of quarters in his priceless right hand. "My wife's meter."

"Nice to see you," I say.

A block later, Ray says, "Dr. Doom, yes? Vincent Price of oncology? Guy who sounds like Joe Pesci trapped in the body of Alvin the Chipmunk, yes?"

I stop. "Ray, what could you possibly have against him?"

Ray shrugs and walks on. But as I look at his back, it's obvious, really. Brilliant as Dr. Bloom is, he's not brilliant enough, not for Ray. Ray wants him to promise he'll cure me for good: *Skip all the pleasantries, buster, and do it.* I'm no different, resenting Ray for not being stronger, as strong as he looks when he's leaping, ducking, rolling over and over, jumping from planes, so certain he'll hit the ground whole.

"Two favors. Please," I say. Ray stops and turns around. Behind him looms the Guggenheim, a spacecraft aglow in the dusk.

"What," he says bluntly, but he looks open to anything.

"Could you pick me up?"

He lifts me quickly, his leather sleeve cold behind my knees.

"And make your skunk face?"

It takes him only a second to remember. He purses his features into a rodent mask and snorts loudly, turning me in circles. I snort back. When he puts me down, I can't stop laughing.

"We are certifiable," says Ray. "We are out where the buses don't run."

In front of the museum, a knot of people wait to go in, stamping their feet like horses, their steamy breath rising in plumes. One at a time, they enter a revolving door that flashes back the headlights of limousines and taxis. When it's our turn, when we pass into the warm sparkling cocoon of the party, separately and then together, I can still feel the weightlessness. Exactly what I wanted to feel yet still such a surprise.

I walk to the center and look straight up. At the top is a blue egg of twilight, electric against the white walls. "Like being inside a tulip," I say.

"More like a missile silo," says Ray. "Where's the bar?"

I'm about to show him the way when something hits me. "How can a pitcher be one-armed?"

"Oh, he's got two, but one is . . . There's only the elbow and then this deformed hand—or I don't know, maybe none. He wears his glove there."

"But the wind-up, the balance . . ."

"Nobody makes a big deal of it."

"I guess you couldn't, could you," I say. "Ray, this guy—will you point him out on TV? I want to see how he does it."

"I just want him to save my team's sorry ass. That's all I want."

I begin to see familiar faces. "I'm going to find Esteban's piece before this place is mobbed. You find the drinks." I set off, away from the crowd.

It stands in its own room: *Coat of Many Colors*, stately and vivid. It is made entirely of the fine, brightly colored wire the telephone company used before fiber optics. From a distance, it's a pure passionate red, but close up, the wires are an orderly tangle flecked with fine stripes of orange, purple, fuchsia, blue. Woven like a basket, like a nest.

The coat is a bell-shaped goddess, wide sleeves beckoning. Back in Esteban's studio, I saw it as a self-portrait: Esteban's garish feminine warmth, his towering joy. But no, of course it's his mother.

The few people in the room admire it from a distance. But I step right in, through the narrow entry. Light pierces the weave, casting a splintered radiance across my naked arms. Above me, the peak is a vortex of stars. Press my face against the side and I can just make out Ray, by the door, holding our drinks. He starts to circle the room. I lean out and wave.

I pull him in and take my champagne; it's in a plastic flute, the kind with the base that always falls off. I raise it. "New pitcher, new season."

He says nothing; I'm being my overly metaphorical self. So I'll ride out the silence, one more unknown, but even in the fractured light, secure inside Esteban's coat, I see Ray looking at me the way he did when he crossed the avenue and called out Jim Abbott's name. He raises his cup—its bottom already lost—and touches the rim of mine.

The Price of Silver

It makes me happy to see that Doris and the cubs have found themselves a great big juicy carcass, a full-grown buck. Snowfall was light this year, so the body count is low. R.B., who scouts the terrain obsessively, tells me he's seen it firsthand: spring pickings are slim. It could be a sign, depending on others yet to come, that the mamas will wean their youngsters on the early side. R.B.'s addicted to prowling the woods, to hunting even when he's not out to kill. I wouldn't be surprised if he's out here right now, watching this very same scene, watching me watch it. Or maybe that's just what I wish.

We've been listening to Doris, all of us, to the frequency that tracks her comings and goings, along with her twins, ever since they left the den last month. She's the most local of our subjects, hanging out on the near slopes of Gannett. So far the signals have been strong and easy to follow, her forays close and fairly routine. I come out to look for her as often as I can these days, whenever I don't have to be at the station. I follow a logging road partway up the mountain, then bushwhack almost randomly, stake out a perch and glass the slopes, close yet not too close to the den. Today my persistence paid off.

I'm careful to stay downwind and keep my distance. One thing that keeps me careful is remembering that guy at the conference in Flagstaff who wasn't. A grizzly sow broke the guy's collarbone and took off a piece of his jaw, but she left it at that, lesson enough for coming so close to her babies. High summer, a field of flowers blooming their heads off. He told me the smell of Queen Anne's lace, even now, fills him with panic. So strange, the things our minds just won't let go of, the things that loom absurdly large and make us quake with fear. I'm not afraid of the dark, of heights or thunderstorms or solitude. What I'm afraid of is a particular kind of pointlessness. Fear of futility. Futiliphobia.

Oh, here's a laugh. The guy who was mauled? He studies salamanders. And now the bottom half of his face looks like it was hit by a truck and then replaced with part of a dime-store mannequin.

Through the binoculars, through all the branches, it's tough to get a clear, uninterrupted view, but if I could see Doris clearly, she could see me, too. So I've hidden myself in a thick stand of lodgepole pine, wedged low between two fat trunks, in a thicket of huckleberry bushes. Berries are months away still, so the bushes don't interest the bears, not yet. Doris and her female cub are eyeball-deep in that elk, but the male sits off to one side, as if it's a restaurant and he's still waiting for a table. *Go on, little buddy,* I'm thinking. *Pull your scrawny butt up to the counter and get your order in.* The scent of raw game reaches me in tendrils, though the carcass could be frozen to the ground.

There's a yin-yang to the climate here in May. A few thousand feet down the mountain, it's full-glory spring; turning off the main road, I drove through meadows of buttercups, shooting stars, and biscuitroot— the valley an orgy of pollination. But up here, even as ferns pierce the dead leaves and begin their slow uncoiling, the shady hollows are bright with snow, places the sun will never quite reach.

Doris stops gorging herself, just for a minute, to cast a look at her reticent cub and issue a soft, sandpapered bellow, invitation to join the picnic. At last he sidles in next to his mother and tears off a strip of something I'm glad I can't see in more detail. *There you go,* I cheer him on, so relieved I almost speak.

What would Doris think if she could comprehend the fuss she's caused, if she could have so much as a mental glimmer of all the paperwork flying around on her account, the way she's talked about behind her shaggy back, by rangers, biologists, and vets, by mothers with kids on trikes, by Game and Fish bureaucrats sitting at plywood desks in Cheyenne who secretly wouldn't give a hoot if the Wind River Range became tier upon tier of golf courses, ski resorts, and woo-woo yoga retreats where meals are garnished with Russian caviar (screw the sturgeon) and orchids flown in from Tahiti? Maybe you'd say that what Doris doesn't know can't hurt her, but you'd be wrong. Because Doris got her little family in hot water. Now she and her cubs, who are two plus change, maybe on the verge of weaning, maybe not, are probably about to be moved. Moving three grizzlies at once is not a piece of cake. Even two, though we do it if we have to. I'm pushing for them to go soon, July at the latest, to get a firm hold on their new surroundings while it's still summer. The clock is ticking. The bureaucrats are doing their jerkoff dance. Ever the world may turn.

Sometimes I wonder how I got here, or rather, I wish I could wonder. In fact, the path was fairly straight. When I was little, I loved this TV show called *Daktari*. Dr. Something (Marsh? Tracy? Wilmerding?) is a noble vet who champions the persecuted wildlife of Africa (that was back when people talked about Africa as if it were a single country, like France or Japan). The noble vet has a cross-eyed lion, a clownish chimp, a jeep with zebra stripes, and the people around him have jolly-ho colonial accents. (*I say there, chap, these bloody poachers must be stopped!*) That's it, I said to myself, sitting on the family couch with its blue fleur-de-lys upholstery, eating my Cap'n Crunch, trail mix of the sixties. That's exactly what I'll do. When I grow up, I'll take care of wild animals in the wild, not in a zoo.

And can you believe it, that's what I've done? Yet it's not at all what I expected. This work is to *Daktari* as, say, Newark is to Paris.

Last night I was at R.B.'s place (the place he borrows) when his wife called from Sarasota. R.B. is nomadic—takes his dogs to Russia, Alaska, wherever there's work; big game or conservation, it's all the same to him—but his wife stays put where life is warm and comfy. That's how their marriage works. Or works for *her*, if I believe his protestations. The wife's existence isn't news to me, but that was the first time she called while I was with him. I guess what bothered me, a little, was that he didn't seem self-conscious about talking to her while I was right there in his kitchen chopping onions. He didn't make excuses or say he'd call her back. He talked to her for a while, and he laughed a lot, which made me wonder. It's not that he ever bad-mouths his wife, not that I'm supposed to think he can't stand her, but sometimes laughing is a proxy for sex. Or it sounds like that. So there I was, hostage to their shared, married amusement, and it began to feel as if I, not Simone, was the distant point of the triangle here. If that's true, fine, but I'd rather not know.

I was silent when R.B. hung up. I could have let him off the hook by changing the subject, but I didn't. And I couldn't look at him.

He leaned across the counter. "Okay, doll, out with it."

"Out with what?" I said. "I'm just making a sauce here."

"You're jealous."

"That's not in my nature," I said. Which is true. Over the winter, while he was in Brazil, then back in Florida, I didn't call R.B. once, didn't wonder where he was, or with what other doll. At blocking things out—some things—I'm better than I used to be. I let him be the one to call, and he did, a few times, telling me he missed me. I think he did, but the calls were more to stake his claim, remind me he'd be back in the spring. For the first time in my life, I preferred being alone to finding someone else. Evenings, if I didn't go to a bar with Jim or Buzz or Vern (all safe), I'd go back to my trailer and read.

"We were talking about the salon," he said. "She's had a bunch of weirdos in this week. One guy walked in and asked if she could shave a hand flipping the bird onto the back of his head. Jesus, the world we live in."

"Florida," I said, "is not the world we live in. Well, not me."

"You *are* jealous."

I looked at him and smirked. "If I'm jealous of anyone in your life, it's Rosie and June. They're the only ones who can kick me out of your bed."

He laughed. "With my blessing." Rosie and Junebug (June when she's good, Bug when she's lazy or sulking) are R.B.'s blueticks, from whom he's basically inseparable, partners in business and crime. They've grown to like me, though. They greet me with cold noses and warm tongues every time I show up. They no longer bark, an honest approval that pleases me. R.B. works a pair of bear dogs, too, the ones that do the serious work when he's here, but they live in a kennel out back. Rosie and June made sure of that.

R.B. leaned over my shoulder to smell the spaghetti sauce. He squeezed my waist, lifting me off the floor just a little, before leaning down to take the big pot from under the counter. I had a flash just then of all the guys' kitchens I've stood in over the past ten years, chopping garlic and onions, drinking wine or beer, exchanging those appetizer kisses, prelude to the meal that is prelude to the bed. Freight train of kitchens, freight train of kisses. For a minute I was at the rail crossing, watching car after car after car pass by, an endless sooty blur. I looked out the window, but the night was too dark to give me a view of anything but me and R.B. behind me, at the sink, staring down into the pot as it filled with water. How much spaghetti, I wondered, have I shared with how many men?

I watch Doris and her cubs for an hour before they eat their fill—though they'll get another meal or two off those bones. Doris sets about covering the carcass, scolding her kids to pitch in. (Her irascible complaints are surely the ursine version of *Who do you think I am, your slave?*) At her mother's urging, G63, the young female we've nicknamed Tipper, drags in a couple of downed branches, kicks up some leaves and icy clods of soil. Her brother, G62, helps out for a few minutes, then sits back and watches, the way he did during most of the feeding. When they're done, it's not like you can't guess there's an extremely dead, mutilated something under all that debris, but unless you're an idiot human (a tourist hiker), you know that meal's been claimed, and you know by what sort of creature. You are outa there.

Doris is both smart and stupid in a way that's helped put her species on the endangered list. No, I take half of that back: she's not stupid, no more than I am. No amount of animal intelligence could enable her to guess, before it's too late, that the idiots in the fancy chalet-style condos who left a shiny white bag of free food for her to find last Thanksgiving are the same idiots who could get her shot by a ranger (if not by the idiots themselves). You can be smart and doomed all the same.

Her only crime was to lead her cubs out of the area we humans have officially spelled out as WIL-DER-NESS (that is, what we've ordained as her rightful territory) and into a new condo complex, built to look out on, and so flirt with, said wilderness. From a mile away, Doris could probably smell the putrid garbage that some guy forgot to load into the arse of some aircraft carrier masquerading as a car. Doris was understandably delighted. She had kids to feed, to fatten for a three-month nap.

By the time Buzz, Vern, and I made it over there, responding to a hysterical phone call from yet another idiot human, the bears were reveling in supermarket offal. They made off quickly when they saw the truck coming toward them. G63 lumbered away with a Chips Ahoy bag in her teeth; her brother, as he followed, tossed aside a large yogurt container. That's how they became Tipper and Danny. Once we name our subjects, they're like family. When we talk about them at the station, a stranger would assume we're gossiping about a bunch of coworkers or cousins.

Doris got her name before the cubs were born, well before I came. Buzz tells me that after they'd collared her, when they released her and she was stumbling, woozy from drugs, back into the woods, Sheldon remarked that she had the figure and bearing of a 1960s sitcom housewife. "Your typical Mabel or Doris," he said. Because she's one of those grizzlies with a golden coat, Doris stuck. Our golden girl, Buzz calls her. She's his favorite.

Sheldon is the team vet. He's a slick guy with a full head of surfer-blond hair, and he just reeks of trust fund (the logos on his shirts alone, forget the second house on Columbia Gorge). It's no secret he regards the biologists on the team as less educated, less skilled, and probably less evolved. (That would be me, Buzz, and Jim; also Vern, who's a plant guy but sometimes joins us if we need a little extra muscle in the field.) Or maybe he just feels outnumbered.

One visit from a bear to a condo might rank as a misdemeanor, but repeat visits—even without hysterical complaints—amount to felony. Doris, who has a perfectly logical head on her shoulders, was back at the condo the very next day, cubs in tow. That time, there was no loot to be had, and maybe she'd have wandered back to the woods without being noticed, except that she happened to show up when a couple of human cubs were riding their bikes in the driveway. She made an instant retreat—but that was a close call no one wants to replicate.

Buzz and Jim decided we'd give her the winter to develop a little amnesia. We badly want bears in this range; there's plenty of space for a larger population down here, but not if they get a taste for Twinkies and fish sticks. The idea was, if Doris returned to the condos this spring, then we'd send her north. Hence our nosy vigilance since she's emerged from her den.

During their first summer, the two cubs were hard to tell apart by sight. Whenever we checked in on Doris, whose signal showed up clearly for most of that season, there'd be talk about whether we should tag and collar the cubs while they were small. Sheldon thinks a radio collar turns a bear into a sitting duck for poachers, but he would never dare say so to Marty Cone, our man in Cheyenne. Marty's attitude seems to be that every mammal in every national park should wear a radio. Tuning in, on one of our routine flyovers, would be like surfing the AM dial at rush hour on the San Diego Freeway. Marty's the anal kind of guy who probably wishes we could stamp them all with barcodes, every squirrel, cougar, coyote, and mouse. "I need to see more organization," Marty is fond of saying, but he says this over the phone, from the tasteless comfort of his office, when he can't *see* a damn thing out here where the real work takes place. To assuage our pride, we call him Conehead, and whenever I speak to him, I picture him wearing the skimpy kidney-brown macramé tie he wore the first time we met and, on his head, the nippled dome of a capitol building, vulgar and white as a wedding cake. This vision keeps me from suggesting that he organize the contents of his lower intestinal tract. Which is good, because Conehead signs off on everything from how much toilet paper we order to whether a pesky bear—that is, a bear who, like Doris, knows that condos and big-butt cars are essentially neon signs advertising fast food—will be trapped, drugged, and either shipped off to Yellowstone (bear Levittown) or euthanized. Killed for exercising common sense.

When I tell him we'd like to see the relocation happen sooner rather than later, he says, "It's a hefty chunk of the budget, this early on."

"Better than a hefty chunk of someone's child who bikes around the corner at just the wrong time."

"No mincing words, that's you, Miss Jardine." He chuckles, his we're-in-this-together laugh. "But let's not jump too fast. See how things play out and we might save ourselves a whole lot of unnecessary expense. And effort."

"You are so right, Marty. Wouldn't want you to put in any overtime, now would we."

That's the end of chuckling from Marty, but after a silence I refuse to break, he says, "Okay. Shoot me a detailed plan. *Organized,* Miss Jardine."

"Well, Mr. Cone, that just happens to be my middle name. Miss Organized Jardine is on the job."

Chuckle, chuckle.

When I get off the phone, Buzz and Jim applaud. "Whoa," says Jim, "are you Mack the Knife or *what.*"

"Yeah, well," I say, "he is still the boss of me."

Our shared contempt is basically childish, but it moves us along, like a current, against the notion that we are merely part of a pipeline, somewhere in the middle. We think of ourselves as lucky in what we do for a living, as mavericks or nonconformists, but we are part of a system that's not a whole lot different on paper than life insurance or widgets.

We never did tag the cubs; another decision deferred. Now, and it's a shock, you can tell those cubs apart easy, because Tipper's grown so much bigger than Danny, even just through the long winter trance. This isn't normal; in the bear kingdom, boys are always a good deal bigger.

So I have to wonder as I see Danny sitting back to let his mom and sister do most of the tidying up after their meal. As they retreat, up through the pines and over a steep ridge, he lags behind. Near the top, before they disappear from view, Doris takes a backward glance but keeps on trucking along. I can't help thinking of that book Mom loved reading to me and my sister, the one where the little bear and the little girl accidentally change places as they follow their mothers in search of berries. Those moms never seemed upset enough to me. Realistically, wouldn't they have been traumatized, reduced to whimpering terror and contrition on the one side, pure bestial rage on the other? But then I guess the book was warning us, whether the author knew it or not, that laggards and daydreamers will be left to their own devices. Mothers will provide, that's their job, but children had better toe the line. This ain't no disco, this ain't no foolin' around!

I haven't been home in three days. I'd like to open my door to the easy attentions of a cat or a dog or even a chatterbox canary, but it wouldn't be fair. When I rented this place—a trailer in the middle of nowhere, plunked down here thirty years ago for some ranch hand who's no longer needed, the ranch house now a rustic hotel—I knew I wouldn't be here often. So today, like most days, I open my door to silence, the sight of my breath in the rattle-bone cold, and my beckoning phone machine. I turn up the thermostat and take a beer from the fridge. I find a bag of taco chips. I sit at the kitchen table, wearing my jacket till the heat cranks up; nights will stay frigid well into summer.

I stare at the machine. It's not that I dread any calls in particular, just calls in general. Since leaving the coast, where I used to work with seals and other ocean creatures, I feel as if the curious comfort of being land-locked, one I welcomed at first in the temporary notion that I'd finally found someplace roomy and wild and deserted enough to call home, has mutated into smug isolation. Not loneliness, not quite, but a way of having to face that I've intentionally closed all the windows and doors of my soul (if you believe in souls, which, if pushed to a philosophical wall, I don't). You'd never know this in public. At work, I'm the one who does the tough stuff, like calling Conehead when we need Daddy's approval to trap a bear or let Sheldon loose to do a "procedure." (Sometimes our work feels like a grown-up version of Captain May I. You can't so much as trim a bear's nails without permission. I exaggerate, but still.)

"Oh God," I say when I play back my messages, because three out of five are from my sister. (The ones from Buzz and Jim, left the day before yesterday, are moot. NO ONE knows to look for me at R.B.'s place, and it has to stay that way.)

Five months ago, Louisa was diagnosed with breast cancer. Before she went in for the biopsy, her doctors told her it would be nothing, and I agreed. She was thirty-six, healthy, not living in Chernobyl, etcetera. So I did my scientific bit, told her about all the quirky benign possibilities, like a waitress reading the off-menu specials: *Tonight we have cysts; we have calcifications; I need to check with the kitchen, but we might still have a necrotic gland or two.* But I felt guilty, because somehow I knew. I just knew. And while I waited for the bad news to whip around and hit me, boomerang style, I couldn't stop thinking how if anyone should have cancer, it's me. Never mind that I'm younger.

Biology is the study of life, right? Yet sometimes I wonder if I chose this field as a grand compensation, not just something I happen to love. Sometimes I feel cut off from life, or from mine. I feel as if what I thought was going to be My Life (the Siamese twin) quietly severed our ties when I wasn't looking, then snuck off on her own and chose a different fork in the trail. Sometimes our two paths cross, so I bump into My Life by accident, and I say, "Here you are! Where have you *been*?" My Life is cordial but cagey. And we hang out together at the same campsite, maybe for quite a while. We boil water from a nearby stream, heat our freeze-dried meals, eat in contented silence. We commune without speaking. We toast marshmallows. We wash our grungy clothing in the stream and hang it out to dry on the limbs of an overhanging birch. We consult our topo maps and hike about, pick berries, swim together, read novels on a sunny rock . . . but then one morning I wake up shivering alone in my sleeping bag. The campfire's out, the coals have crumbled to dust, and once again My Life, that sneaky creature, has struck ahead on a route I can't determine, taking with her all the maps (and the marshmallows, too). I pack up my gear and can only make a random guess at which path she might have chosen. Sometimes all I can do is flip a coin. I have to believe we'll meet up again, though I'm never sure when that will be.

Meanwhile—because you can't help compare—I look at Louisa, and even if I'd never in a million years choose New York or a job that's so completely cerebral, I recognize that she's made a life of color, ambition, the deliberate mess of wanting one true love and kids, the social kaleidoscope of living in a city. She's made some crazy decisions, and sometimes it drives me nuts the way she wears her neuroses and her complaints like colorful floating scarves, but she lives with a boyfriend nearly everyone declares to be a Good Man, she invests her savings, and she seems to have all the right instincts, the nesting ones, the ones I'm missing. She holds her life *tight,* never letting it out of her sight for a minute. So how could *she* be marked?

It's stage one, her tumor, which means there's plenty of genuine hope. Louisa had surgery, then radiation. She called me every few days for a while, and I always called right back if she left a message. Sometimes she cried, and then she'd scold herself for not being a saint. (What I loved was when, in the same evening, Mom would call and go through the very same sequence. *I'm going to lose a daughter! . . . I'm a horrible mother!*) Other times Louisa was hysterically cheerful. *I'm going to be fine, I have to believe that! My job is great, and everyone understands! At least I don't live in Bosnia!* That was worse than the crying. Sometimes I wondered if I should fly out and be there, but I never offered, and she never asked. It wasn't the money; our parents, or even R.B. if I'd asked him, would have picked up the airfare. The truth is, I didn't want to be near the disease. When I came to this conclusion, wide awake in the middle of the night about a month after Louisa's treatment started, I just hated myself. You are a numb, misanthropic, self-serving bitch, I told myself. Now Louisa's going through chemo, which is much worse, but she no longer calls that often. I think she's joined a support group. So I have to worry now: three times in three days?

I finish the first beer and get a second before I pick up the phone.

"Sheldon," I say, "something's not right with that little guy." We're having our weekly meeting over breakfast in Dubois.

Sheldon looks at me skeptically. " 'Not right'?"

"He's too small. I think we should put in for tagging them now, forget about relocation. Figure that part out later."

"Trap them twice?" says Jim. "That seems excessive. I'm not even sure Doris will fall for the trap again. She's no fool."

"I think Sheldon needs to have a look at Danny. A close look."

Sheldon's glance meets mine, but only in passing—en route to the waitress, whose attention he ropes with his best Beach Boy smile. He does a little dance with his wrist to ask for a refill on coffee. She smiles in return and hustles over. Slowly, his handsome gaze circles the table. "Anyone other than Clem have a good look at that cub this season?"

"R.B.'s seen him," I say, though it's only a guess. R.B. doesn't attend our meetings.

Sheldon stares at me. "The houndsman." If he condescends to the biologists, he regards R.B. as inhabiting some sort of intellectual sub-sub-basement. Sheldon is an in-your-face vegetarian, openly contemptuous of hunters, even those who do it to feed their families. ("I've evolved past predator. Anyone can.")

"Yeah. But what would *he* know," I say. "Please excuse me."

"It's just that he's not responsible for these decisions."

Trying hard to lose the sarcasm, I tell Sheldon that I will take *responsi-*

bility. I say nothing more about R.B. I can't tell if Sheldon suspects. I do know he's never forgiven me for refusing to go home with him from a party the first month after I got here. So he has to wonder what I've got going instead. I couldn't refuse him over *nothing.* Not gorgeous, brilliant *him.*

Vern, a peace-loving guy who offers no opinions except when we're talking vegetation, when the bears are eating pine seeds or berries, signals for the check. He offers me a sweet, knowing smile. "Practice at five. Ball field across from the tackle shop."

He knows how to cheer me up, just a little. He's talking about our softball league. Games are about forgetting all the political and personal crap that builds up between us. They're good that way. Despite his gymnified physique, Sheldon throws like a girl. And when I send a ball his way, he sometimes ducks. I'm sorry, but that does give me pleasure.

"If he's ill," I say to Sheldon, "you'd treat him, wouldn't you?"

"Depends."

"On what?"

"That is so complicated, you cannot begin to imagine," he says.

"No imagination, count on me for that." I throw a ten-dollar bill on the table, stand, and grab my jacket. I am shaking. I think about his lousy throw, all the catches he's blown, all the runs he's cost our team. Mild consolation.

"Clem, it's not like I *couldn't*," he says. "You know how Marty is."

"Don't blame everything on Marty," I say. But I know what he means. He means the whole system, the pipeline. Marty's just a valve.

R.B.'s breathing is inaudible; he never snores, as cunning in sleep as he is on a live trail. Maybe stealth is a habit. Against the wall, in their own beds, the hounds sleep, too, but more noisily: an occasional yip, a wet snort. The clock face taunts me with its lurid green: 4:12, fifty-five minutes since I last looked. All I can think about is Danny, that lethargic little cub. Marty called today, not long after the breakfast meeting. He says we're to relocate before another "encounter situation" takes place at the condos. I was still on the phone with Marty, almost speechless at his sudden one-eighty, when Buzz passed me a note. One of the condos belongs to the daughter of a state representative who'd love to see the Endangered Species Act go the way of Prohibition. So just like that, Marty has a green light from the Feds and reluctant support from the Park County sheriff, who'd probably rather mount the bears over his mantelpiece than let them loose in his woods. You'd think we were sending him a trio of known child molesters.

We'll drive the traps up the mountain tomorrow and hope for the best. Sheldon's got a new fast-acting sedative they're using on lions up in Glacier: it has a temporary paralyzing effect, which sounds just awful to me. R.B. can dart them by gun if the traps don't work. Jesus Christ.

R.B. sleeps on his back. His mouth hangs dumbly agape, the skin in front of his earlobes weary and lax, the creases dating him like rings in a tree. I take the opportunity to examine his face, every pore. He's got twenty-five years on me. Within hailing distance of sixty, married, wrinkled, an unapologetic killer. I'm with *him*?

Yet I know exactly how and why he suits me. I like his nose—so big, it's a declaration—and his height, and the strength he never flaunts, and his way of keeping calm no matter what. I know, too, that falling in love is not an option. Because this, whatever we have, isn't "real." It can't last, and I can't let myself even begin to hope that it will. He knows that I know this, that he never has to say a word. That's why it works so well.

I heard about R.B. my first week out here, when I met the rest of the grizzly team and the other pods of biologists, studying everything from pine blight to packs of wolves. Yes, students of LIFE in all the forms it's chosen to take in this part of the world, some of those forms suddenly quite tenuous or fragile. R.B.'s an oddball here. He's a guy who's paid the rent for most of his life by bringing down wild animals, exotic fearsome animals. Twenty years ago, R.B. hunted tigers and elephants. He was a skilled hunting guide to some of the richest men in the world, the one who made sure they took home a prize. But his skills are just as useful to

us, whenever an animal has to be tracked or brought down—sedated—
without the use of a trap. (He says he thinks of this work as "karma cor-
rection." He likes to see if anyone thinks he really means it.)

So I did not look forward to meeting this guy. I couldn't imagine how
I'd collaborate with someone who'd killed for sport; I don't care if his
gun license paid for the microscope on my desk or if deer need periodic
"culling." I know these things and don't want them shoved in my face.

That first week, we were all in the field and it poured for two days
straight. We made camp and sat there huddled in our ponchos and tents,
even though we were drenched to the core. R.B., Jim, and a couple
of interns told jokes. I was poker-faced the whole time. My humor had
been soaked right out of my marrow. I was thinking, *I left the ocean behind for this?* Later, on the trail, R.B. asked if I was a lily-white squirrel-
hugging liberal or just a judgmental bitch. It's hard to shock me, but I
was shocked. All the same, I had to laugh. "Both," I said.

"Maybe 'cause somebody named you after a mollusk."

"It's Clem," I said. "With an *e,* as in *educated.* Clement."

"And are you?"

I get this jokey little question about my name more than you'd think.
"You'll never know me well enough to find out otherwise," I said. "So I
could ask you back, what kind of a mother named you after a fast-food
joint?"

"Touché, doll," he said. "Well, you can call me Rex, or you can call me
Bwana."

"Oh. So either way, you're in charge. How clever is that."

For the rest of the day, we communicated purely through sarcasm,
knowing we'd made an alliance, each of us recognizing in the other the
camouflage of insolence. We're good at pretending we don't give a damn
what others think. Maybe he really doesn't.

On my side, there's a bizarre admiration: what I've come to see is that
R.B. knows animals as well as any conservationist, but he's free of all the
bullshit. We talk a lot about survival and extinction, how people interfere
with both. R.B. says our so-called interference, the selfish heedlessness
we exert on other kinds of life around us, is as natural as any other force

in the cosmos. But we have to face it. If we hunt elephants or tigers to extinction, he says, there's a sadness to cope with—maybe even regret is fair—but don't tell him it's outrageous or criminal or some kind of abomination. Though he's not the least bit religious, he likes to tell the story about the woman at a contentious hearing who stood up and said, more matter-of-fact than belligerent, "Maybe God's just calling all these creatures home." The way a rancher brings in his sheep or a suburban teenager calls her cat out of the night before she goes to bed. This is a famous story in preservation circles, where it's held up as proof of the stupidity and navel-gazing we have to deal with, those of us fighting for ferrets and wolves, lady's slippers and monarch butterflies. But when R.B. tells the story, he shrugs and says, "Who the hell's to say the lady's wrong?"

Maybe meddling to help these animals "survive" is just as benighted, just as selfish, as letting them expire. In Florida, animal-rights activists are trying to stop biologists, a team like ours but more aggressive, from taking panthers out of the most polluted part of the Everglades, from artificially broadening the gene pool with puma sperm, even though such schemes might mean, twenty years from now, the difference between survival and extinction. *Let them be,* the activists are saying. *Just BE.* Which would translate as, almost certainly, *Let them go.*

Louisa and I, we were never taught to let things be or even let things go. Maybe our dad, on his own, would've been a more Zen-like kind of parent, but don't try that stuff on our mom. She may give genteel dinner parties where some of the guests own yachts, but she learned to drive a tractor the minute she was tall enough to step on the gas. She's a scrapper, an adapter, an act-first-think-later kind of woman. We never heard *Haste makes waste.* We heard *What thou doest, do quickly.*

In for a penny, in for a pound. Never *All that glitters is not gold.*

Louisa left me those three phone messages because she's both furious and heartbroken about what the chemo's doing to her body, but not the stuff you'd expect, not the stuff that will pass (going bald, feeling queasy, losing touch with fingers and toes). She needed to rant as maybe you can only rant to family; let out all the stops on self-pity, contempt for hope and courage, loathing for the kind of sympathy offered by all the healthy friends around you. When I called her back last night, she sobbed into the phone that a friend of hers just had a baby in the same hospital where she goes for her treatments, so one day, after stopping in for blood tests, she took the elevator up to Maternity (the floor with the glorious views, of course). Just a week ago, Louisa realized that her period had stopped. She knows it's stopped for good, that her chances of having a baby of her own are, but for a miracle, over. She held that friend's baby and cried, pretending the tears were joy.

I could have said that it might not be for good, that the body's unpredictable, or I could have said, ever so gently but firmly, that she knew this would probably happen—we talked about it while she was having her radiation, how on top of every other indignity and loss she might have to give this up as well—but I listened to her rage and mourn without once interrupting.

"I'm sorry, Louisa," I said when she ran out of words. "I'm really sorry."

She was quiet for a surprising stretch, though quiet in that heaving, sobbing kind of way. She knows me as someone with an explanation for just about everything, or else a retort, and that's what she must have expected.

So finally she said, "Aren't you going to tell me I can adopt, some platitude like that?"

"Lots of other people will tell you that, so I don't need to," I said. "Besides which, you know that." I asked her how Ray was doing with all this.

"He's been away a lot. Working."

"That's too bad," I said. "He calls you, doesn't he?"

"Yes." She blew her nose. "I'm sort of glad he's away right now. I don't think he really wants kids, so maybe this part's a secret relief to him. And you'd sympathize, wouldn't you?" That set her off again.

"God, Lou. Don't you think I want you to have what *you* want?"

"You're my sister. You're supposed to want those things for me."

"You can't have it both ways, Lou. When things get bad, you can't call me—which I'm glad about, I am!—you can't do that and then imply I don't give a shit about you."

"That's what I used to think."

"I know." I paused. Ending the conversation would have punished her for the way she brings up stuff that doesn't matter anymore. But it would have brought all that stuff (grudges, regrets, ugly scenes) back to the surface again. "I guess the point is, what do you think now?"

"I think we . . . I think we're beyond the growing up."

"The growing up? What does that mean?" I asked her. "I'm nowhere near grown up, but I do a good job of hiding it."

"Not that kind of grown up. Hardly! I mean we've reached this place where we understand why it's all different from what we expected and that's just the way it's going to be. We've stopped assuming there's justice."

"Be in the I Don't Know."

"What?" she said, sounding irritated and weary.

"Zip," I said. "Remember Zip?" Of course, I was the one doing the remembering, how life with Zip was my happiest time on the coast. I detoured to a memory of his favorite T-shirt, which said, in letters so small you could read them only when you were intimately close, THE UNEXAMINED LIFE IS NOT WORTH LIVING. He was generous and honest, and completely without meaning to, he made me feel increasingly unworthy.

"Oh, Zip," said Louisa. "I liked him a lot."

"Another good one I let go, right?"

"I didn't mean that."

Don't start in about you, I warned myself. I said, "So. How's life at the big lub-dub?" Louisa works at a glossy magazine called *Artbeat*.

"Uneventful. Thank God. The August issue is thin. Curators are just like shrinks. They go to the beach, every single one, for the entire month."

"Weird," I said, "to have a job where you're always living three months in the future."

"Right now I'd give anything to be living three months in the future.

This hell would be over. If it were August, I'd have all the bad news behind me."

I was hungry and had been making myself a turkey sandwich while we talked. I couldn't hold back any longer from eating it. Better than pointing out that, obviously, all the bad news is never behind you. The *big* bad news is always, in fact, out there waiting to claim you. The worst news comes last.

"I'm interrupting your dinner," said Louisa.

"Not at all. I'm just eating between meals."

Lately, that's our code for having a nervous breakdown. She laughed.

"You laughed," I said, my mouth full. "Are you going to be okay?"

"Menopausal, but okay. I have to be okay, don't I?"

"Smile if it kills you," I said, another of our mother's signature sayings.

"It's a long way from my heart," she said. Still another.

"Maybe we need to update that one," I said. "How about, 'It's a long way from your ovaries'?"

For a minute, I thought she might start crying again, that this was the cruelest joke I could have made, but she said, "That's good, Clem. I like that. I'm going to use it on Ray the next time he complains about a headache or a sore neck."

"I want you to be happy, Lou."

"I believe you," said my sister.

I look at R.B.'s clock: 4:33. Out the window beside the bed (a window smeared with paw prints), a faint chestnut haze gathers above the jagged butte. The sky will go from brown to red to fire to saffron to a bright buttery glow; if you watch like a hawk, you can see just an instant of green, like a new leaf, before the lasting blue appears. I know these colors all too well.

I get up as quietly as I can and go into the kitchen. I stand there pondering: coffee now and get dressed, or water and back to bed? My stealth was useless, since of course Rosie and June are at my side, expectant.

"Good girls," I whisper, bending to stroke their necks. They begin their morning tap dance on the linoleum, hopeful that today involves a hunt: when people rise this early, there's a very good chance. Their tails slap the cupboards in haphazard rhythm.

R.B. groans from the bedroom. He calls out, hoarse, "Miss Inky, get back here." That's his name for me on what he calls my dark mornings. It comes from Inclement, the name he's given my black, insomniac, inside-out self. My inner Tom Waits, the voice of decomposition, decay.

I drink water from the kitchen tap, dry my hands on my T-shirt, and then I am under the covers again, pressing against him gratefully. He looks at the ceiling but holds me close. He is waiting for me to speak.

I say, "How can you ever get happy again after bad news, I mean like permanent bad news, about yourself?"

"What, like about who you are, your character? Like if you find out you're a thief or a cheat?"

"No, no. I'm thinking about Louisa."

R.B. sighs. We've talked about her cancer more than once. "It's normal to freak out," he says. "But she'll get back on the trail."

"Yeah, okay." I decide that I don't really want to discuss the kid thing with him. It might sound like it's about me, not Lou. "But I guess I wonder how anyone gets happy. Tell me, bwana: what is this thing called happy?"

"Inky, you're at it again." He squeezes me hard against his side, rib to rib.

"At what?"

"Don't bullshit me. You are chewin' the wound raw. Ain't she, Rosie Larosa, Miss June?" The hounds are staring at us, resting their long freckled snouts on R.B.'s side of the bed. They know he won't tolerate whining, though prodding's allowed.

"Seriously. Is it a stupid thing to wonder, Moronic Science one-oh-one?"

"Stupid to brood about." R.B.'s free hand meanders toward my hip. "Some people just make their own happiness, like a clean plain hotel bed, and lie right down in it. Hospital corners 'n' all."

"Do you?" I say. "I mean, is that what you do? You seem happy."

"All I do, doll, is get busy. Busy leaves no room for gloom."

"You sound like my mother."

"I'm more nurturing than you give me credit for." He taps the hounds on their noses. "Scoot, girls," he says, and they back off, disappointed but patient. He begins kissing my right ear. "Stop thinking," he says to me. "You are always thinking, thinking, thinking. You're gonna use up that overschooled little brain before its time."

"Thinking's busy."

"Wrong kind of busy." And he takes me down, like a submarine. Down, down, down we go, and finally I stop thinking. *Down periscope,* that's the last thought I have in actual words.

I am riding in the first truck and begging myself not to cry, not in front of Sheldon. He might not notice, because his full attention is on the driving, negotiating ruts in the logging road. He can't see me anyway, since between us sits Dave, the new intern, a towering grad student in ecology (the new, shinier, sexier biology). Dave's head nearly grazes the top of the cab, and he is talking a mile a minute, high from the novelty of what he's just seen. It's his first time out in the field with the whole team, and he is blown away by the operation, from the darting and sedating to the taking of blood and hair samples.

Once the traps were hitched to the trucks, we set off like a gypsy caravan. The traps look like something out of Jules Verne, heavy and cylindrical, mounted on tires. We watch for patches of ice, rare but potentially lethal. With the bears in tow, we can't afford to skid.

I keep thinking of R.B. taking aim at Danny, the dart finding its mark on the cub's neck, the way he slumped to the ground without a moment of combat. Even Sheldon was visibly impressed. The bear dogs were with us, but we didn't need their intimidation. Poor Danny had been waiting, passively, beside the trap holding his mother and sister, who somehow managed to squeeze in together. When we arrived, he looked more bewildered than fearful.

It doesn't help that I was right, that he weighs in at fifty pounds shy of his sister's heft. Sheldon whistled when he held the stethoscope to Danny's chest, the disk buried in his thick dark fur as he lay on the webbing we'd use to haul him up in the air for weighing, then pack him in a cage.

"What is it?" I said.

Sheldon repositioned the stethoscope and listened further. He shook his head. "I need an EKG."

There was too much to do, in too little time, for any of us to stand around quizzing Sheldon about Danny's heart. We had no choice but to get the bears on the road before the sedation wore off too much. I had to show Dave how we label and bag the vials of blood, pack them in the cooler. Vern and Jim were hitching the trucks to the traps, Buzz organizing the equipment. We have it down to a science, this science of ours, but that doesn't mean we can do it in a leisurely fashion. There was a lot of heavy breathing, a lot of cursing, a lot of barking orders, but there was very little talk until Sheldon got off the radio phone. "We're taking them all to the station," he said, "not the relocation site."

So here I am in the truck wondering what the hell we are doing, how the hell we are pulling this off. Dave's puppy-dog enthusiasm, his lack of ambivalence, his exclamations of *wow* and *cool* and *sweet* (sweet!) put me on edge, pulling the tears closer. I wish I had chosen to go with R.B. in his truck. He was trying to catch my eye while Sheldon examined Danny back at the trap site, but I wouldn't let him.

"Call the station," Sheldon says. "Tell them we're fifteen minutes away. Tell them the bears will stay overnight. Make sure they're ready."

Conehead answers, not Vern. He's just arrived from Cheyenne, and now that he knows he's here for more than just some bland local coverage of a routine relocation, I can only imagine that he's suiting up to play the role of some big-zookie game hunter who skipped the gory part but gets to take the credit. I picture him posing with Doris as if he's bagged her, one cowboy boot on her big blond head, that big white cake on his.

"Success?" he barks at me.

"I suppose you could call it that," I tell him, my voice crimped to conceal my emotion. "We're en route with all three."

"Then I suppose you suppose right, Miss Jardine."

I ask for Vern.

"This is so fuckin' cool," says Dave for about the sixty-third time.

"What will be cool," I say when it's clear that ignoring him won't dampen his exuberance, "is when these animals are safe and sound, out of our clutches and back in the woods where they belong."

We are out on the blacktop now, cruising along, though Sheldon's careful not to speed up too much. He lets the wipers run, just long enough to clear the dust off the windshield, then clicks on the radio, low-volume country. All three of us are quiet now, nobody singing along.

"Without surgery, his heart will fail. It's that simple," I say.

"So can they—can you guys do heart surgery on a bear?" asks Louisa.

"There's a vet on the team, and if . . ." I sigh at all the ifs I can't even name.

"If what?"

"If he gets help, he says he could do it."

Danny has a congenital defect called VSD, a hole in his heart, a defect that nowadays, if Danny were a child born with good insurance in a modern city, would be corrected through surgery. A big deal but not that uncommon. From Danny's heart rate, from his respiration and the edema in his limbs, Sheldon's pretty sure he won't live much longer. Weirdly, Sheldon seems less cocky and more certain all at once. Already, he's tracked down a cardiac surgeon in Laramie who says he'll consult for travel expenses alone. Experience of a lifetime. He can be here in two days, with machines and a tech.

The alternative—which even Buzz reluctantly favors—is releasing the little guy without intervention, letting nature take its course.

"So do it," says Louisa. "Get the help!"

"It takes a lot of red tape to get permission for this sort of thing. Never mind the money."

This sort of thing. As if the situation is vaguely routine. Louisa takes for granted that it isn't absurd—all this radical effort to save the life of a single unexceptional animal, nobody's pet, just an anonymous creature from the woods. Yesterday, as I listened to Buzz and Jim and Marty catalog the pros and cons, I said far less than I might have. I felt off balance, even terrified, because to me the choice was obvious when I knew it shouldn't be. Because this creature and his life aren't anonymous to me. Did I cross a line somewhere? To me, Danny's life is priceless—the same life that's worth nothing more than the joy of pulling a trigger to an army of Joe Blow Davy Crocketts who'd use the EPA to wipe their butts.

I'm at my desk in the lab. It's late, and everyone else has left the station. The bears are in a concrete holding pen out back. Doris and Tipper have to be on the road within a day or two—and Danny, if we're simply sending him off to die.

"I'll let you know what happens," I say to Louisa. "But what's with you? What new torture have they devised for you this week?"

"They gave me a drug," she says, "to pump up my white blood cells. It hurts like hell. I feel like some invisible assailant is slugging me, randomly, all over, with a baseball bat."

Among the people I know, only Louisa would use a word like *assailant* so naturally. "Yikes," I say. "Sounds awful."

"It is. I'm going to rent a movie, something funny but not romantic. Maybe something with Danny DeVito or Denis Leary. I need mean funny, not nice funny."

"Is Ray there?"

"He got back yesterday. He's being very sweet. It helps."

"That's good," I say. "I have to go. I have to fill out a bunch of forms."

"Good luck."

"Luck's irrelevant," I say.

"Well, same here," says Louisa.

Why does this conversation leave me sadder, more depleted? Louisa sounds better than she has in a while. Her white cells are set to do battle. Her Good Man is home. He loves her. He doesn't have a wife in Sarasota.

I browse my bulletin board, its scatter of papers: the softball schedule, a long article on forest fires in Yellowstone that I keep on meaning to read, the menu from the nearest pizza joint, a chart of the radioed bears in our unit, their movements since emerging from their dens.

There are only two photos: me posed with a knocked-out bear in the field (I'm lying down in the pine needles, grinning, my arm around the bear as if we're in bed together); me at the Monterey Bay Aquarium, swimming in the kelp forest, all suited up, feeding the fish. Zip took that picture. I like it not because it's flattering—you can hardly tell it's me— but because it's me in another world, reality suspended (though if you look close, you can see the flash, and a silhouette of Zip, reflected in the glass wall of the tank). There are no photos of family. No parents, no Louisa.

Danny has his mother here, but I feel responsible for him. I pull the cot out of the supply room; I lie down, assuming I won't go to sleep. But then I wake to early sunlight, the sound of a key in the lock.

"Hey," says Buzz. He doesn't seem surprised to find me here.

"Hey," I answer.

"Don't sound so cheerful."

When I come out of the bathroom, he's put away the cot. "Have some cardboard java." He hands me a stained mug with coffee from the ancient Mr. Coffee that refuses to die. "They seem okay," he says brightly. "I had a peek on my way in."

"We've fucked it up, though. They should've gone straight to Fox Creek."

"Nah," says Buzz. "Sheldon wants to do some tests on Tipper, then we can have 'em on the road by tomorrow." Buzz is our Boy Scout, the one who acts like everything's fine and dandy, no matter how much scat hits the fan. I used to despise people like that. Now it's complicated.

I don't mention Danny. It looks as if Sheldon and I are the only ones who want the surgery to happen, whatever it takes. In for a penny, in for a pound. No letting go; no giving up.

~

I drive to the diner where I meet R.B. when it's just the two of us, a place the others would never dream of going. It's popular with truckers, the ones who drive the logging rigs over the pass. He isn't there yet. I claim a booth and ask for coffee; it's not much better than the cardboard java back at the station.

At the counter, two middle-aged guys are joking and laughing together, eating platters of eggs with steak and biscuits. Because I have nothing to read, I eavesdrop. They're talking girls and fish. One has a wife; the other doesn't.

When the one with a wife gets up to go to the men's room, the one who doesn't sneaks a backward look and catches my eye. "Morning," he says. He swivels his stool to face me. His shirt strains across his middle, and his face looks older than it should, too many scattershot veins, but he gives me a bright, clean smile.

"Morning," I answer.

"On your own? Join us?"

"I'm waiting for someone. Someone who's always late. But thanks."

"You some kind of cop?" He makes a show of peering at my shoulder patch.

"Game and Fish."

"Ma'am." He salutes me.

His friend returns, sits down, and swings around to face me as well. "I leave for two seconds and you get yourself in trouble with the law, Jack?"

Jack ignores the friend. "Just so you know, officer, the guns on that rack out there are licensed." He nods toward the parking lot. He's flirting, something I'd enjoy if I weren't so tense.

"Not to worry. I'm just a high-minded head-in the-clouds biologist."

Now it's the friend's turn to ask if I'll join them. He makes the time-worn plea that they're two harmless dudes away from home, hungry for a little female company. Jack informs him that I have a date on the way.

I ask where they're from. Turns out they're down from northern Idaho, from mining country, to try a little fishing. When I ask them why now—why not wait for the warmer weather, true summer?—Jack says, "The price of silver."

I laugh. "The price of silver?"

"Shot up to six," he says.

His friend explains to me how mining, up where they live, is practically obsolete—how they're holding down some of the last few dozen jobs—but this spring there's been a sudden demand, a spike in the price of the commodity they blast and wheedle from the earth. Their prosperity's tied to that number, a number that's no doubt published every day in newspapers all across the country. I wonder what it's like to see the value of what you do quantified to the decimal point. Its meaning to the world is out of your hands.

"Wow. Congratulations," I say.

"Oh, it'll sink again. You can count on that. But we figured, why not celebrate now?"

"Get it while you can," says Jack.

And then R.B. slides into the booth. He glances at the miners. "Hey," he says blandly.

"Hey," they answer, in the same neutral guy tone, which must be code for *Yeah, dude, we already knew she was yours*, because just like that, without another word, they salute me in virtual unison and turn back to the counter.

"Make some new friends?" asks R.B.

"That's me, gathering new friends wherever I go."

"Well, if that's what you had a mind to do, you would." I realize he means it. "Why so quiet?" he says in a moment. "You're too quiet these days. Can't believe you had so little to say at the meeting last night. Conehead was wallowing in fine print, happy as a pig in dung. I saw him lookin' at you more than once, wondering why you didn't shoot him down. Not once."

What he's referring to was more of a melee than a meeting. The lot of us were pacing around the lab, trying to figure out how to proceed with the relocation, with Danny. It felt like every wildlife know-it-all inside four counties—Vern's plant-minded colleagues, the ungulate team, even a wolf guy—had shown up to express an opinion, informed or not.

"Wasted breath," I say. "I doubt it matters to Marty or his cronies what any of us think. He wasn't even pretending to listen."

"Oh, I don't know," says R.B. "I think you guys have his ear when the going gets tough."

"Or the learning curve steep."

R.B. stares at me without smiling. "What makes you such a cynic?"

"Protective coloration," I shoot back.

The waitress brings him coffee and a menu. Without opening the menu, he orders for both of us. Then he stares at me again. "I didn't know any better, I'd say you've fallen in love with that bear."

"Would that make you jealous?"

"Can't see any other reason you'd go against what's logical here. One thing you've never been is sentimental."

"I consider that a compliment."

"I know you do, doll." He won't stop staring at me, won't crack a smile. For a man I can never claim as a mate, he's got a scary fix on me. "Inky, watch out," he says. "You're in deep water on this one. I'd let it go."

What Buzz and Jim pointed out is that we don't do the bears any service by fixing Danny up, like a car with a bum alternator, and putting him back out there to thrive and reproduce, maybe have cubs with a defect just like his. So the choice becomes this: play God or play Darwin, wrong either way.

Right there, in the middle of that meeting, I saw the hypocrisy of what we do. Here we are, self-proclaimed lovers of nature, yet our whole mission is to fight its laws and logic. We don't let nature take its course; we struggle to reverse that course. Why make a ruthless exception of Danny?

"Okay then," I say. "How about we do the surgery, then *castrate* the guy? Call it nepotism. Favorable treatment."

Miner Jack and his friend turn around when they hear the c word. I meet their glance. "What we do to hunters who disregard the quotas."

My French toast arrives. I dig in, determined not to talk. I'm not hungry, but I eat because it gives me a way to avoid R.B.'s punishing gaze.

He lowers his voice when he says, "Who do you think you are?"

I look up, stung. It's another echo of my mother, her get-off-your-big-fat-throne retort whenever Louisa or I tried to gain some authority over her (always a losing battle). But the look on R.B.'s face is perplexed, not angry. He says, so earnest that I have to listen, "Are you in this to do the work or get some kind of martyr charge out of everything that fails? 'Cause the work means a lot of beating your head on walls. I hope to God you know that by now."

"Do I ever."

R.B. isn't into power struggles, so he spares me. "Well, doll, as it happens, you just might get your way. There's a *National Geographic* guy in Jackson, a good pal of the surgeon who's gung ho to do this procedure with Sheldon."

I glare at him, but I let him talk. I don't ask how he knows this. R.B. knows everything that goes on in town. He's an all-purpose tracker.

"Conehead loves high-class press. As well he should." R.B. is alluding to the Teddy Factor: the way we win public opinion by trading on just how photogenic the grizzlies are. Whenever someone publishes a letter in the paper about how bears are dangerous or overprized or stand in the way of development and tourism (i.e., jobs), we call up the editor and counter with a Panavision shot of mama and babies frolicking in a starry field of flowers.

"But," says R.B., "Sheldon's motives are one thing."

"Naked ambition," I say. "Good for him."

"So what are yours?"

I shake my head, feigning amusement. This time, I fool him into thinking I couldn't care less. He spears a slice of my tepid French toast and lays it beside the last of his scrambled eggs. A dotted line of syrup runs from my plate to his. I can think of several wry remarks to make about this territorial act, but I am out of witty repartee. This is so incredibly not like *Daktari*. This is more like, what, *Rowan and Martin's Laugh-In*? *The Mod Squad*?

~～

On the day of the surgery, it's hard to tell who brings in more equipment: the surgeon from Laramie who's working with Sheldon or the photographer from *National Geographic*. In our bare-bones exam room, which they've rigged for the procedure, space is tight. It will be a feat to accommodate Sheldon, the surgeon, and his tech, plus a local livestock vet (who has instructions from a zoo vet on how to handle the anesthesia), along with the photographer and the writer. Never mind poor Danny, who's spent a bewildering week in the holding pen. Doris and his sister were taken north and released five days ago.

I did not go along for the release. I made the excuse that one of us had to stay by the phones to handle calls from reporters. In the end, we've bought Danny's life, or his chance at life, with a media fuck. This happens all the time in our work; the best way to hearts, minds, votes, and wallets is through NPR, or *Nova,* or even—the bighorn center nailed this one—the *Wall Street Journal*. So you let the outsiders barge in with their tape recorders and videocams, their oohs and ahs, their never-quite-adequate footwear. You act like you are pleased as punch.

And now, today, when all I want is to be with Danny, as if he were my child, not a subject of my scientific scrutiny, it's my job to hang out with the B-list writers—from two western papers and a magazine for members of a glamorous wildlife organization (the Panda Huggers, we call them behind their backs). Sheldon gave me a list of "talking points" on the surgery; Marty gave me an up-to-date list of the local politicians who are (or are not) behind the protection of grizzlies. "Be darn sure you work in the names of the ones who are pro," he said. To my exasperation, but also relief, Conehead couldn't make it today. His offspring—a real live human child—is graduating from college.

So we have what constitutes a small crowd. We even have hecklers. In the street out front—a street in the middle of nowhere, no TV cameras in sight, maybe an idle passerby or two—stand four people with three signs: GRIZZLIES ARE A THREAT, NOT A TREASURE and PEOPLE ARE A SPECIES TOO and BEARS BELONG IN ZOOS. The fourth person has a megaphone that she is clearly embarrassed to have brought. Out the window, once everyone's in who's coming in, I see her stash it under a bush.

Is it true that grizzly bears are gentle by nature, that only people make them mean? Has this surgery ever been done on a wild animal before? Is it like a bypass? Will he be reunited with his mother? How much will this cost? Is it paid for with our taxes? Isn't the Endangered Species Act due to expire? These are some of the questions I answer while Danny goes under the knife. Over several hours, members of my audience come and go, returning with pizza, doughnuts, pretzels. The office area begins to smell like a sports event: half grease, half perspiration. At one point, the photographer comes out of the exam room to take a leak and grab a slice.

"How's it going?" I ask.

He takes another bite before speaking. "Intense." He wolfs down the rest of his pizza and wipes his hands on the seat of his jeans.

I let myself outside and walk around the building twice. A cold brilliant light emanates from the window to the makeshift OR, but it's a high window, too high for me to see anything more than the fluorescent fixture on the ceiling. The picketers have left. Rage cools fast without an accessible target.

The reporters have run out of questions. Two of them, both women, stand on the concrete steps out front, smoking, chatting about what their kids will be doing for the summer. Inside, two others help themselves to our desks, open their laptops, and start to write their stories. When my phone rings, I have to reach over a stranger's shoulder to answer. R.B. says, "Well?"

I tell him it's not over yet.

"I'm not going anywhere," he says. "Bought some of that white wine you like. Want a movie?"

"A movie? If it goes well, I plan to sleep for three days."

"Sleep here," he says.

"Thank you," I say. What I'm grateful for is that he didn't ask what I plan to do if it doesn't go well.

It's dusk when the door finally opens. The room expels people one by one: first the writer, then the photographer, then the livestock vet.

Beyond them, I can just see Sheldon, his blond hair darkened and flattened by sweat, the blue cloth mask crumpled at his throat.

The faces of the three men who've left the room are slack, drained of energy and will. The photographer says something that makes his colleague laugh briefly. And then the other writers, the ones who've waited with me—four of the original six—crowd around the door, blocking my view.

I sit on my desk and wait. Buzz comes over and stands beside me. He rests a hand, a lingering kindness, on my knee.

"Moment of truth," he says.

I am quiet. I resolve not to say a word until I speak to Sheldon, as if this will promise good news. I refuse to eavesdrop on the conversation at the door, eight or ten feet away. Whatever they're saying, it's hearsay.

The reporters peel away for a moment, making room for the cardiologist from Laramie. He heads straight for the bathroom, inscrutable. The tech wheels a machine out of the room and down the back hall.

On my desk, the phone is ringing again. Buzz looks at me. I shake my head. He lets it ring till the voicemail picks up.

Sheldon comes out quickly, pulling the surgical smock over his head. He throws it hard, an act of violence or emancipation, onto a chair. By the time it slips to the floor, he is standing with me and Buzz. His T-shirt advertises Jamaica; the sweat stains beneath the arms reach all the way to his waist.

"We are fucked," he says to me. "Sorry, Clem."

I start crying before he tells us what happened. Danny did not come out of the anesthesia. Whether the surgery itself might have succeeded is unclear. Sheldon avoids looking at me. He tells Buzz he will go out for a quick dinner by himself, then return to do the necropsy. "No one stick around," he says. "I mean it. I told the vultures to call me tomorrow." He shows no emotion other than mild disgust.

I realize that all the journalists have left, including the *National Geographic* guys. Dave, our hyped-up intern, lurks nervously about but seems to understand it's a time to keep mum.

Finally Sheldon turns to me. "You going to call Marty?"

Buzz says, "I'll do that." He's quietly put an arm around my shoulders.

Sheldon goes into the bathroom. When he comes out, he takes his coat from the rack, as if he's in a tearing hurry. He starts for the door to the parking lot, but then he turns around and comes back toward me. "I'm sorry, Clem. I really am. You said you'd take responsibility, remember that? But it's mine. Just so you know. My responsibility."

"You did your best," I say, and I know he did. But still, in the midst of this agony—worse for him than for anyone else—I can't suppress the cruel thought that his nobility is a pose. He leaves quickly. Before the door closes behind him, I hear him shout "Fuck!" three times at the top of his lungs. What's the matter with me, that I can't feel sorry for Sheldon, that my heart goes out only to the bear?

Dave says, "Wow. What a day. Like, what next?"

"Go home," Buzz tells him, more gently than I would.

Dave looks wounded, but he follows orders.

Buzz and I are alone. The surgery ended less than half an hour ago, and everyone's gone but us. "Want to have dinner?" asks Buzz.

"No, but thanks." I get up from my desk and go over to the exam room. I open the door and switch on the light.

"Oh don't. Really, don't," says Buzz, but he follows me in.

Danny lies on the steel table like a small battered ship washed ashore in a storm. Like all dead creatures, he looks surprisingly deflated. His chest is shaved, a long incision sewn shut in his dark, smooth skin. Bits of tubing and stained wads of gauze lie scattered about his body and on the floor, like windblown debris. On the gray linoleum, two or three partial shoe prints are traced in blood.

"His head is so huge," I say. Grizzlies have massive heads, larger in proportion to their body than in any of the other bears. Even when you know it, this defining point of anatomy, it startles you over and over. So I grasp his head between my hands, the dense fur both coarse and soft, and I look into his eyes. They are open but dull, fogged over. R.B. once told me that if you see your reflection in the eyes of a fierce, predatory animal, one that could tear you limb from limb, you will never be the same again.

I forgot to ask how you will never be the same. Are you cursed; are you wise; are you saved? This won't be my day to find out.

"Clem, let's split," says Buzz. "I'm taking you for a drink."

I let him find my jacket, guide my arms into the sleeves, and lead me to the parking lot. He drives us to a yuppie watering hole with a stunning view of the Tetons. Well, it's stunning by day. Now the picture window is a mirror, in it a gathering of fortunate, good-looking people out on the town. I order a margarita, and then I go to the ladies' room. I call R.B. and tell him what happened. He asks me where I am, and I say that I'm having a postmortem drink with the guys. I wait for him to beg me to come over. He doesn't. He says he's sorry, that he'll see me tomorrow.

As I walk back to the bar, all I can think is *This sucks,* but when I see Buzz from a distance, looking so wholesome and so dejected, stirring his vodka tonic with his little red straw, I know I have to try, just try, to say something nicer than what I'm thinking. Once I'm sitting on my stool, I say, "Serendipity and fluff."

Buzz laughs, nervously. "Excuse me?"

"It's something this really ancient aunt of mine used to say. How she loved 'serendipity and fluff.' The pleasure of trivial nonsense. Her life was like this secret, muted tragedy, but she still had a huge appetite for silliness. Harmless gossip. Beach books. Cotton candy. That is what I'm wishing for right now. Serendipity and fluff."

"Yeah," he says, "we could use that now, couldn't we."

The silence that follows simply mocks our longing for levity. "But hey," I say. "We can eat. And we can damn well drink."

We order burgers. I have two more margaritas. We talk about how we got to this place, these jobs, how much we like Wyoming. It's like two hours of tender small talk, as if we just met, as if we've been dumped by other people and we're each groping for a new beginning. I figure if he wants to take me home with him, I'll go. But he's a gentleman, is Buzz. He drives me all the way out to where I live and promises to pick me up in the morning. "How about I bring the radio receiver? We can drive north and spy on our golden girl."

I say, "Sure."

For a minute or two, we're just sitting in his car, in the dark. It's awkward. Then he gets out, so quickly that I flinch. He's just going around to open my door. Of course. He says, "Drink lots of water and take a couple aspirin."

"Buzz, you'd make a great husband," I tell him.

"I know," he says sharply. "Women who don't want a husband tell me so all the time."

"Sorry."

"No big deal. But forget about the aspirin and you will be."

He waits for me to go inside before he drives away. Typical: I send the gentleman off into the night.

Inside my cold little home, I play back two messages from Louisa, the first one eager, the next one anxious. She's frantic to know what happened with Danny. *You cannot begin to imagine,* I think as I fall onto my bed, fully clothed, not bothering to turn out the light on the table, not drinking a drop of water or taking an aspirin, but then I remember that this is what Sheldon said to me the first time we discussed Danny. *You cannot begin to imagine.* I saw his attitude as nothing more than insulting. What a simpleton I was. Am. And—if I face things as they are, not as I wish they were—will always be. Where is My Life, my nomadic twin, when I desperately need to meet up with her again?

The sheets are so cold. I should get up and turn on the heat, but I don't. What was it R.B. said about happiness as a clean plain hotel bed? The opposite of happiness isn't unhappiness, I think as I sink into sleep. It's surrender.

The World We Made

When the Tetons appear, I am thinking of Eva Hesse. The plane swoons slowly forward, a bison sinking to its knees, then soars in a fanciful arc. The whine of the engines rises in pitch and the landing gear drops, a sound that always jolts my heart. "Seventy-five degrees, clear and dry as a vodka martini," the pilot drawls, as if this cocktail of an afternoon were his private concoction. "May I personally, on behalf of myself and your flight crew, wish each and every one of you a beautiful, safe, and happy stay in Jackson. Or if this is home to you—well, lucky you!"

Three months ago, I went to Washington to cover a retrospective of Eva Hesse's work. My sister was there, too, a coincidence, to give a paper on bear census taking in the Rockies. Just to see me, Clem stayed an extra day. A rare collision, a chance to talk without phone haze or time zones between us, without a family occasion to bring on the hornets. We ate lunch at an Indian restaurant and then, though I was sure she'd turn me down—too much to do, paperwork and politics; "an Everest of guano," as she'd once described the worst part of her job—I asked if she'd like to see the show. Unpredictable as ever, she said yes. That was in May; on the way to the Hirshhorn, we walked through the last plumes of falling cherry blossoms. Almost finished with chemo, I was still wearing a wig.

Eva Hesse died of cancer when she was thirty-four. Hers was brain, mine is breast. Mine has not spread—not detectably. They caught it early, and I am considered, even at thirty-seven, lucky. True, compared with Eva. So far at least.

Crossing the mountains from Denver, I keep my face turned toward the window. I want to avoid idle talk from my neighbors, but the scenery on this flight plan happens to be spectacular. In sunlight, the slopes resemble green velour: in some places rumpled like a cast-off gown, in others sedately corduroyed—wherever the paper companies deploy their platoons of ridgepole saplings, forests resolute with monotony. Clem talked about the paper companies with venom. Their power is supreme, she said. They control everyone in these parts, from journalists to fishing guides—even the clergy. They might as well be God; come to think of it, she said, they are.

At this remove, the terrain takes on a brainlike texture, and maybe that's what makes me think of Eva. But mostly the connection is Clem; the last time I saw her, we were looking at Eva's sculpture.

Among the other passengers, I make my way down to the tarmac. Descending an open-air stairway to the bright hot roar of an airfield makes me feel significant, like a starlet or queen: even today it feels shamefully wonderful, the fragrant heat after hours of anesthetizing chill. Wonderful, the searching faces behind the windows reflecting the mountains. Wonderful, so much blue sky pressing so close, the sun on my newly unprotected head. I am letting my new hair show, curls where it used to be straight, reddish blond where it used to be the greenish gold of hay. I am glad to be out from under the airless helmets I wore for months. When the wind touches my scalp, the sensation is startling, cool and astringent.

On the ground, I turn full circle and see the mountains from below. They seem to lean in right at the edge of the airstrip, as if a child drew them there, upright and pointed, crowned with snow even in August, extruding from the earth like whales breaching water. Then I look for Buzz.

On the phone, he asked if he should hold up a sign, but then he remembered he'd be in his uniform, coming from work. Here he is, sure enough, polyester pants and short-sleeved shirt the brown of walnuts, a color to flatter no one; on the shoulder patches, a poorly stitched elk. He is younger than I imagined—a boyish twenty-eight at most: just the age to make me feel indignantly old.

I wave.

"Louisa?"

"Buzz."

He says my name again. He shakes my hand. "Not too bumpy, your landing?"

"Fine. For once I sat on the right side of the plane. For the view."

"It's something, isn't it?"

I nod, and he asks if I checked any bags. When I shake my head, he says, "Wagon's out front." I can tell that he considered hugging me but decided against it. "Oh!" He reaches for my bag. "Slow on the manners here."

Not till we're in the car (the same brown as his uniform, the Game and Fish seal on both front doors) does he say how sorry he is about my sister's death, how he never knew her real well as a person but worked with her, of course, and thought she was one of the smartest women—"oh," he blushes, "smartest *people*"—he's ever met, how everyone here is in shock.

When I thank him, I feel strangely clearheaded. So far, the hardest I've cried was in Denver, between flights. I couldn't contain it, and there was no place in that airport, not a restroom, not a news shop, not a single flightless lounge, where I could be alone to cry. I had known for twelve hours. Now I feel a callow relief, as if I'll never cry again, as if I've inhaled a potent wintergreen balm.

"We'll drive through the park," says Buzz. "It's a little longer, but phenomenal this time of year—well, any time of year, as you can guess."

I thank him again, remembering how the pilot wished me, along with everyone else, a beautiful stay. That much, unavoidably, it will be. Beautiful.

"The boss says you can have this car while you're here, no problem." I thank him a third time. "We put you in Dubois. About twenty minutes from where she lived. Clem's place," he adds, as if I wouldn't know who. "I was there a couple times. She had this great cookout last summer."

"She liked to party," I say.

"Play ball, too. She was a great shortstop. She tell you about the team?" He is warming up, getting his bearings on this terrible task he's been stuck with. I envision Clem's colleagues—biologists, lab technicians, the bureaucratic charlatans she railed against whenever we spoke—all of them drawing straws and this poor guy coming up short. Because in the three years she lived here, she worked long hours. Outside the lab she knew hardly a soul; so she said. For a year or more, she'd been having an affair; I knew this only because I'd grilled her. She said it was mildly scandalous and never mentioned his name. Not Buzz, I decide; he's attractive in a preppie, duckhunterish way, but she'd never have gone for his eagerness to please, his habit of jumpy self-affirmation. Or perhaps that's just his nervousness at being with me.

Clem was physically reckless, her all-or-nothing soul sealed tight in a cactus veneer. The men she liked—a small battalion, and they always liked her back, fell hard for her hardness—were brawny, outspoken types, or sure of themselves in some other way. Buzz reminds me more of my ex-husband, Hugh: dependable, polite. I'd bet his toenails are clean and close-trimmed, his feet soft and white as shrink-wrapped supermarket mushrooms.

Dubois is more than an hour from Jackson, through a slash in the mountains called Twogwotee Pass. Most of the vehicles we pass are trucks: pickups or semis or flatbeds stacked with flayed trees. Most of the pickups carry guns or dogs or both. The main drag of Dubois—its only commercial street—is Wyoming's retort to Walt Disney. On the right, a motel with a hulking plaster bear out front. On all fours, that bear stands eight feet tall. His mouth is open in a livid roar; his teeth drip with blood the color of Paloma Picasso's signature lipstick. Across the street, side by side, the animal clinic and car wash. You enter the clinic through a bison skull, tall as a house. Next door, on the roof of the car wash, a bull moose looks imperiously up and away toward a red-rock butte. His plastic hide flashes back sunshine. The store where you'd buy your ammo, your flies and tackle, announces itself with a fishing pole taller than a streetlamp, dangling a speckled trout the size of a marlin.

By the time we get there, Buzz is talking about how the grizzly team works, how other teams that share the lab in the wildlife station study other animals, even plants. He takes for granted the surrounding fun-house menagerie, ducking without comment below the arch of tangled antlers that beckons guests to the hotel he's chosen for me. Beyond this savage curio, it could be any old charmless pit stop on any old frontier back road.

"Beds are comfortable," he says, reading my look. He insists on carrying my bag. "I got you rooms across from each other—lucky, this time of year."

"It's fine. We're very grateful."

My parents will arrive tomorrow. Coming from Rhode Island, they had a harder time booking flights than I did from New York. It took poor Dad a few hours to make sure the boatyards were covered; August is a never-ending rush.

The room is larger than it would be in the same hotel back east, and the view is generous: red butte and a canopy of cobalt blue, a sky to depend on. I have a cement balcony with two lawn chairs and, inside, a small refrigerator, which I hope will be filled with small hits of strong booze. I am beginning to drink again, and loving it. During chemo, when it would have made me puke, the unremitting sobriety seemed like an insult thrown in for sadistic good measure. So when Buzz asks if there is anything he can do, anything at all, I hand him the ice bucket from the bathroom. He looks happy. I have learned, just recently, to give people things to do in a crisis. Accepting favors is an odd form of mercy.

After he comes back with my ice, he hovers outside the door. "A couple of us were hoping you'd have dinner with us? Later's fine if . . . or if you'd rather not, if you're too tired . . ."

"That's so kind of you," I say. "Thank you." I tell him I need a bath and that I want to visit my sister's place—just for a minute, just to see it. I don't tell him I need to call the police, call Ray, call a doctor to cancel a checkup I'm supposed to be having tomorrow back in New York.

"Yeah. Sure," says Buzz. "I'll take you out there after dinner. You'd get lost if you tried it alone."

"Don't think I don't know how strange this must be," I tell him. "I feel sorry for you—for all of you. It's not—" I'm going to say it's not their fault, but he interrupts me.

"Oh no. Yeah—no. Everybody feels just awful. I mean for *you.*"

And for Clem? I wonder. Do they feel awful for her? Did she make any enemies, people who are secretly relieved she's out of the way?

After I close the door, I switch on the bathroom light. I look at myself in the mirror. "You," I say to my reflection, and I touch it on the nose, "you are now an only child. That's right." Which means, I realize (sick at the glint of relief in my bitter sorrow), that I inherit everything. There will be no showdown over who gets what, the kind of scene that's played too many times in the theater of my father's large, acquisitive family. Silver demitasse spoons from all the major national parks. Among other antiques, a highboy just like one at Monticello. The arrowheads our great-grandfather found while plowing his Minnesota fields (Clem would have wanted those). The Spanish Colonial armor, the trunk of raccoon coats, the tarnished silver cups and faded satin rosettes—dozens—won by cows my mother showed at state fairs during her midwestern youth. Complementing those trophies, dozens of medals won in all the wars fought by my father's long chain of military ancestors (a chain he broke, with reluctance and then relief, after West Point refused his flat feet). It looks as if I'll inherit all that, and this too: the privilege of dealing, by myself, with our parents' eventual senility, terminal illness, or both. Unless they outlive me.

I notice how, in fluorescent light, my scalp gleams unattractively through my new hair. Unless they outlive us both.

I start running a bath. Tub, toilet, and sink are all a gleeful Bermudian green. I empty a tiny bottle of bubble bath into the water, a tiny bottle of

Smirnoff into a glass packed with ice. The steam rises in a cloud of brittle evergreen; it smells like a cat I loved as a child, a gingham cat stuffed with pine needles. Every time I slept with that cat, a needle would poke through a seam and jab me awake. But I never gave up on its thorny love; I mothered that cat till the strained seams along its ears finally burst, disgorging its dry brown innards.

I peel off my clothes and get into the tub when it's half full. I watch the froth rise, from both sides, to bury my shins, my thighs, my navel, my knees. I slump down till the suds cover the scar on my breast and cling to my neck like an Elizabethan ruff. I lean forward, turn off the taps, lie back. I close my eyes and stay that way, sipping vodka, until the water feels chilly and the bubbles thin to a milky scrim like aimless, inconsequential clouds. As my body comes back into view, I suddenly want to know about hers—what she did to it, where it is right now, what there is left to see. I want to see Clem's body.

The last time I saw her, in Washington, she made fun of my wig.

"You know, that thing makes you look like one of the Supremes. A lily-white Supreme. Or Doris Day. Like any minute you'll break into song—like, 'Que Sera, Sera.' "

I laughed. "You try it on for size. I don't mean the wig."

"Oh, we all get it sooner or later, long as we're not struck down by a falling rock or a sniper. It's the world we've made, no mystery there. But if it were me, I'd shave my head."

"And what, flaunt it? Remind everyone of their biggest fear?"

"If cancer is your biggest fear, you're doing all right," said Clem.

Long ago, I realized that idealism had turned my sister into a crank. But her company made me happy—and I still had glimpses of her inviolate tenderness, deep inside her shell. And honestly, I was relieved when she made fun of how silly I looked, because I did look silly. Like most women in my predicament, I'd tried on dozens of wigs looking for my old familiar self in the mirror—couldn't I hang on to *her*?—before I saw that the only thing to do was treat this cover-up like a masquerade or a disguise. I chose two: a long auburn pageboy, very Glenda Jackson, and the one I wore that day, a canary bubble that swooped along my jawbone. My friends told me I looked camp or chic or risqué; I looked nothing of the kind, but it was their job to say so. Not Clem's. Clem picked her own job: calling classmates from grad school who'd gone into medical research. She asked them for the more complicated truths about my drugs, and then she told me, not a single word minced. Risk of leukemia, atrophied muscle and memory, sandblasted liver, neuropathy, menopause early and mean. No having babies. For that, for telling me what I was up against as bluntly my doctors would never have done, I felt grateful.

I order the Home on the Range BBQ Platter and eat every bite: pulled pork, fried chicken, mashed potatoes, and coleslaw. I eat every shred of iceberg lettuce, every sawdust wedge of tomato in the salad. I rip a roll in two and drag it through the gravy left on my plate, the bottled dressing in my bowl. I can tell my hunger makes them uneasy. When your only sister kills herself, you are not supposed to eat like John Wayne at the hoedown. I can't help it. I eat not just to console myself but to do something I can do well when my mind has shut down or would like to. ("Everyone has a mindless thing they excel at," Clem once said. "Yours is eating, mine is sex." I gave her a dirty look and said, "How do you know mine isn't sex as well?" "Because you react like that," she said. "Because you're clearly jealous. But listen, eating's nothing to sneeze at.")

The place we're having dinner would be called a coffee shop in New York; in Dubois, it's a family restaurant. So the menu declares, as if this claim makes it extra-appealing: all those babies in booster chairs, screeching just for the joy of it. The food is fine—I have coconut custard pie for dessert, with a scoop of chocolate ice cream—but I could have wished for less light. The four people who brought me here share the rancid raw-oyster complexion of people who haven't washed or slept or laughed for days. Besides Buzz, there is Sheldon, a veterinarian; Vern, a tall storky man with cratered skin; and Dave, Clem's field assistant, a summer intern from Bozeman. Buzz told me Dave is the one who found Clem. Now that I've met him, I have no idea how to ask how my sister died. He's just a kid, wide-eyed and baffled. I'm sure my parents know how she killed herself—they spoke with the police—but never in a million years would I ask them.

Sheldon talks the most. He tells me a story about how, back in the spring, they performed surgery on a captive cub to correct a heart defect. Clem did the byzantine paperwork to get the procedure approved (permission, absurdly, to save the life of an animal protected by the Endangered Species Act). They found a cardiac surgeon who, just for the novelty and the publicity, talked Sheldon through the operation. They had all kinds of machinery and special expertise. The risks were significant, that was a given. The bear died on the table.

"It was supposed to be a big story in *National Geographic*. But without a happy ending . . ." Sheldon stops when he becomes aware that Buzz and Vern are frowning at him. I want to tell him to go on, just to have time fill up with talk. It doesn't matter that I heard this whole story from Clem just before I saw her in Washington. She called me the day after the surgery. She sounded miserable, wiped out, defeated. But she never mentioned it again, so neither did I.

"I think," Sheldon says now, "well, I think she identified with that bear. I think she felt she died *with* it somehow. I think she thought it had something to do with her karma. She wasn't really the same after that."

Vern rolls his eyes. "Clem wasn't no Buddhist, Shel." Vern is a botanist. Clem bought her jeep from him, and the two of them sometimes went dancing. Just platonic, she said, but Vern had a blues soul. I look at him now and know why it was platonic, no matter how charming and smart the guy was. He wasn't good-looking enough. Clem was vain that way.

"Karma in the *generic* sense," says Sheldon. I remember now how Clem told me, early on in the job, that Sheldon was a good vet but an arrogant SOB. All these people—people I imagined I would meet if I came out to visit Clem—are falling into place, fitting the portraits she drew in our phone conversations, portraits that made me laugh. (Where is the pencil-pushing boss with the comb-over and the macramé ties? Where is the tattooed woman who studies mountain lions but shrieks at the sight of a spider?)

"All I know," says Dave, "is like, day before yesterday, she packed for a week in the field. She had me order this new set of hiking boots from that store she likes in Jackson. She said purple, no second choice, and asked for these special all-weather liners. Man, that is so, like—like it makes no sense, does it?"

"Yeah," says Buzz. "Yeah, she was makin' the usual plans. Like tomorrow's game. She told me she got the dogs, even the Not Dogs for you, Sheldon."

I didn't ask them for explanations or theories. I guess they assume that reaching for reasons will make me feel better. I feel, instead, sort of lofty, as if I am floating above them (despite the leaden food in my gut). Three and a half higher degrees at this table and none of these eggheads knows what even the cheapest TV movies do: that suicide, when it succeeds, wears other well-laid plans. Sort of like a flashy wig.

We take a narrow, twisting road through sparse pines and patchy fields. We cross four cattle guards, which rattle the car loudly, as if to keep us wide awake. This time, Buzz makes no talk, small or otherwise. I'm still thankful for his awkward presence, anything to keep me from being alone.

Clem rented a mobile home on a spread that used to be a cattle ranch but was turned into a fancy lodge. On the way in, there's a kennel of sled dogs; in the winter, guests can ride around in style. Clem said they also keep the coyotes away. As we drive through, the dogs rush to their fence and bark, but no one comes out of the lodge. It's still light, the sun heavy and large down near the horizon. Buzz turns off the motor; we sit with the ticking for a moment. He says, "Want me to stay out here?"

"No. Unless you mind coming in."

"Oh yeah, no, not at all," he says.

I've never been in a mobile home. It feels like a train car, shipshape and economically furnished but plastered everywhere with posters of magnificently rugged places: Barrow, Patagonia, Big Sur, the Río Negro. Clem went to all these places, mostly for work, but it's a shock to see her worldliness defining so narrow a space. Unconscious trompe l'oeil: as if she wished to trick herself out of a claustrophobia that, even in Wyoming, she couldn't elude.

From a telephone conversation this afternoon, I know the police came out here, to look for notes. They found none. No one suspected foul play; this was just protocol. So I cannot chill myself with the thought that Clem was the last one here.

"I'm going to, um . . ." Buzz stands by the table in the tiny kitchen. On the table is a tiny television.

"Go ahead, please." I'm relieved he has something to watch other than me.

At the opposite end is Clem's bed; there, against the pillows, sits the stuffed polar bear she's had since college. I try to remember his name. Damien? Beside the bed is a nightstand with a lamp. The lampshade is covered with a sheer green silk scarf that belongs to me, a souvenir of lost love that I thought I'd misplaced around the time of my wedding (and which should, by its lingering importance, have warned me to back out). I lift the scarf and hold it up to the last light from the window. There is a dark ring in the center where the lampshade gradually singed the delicate silk. "You little worm," I whisper. I lay it back over the lamp and turn it on. My surroundings glow a sweet chartreuse.

I pull the one drawer out of the table, set it on the bed, sit down beside it. One by one, I remove the objects it holds:

An Indian enameled box jammed with earrings, the dangling organic kind that Clem loved, made of feathers, seashells, rough turquoise nuggets, leaves dipped in gold.

A barrette, tarnished silver, shaped like a fish.

A strip of gold condoms in see-through plastic.

A box of matches from our mother's favorite French restaurant in Providence.

A paperback book, *Why Big Fierce Animals Are Rare.*

A tiny delicate skull, jaw and teeth intact.

A pair of ebony chopsticks with abalone inlay.

A card for a dentist appointment in Jackson three weeks ago.

A photograph of Clem, grinning and tanned, seated in tall grass next to a knocked-out radio-collared grizzly bear, one hand buried in its fur.

A large copper bracelet, clearly a man's.

There is more, but my vision is no longer clear. I pocket the condoms (I think of our parents, tomorrow, going through all these same motions, all the detective work of grief) and take the skull over to Buzz.

He examines it and smiles. "Prairie dog. Yeah. Nice specimen."

I return it to the drawer and slide the drawer into the table.

I look again at Clem's bed. Darius; the polar bear's name is Darius. I pick him up and hold him close.

Now it's dark. I ask Buzz to drive me back. I close my eyes and wait to feel us cross the cattleguards. This time, I welcome the way they jar me through and through.

"I know, I know. I'll win the pity sweepstakes now, for sure." This is me, wearing the brave wry face I always wear for Ray. I wore it even through my so-called treatment. (Oncologists: do us all a favor and find another word; as one of my radiationmates put it, "Ain't no treat to none of it, hon.") This is my fault, not Ray's, and it's part of why we finally knew we had to call it quits. The way I felt I had to be; the way he couldn't be.

But we've been apart for only a month, so he's still the one I needed to speak with, desperately, after I heard the unbearable news. I didn't think twice. I left messages for him in three places, even with his agent. Ray travels a lot, and sometimes he's simply impossible to reach. Now I tell him everything. How my shell-shocked mother was the messenger, how I heard my father (a gentle man) throwing and breaking things in the background. Everything, everything: crying in Denver, arriving in the middle of such outrageous beauty, my guilt at recognizing this beauty, the huge greasy dinner I've eaten, the heartburn from eating it. The people my sister worked with. The contents of that drawer.

"These are not the belongings of someone who'd kill herself!" I shout into the phone.

"What would those belongings be?" says Ray, the first thing he's said in some time. He's in L.A.: like me, in a hotel room.

"Dull belongings, I don't know, just . . . not photographs of yourself with a bear! Not *gold* condoms."

"Not gold." He says this quietly, just to repeat it, the way a therapist would. "Well, all that glitters . . ."

"Her life, you mean. Gee, duh. Thanks, Ray." Now I begin to cry.

"I'm sorry. It's just that . . . you always thought she knew so much."

"So what? So she didn't know anything after all? Is that what you mean?"

"That's not what I said."

"Sorry." I stroke Darius, who lies on the hotel bed beside me.

Ray moved out after my chemo ended. Part of the reason had to be that we were apologizing way too much—that is, we were saying too many things requiring apology. We had been together for almost three years. For much of that time, I'd been pestering him about children; he didn't want children. Funny how we broke up once I could no longer physically have them. We had been through too much strife. I think we're both sad, but our lives are more peaceful now. When we talk, we remind each other that we made the right decision.

"I'd be glad to come up there and help you. The shoot's been delayed a week, so I could fly up tomorrow," he says.

"My parents will be here."

"Gee, duh," says Ray, and I have to laugh.

"Thanks, but I don't think it's a great idea."

"No, you're right. It would raise too many questions." Before we say good-bye, he gives me the number of the hotel where he's staying.

We made an odd, even talked-about couple. When they found out that

Ray was a stuntman, the line among my friends was that dutiful Louisa had left Mr. Chips for Mr. T. Brains for brawn. Only that's not how it was. Still, I let the misperception stand. I felt it gave my life more color. That was before the cancer.

I sit on the bed, wondering how I can possibly sleep. My sheets have been folded down, and three Hershey's kisses perch on one of the pillows. When I stand, I discover that I'm sitting on the fourth, now soft and misshapen. Carrying Darius with me, I open the minifridge and see that the tiny Smirnoff I drank has been replaced with two. I like this hotel after all.

Buzz left me with the station wagon and directions to the airport. My plan was to walk down the street and have breakfast while looking at a map, then drive into Jackson and find the funeral home that has my sister's body. Where she is, that much I know. If I survive that, I will find lunch and eat too much of it. Then I'll pick up my parents. After that, I can't imagine a plan of any kind.

I didn't figure on the scruffy guy with the dogs waiting by the antler archway. "Hey," he says pleasantly enough. The dogs, a pair of big freckled hounds, are already sniffing between my legs. Briefly, I touch their sleek heads. I say hello but keep on walking.

"You're Louisa," he says, in a tone that implies I might not know it myself.

I look him over. Of all the men I've seen out here, he comes closest to cowboy. He wears a sweat-stained felt hat with an asymmetrically curled brim, something like a Stetson, but it's more the way he stands that makes me think he rides horses. He needs a haircut, a mustache trim, new knees for his jeans. His incongruously clean white T-shirt reads, in big brown letters, FAUNA.

"I'm subbing for your sister," he says. "They asked if I'd come by and see if you wanted to join us. You don't, they'd understand."

I touch one of the antlers. Smooth as new skin. I look at my watch. It's ten o'clock on a Saturday morning. I don't know what on earth he's talking about.

"Softball," he says. "Some folks come from two hours downstate, or I'm sure they would have canceled." He pauses, but still I'm speechless. "They hope you don't mind."

"How could I mind?"

"Your sister would have minded."

I look at the antlers again. "Doesn't anybody find this barbaric?"

"Barbaric?"

"It's like a great big souvenir of carnage."

My mystery companion laughs. "Doll, these antlers get molted. No blood spilled to make this bric-a-brac. Does anyone think it's *tacky* is the question."

I follow him to his truck (guns, no surprise; the dogs run ahead of us and jump in back). He tells me his name is R.B. "We'll just stop at the station and pick up the dogs."

I glance at his hounds, confused.

"Hot dogs," he says. "For the barbecue after the game."

I remember what Buzz said: how Clem took care of this task just two days ago. *The usual plans.* I see her putting them in the fridge at her lab, alongside petri dishes growing invisible things and tubes containing the blood of rare animals.

We ride five minutes without talking. In my head, I'm asking questions about the sights we pass. It seems shameful to be curious about them.

R.B. is friendly but quiet. Once in while he looks over at me, perhaps to check if I'm crying. What would he say? Being with the sister of his dead colleague doesn't seem to put him on edge. At the station, a low cement building that sprawls into a grove of scrubby trees, he doesn't ask if I want to go in. He comes out with a brown grocery bag and sets it between us.

I peer inside. On top are the Not Dogs for Sheldon. Enough silence. I say, "You can get Not Dogs in Wyoming?"

"Jackson," says R.B. "Whether or not that's Wyoming anymore is a matter of some debate."

He drives back the way we came and stops at a public schoolyard.

"Anytime you want me to drive you back to the hotel, I will," he says. "We all just want to take care of you while you're here."

And afterward? How about then? "Thank you," I say.

The Fauna are one team; the other, as logic would have it, the Flora (Vern, the botanist, wears one of their T-shirts, white on green). From nearby wildlife stations, these are the personnel entitled to wear the ugly uniform I saw on Buzz and, in a photo my mother framed, on my sister.

"Rosie. June." R.B. wedges a cooler under one arm, carries the grocery bag with the other, and starts toward the diamond. The dogs follow, and so do I. I'm grateful when he does not introduce me around. (Most of these people, I figure, knew my sister as an every-other-weekend shortstop, nothing more.) He leads the way to the bleachers. "Want to play? You can join the Floras. They're pathetic if the prairie grasses guy don't show."

"Oh no. I'd only make it worse." I can see Vern headed our way.

R.B. nods. "Just checking."

Vern shakes my hand and asks if I'm doing okay. I say I am. People are stretching out tendons, jogging around the bases, tossing balls randomly about. *Smack . . . smack . . . smack.* The ball lands in glove after glove after glove. An easy rhythm. A pregnant woman and two children have the bleachers all to themselves. What am I doing here? Suddenly, I ache for Ray.

Clem's team takes the field. The Flora sit on a long wooden bench behind home plate. A man I haven't met is on the pitcher's mound. He has a loose build, not the least bit athletic. Buzz is at first base, Dave at second. Sheldon stands in the outfield. After the pitcher plays catch for a bit with the catcher, he says in a ministerial tone, "This one's for Clem." It's a strike. The pregnant woman applauds.

I sit at the top of the bleachers; no one joins me. I watch an inning and a half, absorbing nothing about the game except that it's oddly businesslike, with none of the goofball camaraderie you expect in amateur sports (not that I play sports of any kind). Then I realize that the players who know about my presence have probably made an effort to mute the normal shenanigans. When R.B. comes in from the outfield, I climb down.

I don't have to say a thing. He meets me with "I'll just let 'em know I'm out of the order. Meet you at the truck."

As soon as he gets in, he says, "That was definitely weird. I'm sorry."

"Whose idea was it to invite me?"

"Mine." He drives without looking at me. This allows me to examine his large, battered-looking nose and his big hands on the wheel. "Thought I'd give you that place."

When I say nothing, he adds, "Clement liked the games a lot. She was a real show-off. I thought this way you'd be able to look back and see her there. Wouldn't kick yourself later that you hadn't asked more about her life in these parts. She told me you wanted to visit sometime."

"So here I am. A little late." I ask if he knew Clem well. I ask if he thinks any of the people I've met knew her well.

"I knew her pretty well. I did," he says. "She was good company. Nobody didn't think so, I can tell you that. Even people who found her . . . a challenge."

Who was in love with her? That's the question I really want to ask. Because everywhere she went, somebody fell in love with Clem. It seemed to be a rule of physics. And what, I think, will rush to fill the void?

"You don't have to talk," says R.B.

"I know." Do I sound angry? (Does it matter?)

I look for and see his wedding ring. But on his right wrist, I see a band of paler skin, the ghost of a bracelet.

"Who was the pitcher?" I say. "The guy who mentioned her."

"Dung-beetle paper-pusher up from Cheyenne, the guy they all report to. He's here on account of her death. He'll want to make nice with your parents. He liked your sister fine, but he's got lawsuits on the brain."

I could assure him that my parents are too Old World to sue, but right now I can't bear to think about them. "You're a biologist, too? A bear guy?"

He hesitates. "My job's to track whatever animal I get told to track. Rosie and June do a lot of the work. I chaperone." He raps a knuckle on the window behind us; his dogs snuffle and lick the glass where he touched it.

We reach the hotel. "How did she kill herself?"

He parks. "Leavin' no doubt she meant to get the job done." Now he does look at me. "You mean method?" He reaches across the space between us and puts a big hand on my knee. "She gassed herself in the fieldwork Rover whilst overdosing on the anesthetic they stocked for that little cub's surgery. Rigged an IV from the rearview mirror. She was always learning things. Stupid ingenuity. She was hours dead when Dave showed up next day and opened the garage." He slowly pulls his hand away. He gives me a worried, tender look, which goes against the grain of his weather-beaten face. "I'm the first to tell you that?"

"Yes," I say. "So then, if I . . ."

He puts the hand back on my knee. "If you want to see her body, it's sure to be nice and tidy." He has Clem's sense of humor.

"Well. That's good to know. How considerate."

"Ain't it," he says. "I'd go now, if I was you. I can give a call, let the funeral home know you'll be along."

"Would you?" Tears start, but I will them back. I had planned to show up without telling anyone.

As I reach to open the door, he says, "You'll be here a day or two. Yes?" When I nod, he nods, too. "I have a few things of hers. I'll get them to you later." He looks at his watch. I understand that he doesn't want to talk anymore right now, doesn't want to answer more questions—though if I asked him, I know he would.

"You'd better get back to the game," I say.

"Game doesn't matter," he says.

$\backsim$

Never again will the scent of hyacinths touch me as sublime. In this place, it's become a virulent stench, with a purpose obscure to no one. Turns out that even in an airy town like Jackson, the funeral home has no windows. Secret society of death.

The director murmurs his scripted condolences; she could have died of a stroke, in a plane crash, gunned down on the street. He sits me on a tweed couch facing a table with an open Bible. I fix my gaze on a small painting of mountain scenery, homely but safe. When the director returns, he tells me that bodies to be cremated are kept in the garage; would I mind viewing her there? No, I tell him. After all, I think but keep to myself, she died in a garage.

Without a word, a teenage boy leads me across the parking lot. The doors to the garage are wide open. Though it's empty now, it has space for three hearses. Once we are inside this place, the boy tells me to wait. I obey, standing in one of the concrete bays, next to a dark oil stain. I watch him unlock a heavy door at the back; as he pulls it open, a cloud of frigid air spills out around him.

He wheels out a gurney carrying an oblong cardboard box, like a florist box, only six feet long. He removes the lid and leans it against a wall. He walks past me and says, "I'll be out there." Numb, I watch him leave. I'm glad he leaves the garage door ajar. He stands on the sunny pavement and lights a cigarette.

Clem is my first dead body. I've heard again and again—mostly from friends who've lost other friends to AIDS—that it's essential to see the corpse of someone you love, especially someone who's died undeservedly young; how it will confirm the way nothing else can that he or she is no longer here. The body won't look like the person you know, the self of that person, at all. This tells you there has to be a soul because something's missing; what else could that something be?

The first thing I know, when I see her, is that this is not a piece of advice I will ever pass on.

Except for her violet lips, Clem looks as if she has just come in from the cold, from skiing or skating, frost on her lashes. Unadorned, uncamouflaged, she is covered to the neck with a sheet—or, I suppose, the sheet has been folded back from over her face. There is a blackish clot beneath her left nostril. On top of her head, inconspicuous because of her dark hair, there appears to be more of the same dull black substance. Blood, of course, though it looks more like tar. (The way she killed herself was bloodless, but there has been, by law, an autopsy.) What's wrong here, what shocks and dismays me, is that in fact she still looks so much like the self I knew. Her lips may be unnaturally dark, but they are Clem's lips all right. Still an old familiar self, like the one I searched for while trying on wigs. *Well, here you are!* I exclaim silently when I look down at my sister. *And to think I was so worried!*

I look hard, I can't say for what, but there's something I've clearly missed. It's as if, against all common sense, I need to memorize this image of Clem. As if this Clem is essential to the Clem who will inhabit only memories now. I begin to speak—babble, really (though quietly, conscious of the boy who waits in the driveway). I am beseeching, cursing, adoring, my vacillating passions more suited to a lover than a sister. I know that as soon as I stop looking at her, I'll be looking at a void, not the transient void of the woman who captivated, who magnetized, the men—that void will be filled because, as Clem would say, indifferent nature gets her way—but the void left by the departure of my genetic alter ego. It's like someone's gone and severed my shadow.

I notice two things I never noticed before: as ever unlike me (even now, with my follicles corkscrewed by intravenous toxins), she has gray hairs. And under an eyebrow, there's a tiny mole I don't recall. I always wanted her beautiful eyebrows—her most elegant tease.

My parents look wan and spent, specters of exhaustion. I make the mistake of telling them I've been to see Clem; do they want to see her, too? I make this offer timidly. I say I'll drive them.

The look my mother gives me is one I haven't seen since I was a teenager. "Honey, I saw that girl in. She can bloody well see herself out." Mom begins to walk through the terminal like a general toward war.

She's always conflated grief with rage. "First you. You. Your damn disease. And now this. Now this. *This!* The whole way out here, your father said not a God damn word. What could he say? That he spent thousands upon thousands of dollars to educate this daughter, to turn her into the next Jane Goodall or whatever, that we gave her everything she could want, that . . . Well, until you have children you can't imagine." In other words, I will never imagine.

We arrive at the carousel as luggage begins to plummet down the chute.

My father, whom I can hardly bear to look at, says, "My daughter was Halley's Comet."

"That's what you have to say? What kind of baloney is that?" snaps Mom.

He shakes his head swiftly, dismayed that Mom doesn't get it. Clem's life, he means, was a brief, beautiful arc. A rare drama, compressed in time. I see in an instant that he will romanticize her life. It will have been complete, a predetermined path. "Please show some respect," he says to Mom.

"Well, did she?" Mom answers. "Did *she*?" To her, Clem's life was far from complete, was made a travesty. My parents are not religious, and suddenly I see a different kind of destruction looming. I have that sick feeling you get when you switch on the news and can tell right away, before you hear so much as a phrase, that something just awful has happened in the world, is happening still.

"Will you excuse me a minute?" I say. "Wait right here. Please."

At the pay phone, I say to Ray's hotel voicemail, "I changed my mind. If you could still come, you'd save all our lives." Except for Clem's. I make myself dwell on the notion that letting him do this favor is somehow merciful. I see my mother from afar, pacing the circuit of the carousel, keeping her distance from Dad. I see my father, superfluous raincoat over one arm, an agony of stillness. My ex-husband, so well mannered, would have known what to say. But Ray—Ray will know what to do.

There is a brief, strained remembrance in the field outside Clem's trailer. About two dozen people show up (the sled dogs go nuts as car after car bumps past the kennel). Sheldon and Clem's fellow biologists come. I recognize several faces from the softball game, including the dung beetle from Cheyenne, my sister's boss. Before anything begins, he gets a verbal pistol-whipping from Mom. How in God's name could the man have an employee in such a state of mind and be utterly oblivious? What was going on at the office, for Pete's sake, that Clem would feel so much despair? She has a mind to write his superiors in the government! He bows his head and nods. He keeps on mumbling how sorry he is, what a loss it is to everyone there. As my mother scolds him, my sister's colleagues watch. Their passive approval is so pungent, you could distill a perfume.

But R.B. isn't here. I ask Buzz if he's coming. "Oh," Buzz says, looking embarrassed, "he doesn't work so closely with us. He shows up when we need him, but he's not really a part of the team. I'm sure he liked Clem, yeah, I know he did, and it's nothing personal he's not here."

That's when I'm certain he was the scandalous affair. In my pocket, I have the copper bracelet; I was going to hand it to him, without comment, to see if it would make him tell me things he wouldn't tell me yesterday. I keep looking toward the turnoff from the road. I can't believe he won't show up. But he doesn't. While Buzz tells everyone how smart and funny Clem was, how she made them laugh, how much they'll miss her, and while Vern reads from Edward Abbey, and while Dave tells everyone what a great dancer she was and how he'll *really* miss her awesome margaritas (a soliloquy he would squelch if he could see my mother's face), I squeeze the bracelet hard, until the soft metal begins to yield.

Ray is beside me: not touching me, but he's here. He arrived late this morning, and already he's gone through Clem's belongings at the wildlife station. Other than a couple of snapshots, a folder of letters from old colleagues, all business, there's nothing personal. Buzz went through the files related to the bears.

Clem's boss, who's clearly aimed at getting the last word, says, "She sure was smart, as everyone here's been saying. And one thing she knew, maybe better than most of us, was the meaning of work. In the old-fashioned sense of the word." He talks about her long hours and her dedication and her passion for wildlife, as if she's there and he's giving her a medal, and I think, *You pathetic moron. What do you know?* It's my sister speaking, right there in my head. And she might as well be talking to me.

Clem had never heard of Eva Hesse, which wasn't a surprise. Outside the museum, before we went in, she paused to look at the sculpture by Rodin. "Him I like," she said. As we entered the show, I told her a bit about Hesse's life and art. "No one before or since has ever made work like this," I said. "No one could ever imitate this work."

"Work," said Clem. "Work." She smiled a peculiar smile as we walked into the first room. I couldn't tell if she was mocking what she saw.

I followed her. "You don't see this as work?"

"I'm just thinking, okay, so it's possible to be dead all these years like this woman's been, but here's her actual *work*, what she did, still here. People write about it in magazines, people pay to see it, under all these fancy lights. She's long gone, but she made these things, she didn't just *think* about them, and here they are, with a life of their own. So much work in the world is finished—I mean, kaput—the minute it's done."

"Work doesn't have to be concrete to last." Such an older-sister thing to say.

"Even if it is," said Clem, "no guarantees there, either, right?"

"No."

"You can't predict what lasts."

"Of course not," I said, irritated. I did not want her cynicism to intensify the dour palette of the show, its hues of duct tape, barbed wire, old snow, gunmetal, creosote, ash. "Just look. Stop talking for a minute and look."

"Fair enough," she said. And she walked with me through that show, silent, for over an hour. I'm the one who didn't look; who didn't listen.

~⌒~

After the boss finishes his little speech, an appalling silence sets in. Some people glance at my mother, wondering if she's going to stand for Conehead's absurd commemoration. Finally, Dad says to everyone, "Thank you for coming. Thank you for honoring our daughter." No one's organized a reception of any kind; there are no casseroles or brownies or free jugs of wine. Some people shake my parents' hands. Some of them hug me. They drive away, and the dogs go through their commotion all over again.

"Take your parents back to the hotel," says Ray. "I'll start in here." He goes into the trailer.

My parents have already walked around inside. My mother opened the two closets, every drawer, even peered under the bed. "She cleaned up all the evidence, whatever it might've been," Mom said tersely. "Well, I always knew she was gifted at whatever she chose to do."

For the first time in an hour, my father breaks his silence. "We're going to go now, back to our room, May. We're going to let this young man clean up our daughter's belongings. He'll have them shipped to our house, the ones worth saving. I've had enough for today." He takes Mom's arm, and for once, he's in charge.

They sit together in the backseat of the borrowed station wagon as I drive back to Dubois. This is when they cry. I say not a word. It's as if I'm a stranger, a hired driver, until my mother squeezes my shoulders from behind, once I've stopped the car in front of the antler archway. I don't even turn off the engine. They get out, and I head back to Clem's place.

Ray has boxed up her books and emptied her clothes into a pair of black garbage bags.

"Wait!" I cry. "I have to look!"

"You take the kitchen," he says firmly. "The jewelry, the things on her bureau, I've put them in a box you can take back to the hotel. You can go through those things later." He walks over to me and holds me as if to restrain me, though I'm more or less paralyzed. "This is just the worst thing, the very worst thing."

"Yes, it is," I say. He rocks me a little.

"I miss you so much," I say.

"I miss you, too," he says.

I feel crushed and buoyed all at once. "But I guess . . ."

"Yes," he says quickly before I finish. "That's part of what makes this so bad. She's drawn me back, the little bitch."

I'm suddenly seized with the panicky delusion that this was why she did it, that she wanted me back with Ray . . . or that she did it because she thought that if she died, I couldn't have a recurrence, I'd have to be cured. It was an elaborate scheme to make me happy, to fix my fate. It was all about me. And if this was true, shouldn't I make it so? Shouldn't I *be happy*? Otherwise, what's left? Will nothing remain of her life?

"Tomorrow you can go," I say. "You should."

We're standing apart now.

"I may have no choice." I know he means that the movie may start shooting, but still I feel hurt. It's as if someone else is controlling all my reactions to everything around me. Clem, I think. That's who.

At the hotel, a package waits for me at the desk, one of those padded brown mailing envelopes. *For Louisa Jardine.* No return address or name. I take it up to my room. Ray is driving the bags of clothing and boxes of books to my sister's office. Buzz will take care of them.

I listen at my parents' door, across the hall. I hear the TV, the din of a sports event. No voices. I open and close my own door as quietly as I can. In the envelope is a sheet of paper bearing my sister's handwriting, a Fauna team T-shirt, and a note to me in a clumsy masculine hand. *Louisa: I figured this note wasn't mine to keep secret. The T-shirt was hers. I don't like funerals, even for people I liked as much as I liked her. I really did. Sorry.* It was from R.B. This was what Clem had written:

This is where I tell you the obvious. That it had nothing to do with you. It had nothing to do with anyone, that's the problem. No one mattered that much, I finally understood. Not that they didn't deserve to matter a whole lot. Especially you. But (you know the rest). I think I made the mistake of expecting people to contain me. A myth. People can't do that. Just the way rock cannot contain water, water cannot contain air, air cannot contain fire. It's elemental.

The things I will miss are predictable: laughing, fucking, champagne, dancing, first shower after camping, first sunset of real winter, first dawn of honest-to-god (whoever he thinks he is) summer. Go on here and I could dissuade myself. Dissuasion (a real word?) is not the business at hand. I've been through that a few times before. It's getting old. I know the dreams I should be wanting. Should: again, the problem.

All day today I've been looking at graphs. My life is a graph where ambition levels off, desire spikes, and passion plummets.

I'm sorry for the mess. But I imagine you can stay outside of it. Please do that. Please don't get all confessional with everyone. If you meet my parents (I hope you don't but what does it matter?) don't tell them about us. My mother thought there were too many men in my life already. She thought the right one would "steady me." (Like I was a horse in need of a little dressage.) Talk about me to anyone who cares to talk about me as if I led a wild, never boring life. (True!) Pain is a detached thing, like an outbuilding, the constant dullness of it irrelevant to the overall estate of pleasure but bringing down property values all over the place. No. It's like the bass in a good song. At first you don't feel it, but in the end it's what you're dancing to. But we talked about this. I don't (quite) believe I was never loved. It's not about that. I feel sorry for my parents in that respect but what would be the point of telling them? I don't think anyone needs me however. Those poor bears do not need me, no more meddling from me. Too bad for them I'm replaceable. Karma, though I hate the hare krishna aspect, had a lot to do with it too. This body (you'd argue, and thanks) just never seemed right (habitable). A mistake on the assembly line. Work (mine) put an exclamation point on that discomfort, the way nothing ever seemed to fit. Seeing the bears close up convinced me. They know where they fit. I'd like to have been a bear instead. Even Danny. Poor little Danny. You knew that would happen. You were right. I gave you so little credit on so many things.

My thoughts closed into a circle. I need to break out of that circle. The other night I rented Hamlet. I did it to see Mel Gibson, see if he could cheer me up, that great ass of his in tights, but I got into Hamlet, the guy Shakespeare created. Good questions lead to a bad end. Did I have 33 years too many? No way. But it was high time, and 33, that's a mystical number if you're so inclined.

Shel's just left the lab: my next to last goodbye. I've always liked this place when it's all mine. So here I go. You go too, wherever you belong. I love the way you roam and it seems so easy. I wish I'd been made that way too.

That was it. No sign-off, not even her name.

And there was no mention of me. No reference at all. "You worm," I say out loud. "You *monster*." My hands are shaking. I throw the letter down on the bed, as if it's scorching hot.

An hour later, Ray comes in. He is carrying the box of Clem's personal belongings for me to comb through. I have the urge to carry it out onto the balcony and throw it over the edge. I let Ray set it on the dresser.

He sees my swollen face. He sees the letter on the floor, where it's fallen. He sits beside me on the bed and reads it.

"It's like I didn't even exist," I say.

"What would you like to have seen?" Ray asks. "That she knew you wanted her to stay but it didn't matter? Like, fuck Louisa, who gives a damn what becomes of her? Wouldn't that hurt just as much?" The bottom line, he points out, is that nothing and no one were indispensable to Clem.

Funny how Sheldon was right about the karma. Clem would not have been pleased about that.

By FedEx, Clem's ashes arrive at our parents' house ten days after her death. Mom calls me at work. "Well, I signed for her 'cremains' this morning. I said to the guy, 'You know what's in this box? My dead daughter.' I thought he was going to vaporize from shock right there on my doorstep." Her laughter is pure contempt. " 'Welcome to the modern world, young man,' I said. 'Death by Federal Express.' He could not get out of our driveway fast enough."

My mother's weakness is her scorn, but her strength is her practicality. She's the one who decided right away on cremation, and she's the one who decides what to do with the ashes. "To hell with the family plot," she says. "The last place your sister was happy—if she ever was happy, that girl!—was the ocean. I'm putting her there."

Once more, Ray flies east. His shoot is over; he insists. He volunteers to drive the boat, and we head straight out into Narragansett Bay. The weather is sunny, the water calm. The surface of the bay glitters like an eye. He guides us between all the Saturday sailors: the stately sloops, the flashy speedboats, the lasers, whalers, and dinghies. The skippers and passengers greet us with waves and entitled smiles, the shared good fortune of those who ride the waves for sheer amusement. A few people recognize my father and hail him by name.

"For God's sake, can we get any privacy out here?" says Mom.

Dad has no comment. He rides in the bow, ignoring us all, Napoleon en route to Elba. Just before we stepped into the boat, he told Mom that he thinks touching the ashes is unspeakably obscene. "Then you don't have to," she said. "The rest of us will do it."

Ray speeds up, taking us so far from the shore that we can hardly see it anymore. At last, he slows down and gives me a look. *Here?* I nod. It takes me a moment to venture standing, but soon I am used to the motion of the deck. I turn on my boom box. The tape that plays is *Uprising*, a favorite of Clem's. She loved Bob Marley. I read a passage from Thoreau about the solace of nature when other people simply become unbearable. Together, Mom and I take the plastic bag from the box and undo the twist tie that holds it closed. We are about to reach into the bag and take hold of Clem by the handful, to fling her astern, but something stops us. Instead, we take the bag and, kneeling down, leaning as far over as we can, we empty it in one declarative motion. Most of the cinders fall, though others blow free. Clem, or the matter that was Clem, plummets like a gray cloud down into the depths, out of sight. The weight of the ashes takes me by surprise; only a vague, indecisively shaped film remains on the surface. Ashes, I realize, do not dissolve. Clem was right: she will be dispersed but never contained.

I reach into the satchel I brought along, unfurl the Doris Day wig, and fling that into the water as well. It floats. "What in tarnation is that?" asks Mom. She knows perfectly well what it is; she just wants to know what it's doing here. It's my turn to give her a look she hasn't seen since I was a teenager. I tap Ray's shoulder and he starts back to shore. When we arrive at the dock, Bob Marley's still playing. As Dad steps off to secure the lines, he says tersely, "You can turn that fellow off now."

That's when it occurs to me that Bob Marley died young, too—from cancer, skin cancer invading the brain. Which makes me think of Eva Hesse. Which brings me back to myself, my fear. Bob, Eva, me.

"Everything's an omen, I can't stand it," I whisper to Ray. I explain the connections. We are following my parents, at a careful distance, through the boatyard toward the parking lot.

Ray stops. "Superstition's the easy way out."

"Out of what?"

"You can't help secretly thinking, even hoping, that she took your place." He laughs, just barely. "Well, she did no such thing. Not when she was born. Not now."

My mother is already in the car, at the wheel. She'll want a martini as soon as we get to the restaurant. Who wouldn't? My father stands guard at her open door, waiting for me and Ray to catch up. As we get closer, I see that she's holding his hand. They make a picture of lives that flow together and apart, together and apart. I see their marriage as something like a double helix, two souls coiling round a common axis, joined yet never touching. Our lives, Clem's and mine, made that shape too, for a time.

The Last Word

2005

I take out plates and glasses for two before I remember Henri, who will certainly want to join us. As I place his cushion on a chair, I realize that I'm glad he's here, that I'm wondering if it was foolish to invite this man for lunch—not because I'll feel unsafe with him but because I'm not sure, after all, that I want to talk about the things I'm certain we'll talk about.

Henri is my godson. He's six, but he thrives in the company of grownups. He can sit for hours in a restaurant, engaged by the chitchat and gaiety of adults as they drink wine and soak up the pleasure of sitting together while others do the work to keep them sated and happy. He interrupts now and then with whimsical, irrelevant remarks, but he never crawls under the table or complains that it's time to leave. Already, perhaps because he's such an urban kid, he knows that blunt or wicked observations about nearby strangers—their silly garments, rude habits, unflattering hairstyles—are to be delivered in a whisper, behind a cupped hand, straight into a grown-up's ear. He's the sort of child whom the maître d' will praise as you leave. "What remarkable manners!" "That's quite a son you have there." (And if they choose to believe he's mine, my son, I never correct them; neither does he.) He earns off-menu treats from the chef, even gifts. Two weeks ago, Henri's father brought him along to a working lunch, a staged conversation with a *Times* art critic at a fancy Chinese restaurant where all four of us dipped our fingers in bowls of water flecked with petals, where the table glowed in a pink spotlight, where the plates were translucent as dragonfly wings. Henri watched and mimicked the adults' meticulous, self-conscious manners, listened to his father and the critic as if they were telling folktales under the spell of night. As we were leaving, the owner presented Henri with a ceramic tiger. It was a small well-crafted object to which he had pointed, with longing and awe, when we passed a display of Chinese knickknacks on our way in. "Very special boy," the owner said, bowing and grinning. Henri bowed right back and told him that the noodles had been very special, too.

Henri's father, Esteban, is an artist who achieved success when he was old enough, and had struggled long enough, to know how rare, even miraculous, it is to succeed in his field. He believes that he owes this success to me, because I praised his work when I was an editor at an art magazine that can, it's true, mold or shatter reputations and careers. In his eyes, I am the fairy godmother who lifted her wand and changed him from a cabdriver into a coveted guest at collectors' parties, into someone who pays a New York City mortgage, whose children go to a liberal downtown private school. But we genuinely like each other, without having to consider such a debt, and twelve years of hard work since then have made any sense of obligation moot. And then there's Henri. I adore Henri.

He is staying with me for a week while his parents and his older brother are in Haiti, to arrange his grandmother's funeral. Unlike his brother, Henri did not know his grandmother well, so Esteban thought it better, and safer, to leave him with me and my husband. Campbell adores Henri, too—with a nostalgia that reveals how much he's loved being a father from the very moment he became one—and Campbell's two sons enjoy the presence of a much smaller boy. Luke and Max are close in age to Henri's brother, but unlike his brother, they treat him only with affection and generosity. They pull out their old toys; they read him stories; and if they go out with friends, to buy pizza or shoot hoops, they take Henri along, as if to show him off. In return, Henri esteems and validates their adolescent swagger. When he stays with us, the rules relax. Games of soccer are played in the hallway, sneakers abandoned beneath the table, rock 'n' roll songs composed at top volume on Luke's electronic keyboard. Boy Heaven, Campbell calls our place when Henri comes to stay.

Right now, Henri is at the far end of the loft, building a zoo with Lego blocks and faded plastic animals that Luke and Max outgrew long ago but refuse to surrender.

"Hey you," I call out, "come help me set the table for our guest!"

He leaps to his feet. "What's my job! What's my job! What's my job!" he chants as he runs toward the kitchen.

"First, napkins," I say. I fold them and hand them to him one at a time. "Forks," I say. "Knives." They are butter knives, perfectly safe, even if he fumbles and drops them. "Spoons."

He holds the last spoon close to his face. "Handsome nose," he says to his reflection.

"You are so right," I say. When I put him to bed last night, I told him he has a handsome nose. The nose comes straight from his father.

"Will he bring animals with him?" Henri asks.

"No," I say. "The animals have to stay where they live—in the forest or at the zoo."

"But he's their friend, right?"

"He finds out things about the animals—the birds—that help people save them out in the wild."

"Because they're endangered," Henri says, frowning. "Because of global warming." Henri's kindergarten teacher has been talking to the class about global warming. When I picked him up yesterday, he was carrying a collage he'd made. At the center is a photograph of a polar bear on a perilously tiny ice floe; he looks like a woman in a dress that's clearly too small. Anthropomorphize yet further and you'd say he (or she) looks perplexed and sad. Around the bear Henri glued sunsets, whales, and seals, but also a freeway traffic jam, a vast landfill, and a daunting image of factory smokestacks somewhere in China. Along with the collage came a class handout titled *Let's All Do Our Part!* Henri goes around the loft turning out lights after people. Every few hours, he checks the recycling bins, to make sure we are separating refuse as the city requires (regulations his teacher has posted on the classroom wall). Until I gently asked him not to, he'd stand outside the bathroom when anyone was using it, and he'd announce, "You don't have to flush every time!"

"Sometimes that's why," I say now. "Or sometimes it's because of pollution in the water, or because people want to build houses where the birds need to live. Which scares the birds away, and then they have a hard time finding another good home."

"So it's always people's fault." He looks at me earnestly.

"Well, mostly," I say, though I'm not comfortable issuing this condemnation. Should a six-year-old already see humanity as heedless, destructive, and selfish? "But then there are other people who have the job of trying to help the birds. And other animals, too."

"Like the polar bear."

"Yes." And I notice yet again how the current woes of the world, or the woes on which reporters and kindergarten teachers have seized with such alacrity—though this is *good,* we tell ourselves as we thank poor, dear, wronged Al Gore for his crusading—how they hold my sister close to my conscience as well as my memory. It's painful yet remotely amusing. Or Clem would have found it amusing: that her beloved grizzlies—unlike their polar cousins—are staging a comeback, while she is the one who's gone, leaving no descendants. Sometimes I'm haunted by the thought that the work she did twelve years ago wouldn't seem so quixotic, so lonely, today. Would this have made a difference to her?

I place the salad on the counter and cover it with a damp towel. I cut a long loaf of bread across the middle, brush the halves with oil, rub them with garlic, close the loaf, and wrap it in foil. I make sure there's a bottle of wine in the fridge. I don't drink wine at lunch, but today may be an exception.

"Can Darius sit with us?" Henri asks.

"Good idea," I say.

Henri runs to my bedroom—indoors or out, running is his baseline speed—and returns with Darius, a stuffed polar bear whose fake white fur has yellowed over the years, though his glass eyes and velvet nose are still intact. I think of Henri's collage and wonder if it's a coincidence; but then polar bears, like Al Gore, are suddenly all the alarmist rage.

Henri pulls a fourth chair next to his own. He props Darius there— even though the creature's head is well below the tabletop. Henri tells me that Darius won't need a fork or a plate, that he won't eat salad or bread—not even pretend. "Only meat. Seals and fish."

Our guest is a vegetarian, so there will be nothing agreeable to polar bears.

The buzzer startles us both. I speak through the intercom and let Ralph into the building. Henri waits by the door; I unlock it so that he can open it by himself. I hear the elevator descending. Henri runs back to the kitchen, grabs Darius, and returns to his post. I hang back a little, pretending to rearrange the tulips. I put the bread in the oven.

And then I hear Henri introducing Darius to Ralph. Ralph shakes hands with both of them, making the proper fuss over finding a polar bear as a fellow lunch guest in a Lower Manhattan loft.

When it's my turn to greet Ralph—awkwardly, we embrace—I'm still struggling to reconcile his present incarnation with my memory of the man I met, twenty-five years ago, on a visit with Clem the summer she lived in Vermont. He's still youthful and fit, but the sun has roughened his skin, and his hair, cropped fashionably close, is pure gray. Until our conversation on the subway last week, when I recognized him in the strangest of ways, I hadn't seen or even heard about him since that summer.

"This is a treat," he says, setting a backpack on the bench by the door. "Most of my meals while I'm here are Chinese takeout or deli salad bar."

"Well, I can't promise much better than the latter," I say.

"We're not eating a ladder!" exclaims Henri.

"Wiseguy," I say.

Like every guest who enters the loft, Ralph is drawn to the large window in the living room. The view isn't grand or panoramic, but it's very New York: we're just a floor or two above most adjacent rooftops, so we look out on makeshift sky gardens, sunbathers, and air-conditioning turbines. Campbell and his sons call it the "twenty-seven-water-tower view." If you challenge them, they'll count you through it. Sometimes I demand this performance, just for the amusement. They've turned it into a family act, a cross between hip-hop and vaudeville.

"Toto," says Ralph, "I don't think we're in the rain forest anymore." He turns and smiles at me, so warmly that my anxiety dissolves. Here is the man I remember, the friend (and boss) of my sister who radiated kindness as well as confidence, on whom I had a crush for one brief night of dancing to Marvin Gaye on a Burlington jukebox; who, the next day, witnessed what remains my most humiliating moment, the time I nearly drowned at that swimming hole and Clem saved my life before an audience of strangers. Later she insisted I wouldn't have drowned, that what she did—talk me out of a panic—was no big deal. I pointed out that if my situation really *hadn't* been so dire, I'd be doubly mortified. "Okay, so definitely I saved your life," Clem said, "which means you owe me one." Over the next decade, whenever we came together, she enjoyed ribbing me in front of our friends. With a glint in her eye, she'd make offhand remarks like "Wasn't that the same summer I saved your life?" She even referred to it in a toast at my first wedding—telling Hugh that by extension he owed her bigtime. I might have minded, and told her so, but I enjoyed her attention, which I saw as proof of a deep bond between us, never mind that we saw so little of each other, that our lives had grown so differently and distantly busy that we wrote and called less and less often.

Recently, when I tried to conjure the scene of that wedding dinner, of Clem's toast, I realized that I am losing the sound of her voice, that I've already lost the memory of her laugh. It's both comforting and painfully confusing to remember this: that my sister loved to laugh.

Ralph accepts a beer. He sits in a chair facing the view. I sit across from him, with a glass of water. If I have wine now, I'll lose control of my logic—and my emotions.

Henri sits beside me, Darius on his lap. I see Ralph appraising us as a pair. This would be an immediate puzzle, since I am pale and Henri's dark. "Henri is my godson," I say. "My *favorite* godson." I hug him to my side.

Ralph is now looking around at what he can see of the loft, at the objects that overshadow the simple furniture. At the far end, above Henri's Lego zoo, hang Campbell's antique Mardi Gras masks, a collection from his days at Tulane, but most of the walls are taken up by the artwork I own, much of it given to me by the artists I love best. "Wow," says Ralph, and I realize that our hasty, hurtling conversation on the A train, only five stops long, did not fill him in on very much of my life. I wonder if he remembers anything about the life I was living when I met him in Vermont. It occurs to me that in fact he may not have remembered *me*, even when I introduced myself on the train. But of course he remembers Clem. Who wouldn't?

"Henri's father," I say, "is one of the artists I represent at my gallery— at the gallery I share with my partners." I look up, to point out the piece that dominates the loft once you see it. A great web of fine white feathers, knit ingeniously, invisibly together, droops delicately from above, as if the ceiling has become the underbelly of a mammoth gull or egret. I blush, thinking of Ralph's work with birds.

"Wow," Ralph says again. "Now that is something."

"That's my dad's," Henri brags.

"Wow. Your dad has quite the imagination."

"I think the feathers came from a place that supplies pillow makers," I offer, and then feel even more embarrassed.

"You're not offending me here," says Ralph. "I'm not an animal-rights extremist. Please." He stands and begins to look at other pieces of art arranged in the room around us. He asks about a photograph and a sculpture. Certain that he's only being polite, I keep my answers short. "Now here we have something downright avant-garde," he says, pointing to a pair of hockey sticks leaning against the doorway to the boys' bedroom.

"My stepsons. Luke and Max."

"I get to stay in their room, but I don't live here," says Henri. "I live in

Long Island City. I have my own bedroom when I'm at home. I have a bed *and* a hammock. Sometimes I sleep in my hammock."

"I sometimes sleep in a hammock, too," says Ralph. "Outside, even."

Henri nods. "You live in the jungle."

I smile at him, wondering if Ralph and I will be able to have a continuous conversation—or if, secretly, I hope we won't. What was I thinking, inviting him over? And what could the poor guy do but say yes? I'm sure it's clear to both of us that what I want is for him to shed more light on Clem's life—and, by implication, her death. He did know about it; by the second subway stop we passed, he'd told me how sorry he was; what a waste, what a loss, how awful for our parents.

Henri informs Ralph, with obvious pride, that Luke is fifteen and Max is twelve. Max was born the same year Clem died.

"You'll probably get to meet them for about three minutes," I say, "when they come roaring through to drop off their soccer equipment. You won't meet my husband, though. I'm afraid he's spending the weekend at one of those ghastly corporate golf things. He hates them—he hates golf—but it's part of his job."

"Is he in the art world, too?"

"Absolutely not," I say. "For which I'm grateful. He handles real estate investments at NYU."

"Ah!" says Ralph, as if this is a compelling job to someone who spends his life trying to figure out how we can undo the damage we've done to all the wild creatures around us—much of that damage involving real estate. On the A train, he told me he comes to New York a few times a year; he has an office at the Wildlife Conservation Society (the zoo, to those of us who take children up to the Bronx to see giraffes, gorillas, and all the fierce, coldhearted predators that we may be delighted *not* to number among the ever-increasing threats we face as city dwellers who are just too stubborn to flee).

I never thought I would end up pairing off so happily with a man whose livelihood is so unintriguing. I used to think that the man's work has to be part of what seduces you. (You could see Hugh and Ray—a guy who taught high school history and, like me, loved art; and then a stuntman—as two ends of the curiosity spectrum.) But here's the thing about Campbell: five years ago, on our first evening alone together (hard to call it a date at our stage in life), he told me he can take or leave what he does for a living. "You don't need to ask polite questions about my job," he said before we even ordered our meal. "I do it well, and I get a kick out of having this weird talent to which no kid would ever aspire; I mean, I wanted to be a movie critic! But I'm not sorry. It's not my reason for being. It never has been." He didn't need to tell me his reason for being: by then I'd seen pictures of his sons, and I knew, all too well, the story of how he'd lost his wife. Yet even before she died, what mattered most to Campbell was family. Her death changed many things, but not that.

When you're forty-four, childless, menopausal by way of chemotherapy, simply glad to be alive, how can you *not* fall madly in love with a man like that? Who cares what he does for a living? My cancer was, by then, seven years in the past. I couldn't say I was cured, not quite, but I was beginning to think that my future might fit into something larger than a shoe box.

"Hungry?" I say to Henri, and he jumps up.

I place the bread in a basket. I put a platter of cheeses, grilled tomatoes, and olives on the table. Once we're all seated, I serve the salad.

"This looks magnificent," says Ralph. He thanks me effusively again. I repeat how glad I am to see him. I pour myself a glass of wine.

Henri is occupied with Darius, keeping him upright. "No tomatoes, we both do not eat tomatoes," he says when he gets the bear settled. Darius belonged to Clem; he was the "love child," she used to joke, of her first and longest relationship, with her boyfriend from college and beyond. After she died, I found Darius among her belongings, and I made a feeble attempt to track down the old boyfriend. This was well before Google was a household verb, but even so, I didn't try as hard as I might have. I wanted custody of Darius myself. Not even Henri may take him out of the loft.

"Henri wants to hear about your work," I say to Ralph, "and so do I."

Ralph travels back and forth between Brazil and the Great Lakes. He is studying the effects of fertilizers and other waterborne chemical compounds, "industrial effluvia," on bird populations in both areas. I remember now that when I met him he was writing a dissertation on basically the very same subject. It's always amazing to me when people find the thing they were meant to do as soon as they grow up, they stick with it, and their passion never fades. I once believed my sister was one of these people.

As if reading my mind, Ralph says, "These plates are beautiful. They look handmade."

"Yes," I say. "By me. A long time ago. I used to be a potter."

"That's right!" he says. "Now I remember that! You lived in California, and you weren't happy out there."

I laugh. "No. I was a fairly miserable creature. I'm sorry you remember anything at all about me from back then."

"I liked you, though. I did," he says. "You and Clem both had the same . . . feistiness. I asked her about you later, how you were doing, and she said, 'Oh, never worry about Louisa. She'll figure things out. She always does.' "

"She talked about me?" I wonder if he's making this up; Clem used to berate me for my lack of common sense.

"Sure. She talked about your parents, too. Not a lot, but she did."

I hesitate. I don't want to talk about my parents. In a way, they closed ranks after Clem's death. They undertook home improvement projects they'd put off for years, took a cooking class in a foreign country, started going to black-tie benefits, installed an outdoor hot tub; behaved in ways that seemed inappropriately young to me yet struck the rest of the world as a huge relief, a sign of hope. *Good for them*, their friends would say. I understood later that what I really felt was a secret, shameful resentment, that they got to claim the lion's share of all the sympathy and condolence. Even if it's not their fault. Except for Campbell, no one ever asks me if I still miss my sister, if I'm angry or heartbroken, if the way she died—on purpose—still keeps me up at night.

Impulsively, I say, "How's Hector?" When I met Ralph, he had a partner, an equally charming man whose name I remember now only for its classical singularity. For an instant, I can't help thinking of all the things that might so easily have separated them in unhappy ways—not just a breakup but AIDS. "Are you still . . . ? I realize . . ." What do I realize?

Ralph has to finish chewing his bread, but he's nodding. "Hector's good," he says. "He lives in New Bedford for now, with his mother, who needs him. We haven't been together like that for years, but we stay in touch. He runs the aquarium in Mystic."

"Oh," I say, relieved yet stuck. "The two of you were such good friends to Clem. She had a blast with you."

"The party years," says Ralph. "I suppose we're lucky to have had them *and* to have survived them." His smile fades slightly. He digs into a second helping of salad. I notice that he's pushed the dried cherries to one side. I feel as if there's no escaping the sadness, as if I've merely pulled all our separate sorrows into a common center, a whirlpool.

Ralph looks up at me abruptly, catching me off guard. He speaks softly. "She told me about your cancer. I guess you're . . . You look great." The end of this awkward remark sounds like a question. He blushes.

"I'm fine," I say quickly. I knock on the table. "But listen. I didn't invite you here to be so unrelentingly morbid. I'm sorry."

"What's morbid?" asks Henri. Our sober tone has distracted him from the whispered discourse he was conducting with Darius.

"It means thinking too much about dark things," I say.

"What dark things?"

"Sad things."

"What's sad? Are you sad?" He stares at me, alarmed.

"Not now," I say. "We're not sad right now. But sometimes people can be happy and remember sad things at the same time. Or we talk about other people being sad."

"Like my dad. Because Tati died."

"Yes," I say.

"She was very, very old."

"That's true. But it's always sad to say good-bye, even when you know someone had a good long life."

"I *know* that."

Ralph leans across the table. "I love garlic bread, don't you?" He's offering a piece to Darius, which makes Henri laugh. Henri tells him that polar bears certainly wouldn't like garlic bread, even if they did have stoves. Which they don't. And you need a stove for garlic bread. Ralph is in the midst of telling Henri how he's made garlic bread over a campfire when the front door opens wide and in barge my stepsons, shedding clods of dirt from their cleats, bringing with them the mingled smells of wet rubber, boyish sweat, and new grass—which tints their ruddy legs an unreal shade of green. They are snorting with laughter and, having raced up the stairs, breathless.

"Guys! Shoes off!" I shout above their clamorous talk.

They become still for a moment when they notice the stranger in their kitchen. "Hey," says Luke, the older one speaking first. "Hey," echoes Max. They stand there, two large damp boys with roughed-up hair and clothes. Though they share their mother's pale, delicate coloring, it's now obvious that they will both grow into their father's extreme stature; Campbell is tall and bony in a way that makes him look impressive and graceful half the time—but then, just as often, so precarious that surely he must topple to the ground.

When the boys shake hands with Ralph—firmly, making steady eye contact, as their father has taught them—I see how dirty their hands are, how dirty they are from head to foot. But this kind of disorder pleases me; it's a healthy antidote to the sterile, sometimes monastic atmosphere in which I do business, where the one constant is a large, pure-white, resolutely spotless room through which various spectacles and spectators come and go, none leaving a permanent mark. In that world, the colors and shapes and attitudes ceaselessly change, but there is very little dirt. There's not enough patience for dust.

"Are you the bird man?" asks Luke.

"In person," says Ralph.

"Cool," says Luke, simply, conclusively. He turns and lifts Henri onto his shoulders. "We're 'napping you, man." Henri squeals as he is galloped across the loft and into the boys' room.

"Nice to meet you," says Max, and then he shouts out that he gets the bathroom first, and they vanish, all three boys, behind a pair of loudly closed doors. I hear the shower running, I hear muffled synthetic electric guitar; behind me, a soccer ball drops from the hallway bench and rolls past the table to rest at the edge of the carpet that marks the divide between kitchen and living room.

"Boy Heaven," I say.

"Boy Jungle," says Ralph, eyeing a clump of grass on the tile floor.

We stare at each other, first happily, then tenderly, then sadly.

Quietly, Ralph says, "Can we get back to morbid? Because I want to tell you how incredibly sorry I am about your sister."

"I know, and I appreciate it. A lot of time's gone by, and I hope you don't feel—"

"No," he says forcefully. "What I want to say is that I'm sorry I never wrote or called you when it happened. Because I meant to, and I should have. We were good friends. Even though we hardly ever saw each other. When I got my first big grant, I tried to get her to work for me, but she'd made up her mind to stick with mammals. She liked writing letters, and sometimes she'd call. I was so ashamed—I mean, that I hadn't taken some things about her seriously, so it . . . so by the time I screwed up any kind of nerve to get in touch with you, I figured it was too late."

"It's never too late."

"Can I tell you, that makes me feel even worse? Because now it's you who found me. I would never have been in touch. That's the truth."

"And I'd never have been the wiser. Or stirred this up again."

"I'm glad you spotted me. I'm glad to be here." His right hand rests on my left arm. I cover it with my own right hand. I can see the feet of the blue cormorant below the edge of his T-shirt sleeve. I've lost my sister's laugh, but across twenty-five years I've held on to the image of this fairly plain tattoo: on the subway, that's what I recognized, not Ralph's face. He was standing across from me, facing away, just your typical stranger on a crowded train, but his right arm was raised to hold the steel bar. The short sleeve had pulled back toward his shoulder, and there it was, upside down but distinct, the blue cormorant flying across his biceps. I still can't believe I had the courage to tap him on the shoulder.

I give him another beer and pour myself a second glass of wine. "I made brownies. Would you like a brownie?"

"Good lord, yes! Who says no to brownies?"

"Leave it," I say when Ralph begins to clear the table. I hand him a plate with a brownie and lead him back to the living room.

I see him eyeing the ceiling, the inverted parachute of feathers. I say, "It's called *Host*. I hope it doesn't seem cruel or thoughtless to you."

"Let's stop acting like I'm a saint, okay? I am anything but."

I sit on the couch and begin to eat my brownie. It's undercooked in the middle, too dense, but it fills the need for something solid and rich, something to weigh me down. I say, "No matter how many things Clem did to shock me—the guys she shafted, the crude way she talked about people she'd written off—I thought of her that way a lot of the time, as a saint. Because of her work, I guess. How important she thought it was. How other things mattered less. But maybe all the good work . . . maybe it felt . . . I think she worried it was pointless. A kind of hubris. Though she would have made fun of my using such a big word."

Every so often Ralph's gaze shifts to the sky outside the window, over my head, but I know he is also intent on our conversation. "All 'good work,' " he says, "feels foolish at times. Naïve and stupid. That's part of the territory. She knew that."

And how about work that really *is* foolish? I think. How about parsing and praising the glories of art? Isn't art, strictly speaking, just another form of human excess, even waste? Shouldn't it seem pointless once you think your whole world's been changed by (for example) cancer, then by your only sibling's death, then by a terrorist act? Is it "good" to go on doing the same old oblivious thing, to still enjoy it no matter what? Does perseverance steady the world?

"I don't know what she knew, if you want to know the truth," I say. "I want it not to matter, but it does."

"Of course it matters."

Max bursts out of the bathroom and makes for the bedroom, wrapped in a towel, trailing water across the floor. He trades off with Luke; both doors close again. I hear Henri exclaim "Dude!" in his high-pitched voice. When he's around Max and Luke, he seems to drink the very air around them.

Ralph stands up, and I panic at the thought that he will leave. But he says, "I brought you something." He goes through the kitchen and gets his backpack, from which he pulls a manila envelope. "I found a few of your sister's letters in my office. The others are probably gone—I'm a nomad—but you can keep these."

The envelope yields a sheaf of paper, a dozen sheets torn from spiral notebooks, blue lines covered with row after row of my sister's oddly ingenuous printing: self-consciously neat, each letter distinct, the handiwork of a pupil eager to please. I close my eyes for a moment and hold them in my lap, both hands flat on the surface of the first letter. I look down. *May 15, 1981.*

"The year after we met," says Ralph. "After I met you, too, I guess."

"Alaska."

"She wrote me from so many places."

"Amazing places." I start reading; I can't help it. She was twenty-one, a year of college left to go. She'd won a summer internship with a government agency that monitored the whaling in northern Alaska; Clem had explained that the native people of the region were still allowed to make a living this way. I remember when she set out for that adventure, all the gear she had to buy, the winter-worthy hats and boots and underwear, though it was nearly summer. The whales were moving north across the Arctic Circle, through the fracturing pack ice. She'd be part of the team counting the whales, judging their numbers more by the sounds they made underwater than by their appearance on the surface.

Clem wrote me, too, from all her amazing places, but when I looked for those letters after her death, I found only recent ones, the ones from Wyoming, the ones where she admitted to feeling isolated in many ways yet never sounded desperate. (Such interesting work, I'd think; how lucky she was.) I could not believe I had thrown away all those earlier letters, and sometimes even now—when I visit my parents in Rhode Island—I go through the same closets, the same boxes in the attic and the hayloft, sure that I will find them yet.

Second day and here I am making tea from a snowbank on Point Barrow. I'm in the sled shed, monitoring array B broadcast from Tovak Perch Lead. My 6 hr. watch ends at 1800 and I'm listening to underwater sounds: bearded seals (oogruks—isn't that a great word?), ring seals, belugas, bowheads. Screeching, whistling, clicking, warbling—it sounds like the tropics, like birds and monkeys and cats, insects buzzing, vines dripping, rivers flowing. What is so weird is how totally silent it is UP HERE, except the breaking ice now & then, the crunching of your feet in the snow or the loud eerie blow of a whale when it comes up for air. Long flocks of king eiders mutter past in the sky. It's like all the life's above or below, while the "earth," this narrow plane, is just so incredibly still. At the tiny drugstore, this older lady asked me what I was doing here—not hostile, just curious. I felt myself sort of apologizing for the intrusion, how I know we're from outside this world (like WAY outside!), and she said, "God put you down there with all those trees and oranges and flowers and mountains, and you have a great time. He put us up here and all we have is the animals. That's what we live on. You can just look at the animals, but we have to eat them. We count on them for that." She wasn't complaining, just saying how it is.

I force myself to look up. Ralph is staring out the window. I suppose people who study birds must keep an eye on the sky as often as they can, no matter where they are. I think about the woman in Clem's letter and then about Ralph, how completely different their lives are, how they were both connected to Clem, connected to each other through the letter itself.

Ralph says, "You need a telescope. There's probably much more to see out there than you realize."

"I'm sure. Afternoon liaisons and domestic fights."

"Oh, much more than that, I promise you." He's reaching into his backpack again. He pulls out a pair of large, serious-looking binoculars.

I set aside Clem's letters. The three boys emerge from their lair. They stand at the edge of the living room, staring at the two grown-ups as if they've caught us doing something peculiar. Henri is jumping up and down, leaking absentminded joy. I have a vision of them as two young horses and a monkey, creatures who've ventured into this room from another, more natural world.

"Can we have ice cream? We're like famished," says Luke.

"There are brownies," I offer.

"Brownies *with* ice cream?" Max gives me his most flattering smile.

I tell them to help themselves, to put the ice cream back in the freezer, and not to eat ice cream over the computer. (Another rule—the no-food-in-bedroom rule—that gets suspended because of Henri.)

The eager commotion of hunting and gathering sweets erupts in the kitchen. Ralph is silent, absorbed in scanning the view. "Bingo," he says at last. He beckons me over. He points out the direction and gives me the binoculars. I am shocked at just how powerful they are. I am looking at the frayed weave of a plastic chaise longue several hundred feet away. Beneath it lie a pair of flip-flops, faded but stylish; on one of them, I can read the name of the designer.

"Higher," says Ralph. He adjusts the glasses, his hands over mine. "There. Do you see the nest?"

A parcel of twigs, lodged inside a decorative bit of cornice at the top of an old industrial building. Something moves among the twigs.

Finches, Ralph tells me. Or possibly sparrows. After I've looked for a short while, he shifts the direction of my vigil to a broken flowerpot shoved against the railing of a little-used deck. "And there you have a pigeon nest."

"Wow," I say. "Mystery solved."

"What mystery?"

"You know: where are all the *baby* pigeons? It's the burning question on every New Yorker's mind."

"They're everywhere. You just have to look," says Ralph, who seems not to have heard the urban myth that pigeons arrive on the earth fully grown and ready to be despised—or that they perform a backward version of human migration: raise babies in the suburbs, then move into town.

The boys stampede past us, bearing large bowls of glistening chocolate. Before I can tell them to slow down, the bedroom door closes behind them.

Ralph is searching the roofscape for other signs of avian life. I stand behind him, letting the silence soothe me.

"Ralph, did you have a clue that she'd kill herself?"

He turns around to face me. "Louisa, I want to say no." He sets the binoculars on the coffee table and sits.

"You mean yes?"

"Didn't she joke with you about death? She did with me. About flaming out young, packing it in, making your exit in a blaze of glory. She called it pulling a Patsy Cline."

"That was part of her bravado, I thought. Her need to be fearless," I say. "To impress the guys. Which she did. In spades."

"But that's it. She *needed* to be fearless. Do you need that?"

I think about this for a moment. "I couldn't be fearless if I tried."

"But you don't *need* to be. Do you know what I'm saying?"

"That asserting her fearlessness was . . . a sign of fear?" Now I'm the one facing the view, and I'm beginning to notice how many birds cross the sky at any given moment.

Ralph sighs. "I'm just guessing. That's the best I can do."

Seven years ago, I joined a support group. The loneliness of my Clemlessness—privately, that's what I called it—had become so acute that I could feel it pulling me away, like an undertow, from the people I loved who were still alive. (I angered easily. I wanted to yell at them, "You don't fucking *know*!"—not just about what they might lose but about anything, everything: politics, art, laundry, taxes. I saw them as not just ignorant but smug, not just naïve but stupid.) The group was for "survivors of suicide." I have always shuddered at the use of that word, *survivor,* for endurance beyond anything short of shipwreck or tsunami, something that puts you in violent physical peril. It feels melodramatic to think of myself as a survivor, though that's what the politics of cancer would have me proclaim myself to be. I was sick—invisibly, impalpably sick—and now I'm better; at least until the next thing, or the last thing, comes along. That's how I see it. None of this trumpeting far and wide that I, yes brave and resilient I, am a survivor.

Yet I needed to sense that others were a little in awe of me. I was thirty-six; no one I knew had heard such bad news from a doctor. I wanted to feel—just a little—like a victim of tragedy. Six months later, Clem pulled the tragedy right out from under me—and also gave it back to me, compounded. *I'll give you tragedy,* she said with her death.

For a few years, I held a special, unspoken status; I was owed a degree of tenderness from everyone around me.

As we grow older, however, our tragedies diminish in their grandeur. Not to us, not personally, but in what my father would call the cosmic scheme of things. Because tragedy, like a rare dark flower gone to seed, proliferates all about us. Your boss succumbs to lymphoma. One friend has a stillbirth, another loses an eye. Someone's parents plummet off a cliff while driving on vacation in Scotland. Another friend's sister-in-law, the mother of a newborn baby, drops dead on a treadmill at the gym. You begin to understand that there are no quotas for hard knocks. It's not, alas, like you've used up your allotted share. You're simply growing older and this is how it is. One day you're no longer hearing "Oh my God I can't believe it!" You're hearing "These things happen" and "There but for the grace of God." And the terrible things that befell you first of all? Old news, background noise, forgotten headlines. To everyone else.

I was repelled by the idea of a support group, the naked neediness—but that was precisely my problem. I was desperate to talk about Clem, to have someone listen to my story who didn't think of it as ancient history, a monument crumbling to dust. I'll hear other stories, I thought, and they'll give me some facsimile of comfort. My Clemlessness will find a context.

What I didn't expect was the frantic, keening search for answers. The nine people who sat in the windowless room of the church basement were obsessed with knowing why a father or brother or spouse had chosen death. Even the daughter of a woman who was elderly, riddled with disease and pain, a woman who ended her life with the furtive help of a doctor—even that woman's daughter could not fathom how her mother's hope had come to an end, how the doctor could have "given up" on his patient. The social worker who led the group encouraged these rounds of futile inquisition. "You never stop wondering, that's natural," she'd say, or "It's just not fair, having to go on alone without at least a good, solid reason—even the illusion of a reason!"

After the introductions, when each of us gave our bare-bones story, Campbell and I were the only ones who stayed silent through that first meeting. Clem had been dead for five years, Campbell's wife for a mere six months. Halfway through the second meeting, Campbell leaned forward in his folding chair and said, "I don't really give a damn, at this point, what her reasons were. I just want to know how I talk about her to our children without showing how outrageously angry I am that she betrayed us like that."

Chairs shifted, but no one spoke. Some people nodded. Then the social worker said, "It's good to feel angry—but have you and your boys really felt the sorrow of it, realized the unbearable pain she must have been in, to leave behind the family I'm sure she loved more than anything else in the world?"

"I don't want them to understand that!" said Campbell. "I don't think that's really a priority here! My sons are eight and *five*. Why the hell should they know about somebody else's unbearable pain when they've got enough of their own?"

"Be as angry as you need to be," the social worker said.

"I don't need your permission for that," said Campbell tersely. "The harder question is just how honest I need to be."

"Are your boys in therapy?" our leader asked.

"Of course they are," said Campbell. "What century, what city, is this? It's all I can do to keep them from being put on bubble-gum-flavored Prozac."

The social worker pursed her lips, as if to show the rest of the group how strong she was, to bear the brunt of this rage with so much kindness and patience. Another member of the group said, "Do they talk about their mother? Do they talk about missing her?"

"At this point, no," said Campbell. "Not to me."

"Then you need to initiate those conversations," said the member.

"I do? Really? Our whole life, from the breakfast she doesn't prepare to the stories she doesn't read, is one big miserable package of missing her. One ginormous *duh*, my boys would say."

A young woman, an only child whose father had killed himself after she left for college, began to talk about losing a parent this way. "Didn't he love me enough to stick around? Or should I have stayed at home? Did my mother abuse him somehow and I could have stopped it? Did he have some terrible secret? Didn't he know how guilty it would make me feel?"

"The guilt is huge," said our leader, nodding emphatically. "All of us can agree with that, I'm sure."

After that meeting, Campbell walked off in the same direction I did; awkwardly, we fell in step and found ourselves going downstairs, together, into the Twenty-third Street station. "I'm not going back there," he said as he fingered a palmful of coins, searching for a token.

I said, "Neither am I. I'm not sure what I hoped to accomplish."

"We should probably give it more time," he said. "Shouldn't we?"

"That's what we'd be told if we ever went back to say we're quitting."

We shared a bench on the dim subway platform, both of us waiting for a downtown 6. I could tell, because we were the only ones there, that we had just missed a train. I was beginning to think we might never say another word to each other when, abruptly, Campbell spoke. "You know, when Janie and I used to fight—and I won't pretend it was rare or that I was especially tolerant of her never-ending depression; I was frustrated that she wouldn't get serious help, but still . . . Anyway, when we argued, about anything, we both had a hard time quitting, calling a truce. That was a big weakness we shared. And sometimes she'd finally yell at me, 'You always have to have the last word, don't you? Well go ahead, have it! Congratulations, it's yours!' And she'd stalk off and slam the door."

He looked at me, as if for permission to continue. When he did, his voice was almost plaintive. "So now, you know what's so incredibly awful? It's like she's left me with the *very* last word, the last word of all. Slammed the door and said *Congratulations* one very last time. And when I feel really, really sorry for myself, that's what I focus on: the way she punished me for all those dragged-out arguments when I could have given in, or I could have given her much more slack because she was . . . ill."

I knew how hard it was for him to say that word. I'd composed my own litany: Clem was brilliant, she was accomplished, she was passionate, she was loved, but she was . . . ill. Yet unlike Campbell, I hadn't known. Why didn't *anyone* seem to know? Was she that cunning? Were we that blind?

On the center tracks, two express trains passed in opposite directions. The air they displaced, an artificial wind, blew paper refuse onto the platform at our feet. The sound of the trains diminished slowly.

"Maybe," I said, "she's the one who got the last word. I mean, isn't suicide the ultimate last word, the declaration nobody ever gets to dispute?"

Campbell looked at me intently, almost fearfully. At first, I thought he was appalled. Our train came. We got on and sat down next to each other. It always feels odd, stepping from the murky station into the harsh light of a new subway car. It's like having something stripped away. Campbell said, "Where do you live? Let me get off at your stop and walk you home."

Ralph looks dismayed. Our attempt to unravel this shared mystery has foundered in the same old morass. Same dark, cold, insultingly dull destination where all these conversations come to a halt. I wish that Campbell was here. He understands the morass better than anyone else I know.

"Well!" Ralph says, to break our gloomy silence. "Can I be completely rude and ask if we could have ice cream, too?"

"If there's any left," I say.

The boys did put the cartons away, but there is a complex graffiti of melted chocolate goo across the counter. "Cy Twombly," I say.

"Is that a new flavor?" asks Ralph.

I laugh. "An artist I love." I wipe down the counter, and then I look into the freezer. We have plenty of vanilla, a little Chunky Monkey, some Cherry Garcia frozen yogurt. I divide it all between two bowls. We eat quickly and gratefully, standing in the kitchen.

Ralph sets his bowl down first. "That was a happy summer. For her."

It takes me a moment to understand. "Vermont."

He nods. "She fell in love with that aunt of yours. She talked about her constantly. I didn't quite get the generational thing. She was nearly a hundred, I seem to remember."

"Almost ninety-nine," I say. "She was a vestige of another era, the maiden aunt who outlives everyone else. But that's my father's family. You can't keep track of how they're all related because they live practically forever." I realize what I've said, but Ralph doesn't seem to catch it.

"You know," he says, "your aunt told Clem a secret. She said she had to share it with someone. Clem, I mean."

That someone, I think, was not me. Again, Ralph doesn't see what I'm feeling. Maybe he's nervous now, eager to leave—though he keeps on staying.

"She had a baby."

"What?" I am seized with panic.

"Oh no. No—I mean your aunt."

I try to make sense of this. "But she had no children."

"I think it died," he says. "Or was adopted."

"But that would mean . . ."

"I've lost the details," says Ralph. "There was no husband, I do remember that."

The pleasure of remembering Lucy dissolves back into sorrow. This time, Ralph reads my face astutely. He apologizes. I tell him it's fine. Some secrets—how well we both know this—will never come clean. They tease you with their general shape but refuse to step out of the shadows.

"You seem okay, can I say that?" says Ralph. "I mean, more than okay. This looks like a nice life you have."

"It is," I say. "And so does yours."

"It's the life of a nomad, like I said. I don't mind. There's another guy who shows up in the field sometimes. Our work overlaps, which is nearly perfect. And we're both happy to be around. We're . . . on the same wavelength, I guess." Ralph scrapes the last of his vanilla from the bowl. He tells me then that he's positive; he found out years ago—but just in time to take the drugs that are keeping so many people alive. He'd been on the verge of accepting a major position at a wildlife fund that would have given him administrative power yet kept him in the field.

"I said no, because I figured I wouldn't be alive for a whole lot longer. I'd better stick with what I knew, what I was already good at, the hands-on work, do it until I had no more energy left. No time. So now the joke's on me. I might actually have to think about retirement!" I sense the exaggerated cheer, his polite assurance that the tragic part is past, not to worry if I don't know what to say.

"You were hoping I'd tell you why she did it," he says.

"Yes. I was. But it doesn't matter. It's been wonderful seeing you."

He tells me he feels the same, that we must stay in touch, and I agree.

"Let me take your godson for a tour, up at the zoo," he says.

"He'd love that. The older boys, too."

I retrieve Ralph's backpack from the living room while he puts on his jacket. We kiss each other on the cheek, we hug, and I stand in the doorway until the elevator opens. We wave at each other. The doors close.

I put the bowls in the dishwasher. Standing still, I realize that I do not hear a peep from the boys' bedroom. I knock on their door. When they answer, I open it. Inside, the three boys are crowded together at Luke's computer, their faces rapt and luminous.

They are playing a game where you construct an obstacle course for a hapless little man you must then guide through the course you've built, trying your best to keep him from falling victim to the vagaries of trap-doors, falling airplanes, wayward hammers, boxing gloves that emerge—*kapow!*—from nowhere. You hear alarm clocks, whistles, the classic sound effects of slapstick. It's like Mouse Trap meets the Three Stooges. In the end, the little man is indestructible. If you don't give up, neither does he.

I pick up Darius from the floor and tuck him under one arm; I stack the ice-cream bowls and carry them to the kitchen. Aimless, I go back into the living room and sit on the couch. I set the bear down beside me and pick up the pieces of paper covered with my sister's words. I shuffle randomly toward the end; here is the letter she wrote to Ralph after the day of the hunt. She describes with the clinical care of a young scientist—already having found what she was meant to do—the weapons the men used to kill the animal, the tools they used to haul it onto the ice and reduce its vast anatomy to the stuff of everyday survival. I seem to remember getting a letter from Clem with all this information, too—perhaps skimming what I saw as the gory parts, missing the awe she felt at her own admiration for what had been accomplished.

In a matter of hours, this massive creature is stripped of its skin for muk-tuk, butchered and divided precisely among crew and helpers, loaded on sleds and taken back to town. Women with sharp knives glean all the last fragments of meat from the skull and spine. Finally all that remains on the ice is a large stain of bright red and a few naked bones. When the ice moves out, these will be gone too.

Campbell and I were married for two years before we imagined—out loud, to each other—what Clem's and Janie's last hours and moments were like, once they had turned the final corner, the point of no return.

We rarely drink anything stronger than wine, but friends had given us a bottle of fine golden tequila, which stood untouched in a cupboard for months. And then, toward the end of one exquisitely autumnal Saturday, the boys away with Campbell's parents for the weekend, I suggested margaritas. I bought Grand Marnier and a sack of limes. I made our drinks in a blender with ice and poured them into large stemmed glasses the color of twilight, a wedding present we'd never used.

We were in a festive mood. We had walked aimlessly all afternoon, following the byzantine warp and weft of our neighborhood streets. The shaded alleys were bracingly frigid, the promenade along the river alluringly warm. The fragrance of newly spent leaves and the harbor's salty tides filled us with nostalgia for the past—so much of which we hadn't shared—and exhilaration for the future, less tentative than when we'd met. As we made our way together, in virtual lockstep, I was gratified by Campbell's height, by the feel of his sturdy ribs through his shirt against the fingers of my enfolding hand. He is slim, the way my teacher-husband was, and he has the smooth brown hair of my ex the stuntman, but in so many other physical respects he is reassuringly different.

We took our margaritas to the roof terrace of our building. Remarkably, no one else was there. The sunset was every color a sunset should be. We drank and talked and laughed. It was perfect. We stayed on the roof till the sky matched our glasses. My sister, I remembered but kept to myself, had been famous for her killer margaritas.

In the elevator, returning to the loft, I felt dizzy. My face was taut from too much sun, and I hadn't eaten in many hours. Yet I took the blender from the freezer and filled my glass again. A chicken was roasting in the oven, not quite ready.

In a blink, the tequila went from my head to my heart. As if a valve had literally burst in my chest, I cried, cried, and cried—into my hands, then into Campbell's shirt, and then, after he took away my drink and steered me toward the couch, into a large red pillow.

"You need dinner," he said, sitting beside me to stroke my back.

"I need Clem," I said. "I always need Clem. Even when I don't. I need her to *be*. Halfway around the world, wherever!"

"Yes, Louisa, I know."

"And you need Janie. Say it. It's all right."

"No," he said. "I do not need Janie. Luke and Max might need her, they always will, but they're okay."

"Why did she *do it*," I sobbed, knowing full well that this no longer deserved to be a question. "Where was she, where the hell was she when she thought that was a *good idea*."

"Somewhere she'd thought about going for a long time."

This was something we'd talked about just after we did not go back to the group. It was Campbell who pointed out that, killing herself twice over, Clem had not been waving for help.

He held me while I cried myself out. I pictured Clem, in the garage, then in the cab of the truck, making elaborate preparations, taking precautions: the hose, the IV line, all the seals, all the carefully taped connections. The exhaust pipe. The rearview mirror. A vein in the back of her left hand. The light switch. The pure, merciless dark—or had there been a window in that garage? Was there a moon?

I could see a list in her handwriting: *1, 2, 3*.

As I entertained these morbid visions, I began to smell Campbell's roast chicken. He'd basted it with orange juice, mustard, and the Grand Marnier with which I had made those foolish drinks. I told him to go to the kitchen, to see if it was done.

I followed him. I wiped my face on a dish towel, and I drank a glass of water. I watched him take the chicken from the oven, move it to the cutting board, then check the artichokes.

I took a deep, corrugated breath. "I want to know what tipped her over the edge. It drives me crazy not to know."

My husband looked at me but did not reply. His face was red and moist from the steam in the pot of artichokes. His eyes were sad. He stood motionless at the stove for a moment and then surprised me by saying, "Exactly what do you see when you think about the end of it, the end of her? Tell me."

I told him what a planner Clem had always been. I described the list I'm sure she made. I told him about the lumpy envelope the funeral director handed me: the silver earrings inlaid with black designs, the abalone ring, the black leather thong from around her wrist, its clay beads a souvenir of some pristine faraway place. "She knew precisely how it would all work," I said. "She'd have had that thin smile on her face. She could have been humming. She could have had a cup of coffee in the beverage holder of the truck, to keep her alert, to make sure she didn't mess up. Maybe she left on the dashboard light. Oh God, the radio . . .

"I wish I'd asked to see the truck, everything in it, the way it was. I wonder if she left a last-minute note, there, that we never got to see. The police were idiots."

Campbell nodded slowly, respectfully. He turned off the gas under the artichokes and removed the lid. He stepped back against the sink and folded his arms. "But what if it was more like this," he said. "What if she phoned three friends that evening and she said to herself, *If any of them answer, I won't do it.* But they didn't—she got their machines—and then she went to the fridge and she opened a bottle of wine that she'd meant to save for a dinner with her lover, that married guy with the dogs. She thought, To hell with him. Maybe she thought a glass of wine would cheer her up, shake her loose. She turned on the TV, but there wasn't anything worth watching. She drank a little wine, and she got out some old letters. And then she drank more wine. And maybe she tried her friends again, and maybe they still weren't in. And the radio—yes, the radio. Maybe she turned it on, and there was Bob Dylan. 'Knockin' on Heaven's Door.' Or Bob Marley. 'So Much Trouble in the World.' And she finished that bottle of wine."

He was looking at me fiercely. The chicken, on the cutting board, had slumped to one side.

I said, "And she thought, I'm awake now, I might as well go to work."

"So she did."

"And she turned on the fluorescent lights in the lab, and she felt even lonelier. That Edward Hopper light. And she saw the anesthetic on the counter."

"And she heard something in the garage—a mouse—and she opened the door."

"And there was the truck. Waiting." I shook my head. "But I still can't believe, I just can't believe—"

"Who can?" Campbell reached for me across the narrow kitchen. Briefly, he held my shoulders. "So you see."

"You mean, that I will never know."

"We both know that."

I took two plates from the cupboard. He moved toward the counter, to serve our dinner.

"What about Janie?" I said.

"Let's sit down," he said.

I look up from my sister's letter. Ralph's binoculars lie on the coffee table.

"Oh," I say, aloud. I pick them up. I look out the window. On a roof nearly a block away, I am able to inspect the tiniest buds on the birch tree someone planted bravely in a large wooden box. I search again for the two nests and watch them, one and then the other, till I detect motion. The mother pigeon paces a ledge beside her brood. I can't hear her cooing, but I can see her throat swelling again and again, like a beating heart, as she keeps up her maternal chatter.

I think of my Great-Great-Aunt Lucy's house in Winooski, Vermont. I haven't thought of it in so long. It was shabby outside, pretty and spotless within. But I'm thinking of the bird feeders she hung from the trees in the yard. Maybe, for just that one summer, Clem and Aunt Lucy were soul mates. Absurdly, the memory makes me jealous. They are both gone, long gone.

Like a cop on his beat, the mother pigeon struts her ledge.

"Guys!" I call out. "Come have a look at something!"

Henri, at full tilt, is the first to arrive. I hold the binoculars to his eyes, bending over to get the view right, my head right next to his. "Baby birds," I whisper. His hair smells like the sandalwood incense that Luke burns in a jar on his desk. Beside the jar is a picture of his mother; Max's picture of Janie, a different one, sits on top of his dresser. They still go to a therapist, but only twice a month.

Max and Luke saunter along, barefoot, hair in their eyes, reluctant to leave the hypnotic world of the screen, but then they hear Henri's exclamations of delight. They take turns scanning the skyline. Henri points out the pigeon nest. "Awesome," he says.

The phone rings. I'm pretty sure it will be one of the two fathers calling. Luke crosses the room to answer; he greets the caller happily— "Hey, 'sup, dude?"—and carries the phone back to the window, looking out at the rooftops with Max and Henri.

I stand back, filled with possessive love for all three boys, none of whom is technically, biologically, genetically "mine"—but what does it matter? Before she died, I thought of Clem as mine—my sister—but that gave me no say in her fate. I think of all the sad, desperate people in that support group, the repetitive litany: *my father, my son, my mother, my friend* . . . all the broken illusions that because those people were somehow "ours," we were the ones with the power to hold them.

No one belongs to us, and we belong to no one—not in that sense. This should free us, but it never quite does.

I look at Clem's letters to Ralph from Alaska, a stack of ordinary paper on an ordinary table. I haven't finished reading them, but already I know they hold no clues, no predictions of doom. In all likelihood, they will be the last words of hers—the last that are new to me—I will ever encounter. Seeing them, these words written so long ago, when she was so young, so clear-eyed, so forward-looking, I understand that what I've secretly imagined since her death was that she herself would pop up somewhere—in a dream, in that support group, on a rush-hour subway—and give me a logical explanation.

One, two, three: a list.

And that's when I understand, in every grieving nerve, in the bustling nest of my heart, that in this life, the only life there is—Clem and I disagreed often, but we agreed on that—the last word is mine, and it is a gift.

A NOTE ABOUT THE AUTHOR

Julia Glass is the author of *Three Junes,* winner of the National Book Award for Fiction, and *The Whole World Over.* She has received fellowships from the National Endowment for the Arts, the New York Foundation for the Arts, and the Radcliffe Institute for Advanced Study. Her short fiction has won several prizes, including the Tobias Wolff Award and the Pirate's Alley Faulkner Society Medal for Best Novella. She lives with her family in Massachusetts.

A NOTE ON THE TYPE

The text of this book was set in Ehrhardt, a typeface based on the specimens of "Dutch" types found at the Ehrhardt foundry in Leipzig. The original design of the face was the work of Nicholas Kis, a Hungarian punch cutter known to have worked in Amsterdam from 1680 to 1689. The modern version of Ehrhardt was cut by the Monotype Corporation of London in 1937.